CHANGE

FINDING ANNA, BOOK 5

SHERRI HAYES

Change
Finding Anna Series
Sherri Hayes

ABOUT THIS BOOK

In this long-awaited next installment, Brianna and Stephan are settling into their new home outside of Le Sueur. The river that runs behind their house provides a peace Brianna had never found in the city.

It's been three years since she stood in a courtroom and faced the man who'd held her captive and altered her life forever. Since then, she'd been trying to move on with her life...trying to find her way.

The move was part of that. Too many people knew who Stephan was—who she was. They needed a fresh start.

But demons are funny things. They follow you wherever you go. With the help of Stephan and a new therapist, Brianna will have to face the changes in her life and confront her fears.

CHAPTER 1

Brianna

My heart was pounding in my chest as I raced around the house checking to see if everything was perfect. I needed to calm down.

It had been a little over a month since we'd moved from Minneapolis to our new home, and I was still getting used to the space. That wasn't what had me frantically looking over every surface, checking to make sure I hadn't missed anything, though.

The reason I was plumping pillows and straightening books was because Stephan was on his way home with Lily and Logan. It would be their first time at our new house since we got settled and I wanted it to be just right.

As the thought popped into my mind, I heard Stephan telling me to breathe. Even when he wasn't here beside me, I could still feel him near.

I lifted my hand to cover the necklace I wore around my neck. My collar. With the tips of my fingers I traced the infinity symbol entwined with the heart. It was a symbol of our commitment to each other and our relationship. He was my Dom and I was his submissive.

The muscles in my shoulders began to relax a little and I took a deep, cleansing breath. Everything would be all right.

I placed the book I held in my hand back on the coffee table. Our new house was bigger than Stephan's condo in Minneapolis. It had a huge kitchen, something Stephan had insisted on when we were looking for a new home. He claimed it was so I could spoil him with even more delicious meals.

My gaze turned to the kitchen. Every surface was clean, and everything was in its place. A salad and some cut up fruit I'd made to go with dinner were sitting on the large island that separated the kitchen from the dining room. Stephan had said to keep it simple, and it didn't get much simpler than roast chicken with salad and fruit.

The sound of car doors slamming drew my attention and I rushed to the foyer to greet Stephan and our guests.

Anticipation curled in my belly as I waited the couple minutes it took for them to make their way inside. The door opened and I couldn't help but smile as I saw Stephan cross the threshold. He closed the distance between us before Logan and Lily had made it through the door.

The moment he touched me, I melted into him. Warmth surged through me as he brushed his lips against mine and his fingers caressed my cheek. His scent surrounded me, instantly comforting me. "I missed you, sweetheart," he whispered.

His eyes were full of love as he met my gaze. "I missed you, too, Sir."

"Something smells good," Logan said, breaking the spell between Stephan and me.

Over the last three years I'd gotten to know Logan. He didn't frighten me like he once had. That didn't mean I was completely comfortable with him, but it also meant I didn't want to run and hide when he walked into the room either.

"I made roast chicken."

Lily sighed. "I miss your cooking. It's not the same without you two in the city."

Stephan guided us into the dining room, keeping me at his side. "We're only an hour away. It's not as if we moved across the country."

"Yes, but I can't pop in whenever the mood strikes me anymore."

Lily was pouting, which seemed to amuse Stephan. "Explain to me again how that's a bad thing?"

Logan chuckled, while Lily's mouth twisted. I knew she probably wanted to say something but was biting her tongue. It was the weekend, which meant she and Logan were playing. If she were disrespectful to another Dom, there would be consequences.

Instead of commenting, Lily took the seat Logan offered her.

"I'll help you bring everything to the table," Stephan said, placing a hand on my lower back.

Because I'd kept things simple, it didn't take more than a few minutes to bring the food into the dining room. Stephan carved the chicken while I got everyone something to drink.

Stephan held my chair for me, and then skimmed his fingers along my neck, sending shivers down my spine before taking his own seat. He sent me a knowing grin as he reached for the salad bowl and began loading salad onto my plate. I lowered my head and felt heat creep into my cheeks.

"So, how did the board meeting go?" Logan asked as he piled chicken onto his plate.

"Good, I suppose. Donations are up, but so are costs." Stephan let out a frustrated sigh. "I wish I could do more. I don't like sitting on the sidelines."

Guilt nudged at me. Stephan had to resign because he'd saved me. It wasn't right. I wished there were something I could do to help but considering I still hadn't completely convinced my childhood friend, Cal, I didn't have much hope that I could persuade the general public.

"I wish I had more time on my hands," Logan said. "I've been working way too much lately. This is the first weekend I've had off in over two months."

Lily stabbed a piece of lettuce with her fork. "We thought this new position would mean he'd be home more, but so far I'm lucky if I see him an hour before we head to bed."

Logan nodded. "I'm hoping once I rework a few things, that I can get on a more normal schedule, but the person who was in the position before me was extremely unorganized."

"I'm sure you'll get it sorted eventually." Stephan opened his mouth to say more but was cut short when Lily moaned.

Everyone turned their attention to her. At first, I thought maybe Logan was making her wear a toy or something, but then she shoveled another piece of food into her mouth and moaned again. She was halfway through her second bite when she realized we were all staring at her. "I told you I missed Brianna's cooking. And with Logan working so much, I've been eating way too much takeout. This is heaven!"

Logan and Stephan laughed.

"Here I thought Logan had decided to make dinner interesting." Stephan grinned as he reached for his water.

Lily met Stephan's gaze, then looked at me. Since the incident almost four years ago where I tried to watch her and Logan in a scene and I freaked out, Lily was always cautious when discussing play around me. She knew I was fine with her and Logan's dynamic, but it was Logan doing things to her that was sometimes difficult for me even though I knew everything between them was consensual. Their play tended to be a lot rougher than what Stephan and I did. "My Dom decided to be a little more discreet tonight. I currently have a rather large plug up my bum."

The look on Lily's face said she was quite fine with having a butt plug inserted into her anus. I swallowed and breathed through the anxiety that stirred in my belly. Stephan and I hadn't had anal sex. We'd talked about it once while going through some of his toys, but I didn't know if I'd ever be able to do it. I couldn't say that it would never happen, though. Stephan had worked hard to make me comfortable with a lot of things.

One of those things had nothing to do with sex. He'd encouraged me to ask questions. "Does it hurt?"

Luckily, Lily was used to me asking questions that some people might find strange. "No." She wiggled in her chair. "I wouldn't say it's comfortable, but it's not painful."

Stephan reached for my hand and brought it up to his lips. His eyes sparkled with happiness and I knew he was proud of me.

After that, the conversation drifted back to things in the city. It was only as we were cleaning up that Logan pulled Lily to his side and cleared his throat. "Lily and I have a bit of an announcement to make."

Stephan dried his hands on a towel and reached for my hand. I knew he did that for my benefit. I didn't always handle news well.

Logan looked at Lily and then to us. "Lily and I are getting married and we'd like for both of you to be in the wedding."

"Congratulations!" Stephan gave both Logan and Lily a hug before returning to stand beside me.

Lily walked over to me and took hold of my free hand. "I'd like for you to be in our wedding, but I understand if you're not comfortable participating. I won't be upset or anything."

Even though I knew there'd most likely be a lot of people, which would be challenging for me, I wanted to be part of Lily's wedding. She was the first friend I made after Stephan rescued me. She'd helped me so much. "Can I think about it?"

"Of course." Lily pulled me in for a hug before releasing me and returning to stand beside Logan. "This is going to be so much fun."

I looked over at Stephan, and for a moment, our gazes met and that connection I felt with him had me wishing we were alone. He squeezed my hand and I knew he felt it, too.

Lily didn't seem to notice what was happening between me and Stephan. She was too caught up in her own excitement. "Will you go dress shopping with me?" She didn't wait for me to respond before asking, "What's your schedule like this coming week?"

Stephan

Lily was like a whirlwind. By the time we all called it a night, I was nursing the first signs of a headache.

As Lily had gone on about the need to find dresses, flowers, invitations, and other wedding stuff I had little to no knowledge of, I could feel the tension growing in Brianna. She hadn't signaled to me that she had reached a seven, but if I was feeling overwhelmed, I knew she had to be as well.

Once Logan and Lily retreated upstairs to their room, Brianna and I headed into the master bedroom. As soon as the door closed behind us, I held out my hand. "Come here, Brianna."

Her response was immediate. She took my hand and I crushed her against me, enfolding her in my arms. "What number?"

She didn't answer right away, but I knew she would. "Five, Sir."

I kissed the top of her head, breathing in the scent of her shampoo. "You did well tonight. Lily can get a little carried away."

"I never realized there was so much to do for a wedding." Brianna ran her fingers along the fabric of my shirt. Her touch was so light it almost tickled.

"Neither did I, but then again, this is Lily. You know how she is when it comes to planning a party."

Without warning, I scooped Brianna up and carried her over to the high-backed chair in the corner. It was the same one that had been in her room at the condo. When we'd moved into our new home, we'd discussed her having her own room as she had in the city, but she had no desire for her own space. Given we hadn't slept apart for almost four years, and that I slept better with her beside me, we combined our things into one bedroom.

Brianna snuggled into my lap, resting her head on my shoulder and toying with the buttons on my shirt. This was one of my favorite things, something I looked forward to every night, holding her in my arms as she sat on my lap, just the two of us. It was a time for us to decompress and to communicate anything we needed to. Normally, we had these conversations in the living room, but as we had guests at the moment, the chair in our bedroom would suffice.

She traced her index finger along my collarbone sending a jolt directly to my groin. It was an innocent touch on her part, but it didn't matter. My body knew her and responded. "I want to be in Lily's wedding."

"But?" I could hear the reservation in her voice.

"I don't want to have a panic attack and ruin everything."

Her nose skimmed the side of my neck as she cuddled closer. Purely on instinct, I held her tighter. "You need to talk to Lily about your concerns. The wedding is four months away. We have time to prepare." I tilted her chin up so she could look at me. "I love you, Brianna."

Her sweet smile warmed my soul. "I love you, too, Sir."

I gave her a soft kiss, and then rubbed my thumb along her jaw. "How was your day?"

"Okay." She glanced down, a sure sign she'd done something she didn't think I'd be pleased about. "I spent most of the time you were gone cleaning the house."

I frowned. "You cleaned the house yesterday."

"I know. I just...I wanted everything to be perfect for Logan and Lily."

Several moments ticked by before I responded. While I'd gotten used to how Brianna's mind worked over the years, I still preferred hearing her explanations directly. It did no good to assume. "Why did you think the house needed to be cleaned again?"

"I noticed the windows had some spots, so I cleaned them. Then a few minutes later, I noticed some specs of dirt on the stairs. I kept noticing little things and cleaning them up."

"Do you think Logan and Lily would have been bothered by spots on our windows?" Brianna's OCD tendencies had not abated in the years since we'd met. At first, I'd thought they were a learned behavior from her time with Ian. I wasn't so sure anymore. Then again, the only things she tended to be that way about had to do with cleaning and the space around her being tidy. She never had an issue with her clothes or her hair or anything else for that matter. It was perplexing.

She hesitated. "No, Sir."

I considered my options but decided to let it go for now. "Did you write in your journal while I was gone?"

"Yes. It's hard coming up with my five goals."

Brianna's new therapist, Dr. Katlin, had been talking to her about where she'd like to see herself in five years. She'd asked Brianna to come up with five goals for herself. Each day this week, I'd given her the task of coming up with one thing she'd like to accomplish in that time frame. Ones that weren't sexual in nature, since those types of goals were things we discussed regularly.

"It can be difficult to set goals for oneself, but you have to strive toward something if you wish to achieve it."

"What if I have everything I want?" she asked in not much more than a whisper.

I kissed the top of her head before resting my cheek on her hair. "It's perfectly fine to be content with what you have, but we should always be learning and growing."

She nodded.

I glanced at the clock on the nightstand. It was nearly eleven and we had a long day ahead of us. We needed to get to bed. Lifting Brianna from my lap, we walked hand in hand into the en suite bathroom.

As with the rest of the house, the master bathroom was much bigger in this house than in my condo. It had all the things I'd loved about my condo bathroom, including a huge tub that Brianna and I had already made use of several times since moving in. The other wonderful feature of our new bathroom was our state-of-the-art shower. I could program it so the water was whatever temperature I wanted it to be and I could control the multiple showerheads with the push of a button.

I discarded my clothes and turned on the water before directing my attention to Brianna. She preferred jeans and T-shirts, but often wore skirts and dresses because she knew I liked to have easy access to what was mine.

Pulling her close to my naked body, I reached for the zipper of her skirt and slid it down before slipping my hand inside to cup her ass. The flower covered skirt fluttered to the floor to pool around her ankles. "Did I tell you how much I missed you today?"

She gazed up at me, her hands gripping my shoulders. "Yes, Sir. You did."

"Hmm." I hooked my fingers inside the waistband of her panties and pushed them down her legs to join her skirt where it lay on the floor. Next, I took the hem of the pretty blue sweater she was wearing and lifted it over her head, leaving her clad only in her bra. I could see her nipples trying to peek out at me from behind the material.

Her nipples hardened even farther as I rubbed my thumbs over them with the gentlest of touches. She sucked in a breath when I took them both between my thumb and forefinger and gave them each a pinch.

Grinning, I reached behind her and unclasped her bra, the material falling to the floor, leaving her naked before me.

I cupped her face and brought her lips to mine. Brianna opened for me, and I dipped my tongue inside. It was the first real kiss we'd shared since that morning.

I allowed myself to indulge for a couple of minutes before I released her enough to move us into the shower. There was nothing like Brianna naked with water streaming down her body. I loved watching it fall off the tips of her breast and see how it disappeared between her legs.

She rested her hands on my shoulders, as she looked up at me. "May I wash you, Sir?"

"You may."

She picked up the soap and began working it between her hands. When Brianna was satisfied she had enough suds, she stepped forward. She started with my shoulders, taking her time and massaging the soap over my skin. Slowly, she moved lower, taking care with each part of my body, making sure not to miss a single bit of my skin.

By the time she reached my cock, it was hard and ready for some attention. She took her time as she always did in that area. After four years, Brianna knew what I liked. She moved her hand along my flesh with exactly the right amount of pressure, and then cupped my balls, rolling them against her palm.

The urge to kiss her was strong and I didn't resist it. Tangling my fingers in her hair, I pulled her to her feet and crashed my mouth over hers, taking what I wanted while she continued to pump my erection. I backed her against the tile wall, bringing us directly into the spray, not caring as the water cascaded down my back and shoulders.

Pinning her against the wall, I circled her wrists with my hands and held them against the tile above her head. Brianna arched against me, silently begging for me to give her more.

I bent down, so my erection could slip between her legs. My reward was the soft moan that vibrated from deep in her throat. "Are you ready for me, pet?"

"Yes, Sir. Please, I'm ready." So different from how things had been at first between us. Brianna had finally gotten in touch with her sexuality and had embraced it.

Releasing her wrists, I repositioned my hands at her waist and lifted.

Brianna knew what to do and wrapped her legs around me as I carried her over to the shelf I had specifically designed for this purpose. It was the perfect height with enough room for her to lean back so I could position her however I desired.

Once she was settled on the tile ledge, my cock found its home as if by instinct. No matter how many times I made love to Brianna, it never got old. Feeling her heat surrounding me was a sensation unlike anything I'd ever experienced in my life.

I thrust in and out of her, bracing us both against the tile as the water continued to cascade over us. She held on tight, her fingers digging into my scalp. The zaps of pain went straight to my groin, surging me closer to my orgasm.

Capturing her lips again, I twisted my hand so my thumb could reach her clit. Brianna gasped, and then moaned, digging her nails deeper into my head.

It didn't take long for her to be teetering on the edge and I was right there with her. "Come for me."

Her entire body stiffened a split second before I felt her pussy contract around my cock. I deepened the kiss, swallowing the beautiful sounds of her climax and thrust three more times before finding my own release.

CHAPTER 2

Brianna

Morning was my favorite time of the day. It was a new beginning, a fresh start. And even if I'd had a bad night, things always seemed brighter in the morning.

Of course, a lot of that was because of Stephan. Before he'd rescued me, I'd been lost in so many ways. Not just because of what Ian had done to me, but also because of my father and what had happened to my mother. Stephan had helped me find peace again.

I smiled as I set the table with three place settings and brought the juice and coffee over along with the fruit I'd cut up while the breakfast casserole was baking. Stephan was already at the table, reading my journal entry from yesterday. In addition to coming up with a goal I'd like to achieve in the next five years, I'd also shared some of my fears about having Logan and Lily visit. They'd never stayed in our house before, and even if they were discrete, I knew it was the weekend and they were playing. What if I walked in on something and had a panic attack like I did before?

Stephan was quiet as he read, taking in everything I'd written. I knew we'd talk about it later. Any questions he had, he'd ask me then and he'd usually delve deeper into why I felt or thought the way I did.

It's one of the many reasons I loved him. He pushed my boundaries but was always mindful of what I'd experienced in the past. Dr. Katlin called it desensitization therapy.

"Something smells good," Logan announced as he descended the stairs.

Lily had a huge grin on her face as they made their way to the dining room. "Did you need help with anything?"

"No, thank you. I just have to get the casserole out of the oven, and everything will be ready."

A few minutes later, the timer went off and I removed the casserole, placing it on the counter. Stephan came up behind me and wrapped his arms around my waist. He ran his nose from the curve of my shoulder up to my ear before taking my lobe between his teeth and sucking.

My breath stuttered in anticipation as he flattened his hand over my belly and slipped it under my shirt to rub teasing circles right above my belly button. "My mouth is watering already."

I thought he was talking about the casserole, but I couldn't be sure. His voice was almost a purr as he whispered in my ear and all I could think about was what it would feel like if his hand slipped below the waistband of my shorts.

"Yes, Sir," I said in barely more than a whisper, not even really sure at that point what I was agreeing to.

Stephan chuckled and released me.

The entire exchange hadn't taken more than a few moments, but it left me shaky and trembling inside in the best way. When he touched me like that, I forgot where I was and even who else was in the room.

Before I could get my wits about me again, he grabbed the potholders and carried the dish to the table. I followed him, but he stopped me before I was able to take my seat at the table. Instead, he placed a cushion on the floor next to him and lowered himself into his chair. Without any further instruction, I knelt on the cushion, taking my place at his feet.

Conversation floated between plans for the day and the wedding. Stephan fed my breakfast to me in between taking bites of his food. It was incredibly intimate as he held my gaze each time he presented a new forkful to me, taking care that no crumbs fell and that I'd gotten enough.

No one seemed eager to move once breakfast was over. I suppose that made sense considering there was nowhere we really had to be at any specific time today. Stephan guided my head into his lap and combed his fingers through my hair as they talked. I was content to relax into him and enjoy the moment, letting my eyes drift shut as I listened to the conversation.

It was almost noon by the time everyone rose from the table and began cleaning up. As I finished putting the dishes into the dishwasher, I noticed Lily was getting a little impatient. She was keeping her mouth shut, but with the way she kept glancing at the front door, I knew she was eager to get going.

Apparently, I wasn't the only one who'd noticed. "Think all the bargains will be gone by the time we get there?" Stephan asked.

"You never know."

Both Logan and Stephan laughed, and I couldn't help but grin. Lily lived for shopping. I didn't understand her obsession. Sure, I liked to get new things, but I didn't see the appeal of spending the entire day trying on clothes and shoes.

Stephan helped me wipe down the table and counters while Logan and Lily disappeared upstairs to their room for a few minutes. When they came back down, Lily had changed into a dress that flowed around her thighs. It was white with yellow flowers and buttoned up the front. It reminded me of summer.

"All set?" Stephan asked.

We all climbed into Stephan's vehicle and headed into town. I liked Le Sueur better than Minneapolis. It was smaller and quieter. Plus, there were no reporters.

Stephan drove down main street looking for a place to park. It was a beautiful day and most of the parking spaces were full. He eventually found a place, though, and we all piled out to check out the stores.

Within moments of leaving the vehicle, Lily was pulling us inside one. Although Stephan and I had been downtown a few times, we'd never been to this location. They seemed to sell a little bit of everything . . . clothes, purses, pictures, and even little statues.

After about twenty minutes, we moved on to the next shop. And then the next. I don't think we made it past more than one store without going inside. Lily seemed determined to check out all downtown Le Sueur had to offer.

We'd just exited our fifth, or was it sixth, shop, when Lily let out a squeal. "There it is!"

She was looking across the street. It took me a moment to realize she was pointing at another store.

"Want to be more specific?" Stephan asked.

"The store I was telling Logan about. They refurbish old clothes. Come on." She began marching toward the nearest crosswalk and we were left with no choice but to follow her.

Lily was practically bouncing on the balls of her feet by the time we entered the store. The place was interesting. It wasn't set up like a normal shop. Instead of having racks of clothes lined up near the door, the first thing you saw were pictures of outfits they'd altered— the before and after. It was almost like an art gallery.

We moved farther into the store and the racks of clothes came into view. Again, however, it was different. On one side, there were clothes that looked as if they'd seen better days. On the other, were clothes that looked much more polished.

A young woman, who didn't look much older than me, strolled across the room toward us. "Hello. Can I help you find anything?"

Stephan quirked his eyebrow in Logan and Lily's direction.

"I've heard about what you're doing with vintage clothing and was wondering if you had anything from the 40's or 50's," Lily asked.

"Of course. Follow me and I'll show you what we have in stock."

Stephan let Logan and Lily go first while we followed behind at a slower pace. We lingered about ten feet away as the woman showed Lily the altered items they had for sale. I ran a finger over the lace on one of the dresses with my free hand. It was a pretty blue color and looked like something out of an old movie, except the skirt was shorter and the neckline dipped quite low in the front.

"The blue would bring out your eyes." The feel of Stephan whispering in my ear had butterflies fluttering in my stomach. He liked to do that a lot as he knew what it did to me.

"The skirt is really short."

A wicked grin crossed his face. He removed the dress from the rack and checked the tag. Without a word, he walked over to the saleswoman, with me in tow. "Excuse me. Do you have a dressing room?"

"I'll give you a minute to look around," she said to Lily and Logan before returning her attention to Stephan. "Right this way."

Stephan and I followed her to the back of the store where there was a single door with a long mirror on the front. She unlocked it and held open the door. "Let me know if you have any questions. We do alterations here as well, if the dress doesn't fit exactly right."

Once she'd headed back toward the front where Logan and Lily were, Stephan handed me the dress. "Try it on and then show me what it looks like."

I swallowed and took the dress. Even though I knew Stephan would be right outside the door, it wasn't often I was alone in a public place. On the rare occasions where we went out, I didn't leave his side. If I had to go to the bathroom, I either went with Lily or Jade or I waited until we were home. It wasn't always the most comfortable solution, but there was still a part of me that feared getting taken again.

The door clicked shut behind me and I surveyed my surroundings. It was a small room, no bigger than our powder room at home, with a bench seat, another full-length mirror on the wall, and three hooks.

I didn't want to prolong the experience, so I quickly removed my clothes and slipped the dress over my head. It was a little loose around the waist, but that wasn't as big a problem as the top. The fabric draped over my front and dipped two inches below my breasts, almost to my belly button.

"Sir?"

"What's wrong?" The tone of my voice must have alerted him.

"It's too big."

"Let me see." His voice was right outside the door now.

I reached for the handle and opened the door, revealing myself to him.

His gaze scanned me from head to toe before turning to catch the eye of the saleswoman. He raised his arm, indicating we needed assistance and she came rushing forward. As soon as she caught a look at me, she went in motion. "Oh, that's lovely on you. A little big in the waist and shoulders, but nothing a few adjustments can't fix. Here," she said, grabbing some pins off a nearby shelf. "I can pin it up and you'll be able to get an idea of what it would look like with the alterations."

I stood frozen, not sure what to do.

Stephan, however, didn't hesitate. He moved to stand opposite the woman and took my hands in his so that my back was facing her.

Luckily, she worked swiftly. In less than five minutes, she'd pinned the shoulders back and put a couple of clips at the waist. "There. Much better, don't you think?"

"Much," Stephan agreed. "Take a look at yourself."

I stepped into the dressing room again and faced the mirror. The woman staring back at me looked both sophisticated and sexy at the same time. The extra fabric had been gathered at the waist and shoulders making the V at the front of the dress end two inches higher at the bottom of my breasts. It showed a hint of my cleavage without revealing too much.

Stephan stepped behind me, resting his hands at my waist. "Do you like it?"

"I look like Lily."

He chuckled. "I'm not sure Lily would look good in this color blue." Then he tugged me closer, resting my back against his front. "You look beautiful. Sweet and sexy at the same time."

I felt the blush heating my cheeks before I saw it reflected back at me in the mirror.

Stephan turned to the saleswoman. "How long would it take to do the alterations?"

"For this, it would be about a week. We could have it ready for you to pick up next weekend, if you'd like."

He spread his hand wide over my belly, pressing me against him so I could feel how much he was liking me in the dress. "Sounds great."

The saleswoman smiled. "I'll go write up the paperwork while you get changed. Just be careful not to pull out any of the pins or clips."

She was off a second later, leaving Stephan and I alone again.

He closed the door, shutting us both inside the changing room. Before I could even blink, he had slipped his hand under my dress and was rubbing his fingers along the inside of my thigh.

Anticipation curled in my belly as he continued to caress my skin and I felt myself getting wet.

Then his hand was gone.

I opened my eyes, not even realizing I'd closed them, to find him staring back at me in the mirror.

Without a word, he unzipped the dress and eased it down my shoulders, leaving me in nothing but my bra and panties. I stood there, frozen, not knowing what to do. My body was aching for him, but we weren't alone. Not really.

He hung the dress back on the hanger and handed me the clothes I'd discarded earlier. He used the tips of his fingers, the ones he'd used to touch me, over the bottom of my lip several times before reaching for the door, his gaze never leaving mine. "Get dressed. I'll be right outside."

Stephan

When I exited the dressing room, Logan and Lily were waiting for me. Lily had a knowing grin on her face. Logan quirked a curious brow at me.

I ignored both. "Brianna found a dress, but it needs some alterations."

As if on cue, the saleswoman joined us with paperwork she needed filled out. I gladly took it and the pen she offered.

The door to the dressing room opened while I was writing down my telephone number. Brianna scanned the area searching for me. I met her gaze and a sweet blush coated her cheeks.

I extended my hand and she rushed to close the distance between us, the dress she'd tried on was clutched to her chest. She laced her fingers with mine and I tugged her against my side. It still amazed me how much joy I felt having her near. It made no logical sense, but I was beyond trying to understand it.

Ten minutes later we were on our way to the next store. Lily was obsessed. She'd researched every store in Le Sueur. She knew what each carried and even the owner's names. I was so glad Brianna wasn't like that. She was content to spend her days at home or taking a stroll in the park.

By the time we called it a day and headed home, I was ready to curl up in bed with Brianna and forget about clothes, shoes, or the way fabric draped. Logan, however, didn't seem to mind Lily's shopping. He happily helped carry her bags and gave his opinion when she asked what he thought of a particular outfit.

We'd had lunch at a little café, but by the time we wrapped up for the day it was dinner time, so I picked up a pizza on the way home. I didn't want Brianna to have to cook after such a grueling day.

When we arrived home, Logan took their bags upstairs while Brianna and Lily got plates and drinks for all of us. I carried the pizzas into the living room. By the time Logan made his way back downstairs, everything was ready for us to dig in.

I sat on the floor with Brianna between my knees as we ate. Lily was still buzzing about our day of shopping. Sometimes I wondered where she got all her energy from because she seemed to have an endless abundance of it.

Conversation eventually circled back to Logan and Lily's upcoming wedding. "Do you think you guys could come up to Minneapolis next weekend? I need to start looking for my dress and I need a companion that isn't Logan." She sent a very serious look her fiancée's way. "He's not allowed to see the dress before the wedding."

"Wanting to sneak a peek, are you?" I asked Logan as I leaned back against the base of my chair. Brianna shifted closer, adjusting to the new position. I wrapped my arms around her and placed a soft kiss at her temple.

He shrugged. "I'm not all that big on tradition as you know. I don't really see the point."

"The point is it's tradition. That's all that matters."

Logan tilted his head down and gave her a look. It was a warning, but she either didn't pick up on it or she was outright ignoring it. I didn't know which.

"We'll be spending the night before the wedding apart, too." She paused. "Which reminds me, I need to set up visits to the high-end hotels in the area. Five months really isn't that much time, but I have a few places that owe me favors, so we'll make it work."

She'd been going on and on as if she hadn't noticed the change in Logan's mood. I did. And so had Brianna.

Logan stood. "It's been a long day. I think we're going to turn in."

He reached for Lily and she took his hand. Without another word, they headed upstairs to their bedroom.

Brianna wiggled, her backside brushing against my cock. There wasn't anything sexual about it, however. I knew exactly what she was thinking. "Lily will be fine."

"You're sure?"

"More than likely, Lily knew what she was doing. Even if she didn't, she knows the rules and the consequences." I cupped her face with my hand and brushed my lips against hers.

Her wide blue eyes stared at me. "What will he do?"

I ran my hand down her arm and entangled our fingers together as I answered her question. "He'll most likely spank her. That or orgasm denial. Logan tends to prefer spanking, though, when Lily loses control of her tongue and he isn't willing or able to restrict her speech."

Brianna thought about that for a few moments and I waited while she processed what I'd said. "Why wouldn't he restrict her speech instead?"

The corners of my mouth ticked up. "Given they're here visiting for the weekend and Lily doesn't get to spend all that much time with us anymore, I doubt he'll want to prevent her from communicating with us. That's why I think he'll choose something a little more direct."

She seemed to consider that, and then lay her head on my shoulder.

When she didn't speak for several minutes, I decided to change the subject. "It's early, would you like to watch a movie?"

"Can we watch Buffy?"

I had to suppress a groan. Brianna had recently become addicted to the television show Buffy the Vampire Slayer. I'd downloaded the first season after reading several reviews that had raved about it. We'd watched the first twelve episodes and Brianna had asked if we could get the second season.

It was a good show. Entertaining. But I was pretty sure Brianna had a crush on Angel and I wasn't sure how I felt about that.

Unable to deny her, especially after I'd suggested we watch something. I picked up the remote, brought up Buffy the Vampire Slayer, and settled in for an hour of demon slaying and snarky banter.

CHAPTER 3

Brianna

The best part of waking up was having Stephan beside me. Before him, I couldn't remember sleeping so soundly. He made me feel safe and protected. I knew he wouldn't let anything happen to me and so I could let go and relax.

Of course, it helped that he tended to give me a couple of orgasms every night before we fell asleep as well. That always released any tension I had built up throughout the day. I'd come to realize sex was wonderful. Or maybe that was just sex with Stephan.

After getting dressed, I went to the kitchen to get breakfast started. It was Sunday, which meant waffles and sausage. I had a routine, so it didn't take me long to fry up the sausage and mix the batter for the waffles. Digging out my waffle iron, I plugged it in and lined everything up so it would be ready to go as soon as Logan and Lily came downstairs.

Stephan strolled into the kitchen, freshly showered. He laid my journal on the counter beside the refrigerator, and then began carrying the fruit I'd cut up and the juice to the table. It was then I heard movement coming from upstairs.

"Should I start the waffles?" I asked.

He paused to listen. "Give them fifteen minutes or so, and then you should be good. I'd rather wait for hot waffles than to have them go cold while we're waiting."

Nodding, I moved the sausage to the warming drawer. I didn't want them to overcook or get cold while we were waiting, either.

It was a good thing I hadn't made the waffles because it took Logan and Lily almost thirty minutes to appear. I was starting to get hungry. We didn't usually wait this long after waking to eat.

I took a good look at Lily as she made her way to the table. She looked fine. Normal. That is until she went to sit down. I noticed her take more care when lowering herself onto the dining room chair. Stephan was right. Logan must have spanked her.

Not that I'd doubted him. Stephan knew Logan well. They'd been friends for years and Stephan had trained Logan as a Dom.

Still. I didn't like seeing Lily in pain. I worried about her. I couldn't help it.

"Everything all right?" Stephan asked, coming up behind me.

One thing I didn't do was lie to Stephan. "Logan spanked Lily."

Stephan glanced over to where they were sitting. "Is her bottom a little sore this morning?"

I nodded. "She was really careful when she sat down."

He wrapped his arms around my waist and kissed the top of my head. "Maybe after breakfast you and Lily should have a talk. You can ask her about it."

"Okay."

He gave me a squeeze and released me. "I'll bring the sausages over while you get the waffles ready."

I was quiet during breakfast. Stephan didn't push me to talk. He knew I was concerned about Lily.

Once everything was cleaned and put away from breakfast, Stephan asked Logan if he wanted to walk the property with him before we headed to Stephan's aunt and uncle's for Sunday dinner. I knew it was really just a way for Stephan to give me time alone with Lily.

"So, what's up?" she asked almost as soon as Stephan and Logan were out the door. One thing I'd learned about Lily, she was always direct and to the point.

"Logan spanked you."

"How did you know that? Could you hear us?" she asked.

I shook my head. "No. This morning. When you sat down. I noticed you were . . . cautious."

"Ah." Lily took a seat on the couch and patted the space beside her.

I took a deep breath and lowered myself onto the cushion, facing Lily.

She reached for my hands and held them in her own. "Have you ever been spanked before? When you were a kid, I mean?"

"No. My mom didn't believe in spanking." I looked down at our hands and soldiered on. "One of Ian's friends. He liked to . . ." I didn't finish the sentence, but I didn't need to.

Lily gave my fingers a comforting squeeze. She knew a small bit of what Ian and his friends had done to me, but it was enough. "Do you want to talk about it?"

Did I? Not really. But I never wanted to talk about it. "I just wanted to make sure you were okay. That it was . . . consensual." It was a word I'd learned from Stephan and then was re-enforced by both my therapists.

"Everything we do is consensual. I have my safeword and he'll stop if I use it." She paused and then added, "He's proven that more than once."

"You've had to use your safeword before?" I felt my anxiety rising and did my best to keep myself calm. We were just talking. Everything was fine.

She nodded. "Not recently, but in the beginning when he was just learning, I used it quite a few times. He'd get carried away and focus too long in one spot or tie something too tight." Lily shrugged. "It happens. But the important thing is that when I used my safeword, he stopped like a good Dom should."

Although I'd been with Stephan for over four years, I was still learning, understanding dominance and submission and play. I knew how it worked with us, but it was different for every couple.

"Have you ever had to use your safeword with Stephan?"

I wasn't sure how to answer her question. Technically, I had, but never during sex. Unlike Lily and Logan, Stephan had me use a number scale. He said this way he could better gauge where I was. "Only when something's happened that's triggered a memory or something." I ran my teeth over the bottom of my lip deciding if I wanted to say anymore. "He's really good at reading me."

Lily chuckled. "Stephan's always been like that. It's one of the things that makes him a good Dom."

I nodded. It was true. Sometimes he could sense a shift in my mood within seconds. A slow smile pulled at my lips thinking about one time recently when I'd wanted sex but hadn't been comfortable asking. We'd been sitting in the living room watching a movie. All I did was glance over at him for a second before returning to look at the screen. A few seconds later, he had me on my back with my arms pinned above my head. We never did finish watching the movie.

"You're blushing."

I looked up to find Lily grinning, which only made more heat rush to my cheeks. We'd gotten off the subject and I still had questions for her. "Do you like it when Logan spanks you?"

"It depends." She sat back on the sofa, making herself comfortable. "If it's when we're playing, I like it a lot." She got a dreamy look in her eyes for a moment before she refocused on me. "But play spanking and discipline spanking are different."

The only experience I had with spanking was when I was with Ian and I'd learned over the years that wasn't the best gauge. I doubted Lily had bruises from the spanking she'd received last night, but I figured it was best to ask. "Do you have bruises?"

Lily shook her head. "No. He never spanks me that hard." She paused. "Although, there are some subs who like to be marked like that."

My eyes went wide. "Why?" I couldn't imagine anyone wanting that.

"Some of them enjoy the pain. Others view it as a badge of honor." She shrugged. "It's different for each person."

I twisted my fingers together before looking up at her. "I don't like thinking about you getting hurt."

"Logan would never hurt me. Not really. And a sore backside doesn't count." She stood abruptly and reached for my hand to pull me up. "While Logan and Stephan are off doing whatever it is they're doing, let's get a head start on dress shopping. You have a computer, right? I want to show you this website I found and see what you think."

"Yeah, it's on the nightstand in our bedroom."

She took hold of my hand and we were off.

Stephan

When Logan and I came in from our walk, Brianna and Lily were no longer in the main living area. He headed upstairs to look for them while I scoured the downstairs.

I found them both sitting on our bed looking at Brianna's laptop. "There you both are."

"We figured you'd be a while, so we thought we'd look at some bridesmaid dresses," Lily said.

I strolled over to the bed and glanced at the screen. There was a ball gown style dress with a long slit down the side. It looked rather sexy for a bridesmaid dress, but what did I know?

Brushing the back of my hand along Brianna's cheek, I smiled down at her doing something so normal. I loved seeing her like this. It was so simple, but that was the beauty of it.

"We have about a half hour before we have to leave, so you two need to wrap things up here." With that, I left them alone and went to find Logan.

I ran into him at the bottom of the stairs. "Did you find them?" he asked.

"They're in our bedroom looking at bridesmaid's dresses."

He shook his head and chuckled. "She has wedding fever and we still have five months to go."

I went to the refrigerator and removed a pitcher. "Water?"

"Yes, please," he said and took a seat at the island.

"You know Lily. She's in her element planning a big event and this is her wedding. She's going to go all out."

"I know. And I want her to. I just hope I have the stamina to keep up."

I set a glass of water in front of him and pulled out a stool. "You keep up with her any other time. Why would this be different?"

He took a drink before he answered. "I want it to be perfect for her."

"I can understand that."

A few minutes passed as we sat there sipping our water and looking out at the river that ran behind our house. On warm nights, Brianna and I sat on our deck and watched the water flow. She found it peaceful, and so did I.

"You and Brianna think you'll get married?" he asked.

"I don't know."

Logan turned to look at me. "Never thought about it?"

"I would marry her in a heartbeat if that's what she wanted."

He raised his eyebrows. "She doesn't want to get married?"

"It hasn't come up. She's just now getting her feet under her and finding her way in the world. I figure if it's something she wants to explore; she'll bring it up." I couldn't hide my smile as I remembered some of the stranger conversations we'd had. Brianna had gone from not wanting to ask anything to asking everything. I never knew what topic of conversation we'd discuss from one day to the next.

No more was said on the topic as Brianna and Lily exited the bedroom and joined us at the island. I tugged Brianna to stand between my legs, resting my hands on her hips. "Are you thirsty?" I asked.

She nodded, so after giving her a quick kiss I got up and poured her a glass of water.

"Lily?"

She picked up Logan's glass. "No, thanks. I'm good."

"Stephan said you guys were looking at bridesmaid dresses," Logan said. "Find any you liked?"

Lily hummed. "I've got it narrowed down to a few different styles. It's all going to depend how they look on."

She went on about ruching and cinched waists for a few minutes while the rest of us sat and listened. It was starting to make my eyes glaze over, so I was relieved when I noticed the time. "We should probably get going if we don't want to be late."

Since Logan and Lily would be driving back to the city after dinner, they drove separately. It was the perfect opportunity for Brianna and me to talk uninterrupted. I laced our fingers together, resting them on my thigh. "Logan has a friend who's starting a nonprofit and would like my input."

Brianna didn't respond right away. "Does that mean you'll be going into the city more often?"

"I don't know. It depends." I wasn't sure how she'd react to the information, although we'd been talking recently about me finding another position. It wasn't that I had to work, but as time went on I had less and less to do with the foundation my family established. For the past six months, the only thing I did was attend monthly board meetings. That left a lot of extra time on my hands. As much as I loved Brianna and enjoyed our time together, I knew it was best for both of us if I found another job.

She was quiet for a long time. I knew she was thinking things through. Brianna didn't sulk like some women. She also didn't throw temper tantrums when she didn't get her way. No, Brianna was mulling over her thoughts and feelings regarding what I'd told her.

When she did finally speak, it wasn't about my potential new job. "I want to learn how to drive again."

I glanced over at her. She was looking at the road ahead, not at me. "Brianna."

That was all it took for her to turn in my direction.

We'd known each other for four years and not once had she indicated she had a desire to drive a car. "Not that I object to you learning to drive again, but what brought that up?"

"If you're going back to work, then I want to go back to school. I want to be useful. But I can't do that unless I can drive."

Well, that explained the long silence that had filled the car after my announcement. It wasn't as if we hadn't talked about her going back to school over the years. We had. However, it had always been in the abstract. Something far off into the future. Apparently, the future had arrived.

I couldn't dismiss the grain of fear that settled into the pit of my stomach. Even though I knew I couldn't protect her from everything, I still wanted to. My protective instincts when it came to Brianna were always out in full force.

Logic and reason won the day, however. "All right. I'll have your car brought to the house. We can begin working on some things in the yard. Once you're comfortable there, we can try driving on an actual road."

The sound of skin rubbing against leather assaulted my ears a moment before I felt her head resting on my arm. "Thank you."

I pressed my cheek to the top of her head, my eyes never leaving the road, and took a deep breath. In that moment, I knew my life was about to get very complicated.

We pulled up to Diane and Richard's house five minutes later, the conversation still fresh in my mind. I needed to let it go, though. At least, for now. My relationship with Richard had come a long way. He no longer looked at me as if he were waiting for the other shoe to drop. And he was good to Brianna. That went a long way.

He'd still never asked me anymore about being a Dom. Every now and then, I'd see him give me a long, measured look after witnessing an exchange between me and Brianna, but good to his word, he'd kept his opinions to himself.

Speaking of Richard, he strolled out the front door as I was helping Brianna out of the vehicle. "I hope you all brought your swimsuits. Diane insisted on a pool party."

"We've got ours," Lily said as she and Logan sauntered up beside us.

"We do?" Logan asked.

"Of course. I knew we were coming today and that Diane and

Richard have a pool." She smiled at my uncle. "It always pays to be prepared."

Diane was in the kitchen mixing what looked to be a type of pasta salad. She beamed as soon as she saw us and abandoned her position behind the counter to greet us. She enveloped first Brianna, and then me in a hug. "I'm so glad you're here. I made a new dessert I want you to try."

Once greetings were out of the way, Diane shooed us out onto the back patio so she could finish getting things ready. Brianna had offered to help, but my aunt refused, saying she had everything under control.

I lowered myself into one of the lounge chairs and pulled Brianna onto my lap. She wedged herself between my legs and rested against my chest. Logan and Lily took up a similar position a few feet away.

Richard pulled up a straight-backed chair and sighed as he sat down. "It turned out to be a perfect day. Not too hot. Not to cold. Couldn't ask for anything more in July."

"Hard to believe it was ninety degrees last week."

My uncle nodded at Logan. "I'd rather have that than the subzero temperatures in winter. The older I get, the less I like the ice and snow. Diane and I've been talking about maybe getting a winter house in Texas or something."

"You planning to retire?" I asked. He hadn't mentioned it before, but if they were seriously talking about spending winters down south, that had to be on the table.

"I ain't getting any younger."

That wasn't exactly an answer, but the patio door opened, and Diane began bringing out the food, so I let the subject drop. There'd be plenty of time later to talk.

CHAPTER 4

Brianna

We all sat around a long glass table in Diane and Richard's backyard talking and eating. Well, Lily and Diane did most of the talking. Once it had come out that Lily and Logan were getting married, Diane had gotten really excited and started asking a bunch of questions.

Stephan, Logan, and Richard seemed content to let them dominate the conversation while they dug into their meal. I found I was rather fascinated with the conversation, but I couldn't figure out why exactly. They were talking about dresses and flowers and even honeymoon destinations.

I was focused on their conversation so much that Stephan had to remind me to eat a couple of times.

Once everyone was finished, Diane brought out the dessert she'd made. It was a pineapple upside down cake. The last time I'd had one was when my mom was still alive.

The combination of sweet pineapple and cake hit my tongue and I closed my eyes remembering the last time I'd experience the same flavors.

"Brianna?"

I opened my eyes and turned toward Stephan's voice. There were concerned creases in his brow as he stared back at me.

He reached up and it was only then I realized I was crying. "What's wrong, love?"

"I was just remembering my mom."

The tension at the corners of his eyes eased and he brushed the moisture away from my cheeks. "Did you make this a lot with her?"

"No. Just once. Right before she got sick." Those were the good times. Although looking back, the cancer had probably already been inside her.

He leaned forward and placed a soft kiss on my lips. "Finish your cake and we'll take a walk."

I did as he asked. Luckily, the only person who appeared to have noticed my emotional response was Diane. She gave me an encouraging smile from across the table, and then returned her attention to the others.

True to his word, as soon as I was finished eating my cake, Stephan stood. "Brianna and I are going for a walk."

Lily looked as if she were going to get up from her chair, but Logan placed his hand on her arm, and she stopped. Maybe Diane wasn't the only one who noticed my crying.

"Have fun," Diane said, already beginning to gather the dessert plates to take them inside.

Stephan and I walked hand in hand down the path that led to the river. He didn't say anything until we reached his rock.

There was more white water here than there was at our new house, but I loved them both. The water called to me, and I'd learned it did the same to Stephan.

He circled his arm around me, drawing my head to his shoulder as we sat on the end of the rock as it jutted out over the water. His warmth seeped into my skin and I felt myself breathing easier.

"I still miss her," I whispered.

"I know." He kissed the top of my head. "I still miss my parents, as well. I don't think it ever goes away."

We sat there for a while not saying anything, just listening to the water flowing by. "Sir, can I ask you something about your parents?"

"You can ask me anything, Brianna. You know that."

I knew that was true, but I was still a little nervous asking, although I had no idea why. "Do you think . . . do you think your parents would have liked me?"

Stephan opened his mouth, and then shut it again, thinking about his answer. "My mom was a lot like Diane. She would have embraced you and taken you under her wing. She would have loved cooking and baking with you in the kitchen."

When he didn't say anything more, I had to ask. "And your dad?"

His mouth twisted. I couldn't tell if he was thinking really hard or he didn't want to tell me something. "With my dad it's hard to say. He had a difficult time trusting people sometimes. I have a feeling it would have been an uphill battle, much as it has been with Richard. Although, for different reasons."

"I'm glad Richard isn't mean to you anymore."

He tilted my chin so I could look into his eyes. His thumb caressed my jaw before he kissed me.

It was a slow kiss, long and deep, his tongue taking its time to explore my mouth. My lips tingled and heat spread to every inch of my body. I felt myself getting wet and it had nothing to do with the water below us.

Stephan hummed as he released me. "I can never get enough of you."

"Nor I you, Sir."

He smiled, and then started to get up. I followed his lead, moving back on the rock before standing.

As we neared the edge of the forest that opened to Diane and Richard's backyard, we could hear water splashing. "It sounds as if Logan and Lily are enjoying the pool."

A loud squeal filled the air. It wasn't one of fear, however, given it was immediately followed by laughter. Lily's laughter.

"Want to go for a swim?" Stephan asked as we left the shade of the forest.

"I don't have a swimsuit."

"I'm sure Diane can find you something to wear."

Did I want to go swimming? I looked over to the pool and found Logan and Lily twirling around in each other's arms, smiling as if they couldn't be happier.

I glance up at Stephan. "Will you swim, too?"

He placed a kiss on my knuckles. "I'm sure Richard has a pair of trunks I can borrow."

"Okay."

It took Diane all of five minutes to find an old swimsuit for me and a pair of trunks for Stephan. The top of the bathing suit she found me was a little big as her breasts were a bit larger than mine, so she gave me a t-shirt to wear over it. The shirt was so long, it came down past where the bathing suit bottom ended. If one didn't know any better, it looked like all I had on was the shirt.

I cautiously walked onto the patio where Stephan was waiting, wearing nothing but a pair of long shorts. He spotted me right away and his gaze roamed over me from top to bottom. It didn't take long for that flutter in my stomach to start when he looked at me that way.

Stephan extended his arm, silently asking me to come to him.

Crossing the distance, I took hold of his hand and stood before him. He gave my shirt another brief look, so I explained. "The top was too big."

He released my hand and gripped the hem of the t-shirt with both hands. Before I understood what he was doing, he had the material bunched up and was tying it in a knot at my waist.

Once that was done, he turned me so I was facing away from him. "Much better."

It took me a moment to realize that he was looking at my butt. I felt a blush stain my cheeks.

His chest vibrated as he turned me around and noticed I was blushing. With a quick kiss, he led me toward the pool.

I'd gone in Diane and Richard's pool once last summer. Before that, the last time I'd been swimming was when my mom used to take me to the community pool for lessons. It had taken me a few minutes to get used to being back in the water, but soon everything I'd learned had come back to me.

The water was warm today as I made my way down the stairs into the pool. It wasn't as big as the community pool had been, but it was fancier. They even had a hot tub at one end, although I hadn't been in it yet.

Stephan dove underwater as soon as his feet hit the bottom. When he came back up, he slicked his hair back out of his eyes. Water beads trickled down his chest and I had the urge to lick them off him.

He noticed me staring at his chest and got that gleam in his eyes I knew so well. Closing the distance between us, he pulled me into his arms. Immediately, I felt the hard length of him against my belly. I thought maybe he'd tease me and tell me I needed to behave or even comment on how he'd have me take care of him later, but instead he cupped the back of my head and crashed his lips over mine.

I sucked in a breath at the sudden onslaught as he plunged his tongue into my mouth without warning. The kiss was intense and all I could do was hold on.

Stephan

The woman didn't know what she did to me. One look from her and it sent my body into hyperdrive. I wanted her with every fiber of my being, and it didn't matter that our friends were nearby or that my aunt and uncle could walk in on us at any given time. Logic and reason didn't mean much when she looked at me like that.

And it was even hotter that she had no idea. Even though Brianna was more confident sexually than she used to be, she still didn't understand the power she held over me. She didn't realize that I would lay the world at her feet if I could.

Water splashed on us and I released her. I turned to glare at Logan.

He laughed. "Cool it, lover boy. I don't think your aunt and uncle want that kind of a show."

My gaze whipped in the direction of the house. Sure enough,

Diane and Richard had come back outside. They were deep in conversation and weren't paying us much attention . . . yet.

Reluctantly, I released Brianna. "Why don't you swim a couple of laps."

She nodded and headed for the deep end of the pool. As soon as she was away, I lowered myself into the water, submerging my entire body. I needed to cool off.

By the time Brianna finished two laps, I was feeling more in control of myself. We spent the next hour chatting with Logan and Lily and lounging in the pool.

Diane had brought towels out for us and laid them on a chair near the entrance to the pool. I threw a towel around my neck, and then picked one up for Brianna and began drying her off as best I could. The t-shirt didn't help as it held onto more water than a bathing suit would.

Once we were as dry as we were going to get in our swimming attire, we rejoined Diane and Richard. We still had several hours before evening and no one was in a hurry to leave.

"It doesn't get much better than this," Richard said as he lay back in his lounge chair. Diane, Lily, and Brianna had gone upstairs to wash off and change. They'd been gone for a while, though, which led me to believe they were doing more than just washing and changing. That was good, though. Brianna felt safe with Diane and Lily and she needed to have relationships with other people besides me.

"I just wish I didn't have to go back to work tomorrow. I need at least a week of this," Logan said.

Richard took a sip of his drink. I think it was whiskey, but I couldn't be certain. Since I didn't drink, I didn't pay all that much attention to types of liquor. "It's one of the things I'm looking forward to most when I retire. I can sit out here by the pool every night if I want. No paperwork to do. No rushing to the hospital."

"We can't all be like Stephan." Logan winked at me.

"It's nice for a while, but eventually it catches up to you. I can't imagine what it would be like if not for Brianna." I looked up at the sky, taking in the changing colors as the sun began to move lower in the sky. "Still, a part of me would like to get back to work. I miss managing big projects."

"You could do some traveling," Richard suggested. "I doubt Brianna has seen much of the world. Neither have you, for that matter."

"We drove up to Lake Superior last year and did some exploring. It's not as if we stay at home all the time."

"Maybe it's time you got over your fear of flying."

Logan knew why I didn't like to fly. I'd been in a plane once since I met Brianna and that was to take her to see her mother's grave. It wasn't an experience I wished to repeat anytime soon. "I'll think about it."

Before either could say any more on the subject, I stood. "I'm going to see what's taking the girls so long."

"That's not a bad idea," Logan said. "Lily and I should probably be going soon. We both have to work tomorrow."

I didn't argue when Logan followed me into the house. The downstairs was quiet, which meant they were still upstairs.

About halfway up the stairs, we heard them giggling. "What about this one?"

There was a pause, and then more laughter.

The sight we were met with when we reached my aunt's bedroom wasn't what I'd expected. Brianna and Lily were trying on hats. Some I'd seen my aunt wear before and some that looked as if they hadn't seen the light of day for several decades.

It took a few minutes for them to notice us in the doorway. My aunt was smiling from ear to ear. "Did you boys want to join us?"

"Why are you trying on hats?" I asked.

My aunt waved her hand dismissively as she began gathering the hats and putting them back into the boxes they'd been stored in. "It's a long story."

"I was being nosey." Lily removed the hat from her head and placed it in a box.

Diane chuckled. "Okay, not so long a story."

"It's after seven," Logan said, speaking up for the first time since we'd come upstairs. "We should start heading back to the city."

Lily nodded. "Thanks for letting me try on some of your hats. You have a great collection."

"Anytime."

Goodbyes were exchanged, and I promised to bring Brianna into the city next Friday so she and Lily could go look at dresses. By the time Logan and Lily pulled out of the driveway in their vehicle, I knew Brianna and I should probably be heading home as well.

"You both could spend the night," my aunt said as she packed up leftovers for us. "I put clean sheets on your bed a few days ago."

"As tempting as that is, I have some things to do in the morning that I need to be home for." Even though those things weren't on a hard time schedule, there were several things Brianna and I needed to go over and that would be easier to do at home. As much as I loved my aunt and uncle, they did tend to limit my time alone with Brianna since my aunt always tried to think of ways to include her in whatever she was doing. It was great, but it was contrary to any long, heartfelt discussions.

Diane made sure she packed enough food for Brianna and me to have lunch tomorrow and handed the bundle over to me. I wrapped my arm around her waist and pulled her in for a hug. "Dinner was delicious. Thank you."

She held me close and gave me a kiss on my cheek. "You know you and Brianna are welcome anytime. Not just on Sunday's."

"I know. Maybe one of these days you and Richard can come to dinner at our place. You haven't been there since we moved in."

Diane averted her gaze before looking back at me again. "We didn't want to impose."

While things had been good between my uncle and I for the last year, I wondered if maybe Diane was concerned there would be something at our house that could create a rift again. I'm sure that was the case, however, I had no plans to show my uncle our bedroom or my playroom. Those were the only two rooms that contained anything out of the ordinary.

"It wouldn't be imposing." I figured there was no reason not to leap in with both feet. "How about next Wednesday? That's Richard's half day, right?"

She nodded. "All right. We'll plan on Wednesday. Four o'clock okay?"

I grinned. "Four o'clock sounds perfect."

Brianna returned from the bathroom and came immediately to stand at my side. I rested my hand on her waist. "Diane and Richard are going to come for dinner next Wednesday."

Before Brianna could respond, my aunt spoke up. "If that's okay with you."

"Of course," Brianna said. "Do you like lasagna?"

"I love lasagna. So does Richard."

Brianna smiled.

Richard strolled into the room. "I found that book I was telling you about, Brianna." He handed it to her. I couldn't read the name on the spine, but it looked old.

"Thank you." She took the book from him and cradled it against her chest.

"You're welcome." Richard rocked back on his heels. "I might have a few others that would interest you, although most of my collection are medical journals."

My gaze drifted to the clock on the wall. It was going to be getting dark soon. "We should be going."

Diane gave Brianna a quick hug. "We'll see you Wednesday."

As we were leaving, I heard my uncle ask Diane what was happening Wednesday. Brianna apparently heard it as well. "Will he be mad that she made plans without asking him first?"

"Upset that you're going to cook for him?" I chuckled as I opened Brianna's door and waited for her to slide into the passenger seat. "No. He's more likely rushing to mark his calendar so he can count down the days till he gets to enjoy your cooking."

"It's just lasagna."

I shook my head and shut her door before making my way around the car to get behind the wheel. Brianna always underestimated herself. And her cooking.

CHAPTER 5

Brianna

It was dark by the time we got home. He carried the leftovers into the kitchen and placed them on the counter beside the refrigerator. "Why don't you go write in your journal while I put these things away?"

With Logan and Lily visiting, we'd gotten out of our routine. Normally, I wrote in my journal throughout the day, and then Stephan would read it while I made dinner. That hadn't been possible while we had company.

I went to the study where I kept my journal and sat in the window seat overlooking our backyard. The moon reflected off the water, casting a shadow over the surrounding area.

Opening my journal, I began to write. At first, I'd found it hard to put down my feelings on paper, but the more I did it, the easier it was. This was a safe place for me to express myself. No one read my journal but me and Stephan—and Stephan never judged me. I could be afraid, angry, confused and it was okay. We'd talk about it and figure it out. Together.

An hour had passed before I was done jotting down my thoughts. I knew Stephan was long finished putting the leftovers away. He was giving me time alone.

I took one long look outside the window, and then headed downstairs to find Stephan. He was in the laundry room, taking a load of clothes out of the dryer. He glanced up when he saw me, and then went back to what he was doing. "Finished writing in your journal?"

"Yes, Sir."

He nodded. "Go ahead and get ready for bed. I'll be in as soon as I finish up here."

When I'd first started living with Stephan, we'd sit in his chair every night before bed and talk. We still talked every night, but it wasn't always in his chair. Sometimes, like tonight, it would be cuddled in bed.

The first thing I did when I entered our room was walk over to his side of the bed and place my journal on his nightstand. He would most likely want to read it right away.

Then, I padded into the master bathroom and began getting ready. That meant I needed to get naked. Clothes were not permitted in bed except on rare occasions.

I brushed my teeth and ran a brush through my hair before heading back to the bedroom. Stephan was there putting clothes in one of the dressers. He spotted me right away and a slow smile pulled at his lips. "Get in bed. I'll be there shortly."

True to his word, he finished what he was doing, and then disappeared into the bathroom. A few minutes later, he strolled—undressed—into the bedroom holding a length of rope. Without comment, he placed it at the foot of the bed and climbed in beside me.

As expected, he propped himself up against the headboard, pulled me against him, and then reached for my journal. I closed my eyes, enjoying the feel of him against me, skin to skin. He balanced my journal on his lap with one hand and rested the other on my hip.

I'd written a lot, so it took him several minutes to get through it. Time had taught me to be patient. It had also taught me not to be worried he'd get mad at me for something I'd written.

That had been at the forefront of my mind when he'd first given me a journal. I was always terrified I'd get in trouble for saying how I really felt. Stephan wasn't like that, though. He was the most understanding man I'd ever met.

When I heard him close the journal and shift to set it back on his nightstand, I opened my eyes. "You didn't write about your conversation with Lily."

"I wanted to think about it some more. And . . . and to talk to you."

The hand on my hip began to move ever so slightly. It was comforting but distracting at the same time. Then again, he probably knew that. "Lily said there's a difference between play spanking and what Logan did to her last night. I don't understand how there could be a difference."

"It has to do with preparation."

"Preparation?"

He nodded and brought his free hand up to cup my breast. "If I play with your breasts, lick them, suck on them . . . prepare them, then when I give them a hard pinch it adds to your pleasure." His thumb circled my nipple before giving hit a little tug between his thumb and forefinger. "But if I don't prepare you and just give your nipple a hard pinch without warming you up first, there is only going to be pain."

That made sense. Stephan always made sure I was ready for whatever we did together, but I'd experienced plenty of the other with Ian and his friends. "So, when Logan spanks her not for pleasure, he doesn't prepare her first?"

"Correct." He skimmed the back of his hand down the length of my torso to right below my belly button. "When you spank someone for pleasure, you warm them up. You rub their backside, maybe even give them some lighter swats. It warms up the flesh and turns it a slightly pink color."

"That makes it more pleasurable?"

"It does."

He continued to tease me by running his fingers right above the junction of my thighs. I wanted him to go lower, to touch me. My legs fell open, urging him to take what was his.

"Eager, my pet?" His nose brushed against my ear as his lips sent tingles down my spine as he placed barely there kisses on my neck.

"Yes, Sir."

I felt him smile as he inched his fingers down a little lower. They were now right above my clit. "Are you wet?"

"Yes."

"Show me."

I knew what he wanted. Without a moment's hesitation, I bent one leg and moved so my legs were spread, and I was completely open to him.

He slid down the bed, positioning himself between my legs, spreading me open farther. A satisfied humming sound came from deep in his throat a split second before his mouth made contact with my sex, sending my eyes rolling back in my head.

My head fell back against the headboard with a light thump, but I barely noticed. I was too focused on the sensation his tongue was creating. The next thing I knew, his mouth was gone, and I was being pulled down onto the bed, so I was lying flat on my back.

"Give me your wrists."

I lifted my arms, presenting my wrists to him. Since he'd brought the rope to bed with him, I knew what was coming and I welcomed it. We'd done a lot of exploring with rope and it was something I'd come to love. It was as if the rope was an extension of Stephan, wrapping itself around me, holding me close, protecting me.

Stephan positioned my wrists palms together, so they were touching, and then wound the rope around them both before securing them in the middle. He tested to make sure the ropes weren't too tight before pulling the loose end above my head. The rope tugged at my arms as he hovered above me, securing it to the headboard.

The weight of his body pressed into me, holding me to the bed. I opened my eyes to find him staring down at me.

"You are beautiful, my love. So beautiful. And all mine." He covered my lips with his as his hands began to explore.

My breasts ached as he played with them and I raised my hips, silently begging for more. Stephan responded by giving one of my nipples a hard pinch. I gasped as the pain radiated from my nipple straight to the part of me that ached to have him inside me.

"Patience," he whispered in my ear before abandoning my mouth to work his way lower.

When he reached the nipple he'd pinched, he sucked it into his mouth, soothing it with his tongue. I couldn't stop the moan that escaped my throat even if I wanted to. My body was an instrument and he knew exactly how to play it.

He gave each breast plenty of attention. By the time his mouth left them, they both felt heavy and ultra-sensitive. His chest brushing against my nipples had them pulsing.

I stared into his eyes as he spread my legs wide and positioned himself at my entrance. He captured my lips with his at the same time he thrust inside me.

The sensation of him surrounding me was almost overwhelming. All I could do was feel. Him. The ropes. The way my breasts brushed against his chest with every movement.

One hand held my head in place, his fingers digging into my scalp. The other was splayed across my hip, holding me exactly where he wanted me. He was hitting a spot deep inside me that had me spiraling toward an orgasm.

I held on, trying to focus on not coming. He hadn't given me permission yet.

More time passed. I had no idea how long. I'd lost all notion of time, but I knew I wouldn't be able to hold on much longer. My legs began to shake, and I could feel my internal muscles tightening, ready to explode.

Just as I was about ready to lose control, permission or not, I heard Stephan say the words I'd been longing to hear. "Come for me."

Stephan

Maybe having our nightly talk in our bed hadn't been the best idea.

It's not as if we hadn't done so before, but after spending the afternoon with her in the pool and having to keep my hands to myself for the most part, I couldn't resist. I hadn't wanted to.

After giving Brianna permission to come, she'd screamed out her climax. It would probably have scared the neighbors if we had any close by. And as often happened when Brianna and I had an intense session, she fell into this trance-like state, and had then fallen asleep cuddled in my arms.

I lay there until I was certain she was sound asleep before crawling out of bed, putting the rope away, and turning off the lights. There was a lot still to discuss regarding her journal entry. She'd talked a lot about Lily's upcoming wedding and about our outing in town the day before. It had been a busy weekend with not a lot of down time. I wouldn't be surprised if it took the entire week for us to discuss everything. And that didn't take into consideration that tomorrow she had an appointment with her therapist. That was always guaranteed to bring up topics that needed to be discussed.

As gently as I could, I eased back into bed and pulled her against my chest. She released a soft sigh as she nestled her backside against my stomach. I pressed a kiss to the back of her head and closed my eyes, letting the sound of her breathing lull me to sleep.

The next thing I remember was the feel of lips pressing against my collarbone. I sucked in a deep breath and was rewarded by the sound of giggles.

"What do you think you're doing?" I asked, keeping my eyes closed.

"Giving you kisses."

Without warning, I grabbed hold of her hips and flipped our positions. She was now staring up at me with a huge smile on her face. It was so good to see her this happy.

"Good morning, Sir."

I brushed the hair out of her face and gave her a proper kiss. "Good morning, Brianna."

She ran her fingers through my hair and down my back. I felt my body responding, but I couldn't give in this time. "What time is it?"

"Almost nine. You must have been tired."

I felt a smile tug at the corner of my lips. "Someone wore me out last night."

A pretty blush stained her cheeks.

After another swift kiss, I rolled over and started to get up. "As much as I'd love to spend the day in bed with you, I have some things I need to do this morning and you have an appointment with Dr. Katlin to prepare for."

She nodded and followed me into the bathroom to get ready for the day.

An hour later I was sitting at my desk, drinking a cup of coffee, and scrolling through my emails. Logan's friend had contacted me. He was eager to speak to me and wanted to arrange an in-person meeting to discuss the details. I quickly shot an email back informing him I'd be in Minneapolis on Friday and I could meet with him then. Brianna would be with Lily and it would give me something to do while they were fawning over dresses.

His response came less than five minutes later. We ended up exchanging a few more emails to nail down the time and place before I signed off and headed downstairs.

Brianna was curled up on the couch with the notebook she used for therapy. It was something Dr. Katlin had asked her to start using. Brianna had only been seeing her for a few weeks, so they were still getting used to each other.

The notebook was for her to write down any questions or issues that Brianna wished to discuss during their session. When I'd questioned her about it that first night, she'd explained that she was having trouble opening up to her therapist—that they'd spent almost the entire hour sitting there in silence. This method appeared to be working. From what Brianna had told me, last week's session had gone well.

She looked up as I walked into the room.

"How's the list coming along?"

Brianna scraped her teeth along her bottom lip. "Good, I think. I have three things written down so far that I want to talk about today."

I nodded and sat down beside her. "I spoke to Logan's friend. We've arranged to meet on Friday while you and Lily are dress shopping."

"That makes sense." She looked down at her paper and I could tell she was holding something back. "Tell me."

She looked up at me with those blue eyes that made me want to give her the world. "Lily's going to ask me about the dresses . . . what I think. I'm not good at that."

I brushed the back of my hand along the side of her face. "You'll do fine. Just be honest. Lily can take it."

Brianna gave me the barest nod.

There was still something I wanted to do before lunch. "I'll let you get back to your list. If you need me, I'll be outside." I leaned down and gave her a soft kiss.

"Okay," she whispered as her eyes fluttered back open.

Our property consisted of ten acres, and the house was situated roughly an acre and a half from the road. The nearest house was on the other side of the river. We could see it in the distance, but we'd yet to meet the people who lived there. For all intents and purposes, we were rather isolated.

As I looked out at our side yard, I took some mental calculations as to where and how we should proceed with Brianna's driving instruction. She hadn't been behind the wheel in six years, not since before she was taken.

That wasn't entirely true. She'd tried to drive once about two years ago. We'd been in the parking garage at my condo and she'd tried to back the car out of its space. She'd been taking her time, trying to get her bearings, when another car came up behind her and honked. It scared her and we ended up back in my condo with me rocking her until she calmed down.

Brianna couldn't have that kind of reaction on the road and we both knew it. She'd come a long way since then, however, and I agreed that it was a good idea to try again. This time we were going to take it slow.

I ambled a fair distance away from the house to a rather flat area of ground. It wasn't near the river, which was a plus, and thanks to the landscaper I'd hired, it was freshly mowed. It would give Brianna enough space to get comfortable behind the wheel again.

Pulling out my phone, I called the storage facility where the car I'd purchased for Brianna four years ago was being housed and arranged for them to deliver it the following day. I'd originally planned on selling it, and then buying her a new one when she was ready, but Brianna thought that was wasteful since there wasn't anything wrong with the car I'd bought her.

At first, I didn't understand her logic. What was the big deal if I sold one car and bought a new one when she was ready? Then I'd realized she liked the car I'd purchased for her and was hoping one day she'd be able to drive it.

With that done and a plan in place, I checked the time. It was almost eleven-thirty and we had to be at Brianna's therapist's office at one. There would be just enough time to have lunch and drive into town.

Brianna was one step ahead of me. Plates and glasses were already laid out on the kitchen island when I came through the door. She was digging the leftovers out of the refrigerator.

"Need some help?" I asked.

"No, Sir. I've almost got everything ready.

With the precision of someone who was comfortable in the kitchen, she moved with grace. I washed my hands and took a seat, allowing her to do her thing.

My gaze zeroed in on the way her hips swayed back and forth as she moved. The vision I had of her bent over, her ass in the air as I sank my cock into her had my body overheating. It was too bad I couldn't act on it anytime soon.

Brianna slid onto the stool beside me and handed me a bowl with some of the pasta salad my aunt had made. I took it from her, focused on the task at hand, and willed my erection to go away. There'd be time for that later.

As I was scooping up a forkful into my mouth, I noticed a knowing grin tugging at Brianna's lips. Something told me she knew exactly what I'd been thinking and that did nothing to help the problem in my pants.

CHAPTER 6

Brianna

Stephan sat beside me as I waited for Dr. Katlin to come get me. He'd brought a book with him to read while I was in my session. It would be good if he didn't always have to bring me, if I could drive myself.

Right on time, the door to her office opened and a woman at least twice my age walked out followed by Dr. Katlin. The lady looked as if she'd been crying. My gaze followed her to the door as she exited the room.

"Are you ready for your appointment, Anna?"

My gaze snapped back to Dr. Katlin and I scrambled to my feet. "Yes. Yes, I'm ready."

I walked two steps, and then glanced back at Stephan. He gave me a little nod. I took a deep breath, then followed Dr. Katlin into her office.

The first thing I'd noticed about Dr. Katlin's office was how colorful it was. My previous therapist, Dr. Perkins, her office was full of beige and tan and white. Even the paintings that hung throughout the office were rather plain. That was the complete opposite of Dr. Katlin's office. Everywhere you looked here there was color. Even her couch was a mustard yellow. The only non-colorful things in the room were her large wood desk and the cream-colored carpet.

I took a seat on the yellow couch and waited.

"How are you feeling today?"

"Good." I paused, looking down at the notebook on my lap. "I . . . I wrote some things down."

Dr. Katlin crossed one leg over the other and got her pen ready. "I'm all ears. What would you like to talk about?"

Opening the notebook, I decided to start at the top of the list I'd made. "Logan and Lily came to visit us this weekend."

"They're friends of yours?"

"Of Stephan's."

She scribbled something down in her notes. "They're not your friends, though."

"Lily is my friend." I picked at the tangled edges of the paper. "They're getting married and they want us both to be in the wedding."

More writing. "I see. And do you want to be in their wedding?"

"Yes."

"But?"

Sometimes I didn't know which one was better at reading me or probing for answers, Stephan or Dr. Katlin. "There will be a lot of people there. I don't do well around people."

"When is the wedding?"

"They're getting married on Christmas Eve."

She nodded as she wrote. "Have you talked to Stephan about your fear?"

"Yes. He says we'll work on it." I looked down at my paper, not really seeing it. "I just don't want to have a panic attack and ruin Lily's wedding."

"When was the last time you had a panic attack?" Dr. Katlin asked.

"Forty-one days ago."

Her eyebrows rose. "You recall the exact day?"

I nodded. "We were packing up to move and one of the guys from the moving company startled me. I'd been focused on what I was doing and didn't see him."

"According to Dr. Perkins, most of your panic attacks over the last couple of years have happened when you've been caught unawares. When you've been in a situation where you didn't expect there to be a lot of people or loud noises."

This was true. Stephan and I had even gone to the mall a few times and I'd been okay. Of course, he hadn't left me alone any of those times. "Stephan won't always be with me at the wedding."

More jotting of notes. "Before our next session, I want you to think about different scenarios you might find yourself in at a wedding. Close your eyes and think about each one of them and how you might handle them. Write down the ones that cause you the most concern and we'll see if we can find ways to help you work through them."

"Okay."

We moved on to a few other things I'd written down. She was right. It was easier talking to her if I had the topics written down in front of me. Otherwise, most of the time I couldn't think of anything.

I knew our session was almost up when she placed her notes on the table and uncrossed her legs. "Was there anything else you'd like to discuss today?"

I pressed my lips together debating whether to ask her my question. She'd met with both Stephan and me that first time and we'd talked about our relationship. While she seemed to be okay with Stephan being a Dom, we hadn't discussed any details yet. I didn't know how she'd react.

"This is a safe place, Anna. No judgement."

"I think . . . I think I want Stephan to spank me."

She was quiet for a long moment. "And he doesn't want to spank you?"

"No. I mean, I think he does. He's spanked submissives in the past."

Dr. Katlin looked confused and I knew I wasn't explaining very well.

"I saw Logan spank Lily once and I . . . I had a panic attack. A bad one."

Realization dawned on her face. "How long ago did this happen?"

"About four years ago."

"Four years is a long time."

"I know." Unease settled in the pit of my stomach.

She rested her hand over mine for a brief second before removing it. "Is this really about wanting Stephan to spank you or is it about something else?"

I felt tears prick my eyes. "I know he holds himself back for me and I don't want him to. I want to be able to give him everything and I . . . I can't."

"Anna, I don't know you or Stephan very well yet, but I don't get the impression that he's unhappy with your relationship." She paused. "Are you unhappy?"

Shaking my head, I knew I needed to explain myself. "Stephan loves me. I know that. But he has a playroom I can't enter and that isn't fair to him." I wasn't sure I was making any sense or if she'd understand what I was trying to say.

"You're not allowed in his playroom or you choose not to go in?"

"I'm afraid." I looked into her eyes, willing her to understand. "I'm always afraid."

It was a truth I hated to admit. Anytime we introduced something new to our sex lives, it had to be done slowly because of my fear. Ian had tainted everything. He'd made something that was supposed to be full of pleasure full of pain and nightmares. I wanted so badly to get past it. All of it. That was why I was here. I didn't want Stephan to only use his playroom as a place to store our toys.

"And you think getting Stephan to spank you would get you over some hurdle?"

When she said it like that it sounded silly. "Maybe."

"My best advice is to be honest. Both to yourself and with Stephan."

I was confused. "Honest with myself?"

She nodded. "I think you need to figure out why this is important to you. Is it because you want to make Stephan happy or is it something you want as part of your relationship?"

That made sense. Sort of.

"Why don't you think about what I said, maybe talk it over with Stephan, and we can discuss it some more next week."

I nodded and we both stood.

Stephan was right where I left him, sitting in the lobby outside Dr. Katlin's office reading his book. He looked up when he heard the door open. As he did every time I exited a therapy session, he searched my features for any signs as to how it had gone.

Closing his book, he stood and took my hand.

"Have a good week, Anna. I'll see you next Monday," Dr. Katlin said as we moved toward the door.

One of the things I loved about Stephan was that he didn't pounce on me the minute we left Dr. Katlin's office. If I hadn't shared how things had gone by the time we sat down to talk that evening, he would ask me about it, but he seemed to understand that sometimes I needed time to process my thoughts.

Today was one of those days. I wasn't looking forward to coming up with scenarios where I might have panic attacks at Lily's wedding, but I understood the reasoning behind it. I was better at dealing with things if I was prepared.

The real source of my contemplation, though, was what we'd talked about right before I'd left her office. Why was it important to me? And why couldn't I bring myself to go into his playroom?

I didn't have the answers to either of those questions.

Stephan glanced over at me, his brow furrowing. "Everything all right?

That was the million-dollar question and I didn't have the answer. It had been more than four years. Shouldn't I be back to normal by now? I trusted Stephan completely, and yet there was so much we hadn't done together. Things that I knew he liked—that he'd done in the past.

It would be easy to say I didn't like them and move on, but that wasn't the case. I didn't know whether or not I liked those things because we'd never tried them.

As much as I wanted to talk to him about it, I wanted to get my thoughts in order first. "Yes, Sir."

. . .

Stephan

Brianna wasn't talking to me and I didn't like it.

She didn't always discuss things right away with me after her therapist appointments, but today I could tell something was bothering her. We were both still trying to get used to this new psychiatrist and my trust level wasn't the highest when it came to therapists to begin with.

Then again, my trust level with her previous therapist, Dr. Perkins, had never been high. The woman wasn't my biggest fan, but I put that aside because she was helping Brianna work through her issues. That didn't mean she and I hadn't butted heads over the years, because we had. I was hoping that wouldn't be the case with this one, but only time would tell.

Before leaving town, I needed to stop by the hardware store. If Brianna was going to practice driving, it would be good for her to have a course of some sort.

I parked the car in front of the store and turned off the engine.

"We're going to the hardware store?" Brianna asked.

If it were anyone else, I would have asked if they wanted to wait in the car or go in with me. With Brianna, I already knew the answer. "I wanted to pick up a few things to help you with your driving."

"Oh."

I hopped out of the vehicle and went around to open her door. She stepped out and took in her surroundings. We'd been here once before, right after we moved in, but that was a month ago.

Hand in hand, we headed into the store. We weren't more than ten steps inside before an employee approached us. "Anything I can help you find?"

"Yes, I'm looking for orange cones. Do you carry any?"

"All our safety equipment is in aisle twelve," she said.

"Thank you."

The cones were exactly where the woman said they'd be, along with reflectors, vests, hardhats, and a variety of other safety-oriented items. I released Brianna's hand and grabbed five orange cones.

"Those will help me drive?"

I tucked the cones under one arm and began guiding Brianna toward the front of the store. "I'm going to set them up in the side yard so you can practice driving and parking."

She nodded.

An older man was behind the register. He smiled at Brianna, but her only response was to inch closer to me. I hated that she was still afraid after all this time, but I understood. She'd been hurt. A lot. By more men than I cared to imagine. Her faith in humanity as a whole wasn't all that high, especially when it came to those of the male variety.

Once the transaction was complete, I loaded the cones into the trunk and climbed into the car. Brianna was staring at the entrance to the store.

I reached for her hand and she turned to look at me. "May I go back inside?"

There was no way for me to hide my shock and it took me a moment to answer. "Why do you want to go back inside?"

She pressed her shoulders back. "To see if I can."

"Okay. Sure. We can go back inside."

Brianna shook her head. "I want to go inside. By myself."

My hand froze on the door handle as I turned to face her. A trickle of worry ran down my spine. She hadn't been anywhere outside the house by herself since I'd known her.

But even with my worry, logically I knew this was a step forward she needed to take. If she felt she was ready, I had to tamp down any fears I had and support her. "You have your phone with you?"

She nodded.

"All right. I'll wait here."

The muscles in her throat tightened and released as she went to open the door, her hand shaking. She glanced at me before getting out and I gave her what I hoped was an encouraging smile.

I didn't take my eyes off her as she walked into the building and I lost sight of her. My heart was pounding with increased anxiety as I waited.

Less than five minutes had gone by before she reappeared, and I blew out a loud breath. Brianna was twisting her hands together in front of her, a clear sign she was nervous. She hurried the short distance to the car, opened her door, and climbed inside.

It was impossible to miss that she was trembling. Unable to stop myself, I circled my arm around her shoulders and pulled her toward me.

As soon as her body made contact with mine, all the tension released. She took several deep breaths. "I did it."

I brushed the hair away from her face and tilted her chin so I could look into her eyes. They were glistening with moisture, but I could see the pride there, too. "You did."

"I was scared."

As nervous as I'd been, I was proud of her and I wanted her to know that. "You did good. I'm so proud of you, sweetheart."

Her lips curved up into a smile. "I couldn't have done it if I didn't know you were out here waiting for me."

"I'll always be here waiting for you. Even if it's not in a parking lot." I pressed my lips to hers in a whisper soft kiss. "Are you ready to go home?"

She nodded. "Yes, Sir."

Brianna was quiet on the ride home, but not in a way that I thought something was wrong. When we entered the house, she went right for her journal. I wanted to give her time to put all her thoughts and feelings down on paper, so the best thing I could do was get out of her way for a while. "Go write. I'll be outside if you need me."

I waited until she headed upstairs to the study before returning to the garage and retrieving the orange cones. Her car would be here the next day and I needed to determine the best use of the space we had.

It took me a lot longer than I'd planned, but eventually I mapped out a course for her using the cones, some trees, and some other natural landmarks. The area would allow her to practice and get comfortable behind the wheel of a car again before venturing out onto an actual road.

When I reentered the house, I could hear her talking to someone. Brianna didn't typically talk to herself, so I assumed she was on the phone. Given it was Monday, my guess was that it was Cal. He knew she met with her therapist on Mondays and he made a habit of calling to see how it went. The man still got on my nerves, but we were civil with each other for Brianna's sake.

Given the time, I decided to start making dinner. Brianna was extremely organized when it came to the kitchen. Every week she'd sit down and come up with a meal plan and grocery list. Luckily, on the menu tonight was stir-fry and I could easily accomplish that on my own.

I'd learned a lot about cooking from her over the last three years or so. First and foremost was to lay out all my ingredients before starting. Before Brianna, I tended to remove items from the refrigerator and cabinets as I needed them. This not only slowed the process down, but it also caused a problem if I had to spend five minutes looking for an ingredient while my food was burning on the stove.

With all my ingredients lined up on the counter, I set a pot on to boil for the rice and began chopping the vegetables. The rice was cooking, and I was almost finished with the vegetables when Brianna came down the stairs. I put some oil in the wok and began searing the meat. "Finish your call with Cal?"

She nodded. "I didn't realize it was so late."

I smiled and turned and turned the thin strips of meat so it could sear on the other side. "Have a seat. Dinner should be done in fifteen minutes or so."

Reluctantly, she took a seat. I knew what was going through her head. Brianna viewed cooking as her responsibility. Even though I often helped her here and there, the kitchen was her domain. That didn't mean, however, that I couldn't handle dinner myself from time to time.

"Tell me about your call with Cal," I said. "Did he have anything interesting to say?"

She didn't answer right away, which meant he said something she knew I wasn't going to like. "He wasn't happy I went in the hardware store alone."

Ah. Yes, that did seem like something Cal would get riled up over. As protective as I was regarding Brianna, I also understood that she needed to push her boundaries and that meant taking some risks. Of course, if it were up to him, she would probably have joined a nunnery. "What did you tell him?"

"I told him to mind his own business."

I couldn't help the deep belly laugh that escaped as I dumped the vegetables into the wok. Brianna had picked up a lot of things from Lily and Jade over the last few years and one of them was her ability to put Cal in his place when he needed it.

CHAPTER 7

Brianna

I was about halfway through the book I was reading when I heard someone coming up our driveway. Stephan was upstairs doing research on Logan's friend's company for his meeting on Friday, but I knew he had to have heard it, too. Sure enough, a few seconds later, he made his way down the stairs.

"I do believe your car's here."

While we'd talked about me driving again, I guess I'd assumed I'd practice with his car. "My car?"

He motioned for me to join him as he headed toward the front door. "I called the storage facility yesterday and arranged for them to drive it down today. If you really want to get used to being behind the wheel again, then you should do it in the car you'll be driving."

That made sense.

Stephan held my hand as we walked out to meet the man who'd driven my car and another man who had driven a pickup truck. My hand tightened on Stephan's as the man who'd been driving my car strode toward us. He stopped a little too close for my comfort and held the keys out to Stephan. "She's all ready to go. I even gave her a checkup after you called me yesterday to make sure there were no issues."

"Thanks for driving it here," Stephan said, taking the keys.

"No problem at all." The man took a quick look around. "If you need anything else, you know where to find us." Then the man turned on his heel and jogged over to the pickup truck and hoisted himself into the passenger seat.

We stood there watching until the truck was no longer visible. As soon as they were gone, Stephan handed me the keys. "Let's see how much you remember."

Now?

I felt my eyes go wide.

Before I knew it, I was in his arms and he was resting his forehead against mine. "It will be here in the yard. No other cars and nothing but a few trees to maneuver around."

"You'll be in the car with me?" I knew it was only the yard, but I was nervous. It had been almost six years since I'd driven a vehicle.

"Of course."

I nodded and he placed the keys in my hand. The metal was warm, and I could feel the ridges press into my skin. This was really happening.

Stephan led me to the driver's side and opened the door. When I didn't move to get in, he raised his eyebrows in question.

Pressing my lips together, I forced my feet to move. Stephan would be right beside me. I could do this. It was just a quick drive around the yard.

Once I was in, he closed the door and walked around the vehicle to get in on the passenger side. He clicked his seatbelt in place, and then turned to face me. "The adjustment for the seat is on the side. Marco has longer legs than you do."

Right. Adjust the seat. I remembered that.

Sort of.

It took a few moments to get it to where I could reach both the steering wheel and the gas pedal without having to stretch, but eventually I got it. Then, I put the key into the ignition and started the car. The sound of it starting, although it was much quieter than the one I'd driven in high school, caused me to jerk.

Stephan placed a hand over mine. "Breathe, Brianna. You're doing fine."

I took a breath in and then slowly let it out several times. While it helped, I still felt as if I were balancing on the edge of a tightrope.

"Drive toward the trees over there. I set up a little obstacle course for you."

When I didn't move, he said my name again and I met his gaze. He didn't say anything else, just sat there, breathing with me, until I was ready.

As I eased off the brake for the first time and felt the car lurch forward, I had a surge of anxiety and slammed on the brakes again. He didn't comment, just waited, and after a few moments I tried again. This time I was ready for the movement of the car.

The car rolled a few feet, and then I had to give it some gas. My first attempt at that caused the vehicle to jerk forward and I let out a little squeal.

"It's all right. Just don't press so hard next time. You're doing good."

I tried again and did much better that time. After a few minutes, I began to relax a little. Things were coming back to me. I drove through the obstacle course Stephan had set up before heading back toward the house.

All the air seemed to leave my body as soon as I put the car in park and turned off the engine. I'd been so tense trying to make sure I did what I was supposed to do, and now that it was over all that tension dissipated.

Stephan came around to the driver's side, opened the door, and then practically lifted me out of the vehicle. He held me close and kissed the top of my head as I stood there clinging to his shirt. I'd driven a car again. Granted, it wasn't on the road, but I'd still driven.

I looked up at him and his mouth came down to meet mine. The kiss lingered and I threaded my fingers through his hair. It was only when he pressed me up against the car that I remembered where we were.

Even that thought soon faded away when he popped the button on my shorts and snaked his hand inside. I moaned as his fingers zeroed in on my clit. He deepened the kiss, trapping me between his body and the car while he pleasured me.

With his free hand, he lowered my top and the cup of my bra. His mouth abandoned mine and latched onto my nipple. I felt my interior muscles clench as the sensations continued to build.

He released my nipple and recaptured my lips with his. At the same time, he shifted his hand so his fingers could enter me and the heel of his hand could still rub my clit in the most delicious way. I felt surrounded. Claimed.

His mouth moved to my neck and he began to lick and suck and scrape his teeth along my skin. It did crazy things to me and he knew it. He knew how to play my body.

"Come for me."

With permission granted, I let myself go. Seconds later, my climax hit me.

The rest of the day flew by and before I knew it, I was curled up on his lap. Last night we'd continued talking about Logan and Lily's upcoming wedding and what that would mean for me. He agreed with Dr. Katlin that it would be good to think of scenarios I may have to deal with so I could figure out ahead of time how best to deal with them.

That, however, was easier said than done. I'd never been to a wedding before.

Stephan said he'd help me since he'd been to several weddings. He also thought it was a good idea for us to watch some movies about weddings. I didn't quite understand the reasoning behind that, but he said Hollywood tended to come up with the worst possible situations to create drama. If we could prepare for the worst, then the reality would be easier.

As I sat there with his arms holding me, I thought about all the things I'd written in my journal and waited to see which he'd bring up.

Sometimes it took us all week to talk about my session with Dr. Katlin as he tried to only tackle one topic at a time, so as not to overwhelm me. Unlike my therapist, Stephan tended to push me to get to the heart of the matter.

To my surprise, he asked me about today. "How did it feel to drive again?"

"Scary." I traced the neckline of his shirt with my finger. Since he'd stopped working at the foundation, he didn't always wear button down shirts. "I was afraid I was going to hit something."

He combed his fingers through my hair, sending little tingles down my spine. "It will get easier with practice. I remember when I first learned to drive. I think I almost gave Richard a heart attack."

I'd forgotten that he'd been living with his aunt and uncle by that time. "Was he the one who taught you to drive?"

"For the most part, yes. Although Diane took me out several times, as well."

Then I voiced the fear that had been going through my head since I'd finished my driving adventure earlier that day. "What if I can't get comfortable enough to drive on a road again?"

He kissed the top of my head. "One step at a time. Today was a good first step, but it was only the beginning. You'll keep working at it and see how you do. There's no hurry."

I nodded.

We sat there for a few minutes and I listened to his heartbeat. It was strong and steady, just like Stephan.

Stephan

I never knew what would come out of Brianna's therapy sessions. Sometimes they spent the entire hour discussing one topic. On other days, they'd talk about a half dozen different things. It was those latter times that took a while to unpack.

This week fell into that category. They'd discussed Lily and Logan's upcoming wedding, of course, but they'd also talked about her need to have everything perfect, her desire to go back to school versus her fear of being around people, and then some other issue she'd been extremely vague about in her journal entry. All it said was that she was curious about something, but her fear was stopping her. Given Brianna's history and her reaction to things, it could be any number of items or experiences.

"You mentioned in your journal that you were curious about something but were afraid. What were you curious about?"

She didn't answer right away, and I felt her body tense. "Spanking."

"I thought you and Lily talked about Logan spanking her. Did you have more questions?"

"No." She tucked her head down, so I knew there was more.

I placed my fingers under her chin and forced her to meet my gaze. Raising an eyebrow, I waited for her to answer my unspoken question.

"Lily said she likes to be spanked."

"Yes, she does." Lily loved impact play, whether it was spanking, flogging, or a host of other instruments. She wasn't crazy about canes, but that was the only thing so far that Logan had found she didn't like.

Brianna averted her eyes and I increased my pressure on her chin to bring her eyes back to meet mine. "I . . . I was curious how it felt. Being spanked."

I sat there for a moment studying her face. In the four years we'd been together, Brianna had never once indicated she had an interest in being spanked and I wondered what had brought it on. "You were never spanked when you were with Ian?"

Even now his name made her cringe. It was impossible not to bring him up when talking about anything sexual since her only sexual experiences before me were at his or his friend's hands. But that didn't make these conversations any easier.

"Yes." She pressed her lips together before continuing. "But Lily says it's different. Punishment spanking and play spanking. That it feels different."

"And you want to know how play spanking feels." Several different scenarios went through my mind. Introducing anything new to

Brianna was always a challenge. Even when it was something she said she wanted.

We'd come a long way, however, and I'd learned what tended to work and what didn't.

I released her chin and dropped my hands to the side. "Stand."

She quickly removed herself from my lap and stood beside my chair. I got up, took hold of her hand, and led her to the bedroom. This would be much easier in the playroom upstairs, but she hadn't been in there yet. I wasn't even going to set it up, but she'd said she wanted me to do so.

"Remove your clothes." I left her in the middle of the room to strip as I repositioned the full-length mirror where I wanted it.

When I returned to stand in front of her, she was clutching her arms around her waist. I cupped the side of her face and rubbed my thumb against her cheek. "I will take care of you."

"I know, Sir."

Knowing things would go better if I got her aroused a little first, I slid my hand into her hair, gathered it in my fist, and tilted her head to the side so I could have access to her neck. Nothing sent Brianna's pulse soaring faster than when I paid attention to her neck. She was so sensitive there.

As I nibbled right below her ear, I felt her begin to relax. I cupped her ass with my free hand and massaged her cheek as I pressed her hips against my groin so she could feel my erection. She closed her eyes and parted her lips, lost in the sensations.

Normally, I'd allow her to fall into bliss, but if we were going to try spanking, even on the most rudimentary level, I needed her eyes open. I needed to make sure she was in the here and now. "Eyes open, Brianna."

Her eyes fluttered open to focus on me and I could see just how turned on she was.

I tightened my grip on her hair, knowing it was sending little bites of pain to her scalp, and then I gave her backside a light smack.

Brianna sucked in a breath.

Keeping my focus on her, I did it again.

Her reaction this time was much the same, but I also noticed her pulse had picked up. Not in a way that made me think she was frightened, either.

I landed one more smack to her bottom before releasing my hold on her hair. "Look in the mirror."

She did as instructed.

Once her eyes were on us in the mirror, I placed both hands on her ass cheeks and began roughly massaging them. "Do you feel the difference? This one." I squeezed the one I'd given attention. "is more sensitive now. "

Her gaze was transfixed on what my hands were doing to her ass. The good thing was that I didn't sense any panic from her.

Knowing she was watching, I spanked her right cheek this time.

She tensed up a moment before my hand made contact.

"Relax. Look at me, not at what I'm doing."

Her gaze lifted.

Confident she was watching me and not my hands, I tried again. This time, I got the reaction I wanted.

Not giving her time to think about it, I gave her two more swats in quick succession. Her eyes grew wide and her breathing became more labored. I knew from experience what that meant. If I touched her right now, she would be wet and ready for me.

My erection was straining in my pants, and I didn't want to push things too far on our first try, so I decided it was time to address other things. "Turn around, bend over, and put your hands on the bed."

She blinked twice, and then did as she was told, her blush pink ass staring me in the face. It was a beautiful sight.

Without pretense, I discarded my clothes and stepped up behind her. My hands went directly to her backside. The urge to spank her more was there, but I resisted. She wasn't ready and I wanted tonight to end on a positive note.

With that in mind, I slid my right hand between her legs and confirmed what I'd already known. She was wet.

I took a few moments to explore with my fingers, dipping them inside her pussy and circling her clit. Her legs fell open a little more at my ministrations, which only made me smile.

"Are you ready for me, pet?"

"Yes, Sir—" That was all she was able to get out before I was pushing into her.

I wasn't gentle as I drove my cock into her. She held tight to the sheets as I thrust to keep herself from falling forward. My fingers dug into her hips to hold her steady and right where I wanted her. It never got old being inside her.

The best part was that with the mirror positioned where it was, I was able to get a glimpse of her breasts bouncing with our movements. Between that and having her pink ass right in front of me, I knew I wasn't going to last long.

As I felt my climax approaching, I repositioned one of my hands so that my finger was pressing against her clit. Every thrust had her grinding against it and sending her closer and closer to her own release.

"Come!"

Moments later, her interior muscles contracted around me, and a high-pitched squeal came from deep in her throat.

Feeling her orgasm take her dissolved the last of my control. I let go, shooting my cum into her.

Circling my arm around her stomach, I brought us down on the bed on our sides. I remained inside her, not ready to lose the connection.

She placed her arm over mine and I laced our fingers together as our breathing returned to normal. I placed a kiss on the back of her head. "How does your backside feel?"

Brianna hummed. "Warm."

I chuckled. "Did tonight help you to understand why Lily likes to be spanked?"

"Yes."

I saw her brow wrinkle and I knew she was thinking. I waited.

"I didn't think I'd like it." She paused. "I shouldn't like it."

I propped myself up on my elbow so I could look down at her. "Why shouldn't you like it?"

She shrugged. "I don't know."

Rolling her over, I felt myself slip out of her. It was a small price to pay so I could look her square in the eye. "Remember what I told you. Nothing we do together that we both enjoy is wrong. I love you and you love me. That's all that matters."

CHAPTER 8

Brianna

The sound of rain hitting the windows greeted me as I woke up the next morning. As the drowsiness cleared from my brain, I could also hear the ceiling fan above the bed and Stephan's soft snoring.

I opened my eyes and rolled over. As if drawn by some unknown force, my gaze locked onto the freestanding full-length mirror and the night before rushed back to me. Me standing there, my naked body pressed up against his clothed one, and his hand making contact with my flesh.

At the time, it stung, but I didn't feel anything this morning. No pain or soreness.

The last time Ian had spanked me was two days before I'd met Stephan. He'd used his hand along with a round paddle and had hit me on my butt and thighs. I could still remember how much it had hurt every time he'd slammed the paddle down with enough force to move the bench I was tied to by an inch or so. It had left bruises. Bruises that Stephan had seen when he'd examined me that day in Ian's office.

Because of what happened to me, I shouldn't have liked what Stephan had done last night, but at the time it had been much like

69

when he pinched my nipples or pulled my hair. I couldn't explain it other than knowing that I'd liked it.

But I knew spanking wasn't always like that and for some reason I couldn't get that out of my head.

A hand touched my arm and I jerked.

"Brianna? What's wrong, sweetheart?" Stephan looked worried.

I took a couple deep breaths and waited until my heart slowed to a more normal rhythm. "I was thinking about last night."

Stephan sat up, resting his back against the headboard, and pulled me against him. I rested my head in the crook of his neck. He rubbed his hand up and down my arm. "Tell me what's bothering you."

As usual, Stephan could read me well. "I was thinking about last night . . . and about the last time Ian spanked me."

His hand moved to my hair and he began to pet me in a soothing motion. There were times like this when I wondered if he did it more for him or for me. "Did me spanking you bring up memories? You didn't seem to have any flashbacks last night."

"No, I didn't have a flashback." I thought about how best to explain it. "I was . . . comparing."

Stephan's hand stilled on my hair for a moment before resuming its motion. "Comparing?"

I nodded. "Ian liked to use other things besides his hand, but he used his hand at first that last time."

We'd talked about my life with Ian a lot. He knew Ian used to hit me, along with many other things. If there was a way to use, abuse, or torture someone, there was a good chance it had been done to me at Ian's hands or with his approval.

"Are you feeling guilty again? Last night you'd mentioned that you shouldn't have liked me spanking you."

Was I feeling guilty? I didn't know if that was the right word. "No. I feel . . ." I hesitated, trying to come up with the right word and failing. "I don't know."

He tilted my chin and placed a kiss on the tip of my nose. "Go get yourself ready. I'll meet you in the kitchen."

When I didn't move right away, he raised an eyebrow in question. I hurried out of bed and did what I was told. He'd revisit the subject eventually. That, I knew for sure. Stephan didn't tend to let things go before they were resolved.

I took a quick shower, dried my hair, and got dressed in jeans and a T-shirt. Since it was raining and we had no real plans, I figured we'd most likely be staying in. I was almost done reading my book and I was hoping I'd have time to finish it.

Stephan was in the kitchen as promised. He'd pulled on a pair of jeans that rode low on his hips and a dark green T-shirt. I loved that shirt on him. It brought out the green in his eyes.

He brought two bowls of cereal to the island, placing one in front of me. "Orange juice or apple juice?"

"Apple juice, please," I said. We rarely ever had cereal. I usually cooked, even if it was just eggs and toast.

He sat down beside me, and we ate our breakfast. Other than a few comments about the rain, neither of us said much.

Once we were finished, he gathered our bowls and glasses, rinsed them, and put them in the dishwasher. Then he returned to stand by my stool and placed his hands on my hips. "We're going up to the playroom this morning."

My eyes went wide and I gripped his forearms. I wasn't sure if I was trying to hold him still or make sure he didn't let go of me.

"Breathe, Brianna. We aren't going to play, but I want to talk more about when Ian spanked you."

"O-okay." That wasn't how I'd envisioned spending my morning.

He gave my hips a gentle squeeze before helping me to stand.

I followed him up the stairs to the third flood where he'd set up the playroom. Or at least, started to set it up. He'd been working on it a little at a time since we'd moved in, but since we never used it there really wasn't any hurry to get it done.

Anxiety curled in my belly with every step as we made our way up the stairs. I held tight to his hand, so tight I wondered if I was hurting him. Stephan didn't say anything, though. He just kept walking.

We reached the last step and he pulled out his key. He kept the room locked like he had at his condo.

The first thing that hit me when he opened the door was the smell. It was a mix of leather and the cleaning product we used in the house. I cautiously followed him over the threshold. The last time I'd seen the room it had been empty except for boxes. There were still a few, but most of the contents had either been placed on the walls or were laying on a table along the back wall.

Stephan's hand on my face brought my gaze to his. "I'm right here. You're safe."

I swallowed and tried to remember my breathing. They were just things. I was all right. Nothing was going to hurt me.

My breathing slowed and I leaned my cheek into Stephan's hand. "Good girl."

We stood there for several moments as I relaxed farther. It was a slow process, but Stephan wasn't rushed. He never rushed me.

"Tell me about the last time Ian spanked you. What did he use?"

A prickle of anxiety began to form in my gut, but I tried to focus on Stephan. He was here. He'd protect me. "His hand."

"What else?"

"I don't know what it's called."

He walked backward toward the wall where he'd hung up a lot of his equipment and pulled me along with him. "Do you see it?"

I didn't want to look away from him, but I knew I'd have to if I was going to do what he asked. Tightening my grip on his hand, I turned my head to look.

There were more implements on the wall than I remembered being in his old playroom. Then again, his old playroom at the condo had been much smaller, less than half the size of the room we were in now. Maybe he had them put away.

As I looked at everything in front of me, memories began to surface. Not only from the last time Ian spanked me, but from other times. I did my best to breathe through it. To concentrate on the things I could feel in the present and not allow the past to pull me in. If Stephan hadn't been there with me, I don't know if I could have done it.

Finally, my gaze landed on something that looked similar to what Ian had used on me. "The silver."

Stephan followed my gaze and removed the item from the wall. "This?"

I sucked in a breath. "Yes. But it was . . . bigger."

The item Stephan held in his hand had a black handle and a bunch of little silver beads. Ian's was almost twice the size, including the silver beads that had felt as though a swarm of bees were stinging my legs all at once.

Stephan lifted my hand and placed the silver thing on my palm. It felt strange, but not anything like I thought it would. For some reason, I thought it would be a lot heavier with the beads.

"It's called a silver ball ticker. If you run it lightly over the skin, it's almost like a caress."

Stephan

She was looking at the silver ball ticker as if it might jump out of her hand and bite her. When she'd pointed it out as the instrument Ian had used on her, I was a little surprised. This wasn't exactly the first thing that came to mind when it came to torturing someone. Then again, it did sting quite a bit when enough force was used. And she'd said the one Ian had used was bigger. I'm sure that would influence the result.

"Have you . . . have you ever used it?" she asked, her voice shaking a little. It was subtle, but I knew her better than anyone.

"No. I purchased it not long before you and I met." I didn't need to fill in the blanks. Brianna and I did a lot of sensation play, but nothing that involved impact. I would love to use a crop on her, or even a flogger, but I hadn't felt she was ready. After last night, though, I was beginning to rethink that.

I knew the next question that was coming before she asked. "Will you use it on me?"

"I don't know," I said, taking it from her and replacing it on the wall. "Our play has evolved a lot over the last four years. Anything is possible."

A shiver ran through her and I wrapped my arms around her waist, bringing her body flush with mine. "I know it's scary, but you enjoy our sex life, do you not?"

"Yes. Very much." Her voice was muffled against my shirt, but I heard every word.

I chuckled. "Remember the first time I tied you to my bed? The first time I pinched your nipples? Pulled your hair?"

"I remember."

Looking around the room, I tried to imagine what it must look like to her. To her, everything in this room was a potential torture device. I'd sat for hours listening to her talk about what Ian did to her, how he'd manipulate the most basic things. I still hadn't been able to use nipple clamps on her even though I knew she'd love them because he'd placed them on her and left them for hours, leaving her nipples so sore she couldn't even touch them without pain.

My ire for Ian Pierce knew no bounds and, in a way, I was sad that he was dead. I'd wanted him to suffer, to have his freedom taken from him like hers had been. And even though I regretted his quick and easy death, that didn't mean I'd wanted the man who shot him to pay any more than he already had. Even with the strings I'd pulled through my lawyer, Oscar, the poor man was still sentenced to five years in prison.

"I hate that I'm so scared," Brianna whispered, bringing me back to the present.

"I know, sweetheart." I kissed the top of her head and pulled back enough that I could look into her eyes. "I want you to start coming in here at least once a week."

Her eyes grew wide with panic.

"You don't have to do anything. I just want you to open the door, walk inside, and stand here for at least five minutes." I tucked her hair behind her ear. "Do you think you can do that?"

I watched as the muscles in her throat moved in an exaggerated fashion. "I think so, Sir. I will try."

"Good girl." Tilting her head up, I kissed her. "Since it's raining, I was wondering if you'd like to watch a movie with me."

For the next few hours, we lay cuddled on the couch, my arms around her as we got lost in what was on the screen. Brianna was content to pass the rest of the morning away lounging on the sofa. No drama. No demands to pay more attention to her than the movie. It was wonderful.

Once the movie was over, we made some sandwiches before heading to our workout room. As with most things in the new house, it was larger than the one in my condo. All the equipment was the same, but we were able to spread it out more.

Brianna began on the treadmill, while I did a little weight training. We tried to get in at least three workouts a week, which had been a little difficult since moving into the house. I still hadn't completely unpacked my playroom and Brianna was still working on organizing the kitchen and pantry exactly how she wanted them.

I was on the floor doing sit-ups when I noticed Brianna staring. Her cheeks had a slight flush to them, but I couldn't tell if that was because she was blushing or because of her workout.

As she continued to stare, I felt myself begin to get hard. And the harder I got, the more uncomfortable it was to do sit-ups. Or any other exercise for that matter.

Lying back on the floor, I cupped the bulge in my pants. Her gaze rose to meet mine. "Come here."

She climbed off the exercise bike and made her way over to where I was lying on my back. I patted the mat beside me and she lowered herself onto her knees.

"Were you enjoying the view?" I asked, already knowing the answer.

"Yes, Sir."

I gave my erection another rub as I thought about her getting all hot and bothered watching me. "Remove your top. I want to see you."

Reaching for the hem of her sports bra, she worked it over her sweaty torso and head before dropping it on the floor. Her nipples were like little pebbles. All I wanted to do was suck them, so that's exactly what I did.

A low moan came from deep in her chest as I sucked the tiny tip into my mouth. Such a sexy sound.

When I released the tender flesh with a pop, her pupils were dilated, and I knew the flush that was covering her cheeks and neck had nothing to do with her workout. There was nothing more beautiful than an aroused woman.

I lowered myself back to the floor and pushed the shorts off my hips. My cock sprang free pointing at the ceiling. It was hard and aching and ready for some attention.

Placing one hand at the base of my cock to steady it, I brought the other up to cup the back of her neck. Brianna knew what to do. She leaned down and swallowed my cock.

I'd thought the blowjob she'd given me four years ago had been amazing, and it was. Her technique had been perfect. She knew exactly how hard to suck, lick, and had even been able to swallow my entire length down her throat, something I'd only ever seen done in movies. Now that she was more relaxed and we had a solid relationship filled with love and trust, amazing didn't begin to describe how what she was doing to me felt. If anything, she'd gotten better at it and I hadn't thought that was possible.

She swirled her tongue around the head before sliding back down my shaft until her lips met the skin at the base. Then she swallowed and her throat contracted around me in a way that had me gasping for breath and wanting to pound into her at the same time.

I twisted her ponytail around my fist and began lifting my hips in time with her mouth, increasing the friction. Brianna didn't miss a beat. She relaxed her throat and let me find the rhythm I desired.

Sweat poured from me as I continued to thrust into her mouth at an almost wild pace. I felt my climax approaching and instinctively held tighter to her hair. Her humming response was all it took for me to explode down her throat.

As I eased my hold on her hair, Brianna slowly released me from the warmth of her mouth. When she turned to look at me, she was grinning, and I couldn't help but smile back at her. The little minx loved to service me. She loved watching me lose control, which she knew didn't happen often.

I pulled her down on top of me and crushed her mouth to mine. "You have the most talented mouth on the planet."

"Thank you, Sir." Her pleasure made me happy. I was so glad she was able to find joy in sexual acts after what she'd gone through.

As much as I didn't want to, I knew we needed to get showered and changed. My aunt and uncle would be here in a couple of hours and Brianna needed time to fix dinner.

That didn't mean there wasn't a little time for some multitasking and showers were great for that sort of thing. I stood and helped Brianna to her feet. The faster we got to the shower the better.

CHAPTER 9

Brianna

Dinner with Diane and Richard was nice. Stephan gave them a tour of the house, minus the playroom, and Diane couldn't stop saying how much she loved it. It gave me a sense of pride. I wanted Diane's approval of our home.

After the house tour, we played cards and talked until after dark. It was so normal, and I'd found that I'd enjoyed myself quite a bit more than I thought I would. When they finally left a little after ten, I was drained but content.

Stephan made sure the house was locked up, and then pulled me over to his chair. I rested my head on his shoulder and sighed.

"Happy?" he asked as he laced our fingers together.

I nodded. "It was a good day."

He brought my hand up to his lips and kissed my knuckles. "Yes. I seem to recall several good parts."

Heat spread through my cheeks as I remembered what had happened in the workout room. Just thinking about him in my mouth had my body preparing itself for him. He hadn't been inside me since the previous night and I was hoping that things would lead to that before we went to bed. I always slept better after we'd made love.

And it was making love. The difference between what Stephan and I did, and what had happened to me before I met him, was night and day. Those men had used me, not caring what I wanted or if I was getting any sort of pleasure out of it. Stephan always took care of me. He always put my needs first.

Stephan chuckled as he noticed my blush. "I know exactly what you're thinking about, love."

I turned my head to hide my face in the crook of his neck.

His chest vibrated with his amusement and he kissed the top of my head before making me look at him. "I do love when you get flustered. Your skin turns a lovely pink color. It reminds me of the way you look right before you come."

It wasn't like I didn't know my skin turned a pinkish color from the chest up when I was about to come. There'd been several times when he'd made me watch in a mirror and I'd seen the way my body reacted. Sometimes he even pointed it out. But it didn't help tame the blush I was dealing with at the moment.

He rubbed the back of his hand along my heated cheek. "Do you remember what I told you when we were up in the playroom?"

I swallowed. "Yes."

"How do you feel about what I've asked?" His voice was gentle, soothing, yet firm at the same time.

"I'm nervous." I pressed my lips together and met his gaze. "But I think . . . I think I can do it."

He kissed the tip of my nose and guided my head back to his shoulder. With that small gesture, I knew he was pleased.

I closed my eyes and enjoyed the feel of being in his arms—my safe place.

After a few minutes had passed, he spoke again. "Are you ready for bed?"

As if in response, I yawned.

Stephan laughed. "I guess I have my answer. Come on, let's get you your beauty sleep."

I stood, a little disappointed that it didn't seem as though we were going to have sex but understanding that it had been a long day. He followed behind me, turning off the lights in the living room behind us. Right as I started to head toward the bathroom to brush my teeth, he grabbed me by the waist, pulled me against him and kissed me with enough passion to send my pulse racing. I guessed we weren't going to sleep just yet.

The next morning, I woke with my breasts feeling a little sensitive. Stephan had used the rope to bind my breasts and spent quite a while playing with them the night before.

Not that I was complaining. At the time, it had felt really good. I'd come three times before he'd found his own release and we'd both collapsed in a sweaty mess.

That was why the first thing we did upon waking up was shower and change the bed sheets. He'd helped me wash but didn't take things any farther than that even though I kind of wanted him to. I didn't know what it was, but I always seemed to want him.

About six months ago, I'd asked Dr. Perkins about it. She hadn't really given me an answer. Instead, she'd said something about hormones and addiction. It didn't make sense, but I hadn't asked her to explain.

Maybe I should ask Dr. Katlin.

After finishing breakfast, Stephan headed upstairs to the study and I put the sheets we'd stripped off the bed into the washer. With that done, I began to think of all the things that needed done around the house. I'd changed the sheets on the bed Logan and Lily had used the day after they'd left, but I'd yet to clean the room itself.

I gathered my cleaning supplies and went upstairs to tackle the room. As I was finishing up and thinking about what to do next, I realized I was procrastinating. I'd promised Stephan I would do as he'd asked and spend at least five minutes in the playroom. I needed to be brave and do it.

Logically, I knew nothing was going to jump off the walls and hurt me. That didn't make it any easier.

Leaving my cleaning supplies in the hallway, I walked to the staircase and climbed the steps to the third floor. Every step felt heavier than the last until I was finally standing in front of the door that stood between me and the playroom. Stephan had left it unlocked for me, so I knew all I had to do was turn the handle and walk inside. That was easier said than done.

I must have stood there for ten minutes before I got up the nerve to reach out and take the knob in my hand. And another five before I turned the knob and pushed open the door.

My feet were frozen to the ground as I stared at the interior, but I knew I needed to go inside. That's what he wanted. For me to stand inside the playroom for at least five minutes. I needed to at least try.

I put one foot in front of the other until I was right inside the door. It was only then that I realized I had no way of knowing the time or to figure out how long I was there. I had no watch and there was no clock in the room.

Should I leave and come back?

I didn't know if that was a good idea. I didn't know if I'd be able to get up the nerve a second time in one day. No, I was going to have to guess, which meant I was going to have to stay here until I was sure it had been at least five minutes.

Focusing on my breathing, I looked around and tried not to get lost in my memories. It was impossible to block them out entirely, though. I wished I could forget, but that wasn't possible. So instead, I placed a hand on my collar to anchor me to the present and embraced the emotions coursing through me.

My gaze landed on something leather that was hanging not far from the silver ball thing I'd held the day before. It was about a foot long and about two inches wide.

The flash of a memory hit me, taking me off guard. My legs were spread, held open by cuffs around my ankles. A man, not Ian, was standing between my legs, a wicked look on his face.

I tried to breath like Dr. Perkins had taught me. But my chest hurt. It felt as if the air around me was thick and I couldn't get enough of it into my lungs.

Falling to my knees, I tried to remember Stephan's face. To think about him smiling at me, holding me, loving me. I wasn't with Ian anymore. Those men, they couldn't hurt me. These things couldn't hurt me.

Ever so slowly my breathing returned to normal and I took the opportunity to leave before anything else could trigger another panic attack. I knew the very same thing could happen again the next time, but I'd deal with that when the time came. I understood Stephan's reasoning for having me visit the playroom. I needed to move past my fear and the only way that was going to happen was if I confronted it head on.

Stephan

I'd heard Brianna go upstairs to the playroom and had been listening for any signs of distress ever since. Having her spend time in the playroom was going to be a challenge, but one I felt she was ready for. We'd been playing with rope, sensation toys, and vibrators since she'd returned from living with Cal and Jade. She was comfortable with those things, and given she'd brought up spanking the other day and she'd done well with it, I felt she was ready for the next step.

She'd been up there for almost a half hour when I heard her footfalls coming down the stairs at a pace that let me know she was in a hurry. I stepped out into the hall in time to see her emerge from the stairway. Her eyes were a little wild and as soon as she saw me, she ran the remaining distance and flung herself into my arms.

I held her tight, rubbing my hands along her back. She continued to cling to me, so I swept her up into my arms and carried her into the study. Since my desk chair wasn't really meant for two, I headed over to the window seat. The large window overlooked our backyard and the river that skimmed the back of our property. She loved this spot and spent a lot of time here reading.

Time passed as I waited for her to relax. Eventually, she ran her nose along my neck and sighed. "I had a flashback."

Given her response, I'd figured as much. As eager as I was to find out more details, I waited to see what else she'd say.

"I don't like remembering. I just want to forget."

My chest clenched at the pain in her voice. "I wish I could take the memories away from you, but I can't."

"I know." Brianna tilted her head up to look at me. "And I know I have to face what Ian and those other men did to me. I can't let them control my life and keep me from enjoying things." She scraped her teeth along her bottom lip. "I want to be able to go to Lily's wedding and not be scared. I want to be able to walk down the street. To go to school." She paused. "To drive."

I caressed the side of her face with my thumb. "You'll get there."

She closed her eyes and nodded.

"Tell me about your flashback and what triggered it."

The muscles in her throat moved as she swallowed and then began to tell me what had happened. I did my best to breathe through my anger. I hated learning the details of all the torture she'd been through, but I also knew it was good for her to talk about it.

We ended up ordering pizza for dinner and spending the evening watching television. Tomorrow we were driving into the city. I would be leaving her in Lily's care for several hours and meeting with Logan's friend. As crazy as it sounded, I was a bit nervous about the meeting. I'd never consulted before. Ran an origination, yes, but I wouldn't be the one calling the shots, only giving recommendations.

Still, I was excited to consider this new opportunity. Both Brianna and I had been in a hold pattern of sorts for the last two years. Other than moving into the new house, our lives hadn't changed much.

Friday morning dawned and we packed up and began the one-hour journey into the city. I'd intentionally timed our departure so we would miss most of the rush hour traffic. It worked out well since the bridal store Lily had selected didn't open until ten.

I knew Brianna was anxious about the day, but she hid it well. The only tell-tale sign of her nerves was the way she held her hands in her lap.

Lily was waiting for us when we arrived at the store. She rushed over when she saw us and embraced Brianna in an exuberant hug. "You made it." Before either of us could respond, she took Brianna's hand and began leading her farther into the store. "Bridget, I'd like for you to meet Brianna."

A young woman around Lily's age stood. She had long blonde hair and looked to be around five-six. The thing that stuck out most to me, however, was that she was eyeing me as if she were deciding if I was something she wanted to eat and completely ignoring Brianna and Lily. Not exactly the best first impression from my view.

After eyeing me up and down, she turned her attention to Brianna. "It's nice to meet you."

"Bridget and I have been friends since college. We used to do everything together," Lily said.

Bridget released a dreamy sigh. "Oh yes. Fun times."

She and Lily laughed.

A woman dressed in all black entered the small seating area. "Good morning. Who's my bride?"

"I am," Lily bounded over to the woman and extended her hand in greeting.

The woman smiled. "I'm Carol and I'll be assisting you today." She looked at the three of us, and then back to Lily. "And who do you have with you today?"

"This is Bridget and Brianna." When Lily noticed the woman looking at me, she added, "That's Stephan, but he's not staying, right?"

Such a brat. I don't know how Logan put up with her as a sub. "No, I'm not. I have an appointment to get to." I brushed my lips against Brianna's." I'll be back to pick you up in two hours. Call me if you need me before then."

"I will."

I gave Lily a hard look, hoping to convey that I was trusting her to look after Brianna. It wasn't that I was worried about her being able to cope with trying on dresses, I didn't think anything would come up that she wouldn't be able to deal with in that regard. My main concern was this Bridget person. I didn't know anything about her, I hadn't even known there would be anyone else here today besides Brianna and Lily, and I didn't like that feeling.

As soon as I was out of ear shot, I pulled out my phone and dialed

Logan. "I wasn't expecting to hear from you so soon. How'd the meeting go?"

"I'm on my way there now." I decided to cut right to the chase. "What do you know about Lily's friend, Bridget?"

"Not much. She and Lily were best friends in college, and they've kept in touch ever since. Every year they have a girls' weekend in Chicago and Lily comes home with bags and bags of clothes." He paused. "Why?"

"I met her at the bridal shop."

"Yes. And? Did something happen with Brianna?"

I liked the fact that his first concern was for Brianna. He may not be as protective of her as I was, but he still didn't like the idea of anyone hurting her. "No. It wasn't that." I opened the door to my vehicle and got inside. "She was a little . . . aggressive."

"Aggressive?"

"Maybe that's not the right word. It's been a while since someone looked at me like that."

He chuckled. "Hit on you, did she?"

I rubbed my hand on the back of my neck. "I guess you could say that, although she didn't say anything. It was the way she looked at me. And she'd known I'd come with Brianna."

"Some women don't care about that. You know that as well as I do."

It was true. And I wouldn't have put it past her to have noticed that I wasn't wearing a wedding ring.

Ring or not, I was committed to Brianna. I only hoped that whatever had been going through Bridget's mind, it didn't affect the way she treated Brianna, or she and I would be having words.

I glanced at the clock and grimaced. "I need to go."

"Call me later. I want to know how your meeting goes." He paused. "And don't worry too much about Brianna. Lily will look out for her."

Luckily, the office building I was looking for was only about a mile from the bridal shop. By the time I made it to the tenth floor where Helping Hands was located, I was already two minutes late. Not exactly the best first impression.

I straightened my tie before entering. The reception area was small, smaller than my study at home. An older woman with dark brown hair greeted me. "Welcome to Helping Hands."

"Thank you. I have an appointment with Josh Berkley."

Her smile grew. "You must be Stephan."

"I am." While I figured she might know about the meeting, her response was a little friendlier than that of an average receptionist.

"Come with me. I'll show you to his office." She stepped out from behind her desk and guided me down a long hallway. "I'm Stella, by the way. Josh's aunt."

Family. That explained the overly friendly response. "Nice to meet you, ma'am."

She stopped at the last door on the right, knocked twice, and then opened the door. "Stephan Coleman is here to see you."

"Come in. Come in. I was just getting some paperwork together."

I walked into the office and kept my attention on the man behind the desk. He gathered a bunch of papers into a pile and set them aside before coming to shake my hand. "I'm excited to talk to you about my company. We've been wanting to expand things, but fundraising isn't my specialty. I'm more of a hands-on kind of guy. Sucking up isn't something I do well."

I grinned back at him. "Well, let's see if I can help with that."

CHAPTER 10

Brianna

There was a knock on the changing room door. "Come in."

Carol peeked inside and handed me another dress to try on. This was the fifth one I'd tried on. "Getting tired of trying on dresses yet?"

I grinned as she hung the dress up on the little hook. This one was purple. "A little. How many more are there?"

"This is the last one. I think." I liked Carol. She'd been really nice to me. "Come out when you're ready and we'll see how it looks." Then she ducked back out the door as quickly as she'd come in.

Lily was going with a Christmas theme, so our dresses would be burgundy. However, since the shop didn't have every style of dress available in every color, the color of the dresses had varied. We'd only tried one on that was burgundy.

I was almost finished putting on the new dress when I heard Bridget in the hall. She was . . . interesting. Lily liked her, so that helped, but I still wasn't sure. When Stephan had left, she'd sent me a look that I hadn't understood and then later she'd asked me how long Stephan and I had been together.

There was no time to worry about that now, so I opened the door and stepped into the hall. Lily saw me first. "Ooo. I like this one."

"I don't know," Bridget said from a few feet away. She turned and looked at the back of her dress in the mirror. "You don't think it makes my butt look fat?"

"Men like big butts, so that should be a good thing." Lily turned to me and whispered, "More area to spank."

The hint of a smile tugged at my lips. I knew Lily was trying to include me. Plus, I'd gotten the impression that Bridget didn't know about Lily and Logan's lifestyle.

Bridget huffed. "What do you think, Brianna?"

My eyes went wide. I didn't like being put on the spot. "Um. I . . ."

"Why don't you come take a look at yourself in the mirror," Carol said.

I felt self-conscious as everyone seemed to be waiting for my opinion. The dress was pretty. It was knee length with what Lily called an A-line that flared at the waist. The top half of the dress reminded me of a strapless gown, but it had a sheer layer over the top that came up around the neck. It was pretty and it reminded me of something a nineteen fifties housewife would wear. In other words, it was very Lily. "I like it."

Lily clapped her hands and came to stand behind me. "It has that fifties vibe, don't you think?"

I nodded.

Bridget looked at her reflection in the mirror again. "It does have that retro feel to it. Is that what you're going for?" She twirled. "What about your dress? Have you already picked something out?"

"I did!" Lily turned to Carol. "Do you still have the sample I tried on so we could show them?"

Carol nodded. "Give me a few minutes and I'll pull it. It might be a good idea to try it back on and stand beside your bridesmaids. This way you can see how it all looks together."

Lily was bouncing on her toes again as she waited for Carol to return with her dress.

As promised, Carol returned a few minutes later carrying a long white gown. I didn't get a good look at it before she and Lily went into one of the dressing rooms, but I was sure it was going to be beautiful. Lily knew everything about clothes.

Bridget plopped down on a nearby chair. She leaned back and turned her head in my direction. "Do you live in the city, too?"

I shook my head. "No. Stephan still has his condo here, but we live near Le Sueur."

"So, you and Stephan live together?"

"Yes." I didn't understand why she was asking.

"Are you two married?"

I shook my head again.

"Interesting," she said, sitting up. "But you said you've been together for over four years. He's never asked?"

"No."

"Hmm."

A weird feeling churned in my gut and I didn't like it, but before Bridget could ask any more questions, Lily and Carol exited the fitting room. Bridget gasped and I understood her reaction. Lily's dress was stunning on her. It had a top similar to the bridesmaid dresses we were wearing, but whereas ours were knee length, hers went to the floor. And of course, Lily's was white.

"Well," Lily said, her arms in front of her, palms open. "What do you think?"

"Is there anything you don't look gorgeous in?" Bridget said. "Wow. Just wow."

Lily beamed. "You love it?"

Bridget circled around Lily. "Logan is going to be drooling when he sees you in this dress."

"You think so?" It was the first time I'd ever seen Lily not one hundred percent confident. "Brianna? What do you think?"

"You look beautiful."

Some of the stiffness went out of Lily's shoulders and the smile was back.

"Let's get you three ladies in front of the mirrors together so you can see the dresses side by side," Carol said.

We all took our places in front of the mirrors: Lily in the middle and Bridget and I on either side.

Carol straightened the train of Lily's dress. "Keep in mind the bridesmaid dresses will be burgundy."

A tear slid down Lily's cheek. "This is really happening. I'm getting married."

"Of course, it's really happening. That's why we're here, silly." Bridget bumped her hip against Lily and she laughed.

Carol came to stand beside me so she could look at all of us from the front. "So, is that a yes on the bridesmaid's dresses?"

Lily nodded and laughed. "Yes. They're perfect."

"All right, then," Carol said. "Let's get you ladies back in the fitting rooms. I'll take some measurements, so we can get the dresses ordered. With only five months until the ceremony, we don't want to wait." Then she turned to Lily. "Your other bridesmaid is still coming in on Monday?"

"She is." It was the first time another bridesmaid had been mentioned. There would be three of us?

I tried not to think about it too much as I headed into the dressing room and waited for Carol to come take my measurements. There was no reason to get myself worked up. The other woman could be nice. She was Lily's friend, right?

But I still wasn't sure how I felt about Bridget and I'd spent the last hour and a half with her.

Taking a few deep breaths, I closed my eyes and thought of more pleasant things. I was safe. Lily was nearby. And Stephan would be here to pick me up soon. All good things.

After helping Lily back out of her dress, Carol knocked on my dressing room door. The next fifteen minutes consisted of me getting poked and prodded by Carol to make sure the dress was going to fit my body perfectly. Normally, someone other than Stephan touching me like that would make me uncomfortable, but Carol had a gentle way about her that I liked. In a way, she reminded me of my mother.

Once I was finished getting measured, I dressed and went to join Lily in the sitting area.

"How are you doing?" she asked.

"Okay." I glanced toward the room where Bridget was getting measured. "Bridget keeps asking me about Stephan."

Lily frowned. "What did she ask?"

"She asked how long we'd been together and asked if we were married. I don't know why." I think that's why her questions were bothering me so much.

"I'll talk to her," Lily said.

I tilted my head to the side, confused.

Lily sighed. "Bridget was most likely trying to find out how serious you and Stephan are. As a couple."

"Oh." Now that her questions made sense, I liked them even less.

A few minutes later, Bridget emerged from the dressing room, dressed, and with a big smile on her face. "All that dress shopping has made me hungry. Know anywhere good to eat nearby?"

Lily glanced at her watch. "It's almost lunchtime. There's a café across the street that has great sandwiches."

"Perfect." Before either Lily or I could say anything more, Bridget was on her way out the door. She turned on her heel, still backing toward the door. "Come on. What are you waiting for?"

"You gonna be okay if we have lunch at the café?" Lily asked me.

I nodded. "I need to text Stephan to let him know where I'll be."

Lily nodded and took hold of my hand. "Let's get to the café and you can text him while we're waiting on our food."

Given we couldn't see Bridget any longer, I agreed. I didn't like leaving the store without letting Stephan know, but I didn't see much of a choice. In the end, I thought it was better to stay with Lily than to insist on staying at the store by myself. "Okay."

Stephan

The meeting was wrapping up when I cleared my throat and brought up the one issue I knew I needed to address before jumping into this working arrangement. "How much did Logan tell you about why I'm no longer running The Coleman Foundation?"

During the meeting, Josh had dropped hints that he'd only recently returned to Minneapolis. He'd spent four years in the military, and given the size and scope of his organization, I'd estimated that he'd been back no more than two years. The presses attention had waned significantly at that point, so I had no idea if he knew about Brianna or my involvement with her, Ian Pierce, or anything having to do with the trial.

Josh leaned back in his chair and brought the tips of his fingers together in a point. "Not much." He sat forward again, resting his forearms on his desk. "I did a little of my own research, though, and I have to say I came across some interesting articles."

I could only imagine what he'd found. Some of the worse had me being part of Ian's sex trafficking ring. "The press was very interested in my life for a time."

Silence lingered for several moments. I waited him out. "Whatever happened to the girl?"

"She's currently shopping for bridesmaids' dresses with Lily, Logan's fiancée."

"You still keep in contact with her."

This was the part that seemed to trip people up, but it was best to get it out there. "We live together."

"I see." His face gave no indication of how he was taking the information I'd provided.

"Will that be a problem?" I asked.

He glanced at the door before returning his gaze to me. "I'd like to meet her."

It wasn't the strangest request, but still one I was hesitant about. "She's not fond of people and even less of men she doesn't know."

"She knows Logan, correct?"

"Yes."

He stood. "Great. How about a small get together, then? You and Brianna. Logan and Lily. And me and my wife. We can discuss how best to address the fundraising issue and get to know each other in the process."

It was on the tip of my tongue to say no, but then I decided better of it. "When?"

"How about tonight? You're already in the city. No sense in you making another trip."

"I'll discuss it with Brianna and get back to you this afternoon."

Josh walked me down the hall to the front of the office where Stella was sitting behind the reception desk. "Sounds good."

He offered me his hand and I took it. "I'll be in touch."

I made my way down the elevator to my car. The last thing I'd expected to end up with was a dinner invitation. It made sense the more I thought about it. What better way to gauge whether what the media said was true than to meet the woman at the center of the rumors.

As I was maneuvering onto the road, my phone dinged letting me know I had a message. I immediately found somewhere to pull over. Normally, I'd wait until I was at my destination, but with Brianna out with Lily and in an unfamiliar situation, I wasn't taking any chances.

Putting the car in park, I reached for my phone. The message was from Brianna.

Bridget wanted to go to lunch. We're across the street from the bridal shop at Carly's Café. - Brianna

I released the breath I'd been holding and texted back.

I just left my meeting. I'll see you soon. - Stephan

Placing my phone in the cup holder, I pulled back into traffic. It took almost fifteen minutes to get to my destination and find a place to park. Traffic had increased significantly over the last two hours.

It wasn't difficult to find Carly's Café. The pink sign stood out against the blacks, browns, and grays of the surrounding buildings. There were quite a few people standing around waiting to order their food when I walked inside, so it took some searching to find Brianna, Lily, and Bridget.

Lily noticed me first and waved me over. "You found us."

Brianna's head came up and met my gaze. Her lips curved up into a beautiful smile and my heart skipped a beat. I pulled out the chair beside Brianna and sat down.

Before I could say anything to Brianna, Bridget interrupted. She leaned forward, resting her elbows on the table, her shirt dipping down in the front to show off her cleavage. It wasn't that I was paying attention exactly, but it was kind of hard to miss. "I was hoping you'd be joining us."

I didn't want to be rude, but I had no interest in entertaining whatever Bridget was attempting to convey. Instead, I turned my attention to Brianna. "Have you ordered lunch?"

She nodded. "Yes. I didn't know how long you'd be."

There was still a bit of uncertainty in her eyes. She wasn't one hundred percent positive what my reaction was going to be. But the fact that she wasn't sitting here shaking, unable to meet my gaze, proved how far she'd come.

I grinned, letting her know I wasn't upset, and then held up a hand to flag down a server. A young man hurried over and wrote down my order. I kept it simple since I'd never been to the café before. I figured it was hard to mess up a turkey sandwich.

Once the server had walked away, I asked how the dress shopping had gone. "Did you find what you were looking for?"

Lily launched into a long description of the dress style they'd chosen and how perfectly it matched the theme she was going for. I understood about half of what she said, but given Lily's knowledge of style and fashion, I was confident Brianna would look great in whatever dress Lily had picked out.

Our food came and I tucked into my sandwich. Brianna sat quietly beside me eating the salad she'd ordered. The sandwich was good, and the chips looked to be made in house. Then again, the food had to be pretty good given the number of customers they had.

"Did your morning go as well as ours?" Bridget asked as she picked at her salad.

I could hear the huskiness in her voice and the way her fork lingered near her lips to try and draw attention to her mouth. She was trying to flirt with me. I'd seen the same thing many times over the years, but it didn't have the same effect on me now as it had when I was younger. There was no interest there. My only issue was that she was doing it in front of Brianna.

Wiping my mouth, I placed my napkin over my knee. "It did. In fact," I twisted so I could see Brianna's face. "We've been invited to Josh's house to have dinner with him and his wife."

There was a moment of panic that crossed her face, and then she lowered her gaze. I monitored her breathing, making sure she was able to control her anxiety, while I waited for her response. It took a few minutes, but eventually she looked up and nodded. I knew she'd been going through all the possibilities in her mind and had most likely come to the same conclusion I had. She needed to get more exposure to people if she wanted to accomplish her goals and this would be a good opportunity.

I reached for her hand and brought it up to my mouth for a kiss. "I'll give Josh a call after lunch and let him know to expect us."

"Does that mean you'll be staying in the city tonight?" Bridget asked.

"Probably. I doubt we'll want to drive home that late."

"Tomorrow's Saturday. Maybe we could all meet for breakfast." She turned to include Lily in the conversation. "Logan's off tomorrow, isn't he?"

Lily was trying not to laugh, but she wasn't doing a great job of it. She knew exactly what Bridget was doing. "Yes, he is. I'll have to make sure he doesn't have other plans, though. Logan likes to keep our weekends free."

It was my turn to hide my reaction. Apparently, Lily's friend didn't know about Lily and Logan's lifestyle. That could make breakfast together on a weekend rather interesting.

I picked up the tab and we all headed outside, my hand firmly holding on to Brianna's. As we were nearing the door, I touched Lily's arm with my free hand, letting her know I wanted her to hang back. She paused and turned her head to look at me. "Josh invited you and Logan to join us tonight as well."

She nodded. "I'll call Logan and ask."

Logan and Lily began their weekend play at six on Friday

evenings. Whether they went to dinner tonight and breakfast tomorrow morning would be completely up to Logan.

Bridget was waiting for us when we walked out of the restaurant. "There you are. I thought I'd lost you." She was looking directly at me.

Lily sent me a knowing grin and looped her arm through Bridget's before addressing Brianna and I. "Thanks for coming today. I think the dresses are going to look great on both of you."

"You're welcome," Brianna said. "The dress is really pretty."

Lily smiled, and then turned to Bridget. "I'm in the mood for some ice cream. What do you say?"

Bridget groaned. "You're going to kill my figure and I'm never going to be able to fit in that dress."

Laughing, Lily guided her down the street away from Brianna and me. "You'll just have to spend a few more minutes on the treadmill."

Once they were out of earshot, Brianna released a loud breath. I glanced down at her. "You okay?"

"Yes." She looked down the street, and then at me. "Is Josh nice?"

She'd already moved on from Bridget. I cupped the side of her face and gave her a kiss. "I liked him."

That seemed to be enough for her as she changed subjects again. "I'm feeling tired."

I brushed her hair behind her ear. "I'm feeling a little run down myself. Let's grab a nap before getting ready for dinner."

CHAPTER 11

Brianna

It felt nice being in the condo again. Even though I loved our new house, there was something about the condo that was comforting to me. Maybe it was because this was the first place I'd felt safe. The place where I'd learned to trust again. The place where I'd fallen in love with Stephan. There were so many memories here.

Stephan rolled over and nuzzled his nose into my hair. We'd been in bed since five minutes after walking through the door. The late afternoon sun was shining through the windows, warming our naked bodies. "Hmm. We need to start getting ready or we'll be late."

"How did your meeting go today?" We hadn't talked much in the car on the drive to the condo since he'd been on the phone with Josh confirming that we'd be coming tonight, and once we'd gotten to the condo, talking had been the last thing on either of our minds.

"It went well. I think I can help him get his fundraising up and streamline his operations."

There was something in his tone that told me there was more. "But?"

"No, buts. It was a good meeting." He ran his hand down my side. "I guess I'm waiting for the other shoe to drop, so to speak. After what happened, and having to give up my position at The Coleman Foundation, I'm not sure jumping back into the fray is wise."

I turned in his arms to face him. "Do you want to?"

He hesitated for a moment before answering. "I do. I miss working, helping people. Knowing I'm positively contributing to society."

Stephan was a good man and he had a big heart. It had upset me that he had to step back from his family's foundation because of me. If this was his opportunity to get back to what he loved, I would support him one hundred percent, just as he'd supported me. "How can I help?"

He smiled and pulled me against him. "I love you, Brianna."

I didn't get a chance to respond. Stephan covered my mouth with his and gave me a lingering kiss that had me wanting to feel him inside me again.

His fingers skimmed down my back before cupping my backside. He sighed. "We need to get out of this bed before I forget we have obligations tonight."

Staying in bed sounded like a terrific idea, but that wouldn't be helping Stephan get his career back. "Can we shower together?"

He gave my flesh a squeeze, and then began climbing out of bed. I followed his lead and we made our way into the bathroom to start getting ready.

A little over an hour later, we were pulling up to a two-story townhouse on the opposite side of the river. It looked like a nice house with a large tree in the yard and a front porch that stretched across the entire front of the house.

Stephan took my hand and laced our fingers together. "Are you ready for this?"

"I'm ready, Sir." And I was. More so than I thought I would be.

We walked up three steps onto the porch and Stephan rang the doorbell. Immediately, a dog began barking from inside the house and we could hear movement inside. "Stay," a man's voice said. The dog stopped barking.

A moment later, the door opened to reveal a man who I assumed was Josh Berkley. He was younger than I'd expected him to be. For some reason, in my head, I'd assumed he would be older. He was also shorter than Stephan by a couple inches and had broader shoulders that made me think of football players with those big shoulder pads. "Come on in."

The inside of the house looked more modern than the outside. It reminded me a little of Lily and Logan's apartment, but bigger. Off to the left sat a large golden retriever. His tail was sweeping frantically back and forth on the floor.

"Hi, I'm Josh," the man said, offering me his hand to shake.

I took it because I knew that was what was expected, even though it was uncomfortable for me. "It's nice to meet you."

He smiled and patted the side of his leg. The dog trotted over to him. He sniffed my hand, and then rubbed up against it. "This is Charlie. He likes people."

Stephan held out his hand, letting Charlie sniff him, and then gave him a couple of pats on the head. "How old is he?"

"He turned three last month." Josh said, turning to lead us down the hall. Charlie followed. "My wife, Cynthia, is putting the finishing touches on dinner."

The hallway opened into a kitchen and dining area that looked as if it had recently been remodeled. A woman with blonde hair and brown eyes stepped out from behind the counter to greet us. "You must be Stephan and Brianna. Welcome."

Stephan released my hand so he could shake hers, and then placed a comforting touch on my lower back. "Thank you for inviting us."

I let her take my hand and envelope it with her own. She seemed nice enough, but it was hard to let my guard down with people I didn't know. I tried to remember to breathe.

"Dinner's almost ready. We're just waiting on the potatoes to finish up in the oven." She turned to her husband. "Logan did say he and Lily were coming, right?"

Josh strolled over to the refrigerator, Charlie still in tow. "He said they'd be here." Then he turned to Stephan and me. "What would you like to drink? I have beer, wine?"

"We'll just have water, thank you," Stephan said.

Our host looked to me as if waiting for me to chime in, but I didn't. Stephan had already answered for us. There was no need for me to as well.

After a few moments, Josh realized I wasn't going to answer and went to get glasses out of the cabinet.

"Why don't you two take a seat and make yourselves at home," Cynthia said.

Stephan guided us over to the table and held out a chair for me. I sat down and folded my hands in my lap, not sure what to do with them. Stephan lowered himself onto the chair beside me, and then reached for my hand. "Relax."

Relax. I could do that. It was dinner. And Lily and Logan were coming.

Josh brought two glasses of water over and placed them on the table in front of us. He opened his mouth as if to say something, but the doorbell rang, cutting him off. "That must be Logan and Lily. I'll be right back."

Cynthia was moving around the kitchen, putting the finishing touches on everything. I glanced at Stephan. "Should I offer to help?"

He looked at Cynthia, and then back at me. "I think she's got everything under control."

The sound of heels clicking on the hardwood floor brought our attention to the hallway. Seconds later, Josh and Charlie reappeared with Logan and Lily. Logan was still in a suit and tie, something I rarely saw him in outside of work. Lily was wearing a simple black dress with red heels that were so high I'd probably trip and fall in them if I tried to wear them.

"What can I get you to drink?" Josh asked Logan and Lily.

Like with Stephan and me, Logan answered for the both of them. "Just water for us."

Logan held out the chair directly across from me for Lily and she took a seat. When Logan sat down, Charlie came up beside him and rubbed his nose on Logan's leg, looking for attention. It was obvious the dog knew Logan and liked him as Logan scratched behind Charlie's ears.

"He's putty in your hands, man," Josh said when he brought Logan and Lily their waters. Then he glanced at Stephan and me and added, "He does this every time Logan comes over. You'd think he was Logan's dog instead of ours."

Cynthia chuckled as she set a plate of grilled chicken and a bowl of green beans on the table. "You're just jealous he's paying attention to someone other than you."

Josh laughed. "Maybe."

Our hosts finished bringing dinner to the table and within a few minutes we were all filling our plates and eating. As the lighthearted conversation continued, my anxiety eased. I wasn't sure I could say I was enjoying myself, but I wasn't so stressed I couldn't appreciate my meal.

Cynthia brought a cake out for dessert. "Does anyone want coffee?"

"I'll take some," Josh said.

He looked to Logan who shook his head. "I've had too much already today."

Lily didn't comment and I let Stephan speak for us. "No, thank you, Cynthia."

She returned a few minutes later with two mugs of coffee, one for her and one for Josh as he began cutting the cake and serving it. I had taken my first bite when Josh decided to ask me a direct question. "Brianna, I understand you and Stephan met under some unique circumstances."

I stiffened.

He waited a few moments, but when I didn't answer he continued. "How exactly did you meet? The article I read didn't go into a lot of detail."

Stephan had warned me that Josh may have some questions about our relationship. I'd tried to prepare myself, but it was still a bit of a shock to be asked the question in the middle of a dinner party. I swallowed the bite of cake that now tasted like sand in my mouth.

Josh was waiting for my answer and I knew that whatever I said would probably be the deciding factor in whether Josh wanted to work with Stephan. I felt the enormous weight of it settle in my stomach.

But I had gone over how I'd met Stephan dozens of times over the years, both for the trial and many times with therapists. I could do this.

Stephan

I'd had a feeling this line of questioning was coming. He'd been asking Brianna little questions here and there all evening. First it was our move out of the city. Then it was about how we'd found our house. He was casual about it, but I knew the purpose behind them.

Luckily, Brianna and I had talked about the potential of this happening while we were at the condo this afternoon. I didn't like that it was happening, watching her struggle was never something I enjoyed, but I also knew that if I were in Josh's position, I'd be doing the same thing.

Brianna lowered her fork to her plate and took a deep breath before meeting Josh's gaze. "He rescued me from an evil man who liked to rape and torture me. We found out later that Ian had killed some of the other women he'd owned. If Stephan hadn't saved me, I probably wouldn't be alive today." Her voice shook with the emotion of what she was saying. I was so proud of her.

The silence in the room was deafening. Everyone had stopped eating . . . breathing.

Cynthia was the one to finally breath the silence. "Owned?"

Brianna looked at the other end of the table where Cynthia was seated. "Yes. Ian owned me and another young woman named Alex. We were his slaves."

Our hostess had lost all color in her face.

Josh cleared his throat, clearly uncomfortable. "How? I mean . . . how did . . ." He was stumbling over his words. It wasn't every day you found out the woman you were sitting down to dinner with had lived through horrors you couldn't imagine.

"How did that happen?"

Brianna averted her gaze and took a deep breath. I knew she was struggling, so I took her hand in mine. She was doing so well. "I was sold to a man to pay off my father's gambling debts."

Both Josh and his wife looked stunned. Josh must not have done as much reading as he thought he had on the trial, because most of what Brianna had shared was in the transcripts. However, if he'd only been skimming through newspaper articles, he wouldn't have gotten much. Most of them were focused on her being held captive and my involvement. It still irritated me that many in the press were more concerned that I was part of the story, than the fact that a man had held Brianna captive for ten months.

Logan and Lily were the first to recover. The information Brianna shared wasn't new to them, but it still sent a shiver down one's spine every time she told her story. It was chilling to think of something like that happening today. They both resumed eating their cake and soon the rest of the table followed suit.

There was no more conversation for the rest of the meal as everyone finished their dessert. I leaned in to whisper in Brianna's ear. "Are you ready to go?"

She nodded.

Scooting my chair back, I stood, and helped Brianna to her feet. "Josh. Cynthia. Thank you for a lovely meal. It's been a long day, so we're going to call it a night."

Josh stood. "Could I have a word with you in private before you take off?"

My gaze met Logan's across the table. He knew I was silently asking him to keep an eye on Brianna.

"Of course," I said. Then I turned to Brianna. "Stay with Logan and Lily. I'll return shortly."

Josh led me down the hall to the front of the house and into the room to the left of the entryway. It was a small office, not much bigger than our main bathroom on the second floor of our home. He closed the doors behind us and crossed his arms over his chest. "I wanted to apologize if I upset Brianna. That wasn't my intention."

"If I thought it was, we would have left a long time ago."

He nodded. "I need to ask you one more thing. Some of the articles I read today." He paused and I could tell he was nervous about whatever it was he was going to say. "They said you bought her from this Ian guy."

This was the sticking point for most people. "Yes."

Josh blew out a breath and rubbed his hand on the back of his neck. "Wow. Okay."

"If you'd like to know the details, all you have to do is ask. I did what I felt I needed to do. And if I were in the same position again, even knowing it would mean having to step down from The Coleman Foundation, I would do the same thing."

He stared at me for what felt like several minutes, but was probably more like a few seconds, before he spoke. "I need a little time to think about this."

"I understand. You know how to reach me." I reached for the knob and opened the door. "Have a nice evening. And thank you again for dinner."

When I walked back into the kitchen, Cynthia was hugging Brianna. She stepped back when she saw me, and I could see moisture coating her eyes.

As soon as Brianna noticed me, she came to stand at my side. "Everything all right?"

She nodded.

I met Cynthia's gaze. "It was nice to meet you, Cynthia."

"Thank you both for coming."

Josh strolled back into the room looking a bit shell shocked.

"I think we're gonna head out, too," Logan said. "It's been a long week."

"Of course," Cynthia said when Josh continued to stand there. "I'll walk you all to the door."

Charlie, who'd spent most of dinner lying in the corner on his dog bed, got up to trail after Cynthia toward the front door.

Goodbyes were short and the four of us headed out to where our cars were parked on the street. "I think that went pretty well," Logan said.

"Are you okay, Brianna?" Lily asked.

"I'm okay." She looked up at me. "I'd like to go home, though. Maybe we could take a bath?"

I gave her a kiss. "I think that sounds perfect."

Logan opened his car door and waited for Lily to slip inside. "Lily said Bridget would like us all to meet for breakfast tomorrow."

"As much as I'd like to avoid that situation, maybe it's better to get it over with. If Bridget is going to be part of the wedding party, we're going to have to address the elephant in the room sooner or later. Maybe if she sees more of Brianna and I together, she'll get the message."

My best friend chuckled. "You keep telling yourself that."

I shook my head and helped Brianna into our vehicle. "I'll call you in the morning. We can figure things out then."

The drive home was uneventful. Given the hour, there wasn't a lot of traffic and we made it back to the condo in record time. I pulled into my parking slot and reached for Brianna.

She nuzzled her nose into my neck, and I kissed the top of her hair. "I'm so proud of you, sweetheart."

"Cynthia thanked me for sharing my story."

I smiled. Brianna never saw how amazing she was, how resilient. "Come on, let's get that bath going. I need to unwind."

We were alone in the elevator as we rode up to the top floor. People were already in for the night or they were still out partying. Either way, I was glad for the privacy.

Once we were inside the condo and the door was locked, we made our way into the bathroom. "Get undressed and I'll get the bath started."

Brianna began removing her clothes and putting them in the hamper while I got the water going. Even though we weren't living here full time anymore, I still paid someone to come in once a week to clean. That meant the bathtub was ready to go and we had clean towels on the rack waiting for us.

A naked Brianna stood beside me as I sat on the edge of the bathtub. Her long brown hair teased the tips of her nipples as she stood before me and I couldn't resist sucking one of them into my mouth. Her fingers threaded through my hair as I enjoyed the feel of her on my tongue.

I released her nipple, but not before giving it one last lick. "Get in the bath. I'll be in shortly."

Holding her hand, I steadied her as she stepped into the bathtub and lowered herself into the warm water. She leaned back and closed her eyes.

I unbuttoned my dress shirt and tossed it in the hamper. I swiftly removed my shoes, tossing my socks and pants in the laundry, as well. It felt strange being back in the condo, but familiar at the same time. I was glad I'd decided not to sell it.

Brianna opened her eyes when she heard me approach. She sat up, giving me room to slip in behind her. "Comfortable?" I asked as she leaned back against my chest.

"Yes, Sir." She released a contented sigh.

I wrapped my arms around her waist and held her while we let the water work its magic. We both needed to relax and what better way to do that than soaking in a bath with Brianna in my arms.

CHAPTER 12

Brianna

Something was pulling me out of the deep sleep I was in. I'd been so relaxed after our bath and the orgasm Stephan had given me, that I'd fallen asleep almost as soon as my head hit the pillow. It felt so nice that I didn't want to wake up.

Try as I might, however, something was tugging at my consciousness. I couldn't figure out what it was at first, but as I began to wake up, I realized it was Stephan. He was perched between my legs, licking me.

My legs fell open as if on instinct and he murmured his approval. "Good morning, love. Sleep well?"

He did something wicked with his tongue that felt really good. "Yes, Sir."

With every flick, my body heat rose. He sucked my clit into his mouth and massaged it until I was teetering on the edge. All I needed was a little more and I'd fall off.

Then his mouth was gone.

Before I could register what had happened, I felt his penis at my entrance, pressing into me. "That's it, pet. Take me. Take all of me."

My body welcomed him, and I felt full and loved and protected all at the same time. It was a wonderful feeling and one I've never felt with anyone other than Stephan.

He pressed me into the mattress with his body, braced himself with one arm on the bed, and grabbed the back of my neck with the other as he continued to thrust. I was completely surrounded, and I loved it.

His lips descended to cover mine and he took what he wanted. I could taste myself on his tongue as he devoured my mouth with enthusiasm as he pounded into me. He held my head at the angle he wanted and I could feel his fingers pressing against my skull with exactly the right amount of pressure.

Since my hands were free, I held onto his back, using the leverage to lift my hips to meet his. I loved this feeling of being with him, of feeling both free and captured at the same time.

Stephan shifted his weight and moved his hand that had been supporting his weight so that it was wedged between our bodies directly above where we were joined. I wanted to beg him to touch my clit, to allow me to come, but I couldn't. He continued kissing me with such passion that I was ready to explode from that alone.

Then, his thumb brushed my clit and I nearly cried. It felt so good and I wanted to come so badly.

A strangled cry of desperation tore from my throat.

He released my mouth and moved to my ear. "Do you want to come?" His voice sounded ragged and like he'd been working out in the gym. It was the sexiest sound ever.

"Yes!"

His hand on my skull tightened, pulling some of my hair. It was like an electric current went straight from my head to my sex. "Yes, what?"

"May I come? Please?"

"Such a good girl, you are." He increased the pressure on my clit, and I gritted my teeth. "Come for me, love."

My orgasm started before he'd finished the sentence. It ripped through my body with enough force that I couldn't contain my scream.

When my breathing began to slow and I became aware of my surroundings again, Stephan was hovering over me, a huge smile on his face. He was still inside me.

"I love watching you come," Stephan said. "It's one of the great joys in life to see you fall apart in my arms."

Heat warmed my cheeks back up.

He chuckled and I felt it all the way to my toes. "I love it when you blush, too."

"Was I loud?" I sounded loud, even to myself.

I didn't think it was possible, but his smile seemed to get bigger. "Very. Good thing I soundproofed the walls."

He was teasing me. I knew it. But that didn't help with the embarrassment.

"Hmm." He ran his nose from my neck up to my ear. "So very beautiful."

I swallowed, feeling the tingle of arousal begin to stir again. "Did you . . . did you come?" He was still inside me, after all.

Stephan hummed. "Yes, I did. I came very, very hard."

I sucked in a breath.

He laughed and let himself slip out of me. "As much as I'd love to stay in bed with you all day, we're supposed to be meeting Logan, Lily, and Bridget for breakfast in an hour."

Bridget. I'd forgotten about her. How she'd looked at Stephan. The questions she'd asked. I frowned.

Stephan raised his eyebrows in question.

"Bridget likes you."

Giving me a quick kiss, Stephan rolled over and got out of bed. Then he held out his hand, indicating he wanted me to join him. I scooted across the bed and put my feet on the ground.

Once I was standing next to him, he took both my hands in his and looked me in the eye. "Bridget doesn't like me. She likes my money."

I scrunched my nose up in confusion. Yes, Stephan was rich, but how did she know that? "I don't understand."

Stephan sighed. "I was dressed to impress yesterday in one of my more expensive suits. Given Bridget's rather forward approach, my guess is that she deduced that I had money based on what she knew the suit cost. Someone who made a middle-class income wouldn't likely be able to purchase a tailored suit like the one I was wearing."

It was strange. I'd never thought about how much his suits cost. They were just clothes.

He squeezed my hands and brought them up to his mouth. "Don't worry about Bridget. Lily said she'd talk to her. We'll get through this wedding and we'll never have to see her again."

I tried not to think about it as we showered and got dressed. As we drove to the hotel where Bridget was staying, my nerves started to get the better of me. Normally, we were at the house, or we went to a museum, or something without so much socialization. Even if we went into town to shop, I stayed close to Stephan and we didn't talk to many people other than maybe a server or a store clerk.

The last two days had been all about interacting with people. First Bridget and the lady at the bridal store. Then, last night with Josh and Cynthia. Now we were going to face Bridget again.

"Are you okay?" Stephan asked as he pulled up in front of the hotel. We were meeting everyone in the hotel restaurant.

"Yes, Sir."

He never took his eyes off me even though the valet was standing by the car with the door open, waiting for him to exit. "What number?"

"Four."

He nodded, got out, and walked around the car to help me out. I took his hand and he pulled me over to the side of the door instead of going in. "These last two days have been stressful, I know. You've been doing so well, though. I'm proud of you."

"I'm not used to being around so many people."

Stephan brushed his thumb along my cheek. "I know. But after breakfast we'll head home and the two of us can lock ourselves away until Monday. How does that sound?"

"Can we watch more Buffy?"

He groaned. "You just want to drool over Angel."

I giggled. There was no denying the actor that played Angel was cute, but he wasn't Stephan. If I had to choose, I would choose Stephan every time.

Pulling me into his arms, Stephan kissed my forehead. "Feeling better?"

It was only then I realized that in that short conversation he'd made me forget about my nerves. "Yes, Sir."

"Ready to go inside?"

I nodded.

Taking my hand, he led me into the hotel. The lobby was huge, but it wasn't hard to find the restaurant. We crossed through the seating area and by the front desk to the sign for Chester's Grill. A woman greeted us and showed us to our seats. Logan, Lily, and Bridget were already there waiting.

This time, I tried to see the things Stephan had said. As soon as Bridget spotted us, she turned on the charm—at least where Stephan was concerned. She ignored me, which was okay. I'd had enough socializing for one weekend.

As the meal wore on, I saw Lily's frown increase. She was noticing what her friend was doing, as well. I felt bad. I didn't want this to ruin Lily's wedding. It wasn't fair. I wanted to say something, but I didn't know what.

Finally, Lily spoke up. "Bridget, can I talk to you for a minute?"

"Sure," Bridget said. Then she looked at Stephan and added, "I'll be right back."

My gaze followed Lily and Bridget into the lobby. I couldn't hear what they were saying, but I could tell Lily wasn't happy. And Lily was always happy.

Stephan

"I can't believe she's acting like this," Logan said. "Lily even said something to her before you two got here."

I picked up my orange juice and took a sip as I looked at my best friend. Part of the reason he and Lily got along so well was because she was such a bubbly personality and he was so laid back. It wasn't often he got upset, really upset, but I could see it in his eyes. He was biting his tongue. "We'll get through it one way or another. She won't be the first woman who thought she could get somewhere with me. But I don't want her taking it out on Brianna. That's my main concern."

"Let's hope it doesn't come to that." I sincerely hoped it didn't. When it came to me personally, I could handle a lot. I'd put up with nasty articles and had even lost some friends after the fallout from the trial. But I wouldn't tolerate anyone harming Brianna.

Luckily, I wasn't alone in that. And if Lily's body language was anything to go by, she was giving Bridget a good ear full.

When the two came back into the restaurant and sat down, Bridget looked somewhat chastened. She shot looks at me every now and then, but she'd stopped with the flirting. It was progress.

By the time we said our goodbyes, I was more than ready to go home, and I knew Brianna was as well. We were right outside the city when my phone rang. I put it on speaker. "Hello?"

"Hi, Stephan, this is Josh Berkley. I was hoping we could talk."

A part of me wanted to pull over and take the call so Brianna couldn't hear what he had to say. While Brianna and I had no secrets, my instinct was to shield her from hurt whenever possible. I didn't want to see the look on her face if he said he couldn't work with someone who'd purchased another human being, no matter how noble my intentions were.

But I knew I'd see that look no matter what if that was his decision. She knew about the opportunity. If it fell through, she'd know why, even if I never told her the details.

"Of course."

He was silent for longer than was natural. I waited him out, though. This was his show. His decision. "I thought about what you said last night, and Cynthia and I talked it over this morning." Another pause. "If you're still willing to consult with me about Helping Hands, I'd like to work with you."

I glanced over at Brianna before answering. She wasn't looking at me, but I could see the small uptick of her lips. "I'll contact my lawyer and have him get started on a contract and I'll shoot you an email on Monday with what I'll need to get started."

"I'll look forward to hearing from you."

The call disconnected and Brianna placed her hand on my knee. Covering her hand with mine, I gave it a little squeeze. I didn't release her until I turned onto our driveway.

It was nice to be home. I carried our bag of dirty clothes into the laundry room and tossed them in one of the baskets before joining Brianna in the living room.

Per Brianna's request, we spent several hours watching Buffy the Vampire Slayer and cuddling on the couch. It was nice to decompress. I valued the quiet time Brianna and I shared more than I ever imagined I would. Before her, I was never a big party person, but I did go out regularly with friends, even if it was to various charity events. Since the trial, my invitations to such events had all but dried up. I was surprisingly okay with that.

After breakfast on Sunday morning, I spent a few hours making a list of information I'd need from Josh. I knew the basics of his organization, but if I was going to propose the most effective strategies, I needed to understand all the details of how Helping Hands worked, what their current avenues of fundraising were, and what their goals were for the future. I also left a message for Oscar to begin drawing up a contract.

We left for my aunt and uncle's a little after noon. Cal and Jade were joining us for dinner, which I wasn't looking forward to. Even though Cal and I had formed a sort of truce when it came to Brianna, there was still an underlying animosity there. Brianna sensed it as well, so it wasn't my imagination.

Diane ushered Brianna into the kitchen to help her with the salad she was making, leaving Richard and I alone. "How'd your meeting in Minneapolis go?" he asked, taking a seat on the couch. Normally, we'd be out on the back patio, but it was in the nineties today and humid.

"It went well. We're going to start nailing down the contract details next week."

Richard nodded. "Brianna have any trouble with anything?"

"Nothing major." I debated whether to share what happened with Bridget, but I figured why not. "We had a slight issue with Lily's friend. She seems to be interested in gaining my attention."

He raised an eyebrow. "Does she know you're taken?"

I smiled. Four years ago, my uncle's answer would have been a lot different. "Yes. She met me when I brought Brianna to the bridal shop so they could all try on dresses."

"I see," he said, sitting back, resting one ankle on the opposite knee. "So, she doesn't care that you're spoken for or she doesn't see Brianna as an obstacle to your affections."

"Brianna said she asked her a lot of questions about our relationship. I think she was fishing to see how committed we are."

"And she's a friend of Lily's?" He didn't look impressed.

I nodded. "They went to college together."

"A lot can happen in seven years. People change."

It was true. All the people I kept in contact with from my college days had changed considerably. I knew I had.

Before we could continue the conversation, the doorbell rang, and Richard went to answer it while I headed into the kitchen.

Brianna was placing a bowl of salad on the table, her pretty dress riding up in the back, giving me a glimpse of her thighs. It was hard not to imagine the way they felt wrapped around my waist.

She looked up to find me staring. A slight blush colored her cheeks as she walked toward me. I circled my arms around her and gave her a brief kiss.

"Get a room," Jade said as they walked into the dining area. If it had been Cal who'd said it, I would have been irritated. With Jade, I knew she was teasing.

I didn't relinquish my hold on Brianna. "How have you been, Jade?"

Instead of answering my question, she looked at Cal. I saw a silent communication zing between then, and then he shrugged. She turned back to us and held out her hand. "Cal and I got married."

Of all the things I'd been expecting to come out of her mouth, that wasn't it. Cal and Jade had been together for longer than Brianna and me, but I hadn't heard anything about a wedding.

"When?" Brianna asked.

Again, Jade and Cal shared a look. This time, it was Cal who answered. "We flew to Vegas last weekend and eloped." The expression on Brianna's face must have told him to explain himself. She was one of his closest friends and even I could tell she was hurt by the news. Not because he'd married Jade, she loved Jade, but because he hadn't told her. "It was a spur of the moment thing. We'd been talking about it, but with her family . . . we decided to just get on an airplane and go to Vegas."

Jade's family were an interesting sort. I'd met her parents once. They seemed like nice enough people, but very opinionated. They'd even inserted their feelings on my relationship with Brianna. I couldn't say I blamed Jade and Cal for wanting to avoid the drama that would come with a big family wedding.

Cal's answer didn't seem to pacify Brianna. "Why didn't you tell me?"

"We wanted to tell you in person," Jade said. "Can you forgive us?"

Brianna looked at the ground and shifted her weight. I knew she was hurt, but I also knew she'd ultimately forgive them. Brianna didn't hold grudges.

"Do you have pictures?" Brianna asked.

Jade smiled and hugged Brianna, extracting her from my arms. "Yes, we have lots of pictures. Come, I'll show you."

"Pictures will have to wait. Dinner's ready," Diane said, interrupting.

Even though Diane said pictures would have to wait, we only made it about five minutes before Jade pulled out her phone and began showing Brianna the photographs. The women ooo'd and ahh'd over them while the rest of us ate. I finally had to cut in and remind Brianna to eat her food.

Jade sent me a knowing look and tucked the phone away. "It was a simple ceremony, and everyone was really nice. A lot less stressful than what a traditional wedding would have been with my family."

"Have you told them yet?" I could only imagine how that conversation would have gone.

"They're coming to visit in two weeks. We're telling them then," Cal said.

I hid a smile behind my fork. What I wouldn't give to be a fly on the wall for that conversation.

"I'm sure they'll be thrilled you two finally got married. You've been together over five years, haven't you?" Diane asked.

It was a casual question, but my gaze immediately went to Brianna. She wasn't looking at me. Her focus was on Diane. There were times I could read her like an open book, but now wasn't one of them.

Jade picked up another roll and reached for the butter. "We have, but my parents haven't been the biggest cheerleaders of our relationship from the get-go. It's not that they dislike Cal—"

"They just don't like the idea that I'm defiling their daughter on a regular basis."

"Cal!" Jade chastised him.

"What?" he said. "You know it's true. The first time we went down there, your parents were looking at me as though I'd contaminated you or something."

Richard decided to join in on the conversation. "Won't the fact that you finally married her rectify that?"

Cal snorted. "Doubtful."

Jade rolled her eyes at him. "What Cal means, is that every time we've gone down to visit, my parents have not so discreetly tried to set me up with who they feel is a suitable man." She stabbed at a piece of meat on her plate. "It's embarrassing."

Diane placed a hand over Jade's. "I'm sorry, dear."

"Thanks, Diane. I appreciate it."

Brianna had watched the exchange but didn't comment. She seemed to be taking everything in.

From the talk of weddings and families, the conversation turned to summer plans. Apparently, going to Vegas wasn't enough for Jade and Cal. They were planning to spend a week in the Caribbean over Christmas.

"You'll miss Lily and Logan's wedding," Brianna said, speaking up for the first time since she and Jade were reviewing the pictures.

"They're getting married?" Jade asked, excitement clear on her face. Lily, Jade, and Brianna had all gotten closer over the last few years. They'd even gone on a few shopping trips together.

Brianna nodded.

"They told us last week," I said. "While you were in Vegas getting married." I thought the timing to be a little ironic. What were the odds?

Jade turned to Brianna, abandoning her food. "Has she found a dress yet?"

Brianna smiled. "It's beautiful. She tried it on for Bridget and me at the bridal shop on Friday."

My uncle met my gaze and raised an eyebrow at the mention of Bridget's name. I nodded and went back to my food. There wasn't anything I could do about Bridget. Not at this point, anyway. All I could do was hope that whatever Lily had said to her had finally gotten through.

CHAPTER 13

Brianna

It was dusk by the time we arrived back at the house. Cal and Jade had stayed for a while after dinner and told me all about their trip to Vegas. It sounded almost magical.

Stephan came up behind me and wrapped his arms around my waist. His lips tickled the skin at the base of my neck. "You've been quiet since we left Richard and Diane's."

"I was thinking about Cal and Jade's wedding."

He turned me to face him. "What about it?"

I rested my palms on his chest, feeling his heartbeat under my fingers. "I understand why they eloped, but I'm still sad."

"Because they didn't tell you?"

I nodded.

He glanced out the windows for a few moments before answering. "I think I'd feel the same way if Logan and Lily had taken off to Vegas without telling me. Logan is my best friend and I couldn't imagine him getting married and me not being there."

"I feel guilty, though."

Stephan raised both eyebrows, wanting me to explain.

"Because it's their wedding. It should be for them, not me. I shouldn't feel sad or hurt. I should be happy for them as long as they're happy."

"You can't help how you feel, sweetheart." He pulled me closer, cradling my head against this chest. "It's a beautiful night. Let's sit out on the deck for a while."

Stephan brought matches out with us so he could light the citronella candles. It was August and the mosquitoes were out in full force.

Once the candles were lit, he sat down on one of the lounge chairs and guided me onto his lap. The last of the sun's rays disappeared from the sky as we sat listening to the sounds around us. It was so peaceful. So unlike the city.

"Are you ready for your session with Dr. Katlin tomorrow?" Stephan asked.

"I made a list like she asked. I'm not sure how it's going to help, though."

"Preparation is always a good thing." He paused and shifted me in his arms, so my back was to his chest and I was staring out at our backyard. "I've made a list of wedding movies we can watch that might help us think of situations that may arise."

As the crickets began to sound in the distance, my thoughts returned to Bridget. "Sir? What about Bridget?"

His lips pressed against the top of my head. "What do you mean?"

"I don't know what to say to her when she asks me about us." I took a deep, cleansing breath, enjoying being in his arms. "It reminds me a little of how Cal used to be. About our relationship."

He began playing with my fingers sending tiny electrical currents up my arms. "Cal didn't approve of our relationship because he didn't think I was good enough for you."

"Bridget doesn't think I'm good enough for you," I whispered.

Stephan hesitated before resuming his movements again. "I'm not sure it's that she doesn't think you're good enough for me. I think it's more that she views you as competition and is trying to find out what she's up against."

I thought about what he said and about the questions Bridget had asked, along with her actions over breakfast. "I don't like her."

His chest vibrated beneath me. "Neither do I, love. Neither do I."

We lay there listening to the crickets for a while before blowing out the candles and heading inside. Stephan made sure all the doors were locked while I undressed and brushed my teeth. He was removing his shirt when I walked back into the room. It was still hard to believe he was mine. With everything I'd been through, with all my issues, he wanted me. He loved me.

Stephan saw me staring and motioned for me to come to him. I padded across the floor to stand in front of him.

My heart raced when he pressed a finger along the top of my breast down to the tip before giving it a little flick. They already felt heavier, anticipating what was to come. He had that look in his eyes and I knew we'd be playing tonight.

Leaving me standing there, he went over to the dresser where he kept the toys. I couldn't see what he'd selected, but it didn't matter. I trusted him and knew that whatever it was, he would give me pleasure.

"Climb up on the bed and get on your hands and knees."

I did as I was told.

Out of the corner of my eye, I saw him approach the bed. I was already wet, and he hadn't done anything yet.

He ran his hand down the length of my spine and I could feel it in my toes. His hand cupped my backside before sliding between my legs. "That's my girl. You're so wet for me already."

After a little more exploration with his fingers, I felt the mattress dip with his weight. Then, something pressed against my clit and wrapped around my waist. Seconds later, I felt the vibrations. They were subtle, but it didn't matter.

"How does that feel?" he asked.

"Good, Sir."

As the vibrations continued, I grew wetter. I knew I'd need more stimulation to come. But I also knew he wasn't nearly ready for that yet.

Something soft pressed against my back, moving up and down the length. He was doing it so lightly that I could barely feel it, just like the vibrator. Right as I was getting used to the feeling of softness, I felt the pricks of something sharper. It didn't hurt, but the contract was startling. I sucked in a breath.

The prickling thing followed the same path as the soft thing, but then it went around my body to rub against my stomach. I tried to look to see what it was, but I couldn't get a good look. I thought it was his vampire glove, but it felt a little different.

I didn't get a chance to think about it too much, though, because the soft was back. He kept alternating sensations from soft to sharp, letting me get used to the soft before changing it up. It had my entire body tingling.

The vibrations increased in intensity. I was focusing on that when I felt something new. Suction on my nipple. It was as if something was trying to tug it from my body. It should have hurt, but instead, it only made me wetter.

"That's it. You like that, don't you, pet?" He did it again, pulling at my nipple, sending the feeling straight to my sex.

Then, I felt a sharp sting to my backside, and I couldn't stop the loud moan that bubbled up from my throat. Nor could I prevent the whimper that left me when he did it again.

Stephan

I'd known the best way to introduce Brianna to spanking would most likely be to do it once her body was humming with arousal. Her biggest issue when it came to new experiences was that she let her fear get the best of her. With her body craving more sensations, driving her higher and higher toward climax, her mind shut off and she was able to just feel.

Her ass began to turn a pretty pink. It really was a beautiful sight. I massaged her warmed flesh with my hand before checking between her legs.

She was wet. Very wet.

I didn't want to push it, though, so I gave her a few more solid smacks on the ass before discarding my pants and taking up a position behind her. Lining myself up, I grabbed hold of her hip, making sure to sink my fingers into the area I'd warmed up moments before.

A sound that I could only describe as a purr came out of her as I plunged inside, her body welcoming me. I took hold of her hips with both hands and began thrusting. Closing my eyes, I reveled in the feel of her surrounding my cock. The warmth. The wetness. I wanted to experience this every day for the rest of my life.

As I felt my orgasm approaching, I reached up, grabbing her hair and giving it a firm tug. Her neck arched back at the same time I felt her internal muscles clenching. My girl loved to have her hair pulled. Almost as much as she loved to have her nipples pinched. It was times like this I wish I had more hands.

I increased my speed, pumping into her harder . . . faster. When I felt that surge at the base of my balls, I released my hold on her hip long enough to turn the butterfly up to high. "Let. Go. And. Come. For. Me." Each word was punctuated with a thrust of my hips.

I held tighter to her hair and kept pounding into her until I heard the sound I'd been waiting for. The high-pitched squeal came moments before her pussy began contracting around me. The feeling wasn't something I could describe, and I didn't want to. I only wanted to experience it over and over again.

My own orgasm hit me with the force of a freight train. I felt as if all the energy in my body shot out of my cock and into her. It was exhausting and wonderful and something I'd only ever experienced with Brianna.

As my orgasm subsided, it took me a few moments to catch my breath. I released my hold on her hair, turned off the vibrator, and rubbed the rosy cheeks of her ass. "Are you okay, sweetheart?"

She nodded. At least, I think she did.

Forcing myself to move, I rolled us over so we could lie side by side on the bed. I turned her to face me, wanting to look in her eyes.

There was a healthy flush to her cheeks and her nipples were still standing tall from the stimulation. I brushed the hair away from her face and looked in her eyes. "Talk to me."

She swallowed. "I'm . . . I'm okay."

Her voice sounded a little scratchy. "Lay here. I'm going to go get us some water."

I swiped the glasses we kept in the bathroom and filled them with water from the tap before returning to the bedroom. Brianna was exactly where I left her. I don't think she'd moved at all. Hopefully, that was because she was as exhausted as I was.

"Here," I said, handing her the glass.

She took it and gently raised it to her lips. After a few sips, she looked up at me. "Thank you, Sir."

I smiled. "You're welcome. Drink the rest of it. I'm sure you need it."

While she drank her water, I released the belt holding the vibrator from her waist and set it aside, along with the other toys I'd used. The vibrator was a mess, so after placing it on top of the dresser, I had to go back into the bathroom to wash my hands.

Upon returning to the bedroom, I climbed back into bed. Leaning against the headboard, I drank my own water, needing it as much as she did. I could still feel that orgasm in my toes.

Once she was finished, I put both of our glasses on the nightstand, nestled her in my arms, and pulled the sheet up to cover us. She rested her head on my chest and in typical Brianna fashion, she began playing with the edge of the sheet.

"How are you feeling?" I asked.

"Tired."

I chuckled. "Did I wear you out?"

I felt her lips curve even though I couldn't see her face from this angle. "Yes, Sir."

Kissing the top of her head, I asked the question I needed the answer to most. "How did you feel about me spanking you tonight?"

"It wasn't what I expected." She yawned. "It didn't hurt like I remembered."

I sighed and lowered us down in the bed, keeping her in my arms. "Do you understand more now as to why Lily likes to be spanked?"

She yawned again. "Uh-huh."

I brushed the hair away from her face and pressed my lips to the top of her head. "Get some sleep. We'll talk more tomorrow."

Less than a minute later, I heard her breathing change and I knew she was out. Reaching up, trying not to move any more than I had to, I turned the light off. I'd had a switch installed next to the bed, anticipating situations exactly like this. Closing my eyes, I fell asleep with Brianna in my arms.

As much as I would have loved to spend the morning in bed with Brianna talking about the night before, that wasn't on the agenda. My phone began ringing at eight o'clock sharp. It was Oscar and he needed more details so he could put the contract together.

I spent over an hour on the phone with him before sitting down to eat my breakfast, which Brianna had to heat up for me. Then, almost as soon as I'd finished my breakfast, I received a call from Glenn Trevors. Although he was the president and face of The Coleman Foundation now, we still talked on a regular basis. He respected the fact that my parents had started the foundation and he tended to run any new ideas by me first. I trusted him to run the organization, but I also appreciated being kept in the loop. Even if, legally, I didn't have more say than any other board member.

By the time I finished with Glenn, it was time for lunch, and then off to take Brianna to her appointment with Dr. Katlin. She had her notebook in her lap, prepared for her session. "Did you add more to your list this morning?"

"I want to talk to her about Bridget."

"I think that's an excellent idea. Maybe she can give you some ideas on how to deal with her questions." I'd love it if I were the only one to have to deal with Bridget, but realistically Brianna was going to have contact with her, as well. The more prepared she was, the better. Bridget struck me as someone who wouldn't be above playing dirty to get what she wanted and unfortunately, she seemed to want me.

"Sir?"

"Yes, Brianna?"

She glanced down at her notebook, and then at me. "Are you attracted to her at all?"

I wasn't expecting that question, but I had no problem answering it. "No. She may be pretty, but her personality is a complete turn off."

"But you think she's pretty."

We'd arrived at Dr. Katlin's office and we needed to get inside, but I didn't want to leave it at this. "I think Lily's pretty as well, but I have no desire to have a relationship with her or even have sex with her."

"You played with her once."

"I did and we didn't connect. She's much better with Logan."

I waited to see if she'd say anything more. Instead, she nodded.

"Let's get you inside for your appointment or you're going to be late."

We walked in the door of Dr. Katlin's office at exactly one o'clock. Her receptionist smiled as we entered. "I'll let Dr. Katlin know you're here."

Before we could sit down, Dr. Katlin appeared ready to take Brianna back. I waited a few minutes, and then stood. "I need to step outside to make a phone call. I'll be back shortly," I told the receptionist.

She nodded, and I slipped out in the hallway and into the stairwell. Pulling out my phone, I dialed Lily's number.

"Hey," she said in way of answering.

"You got a minute?"

I heard a door closing in the background. "I kind of figured you'd be calling me."

"How did your conversation with Bridget go?"

She released a loud sigh. "Not as well as I'd hoped. She said she'd tone it down, but I'm not sure I believe her. I mean she was like this in college, going after guys she was interested in full throttle, but I thought she'd grown up. The last few times we've had our girl's weekends she hasn't done more than some light flirting with a few waiters."

I didn't beat around the bush. "She's upsetting Brianna."

"I know." She paused. "I wasn't expecting to be dealing with this on top of all the wedding preparations."

"If she does something to Brianna, I won't be kind."

"I'm hoping it doesn't come to that. But if it does, you know Logan and I have your back. If she makes me choose between her and Brianna, Brianna will win."

Despite the seriousness of our conversation, a smile tugged at my lips. Brianna inspired fierce loyalty. I would protect her with all that I have, even my life, and so would most of the other people who knew her.

CHAPTER 14

Brianna

Cal called me as usual Monday evening. He wanted to know how my appointment with Dr. Katlin had gone and I let slip that Bridget had been hitting on Stephan.

"What did Coleman do?" he asked.

Over the last few years, Cal had done his best to stay neutral about Stephan and our relationship. Sometimes he did better than others and I straightened my shoulders, ready for him to say something I wasn't going to like. "What do you mean? He didn't do anything."

I could almost see him rolling his eyes through the phone. "I mean, did he flirt with her or did he tell her to get lost?"

"He . . . he ignored it." It was the only way I could think to describe Stephan's reaction to Bridget's comments. He'd pretended not to notice.

"He ignored it?" The way he asked the question made it sound like he didn't believe me.

"Yes. He acted like she hadn't said anything unusual."

Cal grunted.

"What?" I hated when he was like this and he was almost always like this when we were talking about Stephan.

"I've known girls like Bridget. She's not going to give up." He hesitated. "Especially if she doesn't view you as a threat."

"A threat?" I swallowed. "I don't understand. Why would I be a threat to her?"

Cal sighed. "I didn't mean it that way. I meant that she thinks she can get Stephan away from you. She thinks she can get him to choose her over you." He chuckled. "She obviously has no idea."

I was quiet for a moment, thinking about what he'd said. "What should I do? Dr. Katlin asked if I trusted Stephan."

He snorted. "She obviously doesn't know him that well if she's asking that. While I'm not his biggest fan, even I know he wouldn't cheat on you. Look, I would let Lily handle it. Bridget is her friend. But if it comes down to it, you may have to tell her to get the hell away from your man."

My eyes grew wide.

"Anna? You still there?"

"Yes."

Cal lowered his voice as if he were confiding some sort of secret. "I know you're not the assertive type, but sometimes you have to mark your territory, so to speak. Jade's had to do it with a few women over the years who've gotten a little too flirty with me even after I've told them I'm with Jade. You and Stephan . . . you have a unique relationship. Not everyone is going to understand that."

Including him. He didn't say it, but it was implied. "So, I should let Lily handle it, but if she can't I should mark my territory?"

He chuckled. "Yeah."

Okay, I was even more confused than when we'd started this conversation.

"Don't stress about it too much. I'm sure Lily will figure it out. Bridget's her friend, right?"

"Right."

"It'll be okay, Anna," he said.

I nodded, even though he couldn't see me.

Silence lingered longer than was natural before I asked about something else. "Cal, what's it feel like to be married?"

"I don't know. I mean, overall things haven't changed much, but I kind of like the idea that Jade is mine in the legal sense." He laughed. "Maybe that makes me a caveman or something, but I get a thrill seeing my ring on her finger."

I bit the inside of my cheek as I considered what he'd said. Instinctively, I touched my collar. It was the symbol that I was Stephan's and he was mine. But it was also something private. No one besides our friends knew what the necklace I wore meant.

That wasn't exactly true, now that I thought about it. I was pretty sure Richard, and maybe even Diane, knew about my collar, but they were Stephan's family.

But it wasn't the same as being married. I knew that.

"Why did you decide to get married then . . . if it didn't change anything?" I asked.

He didn't answer right away, and I thought maybe I'd asked something I shouldn't have. I was about to apologize when he spoke. "You can't tell anyone." Again, he snorted. "I know you're going to tell Stephan. I mean you can't tell anyone else. Not even Lily."

"Okay." I was glad he clarified his statement because he knows I don't keep secrets from Stephan.

Cal blew out a breath. "Jade's pregnant and we wanted to be married before we told anyone, including her parents."

Jade was pregnant?

Images of a little boy or girl running around Cal's house filled my head. Jade holding a baby, rocking it to sleep. I couldn't help but smile.

"You're too quiet. Say something," Cal said.

"I'm sorry."

"Why are you sorry? Are you not happy for us?"

"No," I said, shaking my head. "I mean, yes, I'm happy for you."

"Then what are you sorry about?" he asked, confused.

"I got lost in my head. Thinking about you and Jade and the baby." The images were still floating around in my head and I couldn't help but smile. Jade would be a great mom.

"I've been doing that a lot lately myself." I could hear the smile in his voice. "I can't believe I'm going to be a dad."

"You'll be a good dad, Cal. I know it." My voice shook a little as I said the last part. Cal would love and protect his child. That I knew beyond a shadow of a doubt. His child would never have to worry that they would be sold into slavery in order to pay off their father's debt.

"Thank you, Anna," he whispered, his voice full of emotion. After a minute, he cleared his throat. "I should probably go. Jade will be home any minute."

"Okay. Tell Jade I said I'm happy for you both."

"I will."

I sat on the windowsill looking out at the river. Cal and Jade were going to have a baby. Would they ask me to babysit? Would I be able to? It frustrated me that I didn't know the answer.

While I'd gotten better, there were still times I had panic attacks and I couldn't always predict when they'd happen. I couldn't do that if I was watching a child. They would be dependent on me for their safety and protection.

I had no idea how long I sat there in the window thinking, but eventually Stephan came to find me. He knelt beside me, taking my hands in his. "What's wrong, love?"

"Nothing." He looked doubtful, so I added, "Cal and Jade are going to have a baby."

He blinked several times. "Jade's pregnant?"

I nodded. "Cal said I could tell you but no one else. Not even Lily."

Stephan grinned. "Smart man."

"He said that's why they got married so quickly."

"Given Jade's family situation, that makes sense." He pushed himself up to his full height, and then helped me to stand. "Were you planning to cook tonight, or would you like to order take out?"

It was my turn to blink. "What time is it?"

"Almost five. I was beginning to worry when you didn't come down."

I did a quick rundown in my head of what I had in the refrigerator. "I can make a quick stir-fry."

He gave me a quick kiss. "Sounds perfect."

· · ·

Stephan

Brianna began pulling things out of the refrigerator while I set the table. I'd been working out on the deck while she talked to Cal in order to give her some privacy. When almost two hours had passed and she hadn't appeared, I'd begun to worry. Cal had gotten better at not upsetting her and Brianna didn't rattle as easily, but I always tried to be home whenever they talked.

Twenty minutes later, we were sitting down to our meal. Brianna had brought down her journal before her conversation with Cal, but I'd waited to read it. Her latest journal entry had focused on Sunday dinner at my aunt and uncle's. She'd talked how she felt finding out Cal and Jade had gotten married without telling her.

As much as I didn't fully understand her friendship with Cal and why she put up with some of his antics, her hurt and even anger, although that's not the word she used, was evident. I was glad he told her the reasons behind their rushed decision, but even still, I knew it wouldn't completely take away the hurt. If he'd asked Brianna not to say anything, he knew she wouldn't. Or at least he should. Brianna was loyal to a fault.

I finished reading her journal entry, and then set it aside. "I found us a wedding movie to watch tonight. I think you'll enjoy it."

"What's it called?" she asked in between bites.

"27 Dresses. It's a romantic comedy about a woman who's been a bridesmaid twenty-seven times."

She looked at me in disbelief. "She's been to twenty-seven weddings?"

"That's what the synopsis said. I guess we'll have to watch and find out."

We finished eating our dinner, cleaned up, and got comfortable on the couch with Brianna tucked into my side. I scrolled until I found the movie and pressed play.

As we watched, I tried to pay attention to potential scenarios that may crop up at Lily and Logan's wedding. To my surprise, the movie wasn't bad. Romantic comedies weren't my favorite, but this one had some funny moments and the romance wasn't over the top.

Brianna didn't take her eyes off the screen for the entire movie. She laughed several times and I even heard a couple of sighs. My girl was a romantic.

She had a smile on her face when the credits began rolling. "I liked it."

I chuckled. "I could tell."

"What did you think?" she asked.

"I thought it was pretty good for a romantic comedy. The scene where she tried on all those dresses was cute."

"That was one of my favorite parts." She looked down, and then back up to meet my gaze. "That, and when he tells her he thinks she deserves more."

I lifted her from the couch and moved her so she was straddling my hips. "She did deserve more. She always put everyone else first."

Brianna nodded. "I didn't like her sister very much."

"She did redeem herself a little toward the end." I brushed the hair back behind her ears. "What did you think about the weddings themselves? There were the big receptions at the beginning."

"You'll be with me at Lily and Logan's reception."

This was true. And unfortunately, this movie hadn't shown a lot of what happens behind the scenes between the bridesmaids. "I'll see if I can find a movie that has some scenes of the bridesmaids getting ready. That might provide us with some situations that may arise."

I rubbed the small of her back, sliding my hands under the fabric of her shirt and reveling in the softness of her skin against my palms. Brianna leaned forward, resting her head on my shoulder. "I can't believe Jade is going to have a baby."

Four years ago, Brianna jumping topics would have surprised me. Now, it was par for the course. When we were sitting in the evenings talking, she tended to say whatever popped into her head.

"A baby will be a big change for them, but I'm sure they'll adjust. I think Jade will be a fantastic mom. She keeps Cal in line." I couldn't stop the grin from forming.

"He's gotten better. I don't think he hates you, anymore."

Her breath wafted over my neck causing other areas of my body to sit up and take notice. I ignored them, though. We needed to talk. The rest could wait. "He's gotten better at hiding his disdain for me, but I don't believe his opinion of me has changed all that much over the years. He'd still prefer it if you hadn't chosen me."

"But I did choose you," she whispered, her fingers tracing the collar of my shirt.

I ran my hands higher up her back, stopping right below her bra strap. "Something I will forever be grateful for."

We sat there for a while holding each other before she spoke again. "What would have happened if Cal and Jade didn't get married and her family found out about the baby?"

"I don't know. Families are tricky. Sometimes they don't react rationally."

"Like Richard when he found out about me." Her fingers were sending little shockwaves from my neck straight to my groin and it was getting harder to ignore. A simple touch was usually all it took from Brianna and I was ready and willing.

To give myself a little reprieve, I picked up her hand and brought it to my lips for a kiss. "Yes, like Richard. People are shaped by their experiences and beliefs. Richard believed I was hurting women and given his profession and what he'd seen, he was outraged." I lowered our hands but kept hers firmly laced with mine to keep the temptation at bay. "Jade's family seems to have a view of what her future should look like and the type of man she should be with. Cal isn't their first choice, so if they would have found out about the baby, it's possible it would have caused a greater rift between Jade and her family."

She was quiet for several moments. "I've never been around a baby before."

I hadn't really thought about it, but neither had I. Being an only child, there were no other children in our house and Richard and Diane had never had children of their own. I'd been around a few toddlers over the years, but never babies. "It will be a new experience for both of us."

Brianna pressed her nose against my neck and inhaled. "I love the way you smell."

My chest vibrated with amusement. "What do I smell like?"

She hummed. "You."

That didn't exactly answer my questions, but it was adorable none the same.

"I told Dr. Katlin I drove around the yard last week." We'd switched topics again without warning. "She said she was happy I was working toward driving again, but not to rush getting on the road until I felt I was ready." Brianna glanced up at me, meeting my gaze. "She's worried I'll have a panic attack while driving and hurt someone."

"Is that what she said?"

Resting her head back on my shoulder, she sighed. "Not exactly. She said there was no need to rush. That while driving was a good goal to work towards, she was more concerned that I focus on handling my anxiety in certain situations."

I couldn't fault Dr. Katlin's reasoning. It was rare for Brianna to find herself in a situation where there wasn't someone to drive her where she needed to go, but there were times when she found herself in, what to her, was an uncomfortable situation that could easily spike her anxiety. Addressing that would make most of the normal tasks many people took for granted much easier for Brianna.

Making her sit up so I could look her square in the face, I cupped her face. "You have come so far since the first day we met. I know you want to drive again and Dr. Katlin's right, there's no rush. But I don't think it's because she's worried you'll hurt someone."

"I could, though," she whispered.

"Yes, you could. So could I." I ran my thumb over her bottom lip. "Driving comes with risks. All we can do is prepare ourselves the best we can and try to be as safe as possible."

She glanced down before meeting my gaze again. "I want to drive, but I don't want to hurt anyone."

"I know, sweetheart." I pressed my lips to hers in a barely there kiss. "That's why you're going to practice in the yard until you feel comfortable before going on the road, and even then, I'll be with you until you feel okay on your own."

Some of the tension that had built up released from her shoulders. "I love you."

I grinned. "I love you, too."

The sweetest smile crossed her lips. "Can we play again tonight?"

Tossing her onto the couch next to me, I climbed over her, pinning her down to the couch. "You want to play?"

She nodded. "Yes, Sir."

As her eyes sparkled up at me with excitement at whatever I had in store for tonight, it was hard to believe this was the same woman who'd once feared anything to do with sex.

CHAPTER 15

Brianna

I stood at the bottom of the stairs that led to the attic and willed myself to stay calm. It had been a week since I'd been in Stephan's playroom and I couldn't put it off any longer. Stephan was on the phone with Oscar going over the contract they were sending to Josh, so they would be a while. It was the perfect time for me to accomplish the task Stephan had set out for me. But try as I might, I couldn't get my feet to move.

What had happened last week kept cropping up in my mind. I hated having panic attacks. I hated remembering.

Dr. Perkins said that I had to face my fears in order to overcome them. It was the one thing she and Stephan agreed on.

What Dr. Katlin would say in this situation, I didn't know. While I liked her, I was still unsure how she felt about dominance and submission. As a concept, she seemed to be fine with it, but I'd learned that not everyone was okay once they realized Stephan was my Dom all the time, that it wasn't only in the bedroom. She hadn't asked me a lot of questions about our life together. At least, not about that part of our lives together. Then again, I'd only been seeing her for about two months.

I realized I was stalling. Glancing down the hall, I imagined Stephan sitting there talking on the phone. I didn't want him finding me still standing here at the bottom of the steps when he finished his call.

Turning toward the stairs once more, I took a deep breath and headed up the stairs.

The door was unlocked as it had been since he'd taken me up here. He said it was our playroom, but it didn't feel that way. It felt like his. His toys. His room. His.

Like before, the smell of leather hit me first. I got a hint of cleaning products, but it wasn't as strong as the last time. The room was brighter than I remembered, but maybe that was because the sun was high in the sky and it was the middle of the day. Ian's room was dark. It had no windows and almost everything was black or red.

A shiver ran down my spine. I didn't want to think about Ian or his playroom. Nothing fun happened in there.

My gaze landed on the St. Andrew's cross along the wall. Stephan's cross was a light brown color, made of wood. Ian's was wood, too, but it had been painted black. The other difference I noticed was that Ian's had metal chains to hold the wrists and ankles. Stephan's cuffs were made of leather.

For some reason, I was drawn to them. I crossed the room and ran my fingers over the soft leather. Stephan usually used rope to bind me, but these cuffs didn't feel as if they'd hurt. I doubted they'd dig into my skin like the metal would.

A flash of being tied to Ian's cross flashed through my mind for a second, but I pushed it away. I hated Ian. He may be dead, but I hated him. He'd taken so much from me—my freedom—my innocence—and even my ability to trust.

He made me afraid and I hated him for it.

The tips of my fingers brushed against the wood and I tried to think about the cross as an object of pleasure and not pain. More flashes came and they weren't pleasant. I jerked as the memory of a whip with barbs on the end sliced through my back as my wrists and ankles were tied. Blood dripped down my back as pain seared through me.

Then, when I thought it couldn't get any worse, I'd felt his penis enter me. Not my sex, but my anus. I'd screamed and he'd laughed. I could still hear him in my ear.

"Brianna?"

I blinked and looked up. Somehow, I'd ended up on the floor, curled into a ball. Stephan was kneeling and looking at me, worry etched in his face.

Scrambling, I crawled to him and wrapped my arms around his neck, squeezing tight. He circled his arms around me and settled me on his lap. I buried my face in his neck, unable to get close enough.

"Shh. I've got you."

He rubbed up and down my back, soothing me, and eventually it worked.

We sat there for a while until I calmed down. It was only then I realized that he was leaning against the St. Andrew's cross.

I looked up at it and he noticed. "It won't hurt you."

"I know," I whispered. When I wasn't overcome with memories, I knew the things in this room wouldn't cause me harm. The problem was that most of them were tied to a memory . . . a bad memory.

"Tell me what happened."

"Flashback," I mumbled against his neck.

"Having to do with the St. Andrew's Cross?" he asked.

I nodded. "I hate that I can't look at anything and not remember when it was used to hurt me."

He sighed. "I think we need to start disassociating these things from pain to pleasure for you like we did with the rope and with spanking."

That sounded good, but I didn't know how he was going to do that.

Instead of answering, he kissed the top of my head. "It's been a long day. I'm going to order us a pizza and we'll watch some Buffy."

I knew then how much my panic attack had affected him.

An hour later we were huddled up on the couch eating pizza and I was trying to forget about what had happened in Stephan's playroom. We were halfway through our second episode of Buffy when the phone rang. Stephan paused the television and went to answer it.

Feeling better, I cleaned up the remains of our dinner and put the leftover pizza in the refrigerator before throwing the box in the garage. When I walked back into the house, Stephan was leaning against the kitchen island waiting for me. Something was wrong. His shoulders were stiff, and he stood with his hands in his pockets. He almost never did that.

I went to him. "What's wrong?"

Stephan tucked a strand of hair behind my ear, but he didn't speak.

As the silence lingered, my anxiety increased. "Please."

He searched my eyes before releasing a deep breath and releasing it. "That was Emma on the phone."

The hairs on the back of my neck stood on end. Emma had been my lawyer during the trial, but I hadn't heard from her in years. Once everything was over, I hadn't needed her. I had no idea why she would be calling. "What did she say?"

"She received a call from the prison." His thumb moved back and forth over my jaw. I didn't know if he was trying to comfort me or himself. "John was taken to the hospital with chest pains. They think he had a heart attack."

My heart was beating a mile a minute. I hadn't had any contact with my father since visiting him in the prison with Cal. Finding out he may have had a heart attack sent mixed feelings through me. No matter how much I didn't want to see him again, he was still my father. The thought of him dying sent a chill through me.

Stephan placed a firm hand on my hip. "He's stable for now. He had you listed as his emergency contact but had no valid contact information for you, so they called Emma."

I nodded, unable to form words. A good daughter would probably rush to his side, but I didn't want to see him. Even after four years, I couldn't forgive him for what he'd done, or what he didn't do. "I don't want to see him."

Some of the tension left Stephan's body and I realized that he'd been worried I'd want to go visit my father. He pulled me to him and pressed his mouth to my forehead. I closed my eyes and let the warmth of his lips flow through me.

"It's been a long day. The rest of the show can wait till tomorrow." Without another word, he took my hand and proceeded to make sure the doors were locked and to turn everything off.

Normally, he'd send me to the bedroom to get ready while he shut everything down, but tonight he kept me close. He followed me into the bathroom, brushing his teeth beside me and only leaving me alone long enough for each of us to use the bathroom.

We both discarded our clothes and burrowed under the sheet. He circled his arm around me, pressing my back to his front as we laid on our sides.

"I will always protect you," he whispered in my ear. "Always."

"I know."

Stephan

I didn't sleep well. It was well after midnight before I relaxed enough to fall asleep. Even then, I kept waking up to check on Brianna.

When I'd heard Emma's voice on the phone, I'd known whatever she was calling to say wouldn't be good. To be honest, my first fear was that she was calling to say John was being released for some reason. Brianna was getting her life back on track. She didn't need to be looking over her shoulder, waiting for her father to turn up.

Finding out he'd had a heart attack and was in the hospital, had sent my brain into overdrive. I ran through all the different reactions Brianna could have to the news, including wanting to go visit him. While I didn't think that would happen, I'd been preparing myself, nonetheless.

And even though Brianna had said last night that she didn't want to see him, I was still uneasy about the situation. Not about John. I couldn't care less about him. He could and should rot in prison for the rest of his days. I worried about Brianna and how she would react when, one day, we got the call that her father was dead. She still loved him. He was her father, after all. She just didn't understand, nor did I, how he could have allowed her to be taken and didn't even report her missing.

At six in the morning, I gave up on sleep, put on some pants, and went to the kitchen to get some water. The sun was already up, so I headed out to the deck to get some fresh air. Brianna wouldn't be up for at least another hour.

I pulled out my phone and dialed.

"Hello?" Cal sounded half asleep.

"I figured you'd be awake by now."

A loud yawn came through the phone. "I am. Kind of. Is something wrong with Brianna?"

"Yes." I paused, letting that sink into his sleepy brain. Brianna had said he wasn't a morning person. "Emma called last night. John was admitted to the hospital with chest pains. He has her listed as his emergency contact. They contacted Emma when they couldn't find a current contact number for Brianna."

I heard him set something down, probably a cup of coffee, with a little too much force and mutter a curse. "How is she?"

"Sleeping at the moment. She took the news better than I expected, but I'm not sure if that will change once the shock wears off." As much as I didn't like Cal, I didn't doubt his commitment to Brianna or her wellbeing. He wanted her to be safe and happy, too. We just happened to have different ideas on what that looked like. Namely, he didn't see me in that picture. "Are you and Jade free for dinner tonight?"

He didn't hesitate. "We can be there by six-thirty."

As I disconnected the call, I noticed Brianna standing in the doorway. She'd wrapped her robe around her body, the silk brushing against her legs about four inches above her knees. Her hair was tousled from sleep and she still had a crease from her pillow on her cheek.

I tucked the phone into my pocket and beckoned her to me. "How long have you been standing there, love?"

"Not long." She bit the inside of her lip. "Was that Cal?"

"Yes. He and Jade will be joining us for dinner tonight."

"I'll make a roast. It's Cal's favorite."

Running my hands through her hair, I tried to straighten it. "How did you sleep?"

"Okay."

I tilted her head up so I could look in her eyes. "It's early. I thought you'd sleep longer."

"I woke up and you weren't there." She frowned. From any other woman I would have thought she was being coy, but Brianna didn't do coy. She was stating a fact and letting me know she was sad about it.

"I couldn't sleep and didn't want to wake you."

Her frown deepened. "Why couldn't you sleep?"

Pulling her into my arms, I kissed her temple. "I had a lot on my mind, and I couldn't get it to shut off."

"About John?" Of course, she'd get to the heart of the matter.

"Yes. Him and how you'd feel if something happened to him." I avoided saying when.

She stared out at the river for a while. "When I think about John, I can't remember the good times when I visited him in the summers. All I can see is when he came to the condo and tried to take me away from you."

I held her tighter.

"Can we have my name removed as his emergency contact? I don't want to know if anything happens to him. I don't want to know if he gets hurt. Or . . . or if he dies." She choked on the last part and it nearly broke my heart.

I cupped her face between my palms and brushed my lips against hers. "Let's get some breakfast, and then we can see about calling Emma and asking her about our options."

As it turned out, it wasn't as straightforward as I'd hoped. Given what had happened and John's role in it, Brianna never should have been added as his emergency contact in the first place. Emma said it was likely that he'd gotten someone to 'do him a favor' and put Brianna's name on the paperwork.

Getting her name removed was going to take some work. Emma

was going to contact the Adult Victims Parole Advisory Board to see if they could help. Best case scenario, we could have things cleared up in a couple months. If things didn't go our way, and given John seemed to have friends who were still willing to pull strings for him, we could be looking at three years before her name could officially be removed. It wasn't what either one of us wanted to hear.

After speaking with Emma, I knew we needed to do something positive. It was a beautiful day, so it was the perfect time for Brianna to practice her driving skills. She was nervous at first, but with every minute she spent behind the wheel she got better.

"Try parking between those two trees." There were about two car lengths between the trees, which would give her plenty of room to try her hand at parallel parking.

It took three tries, but she was finally able to get the car to go where she wanted it. "I did it."

The smile on her face was priceless. All the worry lines from earlier that morning were gone, which is exactly what I had hoped would happen. "You did."

To my surprise, she put the car in park and unbuckled her seatbelt. "May I sit on your lap, Sir?"

The instant she made the request, my cock began to twitch. "You may."

She lifted her leg over the center console and straddled my lap. I rested my hands on her hips, positioning her crotch directly over the bulge in my pants.

Her eyes sparkled with joy. "I'm getting better."

"You're doing well. A little more practice and we can give the road a try."

"Do you think I'll be ready to drive by myself by winter?" she asked.

"Why winter?" I hadn't realized we were on a specific time frame.

She averted her eyes, looking outside the car. We were on an area of our property where there were no houses in sight. It was a beautiful day and there was a nice breeze blowing off the water. "I was looking for GED classes and there's one that has openings not far from Le Sueur starting in January."

Brianna had mentioned she'd wanted to go back to school, but I hadn't realized she'd been looking at classes. "And you want to go."

"I do."

I made her look at me. "If it's what you want, we'll do everything we can to make it happen. If you can't drive by then, I'll drive you."

She opened her mouth to speak, but I covered her lips with my finger.

"However, we have five months till January, which means we have five months to practice."

Her lips curved up into a smile, and then her tongue darted out to touch the finger I still held over her mouth. It was such a subtle gesture, but it changed the mood in the car. I pressed my finger into her mouth, and she began sucking on it as if she were sucking on my cock.

I closed my eyes and groaned as the memory of the last time she'd taken me in her mouth came back to me. Reaching between us, I slid my hand under her skirt and zeroed in on her clit. Her panties were already wet as I ran my thumb over the fabric.

"You're very wet."

She hummed sending more sensations from my finger straight to my groin.

I took a quick glance around, confirming once again that no one else was around, before removing my finger from her mouth and laying the seat back as far as it would go. "Unfasten my pants and pull my cock out."

Brianna unbuttoned my pants, and then lowered the zipper down. The confining space meant it took her a few minutes to move the fabric out of the way so my erection could spring free. She skimmed her fingers against my length, and I had to grit my teeth.

Gripping the back of her neck, I pulled her down on top of me and crushed her mouth to mine. Brianna met my tongue stroke for stroke, rubbing her body against me. She was as turned on as I was.

I lost track of time as we kissed and touched, making out like teenagers. Eventually, though, the need to be inside her proved too much to resist any longer. Somehow, I managed to snake a hand between us, push her panties to the side, and line my cock up with her entrance.

"Take me," I growled against her lips.

What happened next had me seeing stars. Instead of gently lowering herself down on my shaft, she impaled herself with it. Within seconds her juices were flowing down my cock as she rode me.

Neither of us lasted long. I drove my hips up to meet her with each downward motion. It was like riding a wild bull, but better.

When I gave her permission to come it was as if the flood gates had opened for both of us. We each let out a strangled cry that would have caused concern had we had neighbors close enough to hear.

As I lay there sweating, with an exhausted Brianna in my arms, trying to regain my breath, I realized how blessed I was. If everything else in my life went away and all I had left was Brianna, I would be good for the rest of my days.

CHAPTER 16

Brianna

By the time Cal and Jade pulled in the driveway, I had already removed the roast from the oven. The table was set, and Stephan went to get the door while I brought the food to the table.

"You made my favorite," Cal said as he ambled over to where I was standing.

"Yes, I—" I didn't get a chance to finish my sentence before he picked me up by the waist and wrapped me in a bear hug. "—did," I said as he put my feet back on the ground.

After a brief and much more subdued hello from Jade, we all sat down at the table. "I'm sorry we didn't tell you about the baby," Jade said after we'd started eating.

"I wouldn't have told anyone if you hadn't wanted me to."

Cal frowned. "It wasn't that, Anna. The doctor said a lot of people choose to wait until after the baby is ten weeks along before telling anyone in case they miscarried. We didn't want to tell anyone in case something happened."

"How far along are you?" Stephan asked. He hadn't said much up until now.

Jade pressed a hand to her stomach. "Around eleven weeks."

While their reasoning made sense, I still couldn't help feeling hurt. "If something had happened to the baby, you wouldn't have told me?"

Cal's brow got a deep crease in it like I was asking him a hard question. "I don't know. We hadn't thought that far ahead."

"We're sorry we didn't tell you, Brianna. We just wanted it to be between us for a while. We didn't mean to hurt your feelings." Jade took hold of my hand. "I was hoping, though, that maybe now that you knew you could help with the baby shower."

"You want me to help?"

"Of course." She smiled. "You're the best cook I know. I wouldn't trust anyone else with making sure the food was perfect. Think we can get Lily to help with the decorations?"

"As long as it's after the wedding, I'm sure Lily would love to help," Stephan said. "She can't say no to organizing a party."

Jade nodded. "It won't be until closer to the due date. There's plenty of time." Then, she frowned. "I hope I'll be able to find a nice dress to wear to the wedding. I'll be six months along by then."

Cal put his arm around her shoulders. "They have great maternity clothes these days. I'm sure you'll be able to find something."

She didn't look convinced.

"I can ask Lily to help if you want," I said. Lily knew everything there was to know about clothes. I'm not sure about maternity clothes, but if she didn't know she could find out.

My suggestion seemed to make her relax some. "Maybe she has a suggestion on where I should look."

I smiled, happy that I was able to help in a small way. "I'll ask."

Cal cleared his throat as he served himself a second helping of roast and glanced over at Stephan. "I heard you were dipping your toes into the business world again."

"Nothing's confirmed yet, but I'm exploring an opportunity." It was obvious by the way Stephan answered Cal's question that the two didn't really get along. Stephan was rarely that formal in his speech anymore.

"I hope everything works out. Give you something to do during the day."

Cal was careful not to attack Stephan verbally or physically anymore, but that didn't mean he didn't get his digs in on occasion. I knew Jade had picked up on his underlying implication as well when I saw him jerk. She'd most likely kicked him in the shin.

When Stephan had stepped down permanently as president of The Coleman Foundation, Cal had been more upset by it than anyone else. I hadn't understood why at first, until he'd mentioned one day during a conversation that Stephan would have extra time to dream up more games for us to play.

He wasn't talking about board games, either. Cal knew that Stephan was a Dom and liked kinky sex. It was what had caused so many problems at the beginning. Even after all these years, I didn't miss that Cal gave me a good once over every time he saw me. I wondered what he would think if he knew Stephan had spanked me the other night.

I couldn't completely stifle the giggle that bubbled up. Everyone looked at me and I felt my cheeks heat. "Sorry."

Luckily, Stephan moved the conversation along, and I was able to wallow in my embarrassment alone. Or mostly alone. Jade gave me a knowing grin. She may not know exactly what I'd been thinking, but she could guess the direction. Mainly because I rarely giggle about anything else. This wasn't the first time I'd had an inappropriate thought at the dinner table.

After dinner, we moved onto the deck. Stephan lit the citronella candles to keep the bugs away, and then eased into one of the lounge chairs. He lifted me onto his lap, and I rested my head on his shoulder, taking up my favorite position.

Cal and Jade sat next to each other, but in separate chairs. They were affectionate, but not as much as Stephan and I were. Stephan was almost always touching me, even in public. I'd seen Cal and Jade hold hands, or Cal put an arm around her, but they rarely did anything more. Not where others could see, anyway.

I was relaxing, listening to Stephan's heartbeat, when Cal spoke. "Were you able to get a hold of Emma?"

My eyes flew open.

"Yes." Stephan's voice rumbled under my ear. "She going to contact a victim advocacy group to see if they can help. It's not a fast process, though, so for now we're in a waiting game."

"That's screwed up. They can't petition the court or something?" Cal asked.

"Apparently not."

"How do you feel about this, Anna?" Jade asked.

"I don't like it. I don't want to see him. I don't want to know if something happens to him. But even if I do know, it won't matter." While that all sounded good, Cal knew me too well.

"Bullshit, Anna."

I startled a little at his outburst and Stephan tightened his hold on me while sending Cal a warning look.

Cal sighed and ran a hand over his face. "You may not want to care, but I know you. You care. Even after all he did to you, you care, and you always will."

"It doesn't matter."

Stephan decided to step in. "Emma's going to contact the prison and see if her name can be put on the emergency contact form instead, but she isn't hopeful given she's not family and Brianna's who John wants listed."

"So, he has more rights than Anna does?"

"Trust me," Stephan said, "I'm not any happier about it than you are."

Cal huffed, but didn't say anything else.

After a few moments of tense silence, Jade asked if Lily had picked a venue for her wedding.

"I'm sure she has," Stephan said. "But she hasn't announced it yet. Normally, I would say The Four Seasons. She loves it there. But they're usually booked at least a year in advance for weddings."

"Well, if anyone can pull it off, Lily can."

Stephan nodded. "Very true."

They stayed until the sun disappeared from the sky. It wasn't as uncomfortable as some of our dinners had been over the years. Cal and Stephan could even have a conversation now without snapping at each other.

We watched from the front door as they backed down the driveway and made their way home. It had been another long day and I was eager to get to bed. My eyes were already feeling heavy.

"You look as if you're about ready to fall asleep standing there." Stephan skimmed his fingers over my cheek.

I leaned my head into his hand, closing my eyes. It felt so natural and so comforting.

The next thing I knew, he was sweeping me up into his arms. I circled my arms around his neck, holding on tight.

"Come on, sleepy head. Let's get you to bed. And hopefully we can both sleep better tonight."

I sighed and relaxed against him as he carried me into our bedroom, laid me on the bed, and slowly undressed me. He left me there, naked, while he went into the bathroom. When he came back to the bedroom, he was naked as well and he slid into bed beside me.

As much as I loved having sex with Stephan, it was in moments like this that I felt precious to him. He pulled the sheet over us and cradled me to his chest.

"Good night, Brianna."

"Good night, Sir."

Stephan

I tried to keep things simple the next three days, giving us both a chance to relax. We took the car out for another drive around the yard, spent some time reading together, and watched a movie. On Sunday we went to Richard and Diane's. Luckily, it was only the four of us and we were able to have a quiet meal together.

Brianna had written about John in her journal on Friday, but that was the last mention she'd made of him. When Emma had called again on Friday afternoon, she'd shared with me what had been said, which wasn't much beyond her checking in to make sure Brianna was doing all right. It was that conversation that had prompted the journal entry.

I kept searching for any signs of distress, but there weren't any. At least, I hadn't thought so until Richard pulled me aside before we left their house Sunday evening. He placed a hand on my arm to get my attention while Brianna was saying goodbye to Diane and motioned for me to follow him into the adjoining room.

Once the door was closed behind us, he sighed. "Normally, I wouldn't say anything, but given the . . . type of relationship you and Brianna have . . . well, I thought maybe I should." He shifted his weight as if he were uncomfortable with the conversation. "Brianna told me about her father being in the hospital. She asked." He blew out a breath. "She asked if I could look at his medical records and see how sick he is."

I wasn't sure how to take this information. "Did she say anything else?"

He shook his head. "I asked if she was sure and she nodded. That was the whole of the conversation."

We could hear voices in the hall and we both knew we were running out of time. "Thank you for letting me know."

Richard opened the door in time to see Diane and Brianna approaching.

"There you two are," Diane said. "We were wondering where you'd taken off to."

Before Richard could formulate some generic reason for us to have snuck off, I brushed past him and addressed Brianna directly. "Are you ready?"

I saw something flash in Brianna's eyes before she answered. "Yes."

"Good night," I said, giving my aunt a kiss on the cheek.

"You two drive safe."

Not five minutes had passed since we left Richard and Diane's house before Brianna asked, "Are you upset with me?"

I glanced over at her, and then back at the road. "No, I'm not upset." And I wasn't. I hated John for what he did to her, but I also understood the conflicting emotions. What I didn't understand was why she would want to know the status of his health if she had no desire to see him. "Did you change your mind about wanting to see him?"

"No. Not really." She was twisting her hands in her lap again. A clear sign that she was nervous. "I'm curious, I guess."

Picking up her hand, I brought it to my lips. I didn't say anything more as I lowered our hands to my lap. That's where they stayed for the duration of the drive.

The next day, I spent the morning reviewing some files Josh had sent over. The contract had been signed on Friday and this week was all about coming up with a game plan. I had to admit, I was excited about getting back to work.

While I was upstairs in the study, Brianna cleaned. The house wasn't all that messy since she did some form of cleaning almost every day, but she said she needed the distraction. I didn't know for sure, but I was assuming Richard was going to look in on John today for her.

Sure enough, after dinner the phone rang and it was Richard. I handed the phone to Brianna. "Hello?"

I stayed close. They didn't talk long, though. The entire conversation lasted less than five minutes.

"Thank you," Brianna said, and then disconnected the call. She cradled the phone in her hands and looked up at me. "They stabilized him and sent him back to the prison. Richard said he was recommended to see a cardiologist to see if he needed to be on medication or if they needed to put in a stent."

She turned to stare out the window with a lost look on her face. I held out my hand for her. "Let's go for a walk."

Brianna placed the phone on the coffee table and stood. She laced her fingers with mine and we headed outside.

A rabbit was munching grass in the backyard about thirty feet from our back deck. He saw us and took off in the opposite direction.

I led us down by the water, one of her favorite places, and walked along the shore. "What are you thinking?"

"I don't want him to die. But I also don't want to see him." She glanced up at me. "That doesn't make sense, right? If I don't want him to die, shouldn't I *want* to see him?"

"Given the circumstances, and what he did, I think it makes perfect sense." I was trying to be neutral here and not allow my feelings toward her father to cloud my judgement. She didn't need my ire for him right now.

She didn't say anything for a while as we walked. The sound of the water was calming. "I want to call Emma tomorrow." She took a deep breath and exhaled. "If they contact her again, I don't want her to call me." She paused. "Even if he dies."

I stopped and pulled her into my arms. My lips brushed against her hair. "Are you sure?"

Brianna nodded.

Kissing the top of her head, I angled us back toward the house. We spent the rest of the evening cuddled in my chair watching television. I didn't question her decision. This was her choice. It always had been.

Since Brianna's panic attack on Wednesday, I'd been thinking about how to help her. So as the new week dawned, I began putting my plan into place. While she spent the afternoon writing in her journal and reading, I headed up to the playroom.

When I looked around this room, I thought of all the possibilities it offered. We played in our room most of the time, which meant I had to plan ahead and bring any toys I wanted to use downstairs in advance. I could never make a spur of the moment decision to switch things up.

When Brianna saw this room, she saw possibilities as well. Just not of the pleasurable kind.

She loved playing. That wasn't the issue.

Strolling over to the St. Andrew's Cross, I considered my options once more. She needed to get over her fear. She wanted to. If that meant working through each toy and apparatus one at a time, then that's what we would do.

Digging into the bag I brought with me, I got to work.

It took me two afternoons. One to get it disassembled and one to reassemble it.

I'd suggested Brianna spend some time out on the deck reading so I could bring everything down the stairs without her seeing what I was doing. It wasn't that I was hiding it from her exactly, but I did want it to be a bit of a surprise. If she knew what was coming, she'd get anxious about it and that was the last thing I wanted.

By the time she came in to begin making dinner the second day, I had everything put back in order. I went to the kitchen to see if she needed any help.

"Can you make the salad?" she asked.

I smiled and went to the refrigerator to get the vegetables. "Are you enjoying the book you're reading?"

"Yes." A blush stained her cheeks and I knew why. As Brianna's sexual appetite has increased, her reading material has gotten steamier. She still wanted to read about the couple falling in love, but the hotter the sex scenes, the better.

"That good, huh?" I teased her. "You might have to read a scene or two to me."

The pink on her cheeks got darker and I chuckled.

We sat down to dinner and I dove into her journal as I ate. Yesterday she'd met with Dr. Katlin and we'd spent over an hour the night before talking through what they'd discussed. To my surprise, she hadn't mentioned her dad at all. Instead, her focus had returned to preparing for Lily's wedding. I had some ideas about that too, but first things first.

We were almost finished cleaning up when I made my announcement. "We're playing tonight."

She finished drying her hands on the towel and came to stand in front of me.

I lifted her chin and gave her a hard kiss before taking her hand and leading her to our bedroom. There was no hesitation on her part. She trusted me completely and I was hoping that would get us over this hurdle as it had all the others in the past.

The moment she noticed the new addition to our bedroom her eyes went wide, and she sucked in a breath. I really hoped this was going to work.

CHAPTER 17

Brianna

My heart wouldn't stop pounding as I stared at the St. Andrew's Cross in the corner of our bedroom. It was the one from his playroom. I didn't understand. What was it doing here?

But even as the thought crossed my mind, I knew. He'd said we were playing tonight. And looking at the large wooden X in our bedroom, I knew that would be part of our play.

He stepped in front of me, partially blocking my view. "What number, Brianna?"

I swallowed and it felt as if there was a lump in my throat. "S-seven."

With the gentlest of pressure, he took my hands and placed them on his cheeks. "Breathe. I'm right here."

His gaze held mine as he breathed with me until my breathing was steady once more and my pulse had slowed.

"Good girl." Still holding my wrists, he began backing toward the Saint Andrew's Cross. I tried to focus on him. To remember that he would take care of me no matter what.

We came to a stop a foot away from the wooden structure. I knew it was there—I could feel it—but I didn't take my eyes off Stephan.

He lowered my hands to the front of his shirt. "Undress me." His voice was soft, barely above a whisper, but it was still a command.

My fingers trembled a little as I released the buttons one by one to reveal his chest and stomach. I'd undressed him many times, but it never got old. I loved being able to touch him, to feel the softness of his skin beneath my palms.

His shirt fell to the floor with barely a sound and I moved on to his pants. I was trying to ignore the imposing item next to us and concentrate on him and what I was doing. It was only a thing and a thing couldn't hurt me.

I kept telling myself that over and over again as I lowered the zipper of his pants and pushed them down his hips. He stepped out of his pants and kicked them off to the side leaving him in only his underwear. The bulge of his erection strained against the confines of the fabric and it called to me.

Unable to resist, I brushed the back of my fingers over it, causing him to suck in a shaky breath. "Take them off."

My heart raced for a different reason this time as I eased his underwear down his legs, leaving his penis pointing directly at me.

Like with his pants, he stepped out of the underwear and pushed them aside. He stood there, naked in front of me for several moments, not saying anything before he took hold of my wrist and brought my hand to his erection. I wrapped my fingers around him, and he moved my hand up and down his length, finding a rhythm he liked.

A bead of pre-come appeared at the tip of his penis and my mouth watered wanting to lick it.

As if knowing exactly what I'd been thinking, he took his free hand, and with his index finger, he gathered up the moisture and brought it to my mouth. I opened obediently.

The salty flavor filled my mouth as he spread it on my tongue. I closed my lips around his finger, sucking, wanting to get it all.

When he removed his finger from my mouth, he skimmed it down my neck to the front of my dress and released the top button. Then the next. And the next. The dress had buttons all down the front and methodically he popped each one from its hole while continuing to guide my hand on his erection.

The cooler air hit my exposed torso causing my nipples to harden against the fabric of my bra. My dress hung loose, open in the front, with my bra and panties peeking out from underneath. I swayed toward him, seeking more of his touch.

He removed my hand from his penis and turned us. I was waiting for him to push me against the wall and kiss me, but instead I felt wood at my back. My eyes widened and my breathing picked up when I felt him lift my wrist. I felt the panic beginning to rise and I opened my mouth to call out my number. I had completely forgotten about the cross.

"Eyes on me, Brianna." His sharp tone shocked me back to the present.

He was staring at me, watching me. I took a deep breath, and then another.

"Good girl. Keep looking at me. Focus on me."

I did as he asked and felt my panic begin to ebb.

Then, I felt the leather encircle my left wrist. I sucked in a breath but didn't get much air.

"Listen to my voice, love. I'm right here. It's just me and you."

I nodded.

"Tell me what you're feeling? What number are you right now?"

"I'm—I'm scared. Six." I was really trying not to get to a seven.

He kissed the skin right below where he had my wrist secured to the wood and I felt a tingle go down my arm. Not a bad tingle, but the good kind of tingle.

"I'm going to secure your other wrist now." It wasn't a request, although I knew I could say ten and he would stop. It had never happened. Not with sexual things. But I knew if I said it, he would stop.

Did I want him to stop?

The scared part of me was screaming yes, but there was another part that knew from experience that if I could get over my fear, I'd most likely enjoy it. All I had to do was not let the fear win.

It was easier said than done.

Leather circled around my right wrist, securing it in place, and I waited for him to bend down and do the same to my ankles. Instead, he stood in front of me, cupped the back of my neck and kissed me.

His mouth teased mine until I leaned forward trying to get more of him.

"That's my girl," he said, his breath tickling my wet lips.

I sucked in a breath as he deepened the kiss and I felt his fingers skim down my sides until he dug his fingers into my hips. All thoughts of anything but Stephan disappeared as he ground his erection against my stomach.

The kiss seemed to go on forever, and then suddenly his mouth was gone, and I was craving more. He didn't leave me hanging for long, though. His lips trailed down my neck, licking and sucking his way to my breasts that were still encased in my bra. He held me in both his hands, kneading my soft flesh. All I wanted was for him to keep touching me.

My wish came true when he pushed the cups of my bra out of his way and guided one nipple into his mouth. A low moan escaped my lips as he sucked. I could feel the moisture building between my legs.

As if reading my mind, he dipped a finger into my panties. "You're so wet for me," he murmured with a mouthful of my breast.

Again, he took his time touching, savoring each of my breasts while massaging between my legs. His fingers slid in and out of me with ease. I wanted more. I needed more.

"Please?" I begged. "Please."

He released my breast and kissed lower. "Is my girl wanting to come?"

To drive his point home, he licked my clit through my panties. I almost came right then. "Please."

He did it again, but lighter this time. "Tell me what you want, pet."

"I . . ." That's all I got out before he started circling my clit with the tip of his tongue. It felt so good, but there wasn't nearly enough pressure. "May I please come . . ." He thrust two fingers inside me, and

I felt my legs begin to tremble. I was so close. "Sir, please, please, please."

Then, as if he were taking a stroll in the park and not kneeling between my legs he said, "Come."

As soon as the word left his mouth, he gave me what I'd been craving. His tongue flattened against my clit, lapping and sucking. It was exactly what I needed, and I screamed out as I came.

Stephan

Seeing Brianna strapped to my Saint Andrew's Cross was a glorious thing. Seeing her coming while strapped to my Saint Andrew's Cross was close to perfection.

Her body shook from the power of her orgasm, but I wasn't quite finished with her yet. I removed her underwear as Brianna was still lost in post orgasmic bliss, which was exactly how I wanted her. She wasn't thinking about the cross or her memories. All she was thinking about was this, us. Exactly how it should be.

Lifting her legs, I held her thighs open and lined myself up with her entrance. I didn't hesitate as I pushed inside.

Brianna opened her eyes and I knew we'd crossed yet another hurdle. I didn't see an ounce of fear.

It didn't take long before I felt my climax approaching. I captured her mouth with mine as I increased my thrusts, grinding my pelvic bone against her clit.

A soft whimper rose from her throat and I knew she was there. I released her mouth long enough to give her permission to come, and then let loose myself. We didn't often come together, but there were occasions, like tonight, when I was able to time things right. There was something about the feeling of her internal muscles clenching around me as I filled her.

The tension that had been building left our bodies in a matter of moments and I felt her legs loosen around my waist. "Hook your ankles around me."

It took a second or two for what I said to register, but soon I felt her legs grip me again. Once I was confident her legs were secure around my waist, I reached up to release her wrists. I freed the first one and kissed the inside of it, placing her hand on my shoulder. She steadied herself as I removed the binding from her other wrist.

I carried us both into the bathroom and set her on top of the counter before unhooking her legs and letting myself slip out of her. "Stay here. I'm going to draw us a bath."

Her eyes were half closed, but she nodded. I knew she was riding high on endorphins at the moment, but I didn't want her to crash once they began to wear off. Hence the bath. Brianna loved relaxing in the bathtub. She'd sometimes spend an hour or more soaking in the water reading one of her romance novels. It was where I normally sent her when I knew she needed to unwind.

After testing the water to make sure it was a good temperature, I dug a hair tie out from one of the drawers and began gathering her hair on top of her head. I tugged a little harder than I meant to as I was attempting to wrap the elastic around her hair, and she made a noise that sounded somewhere between a moan and a squeak. "Did I hurt you?"

She shook her head.

"Words, Brianna."

There was a moment's pause, and then, "No, Sir." I barely heard her above the water running.

If this was the first time she'd done this, I would be worried. But it wasn't. It happened a lot when we had an intense play session.

With her hair secured on top of her head, I removed her bra and helped her off the counter, being sure to stay close in case she lost her balance—I was never sure how steady she'd be on her feet when she was like this. I held her hand as she climbed into the bathtub. She lowered herself into the water and let out a sigh.

I waited until the water was where I wanted it before joining her. She sunk back against my chest, resting her head on my shoulder. I reached for the soap and lathered up my hands.

As I massaged the soap into her shoulders, I took a visual inventory of her body. Other than a few red marks on her breasts from my scruff, she had no other marks, not even from the leather cuffs that had been around her wrists. She hadn't fought the restraints at all, but then again, Brianna enjoyed being bound.

It was something she'd struggled with over the years as she did with a lot of the kinky stuff we did. Given her history, she didn't understand why she liked it. We'd discussed the subject multiple times. She'd even tried to talk to Dr. Perkins about it, but when the conversation had dissolved into questioning whether or not I was pushing Brianna to do things she didn't want to do, Brianna had decided not to bring it up again.

That had been my main issue with her previous therapist. While she helped Brianna work through her social issues and her fear of situations and people, she'd been horrible when it came to assisting Brianna in dealing with her sexual insecurities.

Maybe insecurities wasn't the correct word. Brianna embraced her sexuality in a lot of ways. She communicated her feelings and what she liked and disliked. And she didn't shy away from less than traditional sex. Not only did she love being bound, she enjoyed having her hair pulled, several different types of sensation play, and a variety of toys and vibrators. The only thing that kept her from trying something was her memories. I was really hoping Dr. Katlin would be able to help her with those since she seemed more open to the type of relationship Brianna and I had.

"How are you feeling?" I asked as I soaped up her right arm.

"Okay." Her voice wasn't as dreamy as it had been earlier.

"Are you sore anywhere?"

"My breasts are a little sore."

I chuckled. "Yes, well, I do love your breasts." To prove my point, I gave her right breast a gentle squeeze.

Her only response was to arch her back a little, pushing her breast against my hand.

As much as I would love to continue to play with her, we did need to talk. "How did it feel to be secured to the cross? Did you have any flashbacks?"

She rubbed her hand down my leg. "I didn't have any flashbacks."

Most people would go on to the next question, but I knew Brianna. And she knew me. I wanted more than a single confirmation that she hadn't had any flashbacks.

It took a while, but I waited her out as she gathered her thoughts. "When you started touching me . . . I forgot where I was . . . what I was tied to." She turned so she could look at me. "That's good, right?"

I gave her a quick kiss. "That's very good. It's what I'd hoped."

She nodded. "Ian's cuffs were metal."

Her captor liked metal. From what she'd told me, his playroom sounded as if it had been modeled after a medieval dungeon.

I circled both of her wrists with my fingers, and then lifted them over our heads until her hands were at the back of my head. "I prefer leather."

The new position arched her back, bringing her breasts out of the water. I took the soap, lathered my hands, and began working my way down her chest. As I rinsed the soap from her body, it was tempting to lean down and suck one of her nipples into my mouth. I didn't, though. This was about taking care of Brianna. Bringing her down from her high.

I finished washing her, intentionally making it nonsexual, and then helped her out of the bathtub. After drying off, we both brushed our teeth. She didn't say anything when I handed her toothbrush to her along with the toothpaste. We stood at the double sinks brushing our teeth, looking like any normal couple getting ready for bed.

Once she'd finished brushing her teeth, I picked her up and carried her into the bedroom. The cross still loomed in the corner and I saw her gaze fall on it almost immediately upon us entering. I also felt her grip on my neck tighten. She may have gotten over the first hurdle, but it wasn't over yet. When I touched her, the memories faded into the background. That was certainly a good thing. But it didn't mean the bad memories went away. "It's going to stay there for a while."

She pressed her lips together but didn't say anything as I tucked her into bed.

Lowering the lights, I got in bed next to her and pulled her against my chest. I kissed the top of her hair, breathing in her scent. "I'm right here. Get some sleep."

"Sir?"

"Yes, love?"

She hesitated. "Thank you."

I tightened my hold on her and tucked her head under my chin. "You're welcome, sweetheart."

A few minutes later, I heard her breathing change and knew she'd fallen asleep. It was only then I allowed my eyes to close so I could allow sleep to claim me.

CHAPTER 18

Brianna

Stephan was true to his word. For the next week, we played with the cross in some way almost every night. And even when we didn't, it was there, in our bedroom. I could pretend I didn't know why even the sight of it caused me unease, but it would be a lie. Ian had chained me to a lot of things, but the Saint Andrew's Cross had been one of his favorites.

And now, every time I walked into our bedroom it was there. At first, I tried to ignore it, but Stephan wouldn't let me.

By the time week two rolled around, I was getting better. Seeing it didn't send my pulse racing and my palms sweating in fear. We were making progress and I was grateful. He was so patient with me, and I knew how lucky I was.

It was Wednesday, and that meant it was time for me to make my weekly trip upstairs to the playroom. I hadn't had a panic attack since he'd moved the cross downstairs, but that didn't mean the time I spent in the attic had been easy. Every time I stepped foot in that room, I was at a six or seven.

I'd spent the morning doing some more driving in our yard. I was getting more confident and we'd began talking about leaving the security of our lawn and giving the road a try. While I was anxious, I was fairly certain I could do it. At least, near our house. I didn't think I was ready to tackle traffic in the city.

But I didn't need to. Not yet, anyway. All I needed to be able to do was drive from here to the school and back. We had four months before the class started. Four months to work through my issues.

Blowing out a loud breath, I pushed aside my thoughts on driving and returned my attention to the closed door in front of me. I was stalling. It happened every time. But no matter how long I stood outside the door, it didn't change what was on the other side.

I reached for the handle and turned it, pushing the door open. As always, the scent of leather hit me first as I walked into the room. It was overcast today, so there was no sunlight streaming into the room. The room felt smaller—more closed in.

The space where the cross used to be looked empty. Everything in this room had its place, so to have something so big missing, it was noticeable. I went over to where it had been and turned to look at the room from that perspective. There was a small table to my left. It was empty, but I knew from experience that's where he would lay out whatever tools . . . toys . . . he would use.

To my right was what Stephan had called a spanking bench. It was leather, too. I didn't remember Ian having anything like that, which is why it didn't scare me like the cross or a lot of the implements.

Last week I decided that I'd try to pick up at least one thing each time I came into the room. It's what I'd done with any of the toys Stephan brought down to use on me. He'd always let me touch them first and he would explain what he would do with it and how it would feel.

But there were certain things he hadn't used on me. A lot of things. My gaze fell on three crops he had hanging in a row. One was about the length of my arm and had a piece of leather about four inches long. The one beside it was a little shorter and had a wider, more triangular shaped piece of leather. The third was much shorter and the end was shaped like a heart.

I was pretty sure the middle one was what he'd used on me several years ago to prove that it was the person, not the object, that decided whether an item was used for pain or pleasure. It had been a hard lesson for me and one I still struggled with. My head understood the difference, but sometimes the fear overrode everything else.

Before I could stop myself, I picked up the medium sized crop. It was lighter than I'd thought it would be. The leather was smooth yet stiff, even though I was able to bend it back and forth.

The longer I held it, the more curious I became. Holding my breath, I hit the side of the table with the leather end.

I jumped a little at the sound it made, but I did it again. Ian hadn't been all that fond of crops. That didn't really make the prospect of being hit by one any more appealing.

The more I thought about it, however, the more I wanted to know what it felt like. I'd liked it when Stephan had spanked me. Did that mean I'd like the crop, too?

I didn't know.

As I went to return the crop to its place on the wall, I stopped. I wouldn't know if I didn't try. So, before I could talk myself out of it, I left the playroom with the crop in hand.

Stephan was still in his study and I could hear him talking to someone. He and Josh had been working on a fundraiser of some sort. They were trying to find something that would work with the theme of Helping Hands but would also reach the donors Josh was looking for.

I was happy he was able to work again. Not because I didn't like having his full attention, but because I knew he missed it. Stephan needed to use his talents to help people. More people than just me.

The crop felt heavy in my hand as I carried it down the stairs and into our bedroom. My gaze drifted to the Saint Andrew's Cross as it always did, and then landed on the bed. When Stephan and I had first explored rope, he'd told me that when I was ready for him to tie me up to leave the rope on the bed for him.

My hands shaking, I placed the crop on the mattress and raced out of the room.

As I began preparing dinner, I argued with myself as to whether to go and remove the crop. I could take it upstairs or put it in the closet or even under the bed. By leaving it on the bed, Stephan would know what it meant.

I still hadn't decided by the time Stephan came downstairs. He strolled into the kitchen and wrapped his arms around my waist. "Spaghetti?"

"And meatballs." My voice was higher pitched than normal, and he noticed.

Stephan took the spoon I was using to stir the sauce out of my hand and turned me to face him. "What's wrong? Did you have another panic attack when you were in the playroom?"

"No."

He frowned. "Then what is it?"

"I . . ."

He waited.

"I took one of the crops from your playroom and . . . I put it on the end of our bed."

His eyes searched mine. "Do you wish to remove it from the bed?"

I swallowed. Did I?

"No," I whispered.

He held my gaze for a long moment, and then nodded. "I'll set the table."

I took a deep breath, and then released it. There. I did it. Now it was in Stephan's hands. His decision.

Ten minutes later, we were sitting at the table having dinner. As I twirled spaghetti on my fork, Stephan skimmed through my latest diary entry. We were supposed to go next week to try on our dresses. Our actual dresses this time. The ones they'd ordered for us. That meant Bridget would be there along with the other bridesmaid I hadn't met yet. I was really hoping she wasn't another Bridget. I wasn't sure I could deal with two of them. I wasn't even sure I could deal with one.

"I've met Lily's other bridesmaid, Tess, once before. I think you'll like her," Stephan said after he'd closed my journal and went back to his food.

"I hope so."

After dinner, we cleaned up, and then went into the living room. We sat in his chair and watched another wedding movie. I loved romantic comedies, but some of the movies we'd been watching were over the top. Tonight, we watched a movie called Wedding Crashers. It was funny, but I wasn't sure it was all that helpful in preparing me for Lily's wedding.

"I think I watched that one in college," Stephan said as he turned the television off.

"You watched a lot of movies in college."

He grinned. "Yes, I did."

I snuggled against him. "How did your conversation with Josh go today?"

"We're making progress. I think we're going with a masquerade theme. And if it goes well, it can be an annual event."

We talked a little more about the fundraiser they were planning, and then he tapped my hip letting me know he wanted me to stand. He hadn't said anything more about the crop, so I had no idea if he'd be using it on me tonight or not. As we made our way into our bedroom, he gave me no clue as to how we'd be spending the rest of our evening. I pressed my lips together and waited to see what would happen next.

Stephan

My gaze fell on the crop lying on the end of the bed as soon as we entered the bedroom. I was glad it wasn't the smallest in my collection as that one had more of a sting than the others.

Since she'd told me what she'd done, I'd been thinking over my options for the evening. We'd been working on getting her used to the cross, and we'd made great progress, but I wasn't sure she was ready to be tied to it while I introduced something new. I always tried to make these first-time experiences positive for her.

I began removing her clothes, beginning with her shirt. It was a flimsy thing that tied in the front. I took my time making sure to brush my fingers against her breasts and sides as I parted the fabric and slid it down her arms.

She wore a red bra that matched the shirt she'd been wearing. I could already see the hard tips of her nipples pushing against the lace that confined them. Reaching behind her, I unhooked her bra and peeled it from her body, letting it fall to the floor.

Bringing my hand up, I held the weight of her breast, rubbing my thumb back and forth over her nipple. She closed her eyes and parted her lips as I continued to touch her. Seeing the tip of her tongue peek out from between her lips was something I couldn't resist. I closed the distance between us and covered her mouth with mine.

It was a kiss meant to tease. I ran my tongue over her lips before plunging it inside, only to remove it again and kiss her with only my lips. It was a dance. A dance of lips and tongues in order to have her wanting more.

She swayed toward me, seeking. "Patience, my pet."

Her eyes fluttered open, and her gaze met mine.

I grinned at the glazed look in her eyes.

Brianna's shorts were next. It was one of the great things about summer. I snapped the button on them, pulled down the zipper, and pushed them off her hips. They pooled at her ankles, stopped by the shoes she was wearing.

I knelt before her and removed her shoes and socks, then helped her step out of her shorts. The red panties she wore were the next to disappear. I hooked my fingers into the sides and shimmied them down her legs.

Brianna had been naked before me many times. She didn't get embarrassed or uncomfortable about it anymore. I took a moment to look my fill, admiring the soft curve of her hips and how her nipples were a little darker than her areolas.

Before I tossed my plans out the window and threw her on the bed, I turned and picked up the crop. When I faced her again, I saw her eyes widen a little and her breathing pick up. She remained still though, waiting.

I circled her once with the crop resting in my palm. The next time around, I extended it to trail along her skin, letting her get used to the feel of the leather. I did this several times, moving the crop lower with each pass. "What number, Brianna?"

"Three, Sir."

"You're doing very well." I ran the crop between her legs, rubbing it up and down her slit. "Are you wet?"

"Yes, Sir."

When I removed the crop from between her legs, the evidence was there in front of me. She might be nervous about the new toy, but that didn't mean she wasn't aroused. My girl was as kinky as I was.

"Spread your legs for me."

She widened her stance. I'd thought about having her kneel, but I thought this might be better for our first time.

Making my way around her again, I always kept the crop in contact with some part of her . When I reached her breast, I flicked my wrist.

She gasped.

I watched her closely, making sure she was still with me. She was. And if anything, I noticed signs of enjoyment instead of anxiety. Her lips had parted again, and her eyes were half closed.

The next time around, I flicked her other nipple and got a similar reaction. "Did you like that, pet?"

"Yes, Sir."

We continued the dance for a while and each time I went around her, I used the crop on a different area. By the time I got to the inside of her legs, they were glistening with her arousal. This time I snapped the crop against the inside of one thigh, and then the other in rapid succession.

She sucked in a breath.

If I got that kind of reaction from the inside of her thighs, I was curious as to the reaction I would get when I used it on her clit. I ran the crop along her slit once more, lingering over her clit. Then I flicked my wrist.

Her eyes popped open as did her mouth.

"Did you like that, Brianna?"

She swallowed and her chest rose and fell rapidly. I knew those signs well, but I wanted to hear her say it. "Yes, Sir."

"Would you like me to do it again?"

Brianna nodded. "Yes, Sir."

I grabbed the back of her head and crushed her mouth to mine. By the time I stepped back, she was breathing hard and her gaze was heavy again. That was good because I planned on making her come using the crop.

Not letting her rest, I repositioned the crop over her clit and began a series of strikes. With every one she made a little noise that had my cock straining against my pants, begging to get out. Eventually, I saw her legs begin to tremble and I was concerned she wouldn't be able to hold herself up since she wasn't attached to the cross or anything else.

With that in mind, I threw the crop on the bed and pulled her against me. I positioned my hand over her pussy, thrust two fingers inside her, and began a steady rhythm against her clit with the heel of my hand. "Come for me, sweetheart."

She held onto my shoulders and I captured her lips with mine. It didn't take long before I felt her begin to unravel. Her nails dug into my shoulders as her pussy pulsed against my fingers. I swallowed her cries as she came, letting her ride out her orgasm.

I extracted my fingers as the tension in her body eased. Guiding her to the bed, I picked her up and laid her down on top of it. She gazed up at me as I removed my clothing and joined her on the bed.

Hovering over her, I caressed the side of her face. "Are you all right, love?"

"Yes, Sir. I feel floaty."

I chuckled. She was so cute when she was like this, all soft and pliable.

Placing a soft kiss on her lips, I balanced myself on one elbow and positioned myself at her entrance with the other. I gave her no warning before I pushed my way inside. It didn't matter. Her pussy welcomed me, gripping me tight as if it wanted to hold me there forever.

Our joining didn't last long. I was worked up from playing. While I could have drawn it out, I didn't want to. I wanted to watch her come again first, though.

One of the advantages of being with someone for a while was that you learned how to read them. You learned to notice the signs of when they were close. And you learned what sent them over the edge.

The fastest way to get Brianna to come was to hold her down, play with her nipples, and massage her clit.

"Hands above your head," I ordered.

She released my shoulders and placed her arms above her head.

Shifting my weight, I used one hand to hold down her wrists. The other I snaked between us and positioned it over her clit. Each time I moved, her clit would bump up against my thumb. The only thing left was to play with her nipples. I was out of hands, but my mouth was still readily available. I sucked her nipple into my mouth.

The keening sound began almost immediately. I would have smiled, but I was too lost in my own arousal.

When I felt her muscles begin to contract, I gave her the permission she was waiting for. As she began to come, I tugged on her nipple with my teeth and her squeal became a scream.

I didn't let up until I felt her muscles ease their grip on me. Even then, I didn't release her nipple. I increased my pace, sucking her tit in time with my thrusts.

My orgasm came fast and hard. I held myself inside her until I was spent and collapsed on top of her in a sweaty mess.

Brianna's hands tangled in my hair as I lay with my head on her chest. We needed to clean up and get to bed, but I didn't want to move yet. I wanted to lay here and enjoy being wrapped around Brianna, my cock buried deep inside her, and her fingers in my hair.

CHAPTER 19

Brianna

I couldn't wipe the smile off my face as we drove into the city to meet Lily, Bridget, and Tess at the bridal shop. It wasn't because I was excited to see Bridget again. Or to meet Tess. It was because we'd played this morning.

Stephan had woken me up with feather light kisses that tickled. Then, after he was sure I was awake, he'd informed me he was craving an early morning snack. I was confused at first, but then he'd helped me from the bed and escorted me over to the wooden cross.

We'd played for over an hour with both my wrists and ankles bound to the wood structure. He'd used the crop on me, a dildo, and our newest experimental toy, a little flogger that wasn't much longer than my forearm. I'd come so hard I could still feel it in my muscles hours later. He'd had to carry me back to bed, and we had ended up eating breakfast propped up against the headboard.

"Thinking about this morning?" he asked as he put the car in park.

I looked around and realized we were already at our destination. "Yes."

Stephan unbuckled his seatbelt and brushed his thumb over my heated cheek. A sexy smirk pulled at the side of his lips. "Lily is going to know exactly what we've been up to as soon as she sees you."

That only deepened my blush, which increased his amusement.

He chuckled. "Come on. Let's get inside, or I'll devise more ways to make you blush."

I waited for him to come around and open the door for me. He helped me out and we walked down the sidewalk hand in hand to the bridal shop. Since it wasn't supposed to take more than an hour to try on the dresses and mark them for any alterations, Stephan was going to hang out in the seating area at the front of the store. I felt better having him close, even if he wasn't going to be right beside me the whole time.

Bridget saw us first and I didn't miss how her gaze went to our linked hands. I wasn't sure what to make of her expression, but given the way she'd been the last time we'd met, I didn't like it.

Lily was talking to a woman I didn't recognize. She glanced up and smiled when she saw us. "Tess, I'd like you to meet Brianna. Brianna, this is Tess." Tess gave a little wave to me, but before she could say anything, Lily was moving on. "Now that everyone's here. I'll let Carol know we're ready."

She returned less than a minute later with the saleswoman that had helped us pick out our dresses.

"Ladies, if you'd like to follow me back, we can get you into your dresses." The woman didn't wait for a response. She turned on her heel and expected us to follow.

Stephan leaned down to give me a kiss. "Have fun. I'll be here waiting."

Lily had hung back, waiting on me. She hooked her arm in mine as soon as I was within reach and began marching us toward the back of the store. "You look like you've been up to something naughty."

I felt the heat rise to my cheeks again. "How do you do that?"

She laughed. "What? Know you and Stephan have been fooling around?" She didn't wait for me to answer. With one hand she lifted my wrist, and with the other hand she used her index finger to trace the skin along my wrist. It was a little red from where the cuffs had been.

When I started to look away, she stopped and turned me to face her. I thought she was going to say something, but instead, she placed her wrist beside mine. Looking, I noticed a similar mark on her, as well.

I met her gaze. She just nodded and smiled back at me.

"Brianna," Carol, the saleswoman interrupted us. "I have you set up in this dressing room over here."

I came out of the dressing room five minutes later in my bridesmaid dress. Bridget and Tess were already standing in front of the mirrors. Carol was measuring Bridget and marking where the dress needed to be taken in. I stood over to the side, waiting my turn.

"Hi. You must be Brianna. I'm Tess. Lily's maid of honor." She held out her hand for me to take.

Because I knew it was expected of me, I took her offered hand. I gave her a timid smile. "Hi."

"Lily said you were shy."

I pressed my lips together and glanced over at Lily.

"No worries. Lily and I can talk enough for ten people." She laughed and I couldn't help but grin back. So far, she seemed to be more like Lily than Bridget.

"Did you go to college with Lily, too?" I was hoping she couldn't hear the shakiness in my voice.

She shook her head. "No. Lily and I grew up together. I stole her crayon."

"Are you telling lies again?" Lily asked, coming over to us, a huge smile on her face.

"Nope. Just confessing to stealing your midnight blue crayon."

Lily looked at me. "I still haven't forgiven her for that."

They both laughed and some of my nerves went away. Tess seemed nice. As long as she didn't do a one eighty when she met Stephan, then maybe being in the wedding wouldn't be so bad. All I had to do was find a way to avoid Bridget.

That became difficult to do about fifteen minutes later when Tess and Lily were occupied with measurements for Tess's dress. I was still standing off to the side, staying out of the way, when Bridget emerged from one of the dressing rooms. She had changed back into her regular clothes—a short skirt, cropped top, and what looked to be four-inch heels.

She strolled over to me, her hips swaying. I wasn't sure if that was because of the heels or not, but Lily didn't usually walk that way in heels, and she wore them all the time. "Hi, Brianna."

I didn't like the way she said my name, but I couldn't be rude. "Hi."

We stood there for a few minutes before she spoke again. "I saw Stephan came with you today."

The desire to run away was building, but I knew I couldn't do that.

"You're lucky, you know. To have a guy like that."

I wasn't sure what she meant. And even though I was curious, I wasn't going to ask. I didn't want to talk to her. All I wanted was for her to go away.

Lily glanced over at us, but then Carol asked her something, so she turned away again.

Bridget sighed and it sounded like something from those old black and white movies where the woman would pretend to faint. "If only I could find my own Stephan. How did you manage to find him?"

"He rescued me." It wasn't a secret. A quick internet search of Stephan's name, or mine, would bring up the trial. From there it was only a matter of a little digging. All the details might not be there, but it took about ten minutes to gather the basics.

"Oh, how romantic."

Her response confused me, until I realized that she thought I meant he'd saved me from drowning or something. I didn't correct her.

"Everything okay over here?" Lily asked.

"Just peachy," Bridget said. "Right, Brianna?"

Lily looked at me, but when I didn't say anything she moved on. " Carol's ready for you."

I hurried over to the mirrors where Carol was waiting and took my place on the small, raised platform. Carol knelt in front of me to measure the hem and I glanced at Bridget through the mirror. She was smiling and I didn't like it.

Once we were all back in the clothes we'd worn to the shop, we headed to the front of the building where Stephan was waiting.

"I'm craving sushi. There used to be a place not far from here. We could make an afternoon of it. Just us girls." Then Bridget's gaze fell on Stephan as he stood to greet us. "Oh, I forgot you were here too, Stephan. We don't mind if you come. Right?" She turned to ask all of us, although I wasn't sure she was really expecting us to answer.

"Actually," Stephan said. "Brianna and I need to be getting home."

He extended his arm and I crossed the room to take his hand.

"How'd everything go? Any problems?"

The question was directed to me, but Bridget answered. Sort of. "The dresses look amazing. Don't you think so, Lily?"

Lily was looking at Stephan. They seemed to be having some sort of silent communication. But after a moment, she answered Bridget. "Yes. The dresses are exactly what I wanted."

Bridget looked pleased with herself.

Stephan tugged me to his side and circled his arm around my waist. "Lily, will you let Logan know I'll give him a call later. I have something I want to discuss with him."

We said our goodbyes and made our way to our vehicle. Stephan opened the door for me and helped me inside. Once he was behind the wheel, he reached for my hand and rested it against his thigh. "Why did I get the feeling that Bridget stepped out of line again?"

"I don't know."

He raised an eyebrow. "You don't know?"

I relayed the conversation to him as best as I could remember.

Stephan groaned, and then put the car in gear. "I'm not sure if it's good or not that she doesn't know the reality of how we met. Either way, I don't trust her."

Neither did I.

Stephan

I wasn't lying. There were things I needed to discuss with Logan, and they had nothing to do with Bridget or the wedding. My aunt had called me while I'd been waiting for Brianna. Richard was trying to do some sort of project at the house but needed help. When I recommended he call a professional, she insisted it wasn't that dire. All he needed were a few extra hands and that Logan and I would do.

While I could use a screwdriver and a wrench when need be, I wasn't the handiest of people when it came to household repairs. She refused to tell me what exactly he was working on, mumbling about the backyard and how she'd been after him for years. Then, she'd gotten distracted and said she had to go. It was a strange conversation.

Logan answered on the second ring. "Your timing is impeccable."

I laughed. "Is that so?"

"It is. I was just sitting down to relax a little before heading into town. Daren invited Lily and I to a party tonight."

Daren had called me about the party as well, more as a formality than anything else. He knew Brianna and I didn't play in public.

I tried to focus on that bit of information rather than the first part of what he'd said. It was the weekend, which meant Logan and Lily were playing. I knew him well enough to know exactly what was happening when he said, 'I was just sitting down to relax'.

"I'm sure you'll have fun," I said.

"Already am." I could hear the smile in his voice. He was enjoying this.

My gaze drifted to Brianna. She was in the kitchen prepping dinner. Knowing what Logan and Lily were doing right now had me imagining Brianna in the same position. It was impossible not to, especially when I heard him suck in a breath.

I cleared my throat. "Do you think you could spare a few hours tomorrow? Diane called and Richard is doing some sort of project in the backyard and he needs help."

"Sure. What time?" His response was a little too quick and I assumed it was due to what Lily's mouth was currently doing.

"Diane suggested you and Lily join us for dinner. That way she and Brianna can hang out with her while you and I help Richard."

"Sounds good. Lily wanted to revisit that shop again in Le Sueur. Maybe we'll come down early, and then we can follow you there." He sucked in another breath and I felt my cock stir. "We can be at your house around eleven. That work for you?"

"Sure." I grinned. If I knew Lily, she was doing everything in her power to distract him. "We'll see you tomorrow, then."

The phone disconnected and I placed it back on its charger. I snatched a pillow from the back of the couch before heading into the kitchen. Brianna looked up as I approached.

She was chopping vegetables, which meant nothing was in danger of burning. I did a quick scan of the stove to confirm she didn't have any of the burners on before tossing the pillow on the floor in front of me. It had been a while since I'd done something like this, but Brianna didn't hesitate. She wiped her hands on the towel she'd been using and knelt before me.

I cupped the back of her head and rubbed my thumb over her bottom lip. She gazed up at me, and I nodded. It was hard to ignore the bulge in my pants and we'd been together long enough that she knew exactly what I wanted.

Her hands swiftly released my cock, and I shut my eyes as her mouth closed over the head of my cock. She circled her tongue around, outlining each groove and dip. It felt amazing.

Brianna took her direction from me. I wasn't in a rush. I wanted to savor this.

Looking down, I watched as my length disappeared between her lips and then reappeared again as she slowly bobbed her head. Watching her would bring an end to this quicker, but I couldn't look away. Seeing her like this, on her knees, servicing me, was something that had to be cherished.

I didn't give her any warning other than to hold her head in place, so my erection was at the back of her throat. My cum shot out of my cock, and she swallowed, taking everything I had to give her.

She gazed up at me, a happy smile on her face, as I pulled out of her. I tucked myself back inside my pants, and then placed my hands on both sides of her head. "You are so good at that."

"Thank you, Sir."

I bent to kiss her, tasting the saltiness of myself on her tongue. "Hmm. How much longer until dinner?"

"About forty-five minutes."

I helped her stand, and then picked up the cushion. "Did you need my help with anything?"

She shook her head. "I'm about ready to put everything in the oven."

"I'm going to get a quick workout in, then." I gave her another lingering kiss. "Come get me if you need me."

Brianna nodded and I went to change into my gym clothes. When I came out of the bedroom, she was putting the food in the oven. Her gaze lingered on me as I came closer.

What she was thinking was written all over her face. I loved knowing she was happy. Brianna really was the perfect woman for me. She didn't need or want big parties or expensive things. If all we did was hang out around the house, she was fine with that. And that didn't even take into consideration the sex, which seemed to get better the longer we were together.

I spent the next twenty minutes running on the treadmill. It had been a few days since I'd been in the gym, and I didn't want to slack off too much. I'd be turning thirty next week. The last thing I wanted was to end up with a beer belly or a dad bod or whatever one wanted to call it.

Brianna was setting the table when I exited our home gym. I was hot and sweaty, and I needed a shower before we sat down to eat. As I went to walk by, she turned toward me. I stopped. She looked up at me and asked, "May I kiss you, Sir?"

Smiling, I nodded.

I was expecting a quick brush of lips, but instead Brianna ran her palms up my chest, went up on her tiptoes, and covered my mouth with hers. She licked the seam of my lips and I opened for her. Before I knew it, she was plastered against me, kissing me as if she were starving.

It was obvious my girl was worked up. I wasn't sure if it was from servicing me, seeing me all hot and sweaty from the gym, or a combination of both. Either way, I wasn't complaining.

Lifting her, I carried her over to the island and sat her down. "Lay back."

She released her hold on me and laid back against the cool stone surface.

I didn't waste any time stripping her out of her shorts and panties, letting them drop to the floor and not caring where they landed. Spreading her legs, I settled them on my shoulders and went to work. She was glistening and I could see her clit peeking out from beneath its hood. My guess is it wouldn't take long for her to come.

Glancing over at the oven timer, I saw we had nine minutes before it went off. "When the timer goes off, you may come."

Then I dove in.

By the time the timer rang, Brianna was panting. Her legs gripped my head as she rode out her orgasm.

I grinned and as soon as her hold on my head loosened, I reached over to turn off the timer and grab the oven mitts.

Over dinner, I told her about my call from Diane. "I asked her what the project was, but all she said was it was something in the backyard. And that she wanted me to see if Logan could help, too."

"Maybe it's something with the pool."

"Why not call a pool company? Other than basic maintenance, I know nothing about pools."

She glanced down at her plate and shrugged. "I guess you'll find out tomorrow."

"True."

We ended the night curled up on the couch, watching another wedding movie. This one was about a woman realizing she was in love with her best friend, but he was marrying someone else.

By the end of the movie, Brianna was frowning, and I knew why. All the other wedding movies we'd watched had a happy ending. I'm not sure I would classify this one as having an unhappy ending, but it wasn't what I'd been expecting. The two best friends didn't get together. It was a little depressing.

"Tomorrow we'll have to find a movie with a better ending," I said as we were climbing into bed.

She cuddled against me and pressed a kiss to my chest. "Something with a happy ending."

I tilted her face up and lowered my mouth to hers. "Definitely a happy ending."

CHAPTER 20

Brianna

I made waffles for breakfast Sunday morning and tried to pretend it was a normal day. A month ago, Diane had pulled me to the side and said she'd like to have a surprise party for Stephan's thirtieth birthday. Since then, every week, Richard would find some reason to get Stephan out of the room for a few minutes, so Diane and I could go over the details.

Keeping the party a secret from him was the hardest thing I'd ever had to do. I didn't like keeping anything from Stephan. It was almost a relief that the day was finally here, and I didn't have to keep it to myself anymore. Or at least I wouldn't soon.

Logan and Lily were coming down and following us to Richard and Diane's house. They'd been in on the party preparation as much, or maybe even more so than I had been. The made-up story of Richard needing help with something in the backyard had been Logan's idea. He'd said it was the perfect way to get Stephan into the backyard, and hopefully before he realized what was happening.

Logan, Lily, Stephan, and I were supposed to arrive around noon. Everyone else was getting there at eleven and were parking in a neighbor's field about a half mile down the road. Richard was shuttling everyone to the house in their SUV.

Luckily, there wasn't going to be a crazy number of people. Not only did Diane know I didn't do well in crowds, but Stephan wasn't a big party person either. All in all, there would be twenty to thirty people there. It was going to be a good test for me. There would be a couple hundred at Lily and Logan's wedding and it was less than three months away.

I did my best to distract Stephan after we cleaned up breakfast. Distraction wasn't my strong suit, so I'd asked if we could watch a movie, and then a few minutes in I started playing with the hairs on his arm. It had gotten the reaction I'd wanted, and we'd ended up making out on the couch until it was time to start getting ready.

At ten fifty-five, I heard Logan and Lily pull into our driveway. Stephan went to let them in so I could finish drying my hair. I wanted to look my best today without it being obvious I was making any extra effort.

Lily strolled into the bathroom a few minutes later. "Need any help?"

I shook my head. "I'm almost done."

She looked over my outfit. "I like the dress. The shoes . . . not so much."

Glancing down at my shoes, I frowned. They were simple black flats. The dress was teal with black print along the bottom half of the dress. I didn't understand what the problem was.

"Do you have any nude heels?" she asked.

I scrunched up my nose. "I think so."

She marched into my closet and I followed her.

Lily went directly to my collection of shoes, which compared to hers, was minimal, and surveyed the options. After a moment, she picked up a pair of nude, open toed shoes, that had a one-inch heel. "Here you go. These will look much better."

Since I didn't know fashion like Lily did, I took her word for it and changed into them.

She smiled. "Perfect."

We found Logan and Stephan in the playroom of all places. They were standing over the bench with all his toys. Stephan called me over when he saw me. While the playroom still wasn't my favorite place in our house, I wasn't as scared of it as I used to be.

He tucked me against his side and checked his phone. "It's almost eleven-thirty. We should probably get going. We don't want to be late."

Logan nodded, but took his time exiting the room. Stephan had to slow down in order not to leave them behind.

As we descended the stairs, Lily spoke up. "I should probably hit the bathroom before we go."

"You remember where it is?" Stephan asked.

"Yep. I'll be back in a jiffy."

Logan, Stephan, and I waited for her in the living room. It took her ten minutes. I could tell Stephan was getting antsy, but he didn't say anything.

On the drive to Diane and Richard's, Stephan kept eyeing the speedometer and the clock. Normally, we left in plenty of time, but today we would be pushing it to make it on time. Of course, that was the intention.

Logan had pulled out of the driveway first, so he and Lily were ahead of us, setting the pace. It wasn't that he was going slow. More that he was going exactly the speed limit and not one mile per hour over. Stephan was getting frustrated.

I knew I needed to provide another distraction. "Can we try driving on the road this week?"

It worked. He glanced at me. "I think that's a great idea. You've been doing well in the yard. We can start close to home, and then if that goes well, maybe you could take us into town."

"I'm still nervous, but I don't think that's going to change."

He took my hand in his and gave it a comforting squeeze. "I'll be right there with you. If something doesn't go quite right, we'll figure out how to tackle it, and then try again."

I leaned my head back against the seat and grinned at him. "I love you."

Stephan looked over at me and smiled. "I love you, too, sweetheart."

The conversation had taken some of the tension out of his shoulders. He held my hand the rest of the way and didn't let go until he needed both hands to maneuver into Richard and Diane's driveway.

Logan stretched when he got out of the car as if he'd driven for hours rather than thirty minutes. Then he went to get Lily. He helped her out of the car, slowly, and then moved her to the side so he could shut the door. The movements were all exaggerated, meant to slow things down.

Stephan waited. His manners refused to let him tell them to hurry up, even though I knew he wanted to.

Lily winked at me as we made our way to the front door. Stephan let us in. We didn't usually knock when we came over for dinner on Sundays.

"Hello?" Stephan called out when he didn't see Richard or Diane.

No one answered.

"Maybe they're in the backyard," Logan suggested.

Stephan nodded. "It's possible."

The four of us headed through the house toward the patio. I was so anxious and not all of it was because of the people that were waiting on the other side of the glass doors.

Stephan pulled the slider open and stepped outside.

The patio looked empty until Logan closed the glass behind us. Then, as if he'd rung a bell instead of closing a door, people popped out from behind the shed and trees along the backyard and yelled surprise. Stephan blinked twice. "What's this?"

Diane crossed to us and pulled him in for a hug. "Happy Birthday."

He hugged her back but seemed a little stunned.

Logan patted him on the back. "Were you surprised?"

"Yes." Stephan narrowed his eyes. "You planned this. Lily taking forever in the bathroom before we left. You driving the speed limit when I've never seen you do less than five miles over. Taking your sweet time getting out of the car."

He laughed. "Yep. Had to keep you from speeding here trying to make up time. Would have ruined the surprise."

Then, his gaze fell on me. "Did you know about this?"

I glanced down, feeling a little guilty for keeping a secret from him. "Yes."

Tilting my chin up, he forced me to look at him. "I like my surprise."

Then, he stepped forward and kissed me. It wasn't a peck either, which is all he usually gave me in front of his aunt and uncle. I felt all the nerves and guilt I'd been wrestling with melt away.

"Okay, okay. Enough of that. You'll have time to have fun with your girl later." Daren's voice brought me back to reality.

Last year, he and his wife, Gina, had come to the condo and we'd talked. I knew he was the one who'd told Stephan about me, and that it was because of him that I'd been rescued. It had taken me a while, however, to get over the fact that he'd played with me. Granted, he'd been nicer than most of the other men Ian had shared me with, but it was still difficult to deal with when for me it had been traumatic.

With Stephan's help, I'd begun to feel more comfortable around him. It had helped when he'd explained that some of the things he'd done to me had been a test. Daren was a lot of things, but he wasn't the same as Ian's friends.

Dinner of cheeseburgers, hot dogs, and more side dishes than I could count—Diane must have been up all-night cooking—were laid out on a long table. It was a beautiful fall day and Stephan was smiling. I was happy he'd liked his surprise.

Stephan

The last thing I'd expected was a surprise birthday party. Turning thirty wasn't a big deal. At least, not to me. I had a home. The woman I loved at my side. I was happy.

I knew there were men my age who'd never been in a serious relationship, or who still went out and partied every weekend looking for someone to hook up with. That wasn't me. It never had been me, to be honest.

Brianna stood a few feet away, talking to Lily and Gina. She was doing well. Other than the brief look of guilt on her face when I'd asked if she'd known about the party, she'd seemed relaxed.

It helped that she knew everyone here. Outside of Logan, Lily, Daren, and Gina, Richard and Diane had also invited the executives from The Coleman Foundation, their spouses, and two of my cousins from my dad's side of the family that I'd been close with growing up. It was a small gathering as far as parties went, but as far as I was concerned it was perfect.

Richard came up beside me. He offered me a fresh bottle of water. It was in the seventies today . . . a heatwave for October in Minnesota. "It's hard to believe you're going to be thirty years old. I still remember the day you came to live with us."

I twisted the cap off and took a sip. "A lot has changed since then."

He nodded. "I don't have to worry about you sneaking out the upstairs window."

Richard and Diane had been thrust into parenthood overnight. And not only that, they'd gotten a broody teenager who was racked with guilt. It had been a huge undertaking. "Do you ever regret taking me in?"

"No. You're family and you needed us."

Glenn came over with his wife and we got to talking about the fall gala. I hadn't attended since I'd stepped down as president of The Coleman Foundation, but that didn't mean I wasn't involved. The board had to approve every donation for the silent auction, as well as the evening's agenda. We had a board meeting in two weeks to finalize everything.

When Glenn and his wife slipped off to get a refill on their drinks, Richard noticed that I was watching Brianna. "Speaking of family. Ever think about taking the next step. Settling down."

I shot him a confused look. "I own a house, two cars, and have been in a committed relationship for almost five years. How is that not settled?"

"You know what I mean." When I continued to stare at him, he sighed. "Do you plan on getting married? Having kids of your own? Filling up that nice big house you just bought . . ."

My gaze fell on Brianna. She was blushing at something Lily had said. "She's never given me any indication that she wants to get married." I felt as if I was having déjà vu.

"Isn't that up to you? Given the type of relationship you have?" he asked.

His question wasn't judgmental, so I didn't let it bother me. While Richard had tried to be more understanding of our unconventional relationship, that didn't mean he always understood it. "That's not quite how it works."

"What are you two chatting so intensely about?" Diane walked up and handed Richard a container full of hamburger patties. "Can you put some more meat on the grill? We're down to our last cheeseburger."

He lifted the container. "Duty calls."

Diane waited until Richard was out of earshot before raising her eyebrow.

I knew what she wanted, but I decided to play dumb. "What?"

"Are you and your uncle having another disagreement?" That's what she'd taken to calling the time after my ex, Tami, had convinced him that I'd been abusing her.

"No. Nothing like that."

"Good. I don't like to see you two at odds."

All the way home after the party, I thought about what Richard had said. Brianna and I had an open and honest relationship—keeping my surprise party a secret not withstanding—but did she think the same way Richard did? She'd given me no indication that she wanted to get married. But was that because she was waiting for me to move our relationship in that direction or because it wasn't something she wanted?

I didn't have an answer.

We lay in bed, her head on my chest as I caressed her hair. It was late, almost midnight. The last guest hadn't left until ten, and then we'd stayed to help clean up. It had been a great day hanging out with our friends.

"You and Lily had your heads together for most of the day. What were you talking about?" I asked, seeing if I could feel her out. Maybe whatever she and Lily had been discussing would give me some clues as to her mindset. Maybe that made me a coward to not come right out and ask her, but I didn't want to contemplate how it would feel to ask and have Brianna say no. Or worse, have her say yes because she thought she had to.

"They found a place to get married and she was telling me all about it." She released a dreamy sigh. "It's a renovated barn about fifteen minutes from Richard and Diane's. It sits on a hill and overlooks a lake."

"Sounds pretty."

I looked down to see her smiling. "Lily's going to be a beautiful bride."

"Logan wouldn't care if they got married in a shack. She's been it for him since he laid eyes on her."

Brianna giggled. "Probably." She traced the lines of my abs with her index finger. I'd begun working out more after I stepped down from The Coleman Foundation, so I'd gotten more of a six pack. It still wasn't anywhere near what some of those bodybuilders have, but I was quite pleased with the hours of effort I'd put in. Brianna seemed to be as well.

"I remember the first time they met. Sparks were flying before they knew each other's names. I felt as if I were intruding on an intimate moment as I stood there introducing them." It had been strange. I hadn't known Lily to be speechless before that day.

"She's told me about the night they met." Brianna hummed. "So romantic. It's like something out of a movie."

I couldn't disagree. Him seeing her across a crowded room and asking me if I knew who she was. Me introducing them only to feel as if they were so focused on each other I could have said the sky was falling and they wouldn't have noticed. Yeah, it did sound like something from a movie.

Very unlike the start of our relationship. It had taken weeks for her to stop looking at me with fear in her eyes. Not exactly the stuff romantic movies were made of.

"Well, I for one, can't wait to see you in your dress," I said, bringing the topic of conversation back to her . . . to us. Rolling us over, I positioned her under me. "And out of it."

She circled her arms around my neck, hooking her wrists at the back of my head. "I don't think the barn has a hotel or anything. Will we come back here after?"

"I don't know. Given it's so close to Richard and Diane's we might crash there for the night. I'm sure it will be late, and we'll be exhausted. Weddings tend to do that."

She averted her eyes for a moment before looking back up. "Are they really like the movies we've been watching?"

I brushed the hair away from her face. It was still hard to believe she'd never been to a wedding. "They can be. Weddings tend to bring people together who wouldn't usually interact. That can create situations that degenerate fast."

She was quiet for a few moments and I could tell she was thinking. "I liked Tess."

We'd spent a lot of time the other day talking about Bridget, but almost no time discussing Lily's maid of honor, Tess. "She came to a small fundraiser several years ago. It wasn't long after Logan and Lily began dating, so I think she'd come to check him out."

"It's the maid of honor that usually organizes the bachelorette party, right?" she asked.

"Yes." I searched her eyes for any sign of distress. "Are you concerned about what she might come up with for Lily?"

She pressed her lips together. "A little. But I'd be more worried if Bridget were doing it."

"I agree. I might even have to put my foot down and tell Lily you couldn't attend." It wasn't often I told Brianna she couldn't do something. In fact, I was usually the one encouraging her to step outside her comfort zone and try something she wasn't crazy about. This was different. I would be nervous enough for Brianna to be out for a 'girls' night', whatever Tess and Lily decided that was. If Bridget was planning it? I'm not sure I'd be able to let Brianna out of my sight.

She nodded. "Will Logan have a bachelor party? Since you're the best man, that means you'll be planning it."

"Probably." I hadn't spoken to Logan about it, but I assumed we'd have some sort of bachelor party even if it was just a group of us hanging out at a bar or something. That wouldn't be my first choice, mind you, since I didn't drink, but I knew the other guys in Logan's wedding party did.

"You won't . . ." She'd averted her eyes again, but this time when she looked at me it was to stare at my chest.

Lifting her chin, I waited for her to meet my gaze. I didn't need to say anything. She knew I was waiting for her to finish whatever it was she'd been about to say.

"Will there . . . be other girls?"

It took me a few moments to understand what she was asking, but I wanted to clarify to be sure. "Are you asking me if there'll be strippers?"

She closed her eyes and nodded.

I nudged her legs apart and settled between them, the tip of my cock at her entrance. "Look at me."

Brianna met my gaze. I could see the uncertainty in them, and I didn't like it. "There won't be any strippers. I have everything I need right here. Why would I want anything else?"

With that, I pushed my hips forward, sinking into her. She was all I would ever need, and I set out to prove it to her one thrust at a time.

CHAPTER 21

Brianna

"We're going on the road today," Stephan said as we cleaned up after breakfast.

I swallowed. He wasn't talking about going on a trip.

The panic must have been clear on my face because he cradled the side of my face in his hand and gave me a soft kiss. "You'll do fine."

"What if I hit something? Or someone?"

He smirked. "Considering only a handful of cars go down our road every day, the chances of you hitting anyone are slim." His thumb rubbed against my cheek making me want to close my eyes and lean into him. "And things can be replaced."

I knew he was right. And it did settle my nerves a little. Plus, I knew he'd be right there beside me. If anything went wrong, he'd take care of it like he always did.

A half hour later, I was seated behind the wheel of my car. Being in the driver's seat had gotten more comfortable over the last month. I couldn't say how many hours I'd spent driving around our yard, but it was a lot. If it wasn't raining and the ground was firm enough, I spent at least an hour a day weaving in and out of trees and cones, backing up, practicing turning and parallel parking. And all that practice had led up to this moment. Me driving on the road for the first time in six years.

Stephan clipped his seatbelt into place and nodded to me. I blew out a breath, started the car, and put it in gear.

Backing out of our driveway, I triple checked to make sure there were no cars coming before maneuvering onto the road. As silly as it may have sounded, the road felt different beneath me than driving in the yard. It was a lot smoother.

"We're going to go around the block. Go down to the stop sign and take a right."

I did what he said. It was about a half mile to the stop sign, so not far, and there wasn't another car in sight.

I put on my turn signal as I approached the stop sign. Stephan had been quiet beside me until I came to a complete stop. "You're doing well. Just breathe, love."

Breathe. I could do that. After a few slow and steady breaths, I double checked to make sure no cars were coming, and then turned right.

True to his word, we made a circle around our house—about three miles in total. As I pulled into our driveway once again and put the car in park, I realized my hands were shaking. It didn't matter, though. I'd done it. I'd driven on the road and it hadn't been horrible. We'd even passed another car. Sort of. It had come up to the intersection as I was turning onto our road. Still, I hadn't panicked. I'd kept driving and got us home safely.

As soon as I turned off the engine and got out of the car, I ran to Stephan and launched myself into his arms. "I did it!"

He laughed. "Yes, you did."

After lowering me down to the ground, Stephan cupped my face in his hands and gave me a lingering kiss. I closed my eyes and savored the feel of his lips, his tongue. Stephan could transport me to another world with his kisses alone and I willingly went wherever he wanted to take me.

Our lips parted and I opened my eyes. He was grinning, that pleased look on his face saying he knew exactly what he'd done to me.

"Go inside and relax for a while. I have some work to do, and then I thought we could head to the college and look around. Since it's a weekend, it shouldn't be too crowded."

I spent about an hour reading, and then warmed up some soup I'd made earlier in the week and made a salad to go with it. We sat at the kitchen island and talked about the upcoming fundraiser Stephan was helping Josh with. He was so happy to be working on something he felt was worthwhile again, and I loved that. But Josh wanted Stephan and I to attend the masquerade and I wasn't looking forward to it. I hadn't attended a big event like that in years.

"Logan and Lily will be there as well, so they can stick close to you if I get called away," Stephan said.

"Do you think there'll be a lot of people?" I knew there would be, but it didn't hurt to ask.

He shrugged. "Josh is hoping for at least a hundred. I think we can get more than that, but we'll see. It's the first year, but if we market it correctly there should be a fair amount of interest. It's a great cause."

One hundred people. Or more.

Stephan tilted my chin up and turned my face toward him. "Number?"

"Three."

He nodded and released my chin. "This will be good practice for the wedding. And you'll even get to hide behind a mask."

His smirk caused a warm feeling in my chest. It helped, but it didn't make all the uncertainty go away. With Logan and Lily's wedding, they would know everyone there. Fundraisers were different. It was pretty much a free for all for anyone who had money.

This little voice in the back of my head wouldn't be quiet. "What if I see someone I know?"

It took him a moment to realize what I was saying. When he did, he sat back on his stool and reached for my hand. "Agent Marco tracked down several individuals who'd had connections to Pierce's enterprises. As much as I wish he'd got them all, I know that's unlikely." He paused. "We'll make sure to do some extra self-defense training beforehand and we'll make sure your dress isn't too confining, just in case. But as I said, someone will be with you the entire time, so it shouldn't be an issue."

Before I could think about it anymore, he tugged on my arm, urging me to my feet. I ended up standing between his knees, my chest brushing against his. The mood quickly changed as I rested my palms against him. I could feel his heart under my fingers, its steady rhythm calming my fears. Stephan was my constant. He was my peace.

Our lips met and I melted into him as he spread his hands along my back. I have no idea how long the kiss lasted. It was unrushed and full of soft sounds and touches. I wanted it to go on forever.

When Stephan stared into my eyes and tucked my hair behind my ear, I could see the love in his eyes. It was more than I could have ever hoped for.

"If we don't get going, I'm going to forget about going to check out the school and take you into the bedroom instead," Stephan said.

My voice was quiet, barely even a whisper, but it didn't matter. We were inches away from one another. He heard every word. "I would be okay with that."

He smiled and kissed me once more. "Go get your purse and change into some comfortable shoes for walking. I'll meet you by the door."

The best part about the campus was the trees. They were huge. I couldn't even get my arms around most of them.

We strolled around the buildings, taking our time. Stephan had been right. There weren't a lot of people. At least, not where we were.

It was Saturday, and there was a football game. I would have thought that would mean the place would be swamped with people, but the main campus was almost empty. Everyone was near the stadium.

Stephan asked if I'd like to go to the game, but I shook my head. I didn't think I was ready to be around that many people screaming at the top of their lungs. While I knew they wouldn't be screaming at me, I was afraid something would happen, and my brain wouldn't know the difference.

As we were rounding the corner of one of the buildings, there was a food truck. Almost as if on cue, my stomach growled. It had been almost four hours since we'd eaten lunch.

"I'm getting hungry myself. Let's see what they have," Stephan said.

The man greeted us as we walked up. "Hiya, folks. You leave the game early?"

Stephan shook his head. "No. We're here checking out the campus."

"Well, you picked a beautiful day to do it. Probably not going to get many more like this until spring." The man looked at the trees that were losing their colorful leaves, and then back to us as he got down to business. "What can I get you?"

"What do you recommend?" Stephan asked.

The man's chest puffed out a little as he answered. "We're famous for our mac n' cheese grilled cheese. If you like cheese, then you'll love it."

Since Stephan and I both liked cheese, he ordered one, along with a grilled cheese that had pulled pork on it. Food trucks tended to have a theme and this one's was grilled cheese sandwiches. They had about any version of a grilled cheese sandwich that one could imagine. They even had one with pimento cheese, which didn't sound all that appealing to me.

Once we had our sandwiches, Stephan carried them over to a nearby bench under a tree. He set them down on the bench between us and unwrapped them both. "Which one do you want to try first?"

I had to admit, I was a bit curious about the mac n' cheese one. Picking that one up, I took a bite. I wasn't sure what I was expecting, but the mixture of cheese and carbs was almost sinful. Everything melted together perfectly. I closed my eyes to savor the taste.

"If you keep looking like that, I'm going to have to drag you into one of these buildings and find an open room."

My eyes snapped open. From the look in his eyes, there was no doubt as to his meaning. I tipped my head down and grinned. "Sorry, Sir. It's really good."

· · ·

Stephan

Normally, Brianna didn't call me Sir in public, but we were essentially alone. The nearest person was at least fifty feet away. There was no way for them to hear what we were saying. I was just hoping they couldn't see the bulge in my pants, either.

To keep myself from acting on my desire, I picked up the other half of the mac n' cheese sandwich and took a bite. She was right. It was amazing. Not what I'd expected at all.

We focused on eating for a few minutes, which was good since I needed to allow my cock to settle down. I didn't want to be walking around a college campus with an erection. I wasn't eighteen anymore.

I let her finish the mac n' cheese sandwich while I polished off the one with pulled pork. "It's a nice campus," I said, leading to what we really needed to talk about. "Bigger than what I'd imagined."

She swallowed her last bite and took a drink of water. "I'm glad I'll only have one class, otherwise I might get lost."

"I'm sure you'd be fine either way. Colleges are a lot like small towns. They can seem overwhelming at first, but it doesn't take long to get used to where things are."

More people were beginning to mill about, so I knew that meant the football game was over. To be honest, I hadn't even thought about there being a game, given this was a community college, but apparently even community colleges had sports teams. "Are you ready to continue our tour?"

Brianna nodded.

We ended up walking the entire campus, including by the stadium, which by the time we made it over that way was nearly empty. As we made our way passed all the buildings, I tried to imagine what the place would look like in the dead of winter with snow covering the bushes and trees. I wasn't fooling myself. Letting her attend classes here was going to be a challenge for me. I was so used to being there to protect her. Here, she would be on her own.

It was dark by the time we arrived back at home. I sent her to the bedroom to get ready for bed while I checked to make sure everything was secure for the night. As I came into our bedroom, the first thing I noticed was Brianna. She was naked, kneeling on the floor at the foot of the bed.

Crossing to stand in front of her, I petted the top of her head and felt her relax into my touch. We'd been playing a lot lately. Each week she brought a new toy down from the playroom and we'd been having fun as she learned the pleasure that toys she'd previously feared could bring.

This week she'd chosen nipple clamps. We'd used them once so far, and as I suspected, she'd loved them. I hadn't left them on for long, though, so tonight I was hoping to push things a little farther.

Brianna loved breast play. It didn't matter if I was sucking on them, biting them, binding them with rope, or even using a crop on them. She loved to have her breasts and nipples played with.

I brought her head to my crotch, encouraging her to nuzzle my growing erection. "Are you wanting to play, pet?"

She ran her nose up and down my length. "Yes, Sir."

"Undress me."

Her delicate hands went to work on my pants, and I breathed a sigh of relief when she pushed my jeans and underwear down my hips to let my cock spring free. Bending down, her nose almost to the floor, she removed my shoes and socks before helping me step out of them. The position gave me an excellent view of her ass.

She was finished all too soon and began to stand so she could remove my shirt. As she pushed the shirt up my torso, she placed little kisses on my abs and chest. It took a lot of willpower not to finish removing the shirt myself, but I suffered through the torture of her mouth and let her finish the job she'd started.

Once all my clothing was removed, I took hold of her upper arms and crushed her mouth to mine. Brianna sucked in a breath as our lips met, but she met my tongue stroke for stroke. Her hard nipples raked against my chest sending little electric pulses straight to my groin. I needed to slow this down or I'd end up buried inside her in a matter of seconds.

Ripping my mouth away, I set her away from me. We were both

breathing hard and I needed a moment to get my bearings. "On the bed."

Brianna crawled onto the bed; her ass again tempting me. This time, however, I went with my instincts and gave her cheek a swat with my hand.

She stopped moving, and then lowered her front half to the bed, sticking her ass up in the air. It was almost too much.

Knowing I needed to take control of this now, I took her by the ankles and pulled her down to the end of the bed. She let out a little squeak, but it died in her throat as I flipped her around to face me.

Since we'd begun doing more play in our bedroom, I'd made a few adaptations to our bed. One of those being that I'd added fasteners where I could attach ankle cuffs.

I left her on the bed while I went to retrieve the leather cuffs from the bottom dresser drawer. We'd had to move the toys to a larger space since we'd been bringing stuff down from the playroom. The problem was that even the larger drawer was beginning to fill up, as well.

Returning to the end of the bed, I took her left ankle and wrapped the leather around it, and then secured it to the bed. I did the same with the other ankle, making sure that her legs were spread wide. Her pink pussy was exposed and already glistening with moisture. Leaning down, I gave it one long lick.

Brianna reached for my head, but I pulled back before she could get her hands on me. That wasn't what I wanted.

I kept my favorite rope in my nightstand in case I got the urge to tie her up on a whim. It had come in handy quite a few times and I was glad I had easy access to it now. Securing her wrists, I lifted them above her head and tied the end of the rope to the headboard. I loved her in this position. I had access to her breasts, her pussy, her thighs.

Brushing the hair away from her face, I checked in with her. "How are you doing, sweetheart?"

Her gaze met mine and I could see the excitement in them. My heart was thrilled that we had come so far. "Good, Sir."

I smiled down at her and ran my thumb along her lower lip. She opened for me and I slipped my thumb inside, allowing her to suck on it for a few moments. The feel of her tongue and her lips wrapped around my digit had me longing to feel her mouth around my cock, but I knew if I gave in to that desire this would be over far too quickly.

Removing my thumb, I trailed the wetness down her chin and neck before flattening my palm and running my hand down the length of her body until I came to the junction between her legs. When I stopped, inches before touching her right where she wanted me to most, she lifted her hips, seeking.

Instead of giving her what she wanted, I skirted her pussy and skimmed my hands down her legs. Once I reached her ankles, I began kissing my way back up, alternating sides until I was staring at her center once again. I took another long lick but didn't linger.

When I'd retrieved the cuffs, I'd also grabbed the nipple clamps. Tonight, we were going to see if she could come with them on.

I towered over her and took one of her breasts in my hand, kneading it and tugging on the tip. Her nipple was already hard, but I wanted to increase the stimulation even more before I secured the clamp.

Leaning down, I sucked her nipple into my mouth, circling it with my tongue, and then placed the clamp. She sucked in a breath as it squeezed her nipple.

I repeated the process with the other breast, making sure not to tighten the clamps too much. That was one of the advantages to tweezer clamps and I was glad she'd picked these first, instead of the ones that couldn't be adjusted.

With the clamps in place, I gave the tip of each nipple another lick and then blew on them. One of the main advantages to nipple clamps was that they made the nipples more sensitive. Given how sensitive Brianna's nipples normally were, I was looking forward to seeing how the added sensation was going to affect her.

I checked in with her one more time before taking up a position between her legs. She was even wetter than she had been before, and I couldn't wait to get a taste. I spread her pussy lips open with my fingers, ready to feast on my girl.

Glancing up, I took in the beautiful sight before me. Her rosy pink nipples peeked up through the clamps as her chest rose and fell under her labored breathing. I knew those signs. My girl was on the edge already.

"You may come as many times as you'd like, pet. I want to hear you scream." I lowered my mouth to her and set out to see how quickly I could make her come.

Brianna

"Did you want to drive?" Stephan asked as we left the house.

It was the first Saturday of December and we were headed to the city. The fundraiser for Helping Hands was tonight, but we were dropping our things off at the condo, and then meeting Logan and Lily for lunch. "No. I don't think I'm ready for that."

He nodded and opened the car door so I could get in.

It had been over a month since I'd driven on the road for the first time. Since then, I'd been to town and back several times and had even driven to Richard and Diane's a couple of times. I was getting better, but I wouldn't be taking any long road trips anytime soon. Or maybe ever.

Driving in the yard had been fun. On the road . . . not so much. I would much rather Stephan drive when there were other cars round, but I knew I needed to be able to do it myself sometimes. Even with my continued anxiety when I was behind the wheel, I was feeling more confident that I would be able to drive myself to and from school in January.

On the way into the city, Stephan and I talked about tonight. It would be the first big event I'd been to in years. We didn't think I'd see anyone from my past, but there was always a chance. The people Ian hung around with had money and there would be a lot of people with money there. I was trying to prepare myself, and just in case, Stephan and I had brushed up on some self-defense moves over the last few weeks.

We arrived at the condo a little before eleven and brought all the things we would need for tonight and tomorrow up to the top floor. I loved the condo. I had so many good memories there. But I loved our house even more. We'd spent hours online looking at listings, trying to find the right house. Stephan had known as soon as we flipped through the pictures that it was the one. He'd called the next day to set up a time when we could see it in person.

Stephan hung up my dress and his tux, and then we were back out the door. The restaurant Logan had chosen was not far from downtown. It was a small place, no more than ten tables, but it was packed. Luckily, Logan and Lily were already seated when we arrived.

"I wasn't expecting it to be this busy. It's not even noon yet." Stephan pulled out my chair for me and I sat down.

"Once you try the food, you'll know why," Logan said.

Stephan and I looked over the menu. There were a lot of things I'd never heard of. In the end, I decided to go for something simple . . . tacos. Stephen was a little more adventurous and ordered something that looked like a cross between a salad and a burrito without the wrap. Logan swore it was good.

"You ready for tonight?" Logan asked once the server had taken our orders.

Stephan grinned. "I'm not the one that has to be worried."

Over lunch, Logan and Stephan continued to talk about the masquerade tonight and what a successful evening could do for the organization. I knew Logan had been pooling his resources as well to try and get the word out about the event. He and Stephan had spent several evenings on the phone brainstorming who to send invitations to.

When we were finished, we headed over to Logan and Lily's place.

They'd upgraded from their apartment to a condo two years ago. It was twice the size of their apartment and overlooked a courtyard. I liked it, but not as much as Stephan's condo.

We had several hours before the masquerade. I'd thought maybe Stephan and I would be spending it at the condo much like we had before our dinner with Josh and his wife, but he and Logan must still need to go over things.

Lily whisked me down the hall almost as soon as we stepped in the door. "I can't wait to show you the dress I picked out for tonight. It's going to knock Logan's socks off."

"He hasn't seen it yet?"

She unzipped a long garment bag to reveal an emerald colored dress that went to the floor. It had thin straps holding up the top and a deep V in the front that made me wonder if her breasts would be showing.

I must have stared for too long because a crease began to form across her brow. "You don't like it."

"It's really pretty. But . . . will it cover your breasts? It's really low." I touched the part of the dress I was referring to.

She chuckled. "It covers everything it needs to while teasing at what lies beneath." She beamed. "Logan will love it."

After the dress, she led me over to what she called her hair and makeup station. I'd watched her get ready a few times and it was fascinating the way she could get whatever look she was going for. My mom had died before I'd been old enough for makeup and John had forbidden me from wearing any. Other than the girls I'd gone to high school with, who'd worn way too much of it, I hadn't had much exposure to makeup before Lily.

She sat me down in the chair directly across from the mirror and picked up a bottle of what I thought might be foundation. "What are you doing?"

"Priming your face."

I was confused. "Why?"

Lily tilted her head. "To get you ready for tonight, of course."

"But that isn't until tonight."

She retrieved a sponge from a glass jar near the mirror and put some of the liquid onto it. "Perfection takes time and I plan to make sure you look perfect for tonight. Stephan's going to pick up your dress and you two are going to get ready over here. This way I can do your hair and makeup."

Stephan

"I'll be back soon. It shouldn't take me long."

Logan glanced down the hallway to where Brianna and Lily had disappeared. "I doubt Brianna will even notice you're gone. Lily's been looking forward to doing her hair and makeup for weeks, and since she knows you need Brianna distracted, she's going to take her time."

I nodded and slipped my coat on. It had started drizzling outside on our drive into the city and hadn't stopped. I was hoping it would let up before tonight, but even if it didn't, the hotel had a large awning to keep the arriving guests from getting wet. "Call me if you need anything."

"Get out of here. We'll be fine."

He nearly pushed me out the door, but I couldn't blame him. It wasn't as if Brianna hadn't been on her own with them before. Or at least been on her own with Lily. I knew she'd be fine. That wasn't really the reason for my nerves and Logan knew it.

I pulled up in front of the jewelry store twenty minutes later. It had taken me weeks of searching the internet to find the right ring for Brianna. I'd continued to ask her questions about weddings, and more specifically Lily's wedding, in the guise of trying to prepare her for what was to come. But really, I'd been watching her reactions. I hadn't missed the way she got that wistful look every time we talked about it.

As I jogged into the store, the doubt was still there in the back of my mind. I didn't think she'd say no. That wasn't it. No, what had me more nervous than I'd ever been in my life was the worry that she'd say yes because she thought it was what I wanted. It was, but I didn't want that to be her reason.

A bell dinged as I walked inside and flicked some of the rain off my coat. Two other customers were being helped by Roger, a man I'd known for close to twenty years. He glanced up upon my entrance, smiled, and told me Beth, his wife, would be out to help me in a minute or two.

Less than a minute later, Beth emerged from the backroom. "Stephan, it's so good to see you. You don't come in often enough anymore. How is your lovely girlfriend?"

I'd brought Brianna into the shop about a year ago because there'd been an issue with the clasp on her collar. "She's doing well."

Beth's smile lit up the room as she leaned closer to me as if confiding a secret. "Did I see a ring you ordered in the backroom?"

There was no way to stop my grin. "I certainly hope so."

She patted the back of my hand. "Let me grab it and we'll make sure it's perfect before you present it to your lady. We don't want to give her any reason to say no."

I chuckled as she winked and disappeared into the back once more.

As I waited for Beth to return, I scanned the cases in front of me. They had a variety of items, but most of their selection was rings. It's why I hadn't even considered going anywhere else to buy Brianna's engagement ring. That, and I knew I could trust Beth and Roger to give me the quality I wanted for the ring I hoped Brianna would wear for the rest of her life.

Beth wasn't gone long, but after a few minutes I was getting antsy. I was eager to get back to Brianna and I still had to swing by our condo to pick up our clothes for tonight. On her return, she held a black box and some papers in her hands and placed them on the counter in front of me.

I didn't hesitate to pick up the box and open it. The ring stared back at me. It was simple and elegant. I could have spent more on her ring and a part of me had wanted to—she deserved everything I could give her—but I knew a flashy ring with a huge diamond wouldn't have suited her.

"What do you think?" Beth asked.

"It looks better than the pictures." The ring was custom made.

Roger and I had gone back and forth over email to design the ring, and then he'd sent it off to a friend of his to have it made to my specifications. There was a round stone in the center with smaller stones branching out on each side. I couldn't help imagining it on Brianna's finger.

Roger joined us, finished helping the other couple. He put his arm around his wife's shoulders. "I hope we're invited to the wedding."

I closed the box and met his gaze. "She has to say yes first."

"You're worried she'll say no? This is the same young lady you brought in last year? The one that looked as if she were so in love with you, she would have followed you to the moon and back?" Beth asked.

I released a half snort, half chuckle. "Yes."

"I don't think you have anything to worry about. She'll say yes." Beth picked up the box containing the ring and placed it, along with the paperwork, into a bag. She handed it to me. "Just make sure you make the proposal special. Every woman deserves to have a perfect memory of her proposal."

With the bag in hand, I hurried out to my vehicle, and then headed to my condo. The rain was beginning to let up. I was hoping that didn't mean cooler air was moving in. It was a good thing we were staying in the city tonight in case the weather decided to take a turn for the worse.

The first thing I did when I arrived at the condo was hide the ring. I kept a small safe upstairs in my desk that was perfect. Most of its contents had been moved to the new house, so there was plenty of room for the little black box.

After securing the ring in its temporary hiding place, I retrieved my tux, Brianna's dress, her bag with all her undergarments, and both our shoes. My arms were full by the time I made my way down the elevator and back to the car. It would probably have been easier to get ready at the condo, but I'd needed the excuse. I didn't want Brianna to get suspicious and my girl was very astute. Any major deviation from my normal behavior and she'd notice.

I returned to Logan and Lily's house to find Brianna and Lily sitting on the couch eating little sandwiches, the kind usually found at events like the one we'd be at later that evening. They both looked up when I walked in the door. Brianna set her plate down on the coffee table and came to me.

The first thing I noticed was that she was wearing makeup and her hair was piled on top of her head in a loose sort of bun. As she drew closer, the robe she was wearing shifted with her movement and I realized there was nothing under it. The silky fabric teased with a hint of what lay beneath and the faint pink on her cheeks reminded me of the way she looked when she was breathless from our kisses.

Lily followed her over, but I couldn't take my eyes off Brianna. "Did you get everything you needed to?"

I knew Lily wasn't only asking about the clothes. "I did."

She reached for Brianna's dress and shoes. "I'll put these with my dress. Logan's getting ready in our room, if you want to hang your tux in there."

Once she'd left, I draped my tux over the back of a chair and laid my shoes on the seat before pulling Brianna against me. Her arms wrapped around my waist and I brushed my lips along the top of her head, taking in the scent of her shampoo. She nuzzled her nose against my collarbone.

We stood there for several minutes, neither of us saying a word. We didn't need to.

Lily reentering the room broke the spell we were lost in. "Logan made us some sandwiches. Are you hungry?"

"I'm good. Thank you." I gave Brianna a soft kiss. "I'm going to put my tux in the other room. Go finish your snack."

I waited until she was seated on the couch again before picking up my things and going to find Logan. When I entered Logan and Lily's master bedroom, I heard the shower running, and then abruptly turn off. Tossing my tux on the bed, I dropped my shoes to the floor and was about to head back to the living room when Logan, still dripping wet, strolled out of the bathroom with a towel wrapped around his hips.

"Hey," he said. "I didn't realize you were back already."

"Why didn't you dry off in the bathroom?" I couldn't help but ask. He was dripping water all over the bedroom floor.

He shrugged. "I prefer to air dry."

I rolled my eyes. It was his house. What did I care if he wanted to ruin his floors?

"Put some clothes on. I'll be out in the living room with the girls."

CHAPTER 23

Brianna

I'd forgotten how good he looked in a tux.

Stephan strolled down the hall toward me and I felt my heart skip a beat that had nothing to do with my nerves over tonight. The last time I'd seen him wearing a tux was when I'd asked Jade to help me surprise him. I'd been waiting in a hotel room during The Coleman Foundation's Fall Gala. That was four years ago.

His slow smile sent warmth through my entire body as he took in my appearance. Lily had spent what felt like hours making sure my hair and makeup were perfect, and then helping me into my dress.

Stephan ran his hand over the top of the navy-blue dress, his finger skimming along the top of my breasts. "I'm going to have fun taking you out of this tonight."

A thrill of anticipation rippled through me. Could we skip the event and get to the after?

He chuckled and my eyes snapped up to his. "I know exactly what you're thinking, love, but we do have to go to the masquerade." He trailed his hand down my side and tugged me against him. "I promise to make it up to you later."

"You're going to mess up her hair and makeup," Lily said, sweeping in from the other room.

She'd gotten herself ready in half the time she'd spent on me and she looked like something out of a fashion magazine. Her red hair was pulled back away from her face so it could flow down the center of her back. And even though my gown was strapless, hers was far more . . . daring. It dipped so low in the front that I was sure Logan wouldn't even have to unzip it to get to her nipples.

Maybe that was the point. It was the weekend after all, so Logan had most likely had a say in what she was wearing tonight.

A few moments later, Logan appeared from the same direction Stephan had come. He was also in a tux. Lily walked over to stand in front of him. He looked her up and down, then walked around her until coming to a stop at her front again, his expression softening. I knew what he'd been doing—I'd seen him do it before and had asked Stephan about it.

"Is everyone ready to go?" Logan asked.

We all did one last check to make sure we weren't forgetting anything, grabbed our coats and masks, and headed out the door.

Because we were going back to the condo after the event, Stephan had brought our stuff out to the car as well and secured it in the trunk before helping me into the vehicle. It was a little challenging with the dress. There was a lot more fabric than what I was used to, and it all had to be stuffed into the car.

Once we were on our way, he reached for my hand and squeezed. "There will be roughly two hundred people there tonight. I know a lot of them from the foundation, but there are a few I don't. You are to stay close to me, Logan, or Lily at all times."

"Yes, Sir." That wouldn't be a problem. I was trying not to be nervous about tonight. Stephan and I had talked about it in detail and I'd discussed it with Dr. Katlin. People went to events and parties all the time. It was normal. I wanted to be normal.

We pulled up in front of the hotel and a valet walked up to the car and opened my door while another went to the driver's side to meet Stephan. I stepped out, careful not to trip over my dress and waited for Stephan to finish with his valet. It had turned colder as the day had worn on and I pulled my coat tighter around me.

Stephan strode toward me and hurried us inside the hotel. We checked our coats, put on our masks, and then headed upstairs to one of the ballrooms. I noticed Josh and his wife right away, even with their masks. Josh held himself in a way that stood out in a crowd. Stephan said it was because he'd been in the military.

Josh and his wife were talking to a man and woman who looked to be in their late sixties to early seventies. Both had hair that was grayer than brown.

Much to my dismay, Stephan guided us over to them. Josh noticed us and grinned. "Stephan, I'm so glad you're here. I'd like you to meet my parents, Stan and Deloris." He turned toward his parents. "Mom. Dad. I'd like you to meet Stephan and Brianna. Tonight wouldn't have been possible without Stephan."

Stan held out his hand to Stephan. "Thank you for helping our son. He has a big heart, but things like this really aren't his forte. He'd much rather be in the thick of things getting his hands dirty than hobnob with the rich and famous."

Stephan shook the man's hand but didn't comment.

Before the conversation could go farther, Josh caught sight of Logan and Lily and waved them over. "Mom. Dad. This is a friend of mine, Logan, and his fiancée, Lily. He's the regional director of public relations at one of the largest hospitals in the area and Lily handles all the fundraising events at The Coleman Foundation."

"Impressive," Josh's mother said. "I'm surprised you both have time to plan a wedding."

Logan smiled. "Lily is an amazing event planner. I'm not sure how she does it, but she could make a hoedown fancy if she put her mind to it."

Everyone in our little group laughed.

I stood there listening while everyone chatted for a few more minutes until Josh's parents excused themselves. More people began to arrive, and Stephan suggested that Josh should mingle with his guests. I could tell by the look on his face that he wasn't looking forward to that part of the evening any more than I was.

Stephan guided us around the room, saying hi to the people he knew. Luckily, we didn't stop to talk to anyone as he led me toward a table near the front of the room and pulled out a chair for me. Logan and Lily had followed us. Stephan had said they would stay close, but I hadn't realized they'd be staying that close.

"I'm going to get us some waters," Stephan said.

Logan invited Lily to sit next to me. He placed a hand on her shoulder, and then went off in the same direction as Stephan.

"Are you doing all right?" Lily asked once we were alone.

I nodded.

She leaned in close to me. "Have you tried imagining them all in their underwear?"

Eyes wide, I looked at her. "What?"

Lily chuckled. "They say if you have stage fright, then you should imagine your audience in their underwear. I figure this is similar." She shrugged. "You're nervous in large crowds. Maybe if you imagined them all in their underwear, they wouldn't frighten you so much."

I felt a smile tug at my lips. That was such a Lily thing to say. Unfortunately, that wouldn't help me. "I don't think it would work."

She shrugged again. "Don't know if you don't try."

Stephan and Logan returned so I didn't have to come up with a reply. They sat down on either side of us . . . Stephan to my right and Logan to Lily's left. Stephan handed me a glass of water and took a sip of his own.

We sat for a few minutes, watching the crowd grow. When we'd taken our seats, there had been maybe fifty people in the room. There was more than double that now and people were still arriving.

"I'm going to find Josh. It's almost time to get started." Stephan stood. He tilted my chin up and placed a kiss on my lips before weaving his way through the crowd of people.

To my relief, he wasn't gone long. Stephan returned to the seat beside me, but soon several other people . . . people I didn't know . . . joined us at the table, as well. I'm not sure why I thought it would only be the four of us at the table. There were eight chairs and lots of people. Of course, it wouldn't be just us.

"Number?" Stephan whispered in my ear. He must have noticed me tensing up.

"Four."

He picked up my hand and placed it in his lap. My eyes closed as he began rubbing slow circles into my wrist. With every circular motion, my body relaxed more and I forgot about the other people in the room. Stephan was here. Beside me. He would keep me safe no matter what.

Stephan

I had forgotten how pretentious people at these events could be. Josh had taken the stage to welcome everyone and invite them to take their seats. The food had been good. It was the company that had me counting down the minutes before I could whisk Brianna onto the dance floor.

Two other couples had sat at the table with us. One was older, in their mid to late sixties. I recognized them from previous events. He was an investment banker if I remembered correctly. From the pause right before they sat down and the slow once over they gave Brianna, I knew they knew who I was and maybe even who Brianna was. I thought maybe that would spell trouble, but they weren't the couple that had me counting the minutes until the servers took up the plates and the band began playing.

The woman kept trying to engage Brianna in conversation for some reason; asking her about their home and how she spent her time during the day. She'd not pressed beyond whatever answer Brianna had given her.

Brianna did well. She answered the woman's questions, and then went back to her meal. I'd been watching her closely, waiting for any sign that her anxiety was rising, but other than a few glances around the room, she'd shown no signs of discomfort.

No, the reason for my desire to vacate our table as soon as it was polite had to do with the younger couple seated next to us. The man looked to be in his late forties. The woman, however, could have passed for a teenager in the right clothes and hairstyle. If I had to guess, she was around Brianna's age.

"I was expecting a bigger turnout tonight," the man said after looking around the room for what seemed like the hundredth time. "Networking is key at these types of functions."

While that was true, it wasn't something most people said out loud. "There are almost two hundred people in attendance," I said. "That's a respectable number for the organization's first major fundraiser."

"That's true," the older man said. "The first year always has the smallest attendance. But sometimes that's a good thing. With a lot of people, there's no way you get a chance to talk to everyone."

The younger man frowned. "True. But Cindy and I were hoping to meet the mayor or some senators. Having the right connections makes getting things done in this town a lot easier."

We'd learned throughout the evening that Robert was a real-estate developer. Given his comment, I could only wonder what types of projects he wanted to pursue if he was attempting to get government officials on his side. While I knew knowing the right people did help, there was something in the way Robert talked about rubbing elbows with those in power that had me thinking what he wanted may not be on the up and up.

"So, you said you're getting married later this month?" Chester, the older gentleman at our table, asked Logan and Lily, bring the focus away from Robert.

I was grateful for the distraction, but it was a short reprieve. Cindy began going on and on about her own wedding, showing off her ring and announcing to the table how much her husband had spent on it. Given the age difference, and the way Robert's chest had puffed out at the mention of the money he'd shelled out for the huge rock on Cindy's finger, she screamed trophy wife.

I had met several trophy wives over the years. Some I'd liked and some grated on my nerves like nails on a chalkboard. Cindy was one of the latter.

As soon as the band was set up and began playing their first song, I pushed my chair back and stood. "If you'll excuse us, Brianna and I are going to make use of the dance floor."

Brianna took my hand without hesitation. Not that I expected her to hesitate, but I was surprised by the speed in which she complied. She was as eager to get away from our tablemates as I was . . . maybe more.

I led Brianna onto the dance floor and pulled her into my arms. It had been a while since we'd danced together like this, but it felt as natural as it had the first time. She relaxed into me, letting me move us around the dance floor.

"Better?" I asked as the band transitioned into their second song.

She nodded. "Can we dance for the rest of the night and not go back to our table?"

I chuckled. "We'll see. I'm kind of hoping they get up to 'network' now that the food is being taken away."

Brianna grinned, but it was short lived. "Chester and Margret know who you are." She swallowed. "I think they know who I am, too."

Throughout the evening, I'd noticed some lingering glances from various people around the room. Chester and Margaret weren't the only ones to recognize me. I'd also noticed that not one of the individuals who'd seen me, many of whom I'd known for years from events such as this, had averted their gaze once I'd looked in their direction.

No, if anything, tonight had confirmed what I'd already known. I was no longer welcome in the circles I used to frequent. It wasn't that none of them had secrets or indiscretions, because they did—some of them much worse than mine. It was that mine had become public fodder.

Brianna placed her hand on the side of my cheek bringing my focus back to her. "What's wrong?"

I shook my head. "Nothing. Just wishing I hadn't promised Josh I'd stay till the end of the evening."

"At least we get to dance."

Smiling, I pulled her a little closer, not caring about propriety. "It has been a while, hasn't it, and I do love dancing with you."

We danced for another twenty minutes before Josh tapped me on the shoulder. "Sorry to interrupt, but there are some people I'd like you to meet."

Following Josh across the room, I noticed more stares and even some whispers. It wasn't surprising. I'd moved in these circles to some degree since I was a boy, and once I'd taken over The Coleman Foundation, I'd been the face of the organization.

Josh stopped in front of a group of three people, two women and a man. The man looked to be in his early thirties, while the women seemed a bit older. "Stephan. Brianna. I'd like you to meet Linda Meyers, Olivia Larson, and Lieutenant Carter Johnson." Each of the individuals nodded in turn as he introduced them. "Linda and Olivia run our outreach program and Carter is our law enforcement liaison of sorts. Nothing official, but he helps out whenever we have a matter where we need to get law enforcement involved."

I extended my hand to each of them. "I've seen your names on some of the paperwork, but it's nice to have a face to go with a name. What you're doing will help a lot of people."

"Thank you," Olivia said. "But we couldn't do it without Josh. He makes sure we have the funds we need to help the people who come to us."

As we continued talking about the center, I noticed that Carter wasn't contributing to the conversation. He was paying attention, though. Every time I touched Brianna, his eyes followed the movement.

It made me want to tuck Brianna into my side, but I resisted the urge. This man wasn't like most of the people in the room . . . the ones who would look down their nose at you if you didn't live up to their standards but wouldn't make a scene in public for fear of tarnishing their family's reputation. Carter Johnson was a cop, which meant he'd seen things most people hadn't, and he probably didn't have an issue making a scene if he felt the situation warranted it.

A man came up to the group asking if he could speak with Josh. It broke up the conversation and Linda suggested she and Olivia get a drink. That left Brianna and I alone with Carter.

"We should get back to our table. It was nice to meet you, Lieutenant Johnson," I said, already turning to leave.

"I know who you are." That stopped me in my tracks.

I turned to look at him again but didn't comment. If he had something to say, he could say it. I doubted it was anything I hadn't heard before.

When he spoke again, he didn't pull any punches. "I don't know if you're a saint or a monster."

My gaze didn't waver. "Maybe I'm neither."

He nodded, and then his gaze landed on Brianna. He reached into his jacket pocket and pulled out a card, handing it to her.

Reluctantly, she took it.

"If you ever need my help." He paused, looking over both me and Brianna before settling his gaze on her again. "You can also get in touch with Linda or Olivia at the center. They always know how to find me."

With those parting words, he stalked off.

Brianna and I stared after him. I wasn't sure what I'd expected, but it hadn't been that. Where most of those in attendance had already passed judgement on me—and Brianna for that matter—he seemed to be reserving judgement until he had more information. While I didn't like having my integrity questioned, I also couldn't fault him for his scrutiny.

He hadn't been rude, exactly, just brutally honest.

We swung by the bar to get some water before heading back to our table. The night was still young, but I was hoping all the evenings' surprises were out of the way.

Brianna

Stephan and I ended up back on the dance floor. We stayed there, swaying back and forth to the music until the band announced it would be their last song of the evening.

"I think we're gonna go," Logan said, meeting us halfway between the dance floor and our table. "I doubt people will linger much longer."

Most of the attendees had left during the last hour, but there were still about fifty people engaged in various conversations. Josh, Olivia, and Linda were talking with four men, their wives or girlfriends huddled together at a nearby table. They all looked as if they belonged, whereas I felt completely out of place.

The mask helped. Even though I knew most people were aware of who Stephan was and could figure out who I was as well, the mask gave me something to hide behind. Sort of.

"You did well tonight," Lily said as she gave me a hug goodbye. "And you look amazing. Stephan hasn't been able to keep his eyes off you all night."

I grinned. "It's a beautiful dress."

"The woman in it is beautiful, as well. Remember that." She gave me a little wave as Logan escorted her from the ballroom.

"Do I want to know what she whispered in your ear?" Stephan asked once they were out of earshot.

"Nothing bad. She just told me I was beautiful."

Stephan reached for me, bringing my chest flush against his. He leaned down to brush his lips against mine—our first kiss since we left Logan and Lily's. "Beautiful," he whispered against my mouth before kissing me again.

It was a chaste kiss, but it still left me with butterflies in my stomach. I wanted all these people to disappear so we could be alone.

What I was thinking must have been clear on my face because a slow grin pulled at Stephan's lips. "Let's see if Josh still needs me here, or if we can head home."

I held tight to Stephan's hand as he weaved through the tables. Most of the people Josh had been talking to had left, but he was still talking to one of the men. He perked up when he saw us. "Stephan, do you know Bradley Porter? He's been influential in getting many of the programs at the center off the ground."

"I don't believe we've met," Bradley said. He extended his hand to Stephan. "Josh has told me how you helped put the event together and have been assisting him on other ways to generate funding."

Stephan relaxed at my side and they fell into an easy conversation about the center. It sounded like a nice place with a food pantry for those who needed it, a recreation room for teens, and even beds, showers, and lockers.

From listening to them talk, they were hoping to add counseling services soon. I wondered how Stephan felt about that. He'd never been a big fan of therapy—still wasn't.

It was after eleven by the time we said goodbye to Josh and made our way to the elevator. I breathed a sigh of relief that it was over. While the night hadn't been as bad as I'd feared, I would still have preferred to spend the evening at home cuddled on the couch with Stephan watching a movie or reading.

"We made it," Stephan said as the elevator doors closed behind us.

He circled his arm around me and tucked me into his side as we watched the numbers descend.

I leaned into him, absorbing his strength and letting his scent fill my lungs.

Stephan rested his cheek on top of my head for a moment before the elevator dinged letting us know we'd reached our floor. He dropped his arm from my shoulders and reached for my hand again as the doors opened. We walked out, sidestepping another couple who were on their way into the elevator.

As the other couple passed, I caught a whiff of the man's cologne. My head whipped around, and he looked up right as the doors began closing again. My gaze met his for that moment, but it was enough.

My breath caught in my throat and I froze. I knew that face, those eyes. The smell of his cologne.

Stephan was in front of me in a heartbeat, his hands on my cheeks. I heard him talking to me, telling me to breathe, and I was trying. I was trying to breathe and think past the memories that were clouding my vision. The man. The knife. The pain.

"He likes to cut." The words squeaked from my throat.

I wrapped my hands around Stephan's wrists, digging my fingers into his skin, feeling the texture of it, the hairs on his forearms . . . trying to follow his instructions to focus on him and remember everything I'd learned in therapy. He was my anchor. The one who could pull me back from my fears . . . my memories.

As my vision began to clear and I became aware of my surroundings once more, I collapsed into Stephan's arms. He rubbed my back, holding me to him.

My breathing returned to normal, but I couldn't shake the fear that surged through me. It wasn't fear for me, though. I knew Stephan would protect me. No, my fear was for the woman who'd been with the man.

I pulled back, unsure what to do but feeling the need to do something. While I hadn't gotten a good look at the woman he was with, she'd looked young. Maybe as young as I'd been the first time I'd met him . . . seventeen.

The thought tightened the muscles in my throat. "We have to help her."

It only took a moment for understanding to light Stephan's eyes. He glanced in the direction of the elevator and pulled out his phone. "I need your help."

I had no idea who he was talking to, but he swiftly gave the person a quick rundown of the information. Whoever it was must have asked him if he was sure because he looked down at me, a frown marring his features. "Yes, Brianna's sure. And he has a young woman with him." There was a pause. "I don't know. Young. She had on a lot of make-up, so I'm guessing prostitute or runaway."

Stephan nodded several times. "I understand. I'll do what I can here but see what you can do on your end. Quickly."

He disconnected the call, and then punched in more numbers. "Where are you?" There was a pause and Stephan nodded. "I need you to come back and get Brianna." Another pause. "She recognized someone. Yes. No. He was with a woman. Thanks."

Before I knew it, he'd disconnected the second call and we were on the move. Stephan marched us over to the front desk. As we approached the woman, Stephan positioned me behind him as if to protect me from any fall out.

"Is there a manager on duty? Security?"

The woman took in the two of us—Stephan dressed in a tux and me in my ball gown. We still had our masks on. "Is there a problem, sir?"

"Yes. The man who just got in the elevator with the young woman. I have reason to believe he's going to hurt her."

"Sir, I don't—"

"I've already contacted law enforcement. He's on his way, but I don't want this woman to suffer before he gets here. So, I ask again, is there a manager or security on duty?"

All the color drained from the woman's face when she realized Stephan was serious. She picked up the phone. "There's a man out here that needs to talk to you. He believes one of our guests may be in danger. Yes. Okay. Thanks." She hung up the phone. "He'll be right up."

It felt like forever before a man dressed in a security uniform walked into the lobby from an adjoining hallway. He took in our clothes the same way the woman at the front desk had. "What seems to be the problem, folks?"

Stephan held tight to my hand as he told the security guard the situation. I could tell from the look on the man's face that he didn't believe us. Apparently, Stephan could see the skepticism, too. He reached behind his head and removed his mask. "Do you know who I am?" he asked the security guard.

The man visibly suppressed a sigh. He'd obviously thought Stephan was going to try and push his weight around, but I knew what was coming. This wasn't about using his wealth to get his way. This was about getting the man to understand that this wasn't random and to take our claims seriously. "No, sir. I'm sorry. I do not."

"I'm Stephan Coleman and this is Brianna Reeves. We were in the news a lot a few years ago. You might remember the trial where a young woman had been held against her will for ten months."

The man's brow furrowed, and then he narrowed his eyes. "Are you saying—"

"That Brianna was the young woman? Yes." He gave the man all of two seconds to process that. "And one of the men who tortured her is upstairs in one of your rooms with another young woman."

He only hesitated for a moment before he asked, "Are you sure?"

Stephan didn't hesitate. "Brianna recognized him when we were getting off the elevator. I've already called Agent Marco, the lead investigator on the case. He's on his way, but I don't want something to happen to the woman the man was with while we wait."

A flash of realization crossed the security guard's face as he took in the way I was clinging to Stephan. "You're positive it was him, ma'am? The man who hurt you?"

I didn't bother to correct him that the man had only been one of many. It wasn't important right now. "Yes. I'm sure."

After another moment's contemplation, the man marched over to the front desk. The woman behind it had lost even more of her color having listened to our conversation. She brought up the information in her computer, printed off a sheet, and handed it to the security guard. "Do you want me to call the police?" she asked.

The security guard glanced back at us for a moment before returning his attention to the woman at the desk. "Not yet but keep your radio close."

Stephan

We followed the security guard over to the bank of elevators. Brianna still clung to my hand and I was debating whether to leave her in the lobby when she squeezed my hand, drawing my attention.

I looked down, meeting her gaze. "I need to make sure she's safe."

My gut tightened and churned with the thought of her coming face to face with one of the men who'd tortured her.

"Please." Her voice was barely louder than a whisper, but I didn't need to hear the words. I could see it in her eyes. She needed to make sure this woman was okay.

Sighing, I brought her hand up to my mouth and brushed my lips against the back of it. "You stay close and do not take your mask off."

She nodded.

The elevator doors opened, and we followed the security guard inside. For a moment, he acted as if he were going to ask us to wait in the lobby, but the look I sent him conveyed that we weren't going anywhere.

He squared his shoulders and punched the top floor. A suite. Of course.

The ride up felt like it took forever. Not many things in my life made me anxious, but knowing I'd see one of the men who'd hurt Brianna in a matter of minutes had me wrestling with a mixture of rage and nervous energy.

Finally, the elevator dinged, and the doors opened. We stepped out into a long hallway and the security guard made a right. "There are only two suites on this floor," he said. Once we reached the door, he turned to look at us. "No heroics, okay? Stay here while I make sure the lady is all right."

The muscles in my jaw ached from clenching my teeth as the security guard knocked on the door, announced himself, and waited. It took several minutes for the door to open . . . too long.

Brianna's nails dug into my hand as the man's face came into view. He'd removed his shirt and was currently scowling at the security guard in front of him. "Sorry to bother you, sir, but I was needing to speak with the lady who accompanied you to your room."

The man's gaze fell on Brianna and me. I did my best to keep my face neutral, although given the deep V in the man's brow, I'm not sure I accomplished it. "Is there a problem?" he asked.

To the security guard's credit, he didn't give anything away. "May I speak with the lady? It should only take a few minutes."

"She's not . . . presentable at the moment." His eyes went to Brianna and I knew in that moment that he knew who she was. Or at least he suspected. Every instinct in my body wanted to throw her over my shoulder and get her as far away from him as possible, but I resisted. Brianna wanted . . . needed . . . to make sure the young woman was okay, to save her from the same fate she had endured.

"I can wait for a minute while the lady gets herself presentable. It's no trouble." The security guard smiled. It was friendly enough, but I could tell alarm bells were going off in his head. Good.

"Unless you can tell me what this is about, you're not talking to anyone but me," the man stated, crossing his arms.

The security guard stood his ground. "I'm sorry, sir. I'm not able to disclose that information. If you can get the lady for me, I can conduct my business and you can get on with your evening."

Without warning, the man uncrossed his arms and reached for the door. A loud thump sounded as the security guard's hand connected with the door, but it wasn't enough to stop the door from closing.

The security guard reached for his radio. "Marcy?"

A crackle came through the handheld radio. "Everything okay up there, Jessie?"

"No. Call Trever. I'm going to need back up." Then he pulled a keycard from his pocket and looked at us. "I don't want to wait for Trever. If the woman really is in danger . . ."

He didn't have to complete the sentence. I turned to Brianna. "You wait here."

Brianna nodded and I stepped forward, releasing her hand, ready to back him up.

Jessie shoved the keycard into the slot and waited for the green light. He didn't waste any time opening the door and charging inside.

No matter how much I prepared myself for what I might see, what we found had me leaping into action before I knew what I was doing. The woman was tied to a wooden chair. Half her clothes had been cut and blood was already dripping onto a piece of plastic that was lying on the floor beneath her. She was crying, her makeup streaking down her face.

The man who'd done this to her lunged at Jessie, a knife in his hand. Luckily, Jessie saw it and got out of the way. I moved in to try and grab the knife, but he shifted his weight at the last second and twisted out of my grasp. By the time I got my footing again, he was darting out the door.

Brianna.

I raced out of the room, my heart pumping with pure fear.

Rage surged through me when I reached the hall and saw the man with his hand around Brianna's throat. Her eyes were wide, looking more terrified than I'd seen her in years.

He saw me coming. "Stop, or I'll gut her like a fish."

It was then I saw the knife pressing against her abdomen. I forced myself to remain where I was even though every fiber of my being wanted to kill him.

His lips curled up into a smile. "That's right. You care about this little whore, don't you?"

Brianna sucked in a loud breath when he pressed the knife against her stomach.

He turned his focus to her. "I thought it was you when I saw you downstairs. I remembered your eyes . . . how they used to shimmer with tears when I ran my knife down your throat. Ah, I did love seeing your fear. It was so potent I could almost smell it." He leaned in, his face almost touching hers. "I can smell it now."

I was contemplating my options when Jessie joined us in the hallway. He took in the scene, skidding to a stop inches from the door. "Let her go. The police are on their way."

"Ah, now. That's where I think you have this backward. I'm the one in control here." He tightened his hold on Brianna's neck, pressing her collar into her neck so hard I was sure it would leave an imprint. "We're going to take a little trip," he said to Brianna. Then to Jessie and me he said, "And the two of you are going to stay where you are . . . or she dies. Do you understand?"

"We understand," Jessie said.

I remained silent. There was no way I was letting him walk out of here with Brianna.

She closed her eyes, and I began to worry that she was slipping back into the state I found her in almost five years ago. The one that allowed her to disconnect herself from the pain and survive.

Then he changed his grip on her neck to drag her toward the elevator and her entire body went limp.

Panic took over and I no longer cared about anything else besides making sure Brianna was safe from him. The weight of her body caused the man to stumble and I pounced. In the back of my mind, I registered the sound of fabric ripping, but that was all secondary once I got my hands on him. He was struggling to hold onto the knife, but then Jessie was there, and between the two of us, we managed to get it away from him.

I landed several punches to his face once he was on the ground. The bastard wasn't going anywhere. Not after what he'd done to Brianna and surely would have done to her again had he been able to leave with her.

The man eventually stopped struggling, and as much as I would have liked to continue beating him, Brianna was my priority. I looked at Jessie. "You got him?"

He nodded. "I've got him." And to my surprise, he rolled the man over and secured his hands with zip ties. "He'll keep until the police get here."

With the man secured and Jessie watching over him, I turned to Brianna.

Except she wasn't there.

"Brianna?"

"In here." Her voice, soft and scratchy, came from inside the hotel room.

I ran into the room as fast as my feet could take me and found Brianna on her knees in front of the young woman. Comforting her, even though her own hands were shaking.

"She's hurt," Brianna choked out.

"An ambulance is on its way." I didn't know that for certain, but since Jessie had called for the police, I assumed he'd asked for EMS as well, given he'd seen the cuts to the woman's clothes and body.

I knelt in front of Brianna and placed a finger under her chin, making her look at me. "Are you hurt?"

"My throat hurts. And my side."

Glancing down, I saw the side of her dress had been slashed and blood was soaking the fabric. I released her chin and inspected the cut. There were three horizontal cuts, not deep, and one longer vertical one that was about six inches in length. That was deeper, but still nothing a few stitches wouldn't fix. She'd been lucky.

CHAPTER 25

Brianna

I was still shaking. It had been hours since the police had come and taken the man away. Reginald Wilks. I'd never known his name before today.

Stephan came up behind me as I stared out the window of the condo. It had started snowing, a white blanket covering the streets below. I shivered, and it had nothing to do with the cold.

Wrapping his arms around me, Stephan pulled my back against his chest, resting his chin on the top of my head. He was careful not to put pressure on my side. After the paramedics checked me over to make sure my cut wasn't life threatening, he'd taken me to the hospital to get stitches.

I hadn't wanted to go. I'd wanted to stay with Mel. She couldn't stop crying, even after the police had left and the paramedics had patched her up. Although she'd had cuts all over her chest, none of them were deep. She'd heal. At least, physically. I knew better than most about the emotional fallout from something like that.

"Do you think she'll be okay?"

"Agent Marco said he was going to get her someplace safe for the night. That's what she needs right now. Tomorrow, we'll check on her."

I met his gaze in the glass. "I want to help her. I know . . ." The words got stuck in my throat.

His lips brushed against the top of my head. "How are you doing?"

"My throat still hurts. It feels like I swallowed sandpaper." I'd been choked before and the lasting sensation of your throat being raw didn't go away for days.

"What about your side?" he asked.

"It hurts, but not as much as my throat." That was most likely due to the shot they'd given to numb the area before stitching me up.

Then he turned me in his arms and ran his finger under my collar. I knew what he was doing. He was tracing the red line my collar had made on my skin, imprinting its details into my flesh. "I wanted to kill him," he whispered.

I met his gaze and could see the pain in his eyes. Stephan had seen the aftermath of what had happened to me. This was the first time he'd witnessed it firsthand in real time and what he'd seen was only a small taste of what I'd gone through in the past.

Resting my head on his chest, I circled my arms around his waist and did my best to comfort him.

We stood there for several minutes, holding each other, and I let his warmth seep into my body. When Reginald Wilks stormed out of the hotel room and noticed me, I knew what was coming. A flashback of the last time I'd seen him had paralyzed me as he took hold of my throat and dug the cool metal of my collar into my neck.

But it was the feel of my collar that had kept me from completely falling into the dark abyss of my mind. I clung to the pain, the sights and sounds around me, grabbing onto anything that would keep me in the here and now.

I'm not sure I would have won the battle if not for Stephan. When he appeared, I knew he wouldn't let me be taken again. When Wilks had pressed his knife against me, I'd felt the tip knick my skin. The urge to cry out was almost overwhelming, but I forced myself to stay quiet. I could do it. I had done it in the past.

When he said he was going to take me with him, I knew I had to do something. I had to help Stephan.

Closing my eyes, I tried to push down the fear enough to do something. Anything.

We'd spent hours going over self-defense moves, but none of them had involved what I should do if someone had a knife. They'd always been more of what to do if someone tried to grab me off the street.

Then, as clear as day, I heard Stephan's voice in my head tell me that when all else failed, make yourself as heavy as possible. Become a dead weight. Make them work for it.

So that's what I did. The moment he changed his hold on me, I let my body go.

The knife sliced through my dress and down my side. Tears pricked my eyes as I fell to the floor.

Once I was free of Wilks, I knew I had to get away. Put distance between you and your attacker. That's what Stephan had said.

But I couldn't leave the young woman. She was hurt and I knew she had to be terrified.

I crawled on my hands and knees, not caring about my dress, into the hotel room. It was big, almost as big as the first floor of Stephan's condo. Once inside, I found my way over to the woman. She was sobbing uncontrollably. "Help me. Please."

My hands shook as I untied her. I expected her to try and leave the moment she was free, but it was almost as if she didn't realize the ropes weren't holding her to the chair anymore. She just sat there. Crying.

Stephan tilted my chin up, bringing me back to the present . . . to us standing alone in his condo, shrouded in darkness except for a single light in the kitchen. "Are you ready for bed?"

I nodded.

He laced his fingers with mine, made sure the door was locked, and turned out the light in the kitchen. Stephan didn't leave my side as we got ready for bed. The only time he let me out of his sight was for each of us to use the toilet, and even then, he waited right outside the door and made me do the same while he took care of business.

I couldn't blame him. I didn't. I wanted to be near him as much as he needed to know I was close . . . safe. Tonight had brought home the reality that some of the men who'd hurt me were still out there. Still hurting others.

Stephan removed my clothes and pulled back the covers so I could climb into the bed. Less than a minute later, he joined me.

As soon as his head hit the pillow, he reached for me. He tucked me into his side, caressing my hair and pressing his lips to my forehead. "You're still shaking."

"I can't seem to stop." I held on tighter to him, hoping, somehow, that would help.

It didn't.

"Would you rather talk about it now or in the morning?" he asked.

It was after three in the morning and I should be exhausted after the long day we'd had. And my body was. My body was ready to fall into a deep sleep, nestled safely in Stephan's arms.

My mind was altogether a different story. It wouldn't stop replaying what had happened tonight. And not only to me, but also to Mel. I kept wondering what would have happened if I wouldn't have recognized Wilks. Or if I would have ignored what I knew and stayed safe in my world with Stephan.

Another shiver rocked my body.

"Shh," Stephan whispered. "I've got you. You're safe."

Time ticked by with no sound except for our breathing. I was awake and I knew he was, too. Eventually, my eyes drifted close, exhaustion pulling me under.

Flashes of Wilks's face. His hand around my throat. The knife pressing against me. The sound of my dress ripping. I heard them all as if I were in a theater with surround sound, every sound amplified. Every smell so strong I could taste it in the back of my throat.

Then, I wasn't in the hotel anymore. I was in Ian's playroom. The lights were all on and I was tied to a chair, the straps holding me in place, so I was unable to move even an inch. Wilks was standing over me, knife in hand, and it was already dripping with my blood."

I screamed as he lowered the knife to my stomach.

Hands grabbed hold of my face and I tried to twist away. "No. No. Please. Please, stop."

"Brianna, open your eyes. It's Stephan."

It took me a while to register the voice and what it was saying. Stephan.

I opened my eyes, and he was hovering above me. His hands were cupping my face and he was rubbing his thumbs along my cheeks. "That's it, love. You're here with me. I've got you."

A sob escaped my throat sending a shot of pain through me. I grabbed hold of him and buried my face in his shoulder. He held me as I cried.

By the time I'd calmed down enough to release him, the first signs of the sun were coming over the horizon. We made no move to get out of bed, though. Not for another two hours. Not until Stephan's phone rang, wrenching us from the bubble we'd cocooned ourselves in.

Stephan

Last night did not go as planned. Not by a long shot.

I sat at the kitchen island, watching Brianna make breakfast for the two of us as I contemplated all the ways last night had gone horribly wrong. Leaving the young woman to fend for herself when we'd known what kind of man she was with, wasn't an option. It wasn't in my DNA and it wasn't in Brianna's, either. We could have reported it and left it to security or the police to handle, but even that wouldn't have sat right with me. No one knew better than Brianna and me the damage the man could do, both physically and mentally.

As many times as I'd ran over different scenarios in my mind, I couldn't find a better option. Brianna had wanted to help, even knowing the risks . . . knowing the position she could, and did, put herself in.

Brianna moved about the kitchen with practiced ease. She was at home cooking and I'd allowed her to fall back into what was normal for her, knowing she needed that more than anything.

Even though last night was terrifying, seeing her manhandled by a man who didn't understand how precious she was, I was extremely proud of her. Despite everything, she'd been able to fight through the fear, the panic, and remember her self-defense training. It had provided an opportunity for me and Jessie to act.

No, last night had not gone to plan at all. Instead of standing in front of the floor to ceiling windows of my condo, proposing to the woman I love more than life itself, I'd held her quivering body as she dealt with the trauma of a sadistic bastard hurting her again.

She placed a stack of waffles on the counter and came to sit on the stool beside me. I turned her face to mine and pressed a soft kiss to her lips. "Once we're done eating, I'll call Agent Marco and see how Mel's doing this morning."

Brianna nodded. "Thank you."

I placed another kiss to her lips before picking up my fork and beginning to eat. Brianna followed. We needed to talk about her nightmare, but I wanted to be holding her when we had that conversation. To be honest, I think I needed the connection as much as she did.

We finished our breakfast and while she cleaned up, I made the call to Agent Marco.

"Marco." His voice was clipped and clear even though it was barely eight o'clock on a Sunday morning.

"It's Stephan Coleman. I was calling to see how Mel was doing this morning."

There was movement in the background, and then the sound of a door closing. "Physically, she's going to be fine. She's scared and she's not talking. I even sent a female agent in to see if she'd be able to get through to her, but other than a few sounds she didn't get anywhere."

I glanced at Brianna as she loaded the dishwasher. "Brianna's worried about her."

He was quiet for too long. "Do you think Miss Reeves would be willing to talk to her? I need to get her statement about what happened last night. Yours and Miss Reeves's, too. I should have gotten it last night but . . ."

There was no need to finish that sentence. And I appreciated the fact that he'd let us go home instead of dragging us into the office to make an official statement. "When did you want us to come in to give our statements?"

"Ten o'clock? You know how to get here."

Yes, I did.

"We'll be there. And I'll talk to Brianna about Mel. It will be up to her if she wants to help." I wouldn't push her but given the way Brianna had reacted last night toward Mel, I was certain she'd want to talk to her even if it wasn't to get the statement for Agent Marco.

I disconnected the call, and almost immediately my phone dinged notifying me I had a message. It was from Logan. He and Lily had showed up at the same time as Agent Marco. They'd stayed with Brianna while the paramedics were checking her over so I could deal with the other craziness.

How's Brianna this morning? - Logan

Rough night. Going to see Agent Marco in a couple of hours. I'll call you later. - Stephan

I tucked my phone in my pocket, sat down in my chair, and waited.

Another five minutes passed. I looked over to find Brianna hunched over the kitchen counter.

Standing, I crossed the room in a matter of seconds. I heard her quiet sobs as I drew close and folded her into my arms. She buried her face in my chest, letting the tears flow. I held her until the crying began to ebb, and then I picked her up and carried her over to my chair in the living room.

She adjusted her body to the new position, resting her head on my shoulder and reaching for the buttons on my shirt. I brushed the hair away from her face, some of the strands damp from her tears. We needed to talk. *She* needed to talk.

I didn't bother to ask why she was crying. "I spoke to Agent Marco."

"How is she?" Brianna asked.

"He said she's quiet. She wouldn't even talk to one of the female agents. He wanted to know if you were up to talking to her. They need to get her statement." I pressed a kiss to the top of her head. "Do you feel up to it?"

"Yes, Sir. I can do it." She swallowed. "I want to."

"I'm proud of you, you know. You did so well last night. So brave."

She took a deep breath and released it. "I couldn't go with him."

"I know."

"I would have rather he killed me."

The thought of Brianna no longer being alive wasn't something I wanted to contemplate. A sick feeling filled the pit of my stomach and a pain lodged deep in my chest. I couldn't lose her. "You're here. And he's in custody."

I felt her nod as she gathered the front of my shirt in her hand.

For the next few minutes, I let the feel of her in my arms comfort me. I needed it after her assertion. While I understood it, I didn't want to think about her dead, lifeless. I didn't want her to think about it either.

Once I had my emotions in check, I broached another subject we needed to discuss. "Tell me about your nightmare."

She tensed and I ran my hand up and down her back to sooth her. "I was in Ian's playroom. Wilks was there. I was tied down. I couldn't move."

"How many times did he hurt you?" She knew I wasn't talking about last night.

"Twice."

I breathed through my anger. Hearing what had been done to her was always difficult, but it was nothing compared to her going through it. "Was the nightmare a memory, or something new?"

It took her a moment to answer. "It was Ian's playroom, and I was tied to a chair. But Wilks liked to use the St. Andrew's Cross. He said . . . he said . . . he liked to watch the blood drip." She shivered.

"He's on Agent Marco's radar now. He'll do everything in his power to make sure Wilks spends the rest of his life behind bars." Most of Ian Pierce's illegal business dealings had been off the books, so trying to track down his associates was difficult at best.

"I just don't want him to hurt anyone else."

"I know, sweetheart. I don't want that either. We've got him, though. We know who he is. We have a name, a face. Not to mention the fact that he attacked you in full view of me and hotel security. He'll get what's coming to him." It wouldn't be nearly enough, but it was something.

We sat for a while in the quiet of the condo, in no hurry to get on with our day. But alas, eventually the outside world invaded. "Are you ready to give your statement about last night and try to talk to Mel?"

Brianna tilted her head back to gaze up at me. "Yes." She pressed her lips together as if she wanted to say more. I was about to ask her when she added, "I love you, Sir. I couldn't do this without you."

Cupping the side of her face, I rubbed my thumb along her cheek. "Yes, you could, love. But you don't have to. I'm right here, and I'm not going anywhere."

CHAPTER 26

Brianna

It had been a while since I'd been to the federal building where Agent Marco's office was located. Stephan held my hand as we made our way to the third floor. "Number?" he asked before we exited the elevator.

"Four."

He nodded and gave my hand a squeeze. I knew he was there for me, but I also knew that in a few minutes I'd have to give my statement and Agent Marco would make Stephan wait outside. I knew him well enough to know that.

When we arrived at Agent Marco's office, he wasn't alone. A woman was standing next to his desk, a folder in her hand.

Stephan cleared his throat and they both looked toward the door. Agent Marco stood. "Thank you for coming. Have a seat."

Agent Marco had gotten less hostile toward Stephan after the trial was over. I still don't think he was crazy about the fact that Stephan bought me, but he wasn't on a mission to charge him with anything, either. That could be because of the deal I'd struck to testify against Ian Pierce, but I didn't think so.

"I'd like you to meet Agent Gibbson. She's assisting me with the

Wilks investigation," Agent Marco said pointing to the woman.

Agent Gibbson extended her hand to first Stephan and then me. "Thank you both for coming in. It's always a good day when we can get one of these sickos off the streets."

"Yes. It is," Stephan said, shooting a look toward Agent Marco. Agent Gibbson looked to be in her late twenties, much younger than Agent Marco, and she seemed to have a lot of enthusiasm for her job.

Agent Marco coughed. "Now that the introductions are out of the way, I'd like to get your official statements regarding what happened last night, and then, if you're willing, Miss Reeves, I'd like for you to talk to Mel. Agent Gibbson attempted to speak with her early this morning, but she's not saying anything. We don't even have her last name and every time we try to get near her to take her fingerprints, she huddles herself into a ball in the corner."

"She's scared you're going to hurt her," I said.

"Yes." Agent Marco rested his elbows on the desk and pressed the tips of his fingers together in front of his mouth. "Understandable, given what she went through last night and she doesn't know us." He brought his hands down to lay flat on the wooden surface. "Will you see if you can get through to her? Let her know we're trying to help. I can bring in a psychiatrist—"

"I'll talk to her."

"Excellent." He stood. "Well, then, let's get your statements, and I'll take you to see Mel."

It took about a half hour for them to take our statements, and then they were leading us down a long hallway and into another building. We took a set of stairs to the second floor and down another long hall until we reached the end. There was a single door with a man standing outside.

The man, another agent given his appearance, nodded to Agent Marco as we approached. "How's she doing?" he asked.

"About the same. I checked on her ten minutes ago and she was sitting on the bed staring at the wall."

Agent Marco nodded and reached for the door.

"Can I . . ."

He stopped and turned to look at me.

Everyone was staring at me. I swallowed, still feeling the residual effects of being strangled the night before. "Can I talk to her alone?"

"I don't know—"

Agent Marco cut Agent Gibbson short. "Sure. There's a viewing area in the next room. We can watch from there." He stepped back, clearing the way for me.

I took a step forward, but Stephan held tight to my hand. When I met his gaze, he lifted his hand to my face and rested his forehead against mine. "You know what to say if you need me." He placed a kiss to my forehead and let me go.

After several deep breaths, I reached for the doorknob and twisted.

The door shut with a loud click behind me. Mel was on the bed staring at a spot on the wall. I crossed the room, making sure I wasn't crowding her. "Mel? Do you remember me from last night?"

She turned to look at me, her eyes void of emotion. Then . . . there seemed to be some recognition.

I wasn't used to being on this side of the situation, but I remembered what had helped me. "May I sit with you?"

Mel nodded.

Closing the distance, I sat on the other end of the bed. There was still a good two feet between us. "My name's Brianna. Or you can call me Anna, if you want."

She didn't say anything.

"He hurt me, too. Like he did you. A few years ago. When I saw him going up in the elevator, I knew what he would do to you, so we called security."

Her eyes seemed to focus then. "Your neck."

I touched the red mark that would most likely linger there for the next week. "I'll be okay. My neck is sore and my throat hurts, but I'll survive. So will you."

She closed her eyes.

We sat there for a while, neither of us saying anything. It wouldn't help to push her too far too fast. I could only imagine the onslaught of questions Agent Gibbson had thrown at her. That wasn't what she needed. Not right now. "Last night you told me your name was Mel. Is that short for something?"

She nodded. "Melanie."

"Do you have a last name?"

I saw her tense. "I don't. I don't want them to know. If they know, they'll call my parents and I . . ."

She was getting agitated and that wouldn't help anyone. "It's okay. You don't have to tell me." I paused. "I understand all about not wanting your parents to know."

"You do?" she asked.

I nodded. "My dad was responsible for me being taken." While my father hadn't personally sold me to Dumas, it was because of his debt that the man had decided to take me as payment.

"I wasn't . . ." She glanced down. "I ran away."

"I thought about running away from my dad's house, but I didn't. Then, I was taken. I tried to run away from the man who hurt me, but I wasn't able to. Every time I tried, he caught me."

"The same man who hurt me?" she asked.

"No. He was a friend of the man who hurt me and sometimes he'd let his friends hurt me, too." I was trying to keep things as simple as possible, trying not to go into too much detail. It wasn't about me.

"Oh."

"Do you know the man who hurt you last night?" I asked.

She shook her head. "No. I was cold, and he offered to buy me some food and said he could get me out of the cold for the night. I thought . . ." She met my gaze, moisture in her eyes. "I thought he wanted sex. And he seemed nice. I—" Her words got caught in her throat.

"Have you been on the streets for a long time?"

Mel didn't answer right away, but I waited. Sometimes it took time deciding whether or not to share information. "No," she whispered. "I ran away last week after . . ."

She pressed her lips together so tight they were turning white. "It's okay. You don't have to tell me. But I'll listen if you want to." It was strange being on this side, but it felt good to help, even a little bit.

Again, she met my gaze, and then she looked at the wall. "I ran away because I didn't want my parents to find out." She pulled the sheet around her, holding it as if it would somehow protect her from what she was about to tell me. "My uncle. We were swimming. He . . ." She released a shaky breath and turned to look at me. "I can't tell my parents. I can't." The last part was louder and more forceful.

"The only thing that matters right now is that you're safe."

She didn't react.

The more I talked to her, the younger she seemed. "Mel, can I ask how old you are?"

That's when the tears started.

It broke my heart seeing her like this and I couldn't just sit there and do nothing. I reached out my hand, hoping she'd take it. She did, but then she launched herself into my arms. It was completely unexpected, and I had to fight down my own response to the abrupt change.

She held onto me as if her life depended on it. Then I heard her whisper, "fourteen."

Stephan

I stood beside Agent Marco and watched through the big picture window as Brianna talked to Mel. Sitting on the sidelines wasn't my style, but I knew Brianna was right. She had the best chance of getting information out of the scared young woman.

"Did you hear what she said?" Agent Marco asked.

"No." Mel had hurled herself into Brianna's arms almost knocking Brianna off the bed. I noticed Brianna's hesitation before she'd embraced the young woman.

As soon as Mel had given her full first name, that she'd run away, and that she'd been gone for less than two weeks, Agent Marco had sent Agent Gibbson to run a search with the new information. Brianna may not have gotten everything they wanted, but it was a start.

It also didn't escape me that if she'd run away, that also meant she was most likely a minor. Every time I thought I couldn't detest these men more, they did something to redefine my level of hate.

Time ticked by after that as we watched Brianna do her best to comfort Mel. They said a few words back and forth but they were all too low for us to hear behind the glass.

Agent Marco was beginning to get restless when Agent Gibbson came through the door again. "Melanie Graber. Fourteen. Went missing ten days ago from Corpus Christi, Texas where she was on vacation with her family."

"Fourteen?" Agent Marco asked. "Fourteen?"

There was no masking his anger and I was right there with him. I didn't know how he dealt with these monsters every day.

She nodded and handed him what I assumed was the missing person's information. I glanced over his shoulder to get a look. Sure enough, the girl in the picture was the same girl still clinging to Brianna. The only difference was that the girl in the picture wasn't wearing makeup and had a huge grin on her face.

"Should I call the Corpus Christi PD and let them know we found her?" Agent Gibbson asked.

Agent Marco set the paper down on the table next to him. "Not yet. I want to see what else Miss Reeves is able to find out." He glanced over at me, and then to the two women on the other side of the glass. "I'm especially curious about the uncle."

We were there for another four hours. Even then, Brianna hadn't wanted to leave Mel.

"Are you doing okay?" I asked once we were alone in the car.

"I'm worried about Mel."

I took her face in my hands and made her look at me. "I know, but I want to know about you. How are you?"

"I'm okay. Tired."

Kissing her forehead, I released her and started the engine. "I'll draw you a bubble bath when we get home, and you can rest."

"Can we stay at the condo this week? I don't want to be too far away in case Mel needs me."

We didn't have that many clothes in the city anymore, but we could make do. "Of course."

As soon as we arrived at the condo, I drew her a bath and told her to relax until I came and got her. I stripped out of my clothes, changed into something more comfortable, and ordered dinner from one of our favorite Italian restaurants. Both of us needed comfort food tonight.

I paid extra and had to wait for an hour for the food to be delivered, but it was worth it. The man who brought our meals didn't seem to mind either, once I handed him a very generous tip. "You have a nice night, sir."

"Thank you." I closed the door, locked it, and watched on the monitor as he made his way to the elevator.

I'd ordered all our favorites: lasagna, chicken parmesan, fettuccine alfredo, and a large salad with fresh baked bread. While I'd waited for the food, I'd set the table with plates, glasses, and a pitcher of water. I removed our dinner from the bag and laid it out for easy access, then went to retrieve Brianna.

She was lying in the bathtub with her eyes closed, her hair draped over the back and her breasts peeking up from beneath the bubbles. I felt my cock twitch but ignored it.

"Brianna."

Her eyes opened and she sat up.

"Dinner's here." I extended my hand, offering to help her out of the bath.

She placed her palm in mine and stood, the bubbles sliding down her naked body. After the stress of the last twenty-four hours, all I wanted to do was lose myself in her warmth.

I removed a towel from the shelf and dried her off before clothing her in the robe that hung on the back of the door.

"You got Italian?" she asked when she walked into the main living area.

"I did."

Guiding her to her chair, I pulled it out and waited for her to sit before taking my place beside her. Pouring us each a glass of water, I opened the containers and served us both.

As always, Brianna waited until I'd begun eating before picking up her fork. She took a couple of bites, and then started moving the pasta around her plate. "Is your throat bothering you?"

"No." She glanced up at me. "It is a little, but . . ."

"Then why aren't you eating your food?" I asked. She needed to eat. The only thing she'd had since we'd left the condo earlier that day was a bag of potato chips and a candy bar from a vending machine, and that had been hours ago.

"I'm worried about Mel. I didn't want to leave her. She's all alone."

Picking up her hand, I brought it to my lips and kissed her fingers. "Mel is safe tonight and that's what matters. Agent Marco will make sure of that." Finding out the girl was only fourteen had been jarring, not only for me and Brianna, but for Agent Marco as well. We'd all suspected she was underage the more we listened to her speak, but none of us had been prepared for that revelation.

"I know. I just remember what it was like for me that first night I was here with you. How scared I was."

"Yes, but you were still under the impression that you were my slave then, that you had no choices," I said.

"Mel doesn't have a choice. They've contacted her parents. They're coming to get her. She's going to have to tell them why she left." I could hear her voice rising with anxiety.

"Agent Marco said we could stop by tomorrow and you could spend some more time with her. He said the earliest flight her parents could get was tomorrow morning, so they won't be here until midday."

She nodded.

"It'll be okay. We'll do what we can to help her. I promise." I kissed her fingers again and released them. "And Agent Marco is going to make sure Wilks rots in a prison cell. I really want the satisfaction of knowing he's alive and suffering." I picked up my fork again and pointed it at Brianna's plate. "Now, eat. If you're going to be of any help to Mel, you need your strength."

"Yes, Sir." Brianna picked up her fork and twirled pasta onto it before lifting it to her mouth.

"Good girl. Once we're finished with dinner, I'll clean up while you write in your journal."

She nodded and took another bite.

I was finishing up the dishes when my phone rang. Logan's name flashed across the screen and I knew I needed to answer it. I'd already put him off once today. "Hey."

"Hey, yourself. When I didn't hear back from you, I started to get worried," Logan said.

"We were with Agent Marco most of the day." I filled him in on Mel's situation. He was as appalled by her age as the rest of us.

"Is there anything Lily and I can do?"

"Nothing I can think of. Brianna wants to be there for Mel, so we're heading back to see her tomorrow. Her parents are coming to get her, and I have no idea how that's going to go. She's pretty shaken up."

We talked for a few more minutes. I wasn't in too big of a hurry since Brianna was writing in her journal. I wanted her to get her thoughts and feelings down on paper. Not only would it help me understand how best to help her, but it was good for her, as well.

By the time I finished my phone call and Brianna had completed her journaling, we were both ready for bed. Unlike the night before, I let her go into the bathroom alone to get ready, and then took my turn before joining her in our bed.

Brianna curled into my side as soon as my head hit the pillow. Circling my arms around her, I closed my eyes and absorbed the feel of her pressed up against me. Here. Safe. Mine.

"Sir?" Her voice was barely above a whisper in the darkness.

"Yes, sweetheart?"

"Thank you."

My lips brushed against her hair. "For what?"

"For saving me. For helping me." She paused and I felt moisture hit my chest. "For loving me."

I pressed a kiss to the top of her head, holding my lips against her hair. "Always."

CHAPTER 27

Brianna

I woke up again near morning with another nightmare. This one had been even stranger than the first. It had started off in a hotel room, and then ended up in an alley with Wilks strangling me.

It was him strangling me that had woken me up, gasping. Stephan held me until I'd calmed down, and then we talked it through. Then Stephan had suggested I call Dr. Katlin.

I would have had to call her anyway, since we'd been scheduled to meet at one o'clock and I wouldn't be there, but it was seven-thirty in the morning. Her service answered, and I left a message.

Dr. Katlin called me back ten minutes later. "I got your message, Anna. Did something happen?"

"Yes. We . . . one of the men who hurt me . . . he was trying to hurt someone else. At the hotel after the masquerade."

She asked me several questions. The first was if the police were involved. After I confirmed they were, she continued with the questions. Not about the situation specifically, but more along the lines of how I felt having seen him again and how I was dealing with that.

I told her about the nightmares. She'd listened and told me to try some breathing exercises before going to bed. "This is a new trauma, and your brain is trying to process it. That's going to take time." She paused. "I'm assuming you won't be able to make your session this afternoon?"

"No." I shook my head even though she couldn't see me. "We're staying at Stephan's condo in the city this week. I want to be here for Mel in case she needs me."

"I'll plan on seeing you next Monday, then. But you have my number. If you need to talk before then, call."

"I will."

Stephan was upstairs in his study. He'd left me alone to talk to Dr. Katlin letting me know where he'd be in case I needed him.

He lifted his head from the book he'd been reading, set it down, and opened his arms. I went to him, sitting on his lap. The chair up here wasn't as comfortable, but that was okay.

"How did your call go?"

He brushed a strand of hair behind my ear and a warm tingle went down my ear to the pit of my stomach. It had been two days since we'd made love and I was missing that connection with him. "Good. She said to call her if I needed to talk before next week."

"Did she have any advice about the nightmares?"

I reached for the buttons on his shirt. He'd dressed in a button down again today, something he didn't wear that often anymore in our new home. "She gave me a website. They have some breathing exercises I can do before bed. She said that might help."

He smiled, but it didn't reach his eyes. I didn't like that he was so worried about me. "We'll look at it tonight. We can pull it up on the laptop while we're in bed that way you can go right to sleep after."

I nodded and ran my hand up the front of his shirt. While I wanted to get rid of the nightmares, that wasn't at the forefront of my mind. Last night I'd been exhausted and stressed. The night before, we hadn't gotten to bed until the wee hours of the morning, and I'd been hurt by my encounter with Wilks.

My throat felt better today, even though there was still a faint red mark from where he'd pressed my collar into my skin. The wound on my side was healing. As long as I didn't reach over my head and pull the stitches, it didn't hurt anymore. Everything else was in my head and there wasn't a Band-Aid to fix that.

What I wanted, though, was to forget for a little while. To feel something other than the pain of my injuries, the fear of reliving what had happened, or the worry about what Mel was going through.

We needed to go to Agent Marco's office again, but we weren't supposed to meet him until ten. He was going to let me spend some more time with Mel before her parents got there.

For now, though, we had some time. I should go make us breakfast, but food wasn't what I wanted. I needed him. Needed him to take control and let my mind shut off. Even if it was only for a while.

I met his gaze. "Sir?"

"Yes, sweetheart?"

While I wasn't good at seduction like some of the heroines in the books I read, I knew Stephan. "I want to forget for a little while. "

It only took him a moment to understand. The brown of his eyes got a little darker. He brought his hand up to cover my injured side. "Is it still hurting?"

"Only if I lift my arms above my head."

Next, he skimmed my throat with his fingers.

He didn't ask, but I knew the question anyway. "It doesn't hurt today."

Meeting my gaze, he threaded his hand into the hair at the base of my skull. I let my head tilt back into his grasp without breaking eye contact. He tightened his hold, and it was all I could do to keep my eyes open. I wanted this. I needed it. Needed him.

"Do not be afraid to use your numbers, Brianna. If you reach a five or higher, you are to tell me immediately."

"Yes, Sir. I promise."

The pressure on the back of my head increased as he brought our mouths together. His lips were firm, demanding. He was taking what he wanted, and I was along for the ride.

My fingers dug into his shoulders as he repositioned me to

straddle him on the chair. In the new position, there was no masking his erection as it strained against his slacks. A moan escaped my throat as he rocked my hips against him.

He snaked his hand under my skirt and nudged my panties out of the way to run his fingers up and down my sex, lubricating his fingers before he pressed them inside. My muscles clenched at the intrusion, but then relaxed, welcoming him. This is what I'd wanted. All I could think about was him. The way his mouth felt. His hands. The way his chest scraped my nipples with our movements.

Then, he was slowing the kiss, bringing it into rhythm with the thrust of his fingers inside me. My hips began to move to that same rhythm, pulling me closer to my orgasm. Would he have me come on his fingers or would he change position and remove his pants so I could take him inside?

I got my answer a few minutes later as he turned the palm of his hand to rub against my clit. "Come, pet."

With those words, I let the sensations overtake me and within seconds I was hovering on the edge. He tilted me to the side and scraped his teeth right below my ear. That was all it took to have me gasping for breath as I rode out my climax.

My body was still pulsing when he stood, me in his arms, and placed me on the desk. The next thing I knew, he spread my legs, pushed my panties out of the way again, and slipped inside me.

"Look at me," he demanded.

I met his gaze.

"Number?"

"One, Sir. You feel so good."

That was all he seemed to need. He pulled his hips back and began to move.

Taking hold of my hips, he plunged and retreated with slow, steady strokes. He tugged my shirt down, exposing one of my breasts and sucked my nipple into his mouth. My head fell back as I let myself feel.

Cool air sent another wave of sensation through my body as he released my nipple, wet from his mouth. He picked up the pace, holding my hips steady as he moved, edging us both closer to our orgasm.

Sweat beaded on his forehead and we were both breathing hard by the time he adjusted one of his hands so his thumb reached my clit. I nearly came the moment he touched it. "Sir?"

"Yes, pet?"

"May I . . ." I pressed my hands against the desk trying to steady myself. "Come?"

He didn't answer right away, and I gritted my teeth trying not to come before he gave me permission. I'd only come once without permission and I didn't want to disappoint him again.

Right when I thought I wouldn't be able to hold on any longer, he captured my lips with his and murmured the word I was waiting to hear. "Come."

Stephan

I sent her to clean up while I made us breakfast. Her request for sex had been somewhat unexpected at first, but then I'd understood it. She needed to feel safe. Secure. And while our relationship was 24/7, it was during sex when it was usually at its strongest.

After we ate our breakfast, I jumped in the shower to wash the sweat of our unexpected activities from my body before getting dressed in my last set of clean clothes. We were going to have to go shopping if we were going to stay in the condo for the entire week.

Normally, I'd have Lily do it, but she was focused on her wedding, which was only two weeks away. Logan would have my head if I asked her.

Dressed in a fresh pair of slacks and a dress shirt, Brianna and I headed downtown to Agent Marco's office. Given it was a weekday, there were a lot more people in the building. Brianna held tight to my hand as we were surrounded in the elevator.

Agent Marco sighed with relief when he saw us appear in the doorway. "Mel's been asking for you. She's been pacing her room and refused to eat any of the breakfast we brought her this morning."

"When are her parents due to arrive?" I asked.

"Around eleven-thirty. Their plane lands in an hour."

He led us to the same room as the day before. As soon as the door opened, Mel froze. Then, when she saw Brianna, she ran over to her and hugged her. I couldn't hear what she was saying because she was talking into Brianna's shoulder.

Brianna held her, not saying anything, until the girl calmed down. "Were you able to sleep last night?"

Mel wiped the tears from her eyes and lowered her head as she released Brianna. "A little."

"We'll give you two some time to talk," Agent Marco said, motioning me to return to the hall with him.

Brianna met my gaze. "I'll be next door," I said.

She nodded.

For the next hour, I sat and watched through one-way glass as Brianna talked to Mel. Brianna told her about going to see her counselor and how it had helped her. And that having me, someone who loved her no matter what, had made things easier. Even after everything she'd gone through, she'd found a way to be happy.

It was gut wrenching to listen to. I even saw Agent Marco cringe a few times.

At eleven forty-five, Agent Marco's cell rang. "Marco. Yeah. I'll be right there." He disconnected the call. "That was Agent Gibbson. Melanie's parents are here."

We went to get Brianna and Mel. I had no idea how this was going to go or even if Mel would want us there, but I didn't envy either party. Mel's parents had to be beside themselves. I had no idea how much Agent Marco had told them, but even if he'd told them everything, I knew they truly had no idea what was in store. The nightmares. The fear that cropped up out of nowhere.

Granted, Mel hadn't suffered for ten months like Brianna, but she was also younger. Much younger. The experience would leave its mark.

Agent Marco knocked on the door, and then let himself in, not waiting for an invitation. Both Brianna and Mel looked up at his entrance. "Your parents are here," he said.

Mel griped Brianna's hand in what looked to be a death grip. I saw Brianna let out a loud breath. She had demons of her own she was fighting.

"Will you come with me?"

The shaky timber of her voice reminded me so much of Brianna. It had every protective instinct in my body kicking in and wanting to do something. Anything.

Brianna looked at me and I nodded. I wasn't sure if she was asking or wanting reassurance.

Agent Marco led us back to the side of the building where his office was located. We didn't go there, though. Instead, we got into an elevator and made our way down to the first floor.

No one said a word on the way down. Mel hadn't let go of Brianna's hand. Brianna looked nervous but determined. And Agent Marco stood with his back ramrod straight as if he were preparing for battle.

The elevator doors opened, and we walked down the short hallway. Agent Marco stopped in front of a door and looked at Mel. "Are you ready?"

Mel hesitated, but then she nodded.

He opened the door.

In the room stood a petite woman with short blond hair and a man who looked as if he hadn't seen the inside of a gym in at least a decade. But that wasn't what struck me the most. It was the relief in their eyes when they saw their daughter.

Mel's mother let out a little noise that sounded somewhere between a squeal and a whine before rushing to embrace her daughter. Her dad followed suit, enveloping both in a hug.

Even with her parents' exuberate response, Mel hadn't released Brianna's hand.

"Oh, baby," her mom said, pulling back from the hug enough to look her daughter over. She brushed the hair away from her face and gave her a kiss on the forehead.

With the emotion of the initial greeting over, Mel's parents seemed to register the other people in the room. Agent Marco cleared his throat. "Maybe we could all take a seat."

Mel's mom, unable to let her daughter go, took hold of the girl's other hand and began leading her to a couch along the back wall. Reluctantly, Mel let go of Brianna's hand. She looked back at the loss of contact, almost pleading with her eyes for Brianna not to leave her.

With that in mind, I took two chairs from a nearby table and placed them close to the couch. Mel was sitting in between her parents, but at least Brianna could be close to her.

I motioned for Brianna to take the seat across from Mel, leaving Agent Marco to figure himself out. He'd barely sat down at the table when the door opened again, and Agent Gibbson walked in. She was carrying a folder and a pad of paper. She took a seat beside Agent Marco.

Both agents were solemn as they addressed Mel's parents. I thought at one point Mel's mom was going to need medical attention as Agent Marco laid out the situation in detail and informed them how the case would proceed and what they needed from both them and Mel. From the conversation, I gathered that they hadn't said much to them over the phone other than that Mel had been found.

Agent Marco stood. "I think we have everything we need for now. I'll be in touch once I've gone over things with the prosecutor," he said.

"Can we take her home to Texas?" Mel's dad asked.

"I'd like it if she could stay for another day or so, just in case we need anything more from her. Then you should be able to take her home."

Mel's father nodded as he held onto his daughter's hand.

"Do you all have somewhere to stay?" I asked. Knowing they'd flown in with little notice and not knowing how long they would be here, I doubted they'd even thought that far.

"Yes," her mom said. "We're booked at the Marriott for the night. We'll have to see if we can stay longer. We didn't realize you'd need us to stay."

"Cases like these are complicated. This more than most." Agent Marco hadn't gone into a whole lot of detail regarding Wilks's past other than to say that this wasn't the first time he'd done something like this, and that Brianna had been one of his other victims.

It was probably a good thing he hadn't gone into the fact that had we not intervened, Mel could have ended up in a similar situation as Brianna had. Her parents didn't need those thoughts going through their heads.

The two agents left the five of us alone. As I watched Mel interact with her parents, it felt as if we were intruding on a private family moment. We needed to go and give them time to reconnect. As scared as Mel was, she was going to have to confront her fears. It was the only way out.

I turned to Brianna. "Why don't you give Mel your number so she can call you?"

There was still a pad of paper on the table. I handed it, along with a pen, to Brianna. She scribbled down her cell phone number and handed it to Mel.

The girl took it, folded it neatly, and shoved it in her pocket.

Mel's mom got up from the couch and hugged Brianna, then me. "Thank you, both for saving our daughter. I don't know how we can ever repay you."

"If you're ever down in Texas," Mel's dad said, "come see us. You'll always be welcome."

A hushed silence fell in the room as Brianna walked over to Mel. Silent tears streamed down the girl's face. Brianna knelt in front of her, taking Mel's hands in hers. "You'll be okay. You survived. Remember that. When the memories come, remember you survived."

Mel sniffed.

"If you need to talk, call me. Sometimes talking about it makes it less scary."

The girl collapsed into Brianna's arms.

After a few minutes, her father put a hand on her shoulder. Mel righted herself and brushed away her tears.

"Maybe we could meet for breakfast tomorrow," Mel's mom

suggested. She looked as if she were about ready to dissolve into tears again. I had no doubt she'd probably cry herself to sleep tonight.

"That sounds like a great idea," her father said. "What do you say, Mel?"

"Would you?" Mel's gaze went from Brianna to me.

"Text Brianna with the address of the hotel and we'll meet you there tomorrow morning," I said.

Knowing she'd see Brianna again soon seemed to help Mel relax. It was going to be a rough night. I didn't envy any of them.

Brianna was quiet on our way home. Once we were in our condo, I guided her over to my chair in the living room and situated her on my lap. We needed food, but that could wait. I had a feeling my girl needed to talk.

CHAPTER 28

Brianna

We ended up having breakfast with Mel and her mom for the rest of the week. Her dad had to fly back to Texas after that first day. He hadn't wanted to leave, and seeing the way he was with Mel, gave me hope that one day she'd be okay. She had people who loved her and that was what was most important. I don't know where I would have been without Stephan.

Friday afternoon, Stephan drove Mel and her mom to the airport. It was difficult to say goodbye. I knew Mel didn't really want to leave. She'd finally broken down and told her mom why she'd run away.

The look on her mom's face had been both chilling and comforting at the same time. She'd called that same day and told her husband who then contacted local law enforcement. Mel and her mom had an appointment with a detective Monday morning.

I gave Mel a long hug goodbye as we stood outside security. "Thank you," she said. "I don't . . . I don't know if I'd be going back home if it weren't for you. And Stephan."

"Your parents love you. I think you can talk to them. They may not understand, but that's okay. Stephan doesn't always understand what I went through either, but he still helps me when the bad stuff tries to take over."

"You're so lucky," she said, glancing over her shoulder to where Stephan was talking to her mom. "He's really cute, too."

I ignored her comment on his looks. "I am lucky. You are, too."

Mel nodded. "I guess I am." She hugged me again before joining her mom. "I'll call you."

Stephan stood by my side and we watched as Mel and her mom got in line to go through security. "You doin' all right?"

I looked up at him, then back at Mel who'd turned back to give us a little wave before stepping up to the scanners. "Yes. Just worried about her."

"I think she'll be okay." We waited until they disappeared into the terminal before heading back to our vehicle. "I spoke with her mom. Between that and dealing with Mel's nightmares throughout the week, I think she's as prepared as she can be. She's going to get Mel into counseling." He gave me a pointed look. "I gave her my advice on that as well. I don't want Mel to go through what I did. In her current state, it could lead her to run again."

"Mel likes you," I said, changing to a lighter subject.

"I like her as well."

"I mean likes you likes you." He looked down at me with a confused look on his face and I giggled. It felt good to laugh after the last few days. "She thinks you're cute."

His eyes widened a little. "Aren't I a little old for her?"

"You're only thirty."

We arrived at our car. He opened my door and waited until I was seated inside. "She's only fourteen."

"I don't think that matters. You're quite handsome."

He leaned down, bringing his mouth a breath away from mine. "Handsome, huh?"

"Yes." My breath caught in my throat as he ran his hand up my thigh, stopping to tease the edge of my panties.

"Take them off." Then he backed away and shut the door.

It took me a moment to register what he said but I was already lifting my hips to wiggle my panties off by the time he slipped into the seat beside me. He held out his hand once I'd kicked them loose from my feet and tucked them into his coat pocket.

Stephan didn't say more until we were out of the parking garage. "Spread your legs."

I did, already feeling the cooler air gliding over my sex. As he drove, he reached into his other pocket, removed a small vibrator, and handed it to me. "Put it against your clit and keep it there until we're home. You aren't to come until I put the car in park again."

It was a thirty-minute drive if there was no traffic. Lucky for me, it was still early enough on Friday that we shouldn't hit too much. At least I hoped not.

Within five minutes, I was ready and that was before Stephan placed his hand on my bare thigh and began rubbing the sensitive flesh.

Another ten minutes went by and I was biting the inside of my cheek. "Sir? I don't know if I can—"

"Yes, you can. Keep that vibrator on your clit. I don't want you cheating. I want that clit of yours nice and sensitive by the time we get home."

I closed my eyes and concentrated on what we'd had for breakfast this morning, the book I was reading. Anything other than the vibration between my legs.

The car eventually stopped, and I heard the most glorious words ever. "Now."

My body detonated, fully primed from the long car ride. I struggled to keep quiet, knowing we were in public.

Stephan's mouth covered mine, swallowing my cries, as I rode out the orgasm that seemed to last forever.

He rested his forehead against mine. "I love watching you come."

If I hadn't already been flushed from coming, I probably would have blushed.

Taking the vibrator from me, he put it back in his pocket, readjusted my skirt, and then got out of the vehicle. He came around to the passenger door and let me out. Once I was on my feet, he crushed me to the vehicle and covered my mouth with his. I could feel his erection pressing into my stomach and I knew what was coming as soon as we got upstairs.

He released me with a reluctance that said he wished he could take me right there against his vehicle. I knew he'd never do it, though. Too many people could see, including building security, and he wouldn't want that for several reasons.

Circling an arm around my waist to keep me steady, he guided me to the elevator that would take us to the top floor of the building. We were alone on the ride up, but again there were security cameras, so he kept his hands to himself.

All that changed the minute we walked through the door of the condo. He was on me as soon as the door clicked shut.

I moaned as his lips devoured mine and his hands went to work on removing my clothing. My shirt was first, dropping to the floor, followed by my bra, and then my skirt. The only thing I was left in were my shoes.

Stephan picked me up and carried me to the couch. He laid me down, spread my legs, and dove in with his mouth. My clit was still sensitive from the vibrator and I screamed out as he began sucking, licking, and nipping at my sex. I wanted to come again within seconds.

When I was about to ask for permission to come again, he stood, unfastened his pants, and kicked them from his legs. He got rid of his shirt just as quickly.

He'd been gentle with me all week, afraid to hurt me after my injuries. But the cut on my side was almost completely healed. It didn't hurt anymore, and he could be as rough as he wanted.

Once he was naked, he made himself comfortable between my thighs. This time, he began working his way from the junction between my legs up my stomach to my breasts, kissing and licking his way, taking his time. I threaded my fingers through his hair and arched my back up to meet his mouth.

"Lie still, or I'll have to tie you up."

I stopped moving, forcing myself not to react the way my body desperately wanted to.

His teeth scraped against my nipple and I had to grit my teeth to keep from pushing up into his mouth to beg for more. He took his time, making sure both my nipples were hard and sensitive before he resumed his journey upward.

A faint red line was still visible on my neck and he traced it with the tip of his tongue. As he continued to explore the rest of my neck, his hands returned to my breasts. He pushed, pulled, and twisted them until I was aching to have him inside me. I was more than ready, and I wanted to feel him filling me.

"Are you getting impatient, sweetheart? Do I need to get that rope and tie you down or are you going to behave?"

I hadn't realized until then that I'd started moving my hips against him. "I'm sorry, Sir. I couldn't help it."

"Hmm. That didn't answer my question. Are you going to keep your hips still or do I need to get the rope?"

It was hard to think at that moment. "I don't know if I can stop it, Sir."

To my disappointment, he pulled away and stood. Then, he was lifting me off the couch and carrying me into the bedroom.

He placed me on the bed, and then went to the closet. The few toys we had here were in a chest at the back. It felt like he was gone for ten minutes but was probably closer to a minute. He returned with two lengths of rope draped over his hands. "The rest of the rope is at the house, so we'll have to make do."

Taking hold of one of my ankles, he secured it to one corner of the bed, then did the same with the other to the opposite side. I still had full movement of my upper body, but even that was hindered once he climbed onto the bed and laid on top of me, pinning me down with his body.

Stephan grabbed my wrists and placed them on the bed above my head. "Keep them there. I wanted uninterrupted access to what's mine."

"Yes, Sir—" The words died in my mouth as he picked up where he'd left off. It wasn't long before I was back where I was before, only this time I couldn't move anything but my hands and my head.

By the time he entered me, I think he kissed every inch of my body he could reach between my thighs and my neck . . . multiple times. My entire body felt as if it were humming, alive, and desperately wanting him. I released a cry as he filled me.

He sat on his knees between my thighs, pulling my hips to him and thrusting at the same time. The blanket on the bed scratched against my back, adding to what I was feeling.

Then he started rubbing my clit and I cried out again.

"Are you ready to come, Brianna?" he asked.

"Yes, Sir." I fisted the blanket in my hands trying to hold on.

Instead of giving me permission, he switched hands and began rubbing harder, swirling the moisture around and even pinching my clit. It felt amazing, but I wasn't going to last.

"Come. Now!"

The flood gates opened, and I came. Hard. It started in my sex and vibrated throughout my limbs. I arched my back and screamed out my release.

Stephan

I loved watching her fall apart beneath me. Who was I kidding? I loved watching her climax no matter what position she was in.

Seeing her had brought my own orgasm racing to the surface and within seconds I was shooting my cum into her. I collapsed onto the bed, keeping most of my weight on my arms as I caught my breath. Sex with Brianna was fantastic. I couldn't get enough of it. Of her. She was an amazing submissive and a great partner.

"Are you doing okay?" I asked, looking at her.

Brianna released a contented sigh. "Yes, Sir." Gazing up at me, she asked, "Can I touch you again?"

I smiled. "You may."

She circled her arms around my neck, and then ran her hands down my back.

Her lips parted and her eyes closed, relishing being able to touch me again. It was too cute, and I didn't resist my urge to kiss her. "How are you feeling?"

"Good." She smiled up at me.

"Nothing's hurting? Your side? Your neck?" I asked.

"No, Sir. All I feel is you."

I chuckled, gave her another quick kiss, and pushed myself off the bed. She looked a bit disappointed, but we did have some things to do before tomorrow. I traced the crease in her forehead with my thumb as I gazed down at her on the bed. "We'll have more time later, love, but we need to go over the plan for tomorrow and I have a few calls to make. I promise tonight when I make love to you, you can touch me the entire time."

The rest of the day was full of phone calls and coordinating things. Tomorrow afternoon was the final dress fitting for the wedding party. I was dropping Brianna off at the bridal store, and then joining Logan and the two other groomsmen across town to make sure no last-minute adjustments needed to be made to our tuxes.

It would have been nice if we'd been able to wear the tuxes we already owned—Logan and I at least—but Lily had vetoed that idea. Other than the lapel being skinnier, I didn't see a difference in the tuxes she'd picked out for us to wear for the wedding. She insisted there was a difference, though, so off we were going to the tailor.

I knew part of my mood had to do with the fact that instead of picking Brianna up after the appointment and heading back to our condo, she would be going with Lily and the other women to dinner, and then to a club. Brianna wasn't excited about going to either as she hated crowds and loud music, but she hadn't wanted to disappoint Lily. Logan assured me he knew the owner of the club and that everything would be fine. I really hoped he was right.

Saturday morning came way too soon. We ate breakfast, got in a workout, and spent some time curled up on the couch with our books before it was time to leave.

At one-thirty, I dropped Brianna off at the bridal shop, giving her a long kiss goodbye. "You have your cell phone. Call me if you need to. I'll come get you."

"You'll be at Logan's bachelor party. I don't—"

I raised my eyebrows.

"Yes, Sir."

"Good, girl. Try to have a good time." I was going to leave it at that, but then changed my mind. "And if Bridget starts trouble, say something to Lily."

She nodded.

I waited by the curb while she walked into the bridal shop. It was hard to drop her off and leave, but I knew I was going to have to get used to it if she went to school next month. I couldn't go to her classes with her.

Well, I probably could, but I also knew she needed to do it on her own. As her Dom, I had to do what was best for her even if it wasn't what I wanted.

Logan was already inside the store when I arrived. I didn't see the other groomsmen, though. As soon as that thought crossed my mind, Michael strolled through the door. He was shorter than both Logan and I, around five eleven, and had curly red hair. Logan had struck up a friendship with him when they'd had to work together on a project in college. He was a nice guy. A little shy, but easy to get along with.

"Hey," he said, removing his coat.

Before either of us could answer, the man who'd helped us before with the tuxes came around the corner. "Good afternoon, gentlemen. Do we have everyone here?"

"Not—" Logan turned as the door opened again and Caleb walked through. "I hope you don't cut it this close on the day of my wedding."

Caleb chuckled. "No worries. Besides, Stephan's the one that will have the ring. Even if I don't make it, you'll still be able to put a ring on it."

The tailor showed us where we could hang our coats, and then led us into the back where the fitting rooms were. He already had our tuxes lined up. "Mr. Mattson, would you like to go first?"

"Sure." Logan took the tux and disappeared behind the curtain.

Handing another tux to me, he pointed to one of the other rooms. "Let me know if you have any issues."

I heard him handing out tuxes to Michael and Caleb as I stripped out of my clothes and donned the tux. Given how often Logan and I wore tuxes, or as often as I used to wear a tux, we were dressed and ready to go well before Michael and Caleb.

The tailor marked a few minor issues with Logan's tux before turning his attention to me. He was just finishing up with his inspection of mine when Caleb made his way out of the fitting room. "I don't know how you wear these things all the time, Logan." He pulled at the bow tie around his neck.

Logan laughed. "You get used to it after a while."

Caleb frowned. "I'm not sure I could get used to it."

As if on cue, Michael appeared, his bow tie draped over his shoulders. "I have no idea how to tie one of these things."

The tailor stepped up and quickly sorted the tie out with more practiced ease than even I was capable of.

It took about ten more minutes and then we were all able to get back into our street clothes. Again, Logan and I were the first to emerge. We each handed the tuxes to the tailor. "I'll have those fixes done for you by the middle of the week. You can pick it up on Thursday," he said to Logan. Then he turned to me. "Did you want to take this with you today, or would you prefer to pick everything up together?"

Logan glanced over at me, and then back at the tailor. "I think it would be easiest to pick everything up together on Thursday."

"I'll make sure everything is ready to go for you Thursday, then." Michael and Caleb came out of their dressing rooms and handed over their tuxes. "Is there anything else I can help you gentlemen with today?"

"I think we're good. And we'll see you on Thursday," Logan said.

Everyone followed Logan back to his place, so they could park their cars. A vote had been taken and we were heading to a local sports bar. Caleb had wanted to go to a strip club—he claimed it was tradition—but luckily, he was overruled.

I hadn't been overly excited about the idea of going to a bar, so I'd selected a sports bar instead and one I'd been to before with Logan. They had good food and the atmosphere was a decent mix of bar and restaurant.

Given I didn't drink, I was the designated driver for the evening. I knew Logan wouldn't get plastered and I doubted Michael would either. Caleb was the one I was concerned about. He struck me as the life of the party. Basically, the opposite of me since I'd much rather be spending the evening hanging out at Logan's house and calling it good.

We found a high-top near the bar that would seat four and sat down. A server who looked to be in her early twenties sauntered over to the table. "How are you guys tonight?"

"Better now that you're here," Caleb said.

To my surprise, she didn't seem to be put off by his remark. She grinned at him and gave her hair a little flip. "What can I get you guys started with tonight?"

Caleb went to open his mouth again, but Logan cut him off. "I'll take whatever you have on draft and if you could get us some menus?"

"Sure thing." She winked at Logan, and then turned to Michael.

"Same."

Of course, Caleb had to order a Sex on the Beach. I doubted that was his drink of choice, but it got the reaction that he wanted. The server blushed.

She looked at me, the flush in her cheeks still evident. "Ice water, please."

Nodding, she turned on her heel and walked away, a little more swing in her hips than what was natural.

"You're not drinking at all?" Caleb asked. "We're gonna be here for a while. One beer won't kill you."

"I don't drink," I told him.

He looked disbelieving. "You're kidding."

"I'm not." I had a feeling this was going to be an interesting evening and I couldn't wait for it to end.

CHAPTER 29

Brianna

The music was giving me a headache. We'd been at the club for over an hour. Lily had dragged me onto the dance floor twice, so far. I'd hated it. There were too many people, and one guy had put his hands on my hips and tried to get me to dance with him.

I'd frozen, not knowing what to do and Lily had to come to my rescue. After that, she hadn't asked me to go on the dance floor with them again.

I sat in the VIP section by myself, sipping on a glass of water. All the others were drinking, even Lily. We were going to take a cab back to her house when we were done for the night.

So far, Bridget had left me alone. She'd given me a couple of strange looks, especially when I ordered water instead of a drink, but that was about it. Since a lot of people looked at me weird, it wasn't a big deal.

Tess plopped on the couch beside me. She'd been on the dance floor with the rest of them. "The DJ tonight is really good."

I nodded, not sure what to say.

"You're hating this, aren't you?" she asked.

"It's okay. I just don't like big crowds and—"

"And there are lots of people here."

"Yeah."

She tilted her head to the side and twisted her lips as if she were thinking really hard about something. Then, she set her drink back down on the table and turned to me. "We could dance right here. We don't have to go down to the dance floor."

"That's okay. You don't have to. I'm okay. Really."

Tess glanced at the dance floor and back at me. "Do you not like to dance? Or is it the crowd?"

"The crowd, mostly." I scraped my teeth along my lower lip. "I only ever dance with Stephan."

"Hmm." She took another drink, and then stood. I expected her to head back out to the dance floor, but she held out her hand instead. "Come on. Give it a try, at least?"

I thought about it for a moment, and then put my hand in hers. She led us a few feet away from the table, dropped my hand, and began to move her hips.

It was a little awkward at first, but no one seemed to be paying attention to us here in the corner and so I started to move, too. One song led to another, and after a while I began to relax. Soon, I realized, I was actually having fun.

We danced for a few more songs, and then went back to the table to cool off. The club was warm with everyone in it, and dancing only made it worse. We were both thirsty.

"You're a really good dancer," I said to Tess.

"So are you." She picked up her drink and downed the rest of it.

I picked up mine to do the same, but she stopped me. When I looked at her, I could tell something was wrong. I glanced around our immediate area, but we were alone in our little area. No one had been in our VIP section the entire night except for our little group and the server that brought our drinks. "What's wrong?"

She took my glass out of my hand and held it up in front of her. "You just had water, right?"

"Yes."

"Nothing else? No Mt. Dew or flavoring of any kind?" she asked.

I shook my head. "No. Just water."

Then, she held my water up so I could see it, too. "Do you see the yellow?"

It wasn't obvious when the glass had been on the table, but now I saw it. There was a yellow tint to my water that hadn't been there before. "What is it?"

She set the glass down on the table. "I don't know, but you're not drinking it."

Tess flagged down our server. "Can we get another water? There seems to be something in this one."

She held the glass up for the server to see, and then placed it back on the table off to the side.

"I'll get you another one."

Once we were alone again, I asked the question that had been rolling around in my head. "I don't understand. How could something have gotten into my drink?"

"I don't know, but the only people who've been over here are you, me, Lily, Bridget, and our server. You and I were dancing, and I don't think Lily would put something in your drink. I also don't think it was our server. If she was going to put something in your water, why not do it before delivering the drink in the first place?"

She didn't say it, but she didn't have to. That left Bridget.

The server returned with my new water as Lily danced her way back to where we were sitting. She giggled as she practically fell onto the plush chair. "Can I get a water, too?" she asked the server. "I'm dying of thirst after all that dancing." Then she saw the other water on the table. "Oh. I guess you already brought an extra one."

"No!" Both Tess and I shouted at the same time.

Lily looked taken aback, and then confused.

"I'll get you another water," the server said to Lily. Then she looked at Tess. "Did you want me to go ahead and take this?"

Tess seemed to be weighing the options. "That would probably be safer."

Nodding, the server took the yellow tinted water and left us alone.

"What's going on?" Lily asked. All the playfulness from a few minutes ago was gone.

"Someone put something in Brianna's water while she and I were dancing," Tess said.

"What?" Lily looked at me, and then at Tess. "Who?"

"We don't know," I said.

I didn't want to accuse anyone, but Tess didn't seem to have a problem doing so. "But we have our suspicions." She nodded toward the dance floor where Bridget was currently grinding herself against a blond guy not far from the VIP area.

Lily's eyes went wide. "You think Bridget put something in Brianna's drink?"

Tess laid it out for her. "You didn't do it. Brianna and I were dancing. That only leaves Bridget. No one else has been over here tonight besides the four of us and the server."

Lily's eyes narrowed. "I've had enough of this."

She stood, marched back onto the dance floor, and right up to Bridget. The other woman tried to pull Lily into the dance until Lily pushed her hand away. We couldn't hear what was said over the music, but neither Bridget nor Lily looked happy by the time Lily walked away.

"What happened?" Tess asked when Lily rejoined us.

"I told her she was no longer welcome at my wedding." Lily downed the water the server had brought in her absence and slammed it down on the table. "Damn. I need something stronger."

"I'm sorry." I hated causing trouble.

"This is not your fault, Brianna," Lily said.

"No. It's not," Tess echoed.

Lily looked around the club. "I'm ready to get out of here. The boys should still be out, so we'd have the house to ourselves."

Tess nodded. "Sounds good to me."

Lily let the bouncer who'd been monitoring our VIP section know that we were leaving, and then we went out front to catch a cab. It was only around nine o'clock, and there was still a line of people outside the club waiting to get in.

Everyone was quiet on the ride back to Lily's. The house was dark when we got here apart from a light in the foyer. We each hung up our coats and slipped off our shoes before making our way into the kitchen.

Lily pulled two shot glasses out of the cabinet and poured an amber colored liquid into them. She downed one, handed the other to Tess, and poured herself another.

I know she said I had nothing to apologize for, but I was still sorry her bachelorette party had been ruined. And that she'd lost a bridesmaid. I wanted to make it better for her, but I had no idea how.

Stephan

It was after eleven by the time we pulled up in front of Logan and Lily's house. We probably would have stayed longer, but the sports bar closed at eleven.

As we got out of the car, Caleb tripped over his own feet, almost falling into Logan's hedges. He was drunk and would probably pass out as soon as he was near a bed.

"Careful. You damage the bushes and Lily will have your head," Logan said. He was a little tipsy, as was Michael, but they were both still fully in control of their bodily functions. I wasn't so sure about Caleb. He'd had four beers and I don't know how many shots on top of the Sex on the Beach he'd originally ordered.

"Wouldn't want to do that," he said, slurring his words.

We'd been too distracted by Caleb's lack of coordination that we hadn't noticed that the girls were back. The club they'd gone to didn't close until two in the morning, so we hadn't expected them back so soon.

Logan unlocked the door and headed into the house. We found Brianna, Lily, and Tess on the couch. Brianna was on one end, curled up in a ball. Tess was at the opposite end with her head tilted toward the sky, and Lily's head in her lap. They were all sound asleep.

The four of us stood there staring at them for a few minutes, until Caleb broke the silence. "I need a bathroom."

"Down the hall to the left," Logan said.

Logan carried Lily up to bed, and then made the guest room up for Tess. Given the two empty wine bottles on the coffee table, they'd both been drinking. Or at least, I hoped it was both. That would be a lot of alcohol for one person.

Tess was groggy when Logan woke her to tell her he had the guest room ready for her. Luckily, she didn't fight him on it and followed him upstairs.

Michael and Caleb were crashing in the basement since neither of them was in a condition to drive and I wasn't driving all over town at this time of night.

I waited until the others had vacated the room before gathering Brianna in my arms. She stirred briefly, saw it was me, smiled, and then laid her head on my shoulder with a sigh. As I was heading out the door, Logan came down the stairs. "I'll call you tomorrow once I talk to Lily and find out what happened."

"We're going to Richard and Diane's around noon."

He nodded and locked up behind me.

Brianna didn't stir again until I took her out of the car. Her eyes fluttered open. "Sir?"

"Shh. We're at the condo. It's late. We'll talk tomorrow."

She yawned. "Okay."

I removed her clothing and helped her into bed. When she hadn't woken on the ride home or on the elevator ride, I'd thought maybe she'd indulged in some alcohol, but I didn't smell any on her breath.

"Sir?" she mumbled as I laid down beside her.

"Yes?"

"I don't like loud music." Then she rolled over to her side and fell back to sleep within seconds.

I chuckled, turned off the light, and closed my eyes. Whatever had happened, we'd deal with it tomorrow. Right now, we both needed sleep.

For the first time in a week, Brianna slept through the entire night. "Good morning," I said when I noticed she was awake.

"Good morning." She yawned. "What time is it?"

"A little after nine. I let you sleep in since I didn't know what time you, Lily, and Tess fell asleep."

"I don't know either. We were talking, and then I started getting tired, so I closed my eyes."

I nodded. "Logan and I found all three of you passed out on the couch with two empty bottles of wine nearby."

She knew what I was asking. "Lily and Tess drank them. And some shots."

I raised an eyebrow at that. "Lily drank shots?"

Brianna nodded. "She was really upset."

Lily was not one to drink shots. She preferred cocktails and wine. "What happened?"

As soon as I asked the question, Brianna averted her eyes and began twisting her hands in her lap. I knew I wasn't going to like whatever it was she was about to tell me.

"Can I go to the bathroom first?" she asked.

I was tempted to say no, but I nodded. "Go, and then join me in the living room. I want to know what happened last night before we sit down to breakfast."

"Yes, Sir."

Turning on my heel, I left her to take care of business and freshen up before having our talk. I was tempted to call Logan and see if he'd spoken with Lily yet, but I'd rather get the story from Brianna first.

I was sitting in my chair waiting for her when she walked out of our bedroom. She'd thrown on a pair of yoga pants and a T-shirt. I could tell by the way she was carrying herself that she was dreading what was to come, but I had no idea if that was because she'd done something she knew I'd be upset about or that something else had happened. Given Brianna was a good girl, my bet was on the latter.

That, and the fact that Bridget wasn't passed out in the living room last night with the rest of them.

Brianna climbed into my lap, but she didn't rest her head on my shoulder like she did when we were chatting about our day or life in general. She sat up, hands in her lap. I decided to cut to the chase. "What happened last night?"

"Lily had arranged for us to be in the VIP area so we could get away from the crowds. I was sitting there by myself, but then Tess came and asked me if I wanted to dance with her in the VIP area, so I didn't have to be with everyone else." She glanced up at me, and then back down. "I tried to dance with Lily on the dance floor with everyone else, but it was too much. A man tried to get me to dance with me. He held onto my hips and . . . and I froze."

As much as I didn't like the thought of another man's hands on her, I also understood how those types of clubs worked. "What happened?"

"Lily saw and stepped in. I went back to the VIP area after that."

While I was glad she'd shared that with me, it didn't explain Lily's reaction. "What else?"

"Tess came back, and she convinced me to dance with her. We stayed in the roped off area and danced by ourselves."

The muscles in her shoulders tensed and I knew something was coming, but I didn't know what.

"When we went back to our table to sit down, I reached for my water. Tess stopped me."

I turned her chin, so she was looking at me. "Go on."

"There was something in my water."

"Define 'something'."

"I don't know," she whispered. "It gave the water a yellow tint. Tess had the server get me another water."

It didn't take me long to conclude Lily must have realized. I knew how VIP sections at clubs worked. If you were on the list of VIPs, then you didn't get into the area. There were only four members of their party, so no one else would have been let in besides employees. "Did you all confront Bridget?"

Brianna tried to avert her eyes again, but I tightened my hold on her chin and she refocused on me. "Lily did. She never told us what she said to her, but we left the club shortly after that. Lily drank two shots as soon as we got to her house. She said Bridget was no longer in the wedding."

Well, that was good news. "You didn't drink any of the tainted water?"

She shook her head. "No. It wasn't yellow before we started dancing."

Most drugs people slipped in drinks were colorless. That's why they were so hard to detect and often went unnoticed by the victim until they started feeling the effects.

I released her chin and reached for the phone and dialed Logan. He answered on the first ring. I got right to the point. "Did Lily tell you what happened."

"Yes. Is Brianna okay?" he asked.

"Yes. Thanks to Tess." I paused. "I wish we knew what was in the water and that she put it there."

"Well, the what might be doable," Logan said. "I called my friend who owns the club, and he said the server brought the tainted glass to him last night and he took a sample. He said they do that anytime something like that is brought to their attention, in case police end up getting involved."

"Does he have a way to find out what it is?" If he didn't, I could find someone.

"Yeah. He has a friend that can test it for the common street drugs. I told him to go ahead. Even if we can't nail Bridget, I want to know what it was."

"Agreed." Then I thought of something. "Does your friend have cameras in the club?" Who knows, they might get lucky and have caught her on tape.

"He does, but not from every angle. I can have him check, but I doubt it's going to prove anything. At least, not legally."

"Let me know once he finds out what it was."

I disconnected the call and immediately dialed my lawyer, Oscar.

He answered on the third ring. "It's Sunday, you know. Some of us like to take a day off now and then."

"Someone spiked Brianna's drink last night at a club," I said, getting right to the point.

His tone changed immediately. "What do you need me to do?"

"We think Bridget, a friend of Lily's, is responsible. We haven't found any evidence to prove it yet, but we're working on it." I let that sink in before I continued. "I want to find out everything I can about this woman and if she has any history of doing this kind of thing. Lily's kicked her out of her wedding, but something tells me she isn't just going to go away quietly."

"I'll call my guy as soon as we hang up and let you know as soon as he has something."

"Thanks, Oscar."

Once I ended the called, I turned my attention back to Brianna who was still sitting in my lap. She looked guilty for some reason.

"Talk to me, sweetheart. What's wrong?"

She looked up at me through her lashes. "I keep thinking this never would have happened if Lily hadn't asked me to be in her wedding. If she'd asked someone normal, then Bridget wouldn't have reacted the way she did, and Lily wouldn't have lost a bridesmaid a week before her wedding."

"You didn't do anything wrong. This is all on Bridget. She's been trouble since we met her the first time you went dress shopping. None of this is your fault."

"Tess and Lily said the same thing."

I tucked a strand of hair behind her ear. "They're both very smart ladies."

Brianna's lips began to pull up with a hint of a smile.

Cupping the back of her head, I pulled her in for a kiss. "How about some breakfast. I'm starving."

This time I got a genuine smile out of her. "Yes, Sir."

CHAPTER 30

Brianna

It was the day of the wedding and I was doing my best not to panic. Again.

This happened every time I experienced something new. Both Stephan and Dr. Katlin said it was normal, but that didn't make it any easier. Or make me feel less out of place.

Last night, we'd all met at the barn where the wedding would take place. Using the term barn was misleading. Sure, on the outside it had the shape of a barn and the inside was big and open with high ceilings, but that was where the similarities to a shelter normally meant for animals stopped.

There were crystal chandeliers hanging from the ceiling and the entire floor was covered in a wood planking that had been polished to a high shine. Tables were set up in the center with a raised platform along the back wall. It was beautiful and I could see why Lily picked it.

The wedding wasn't until three-thirty in the afternoon, but we had to be there early to start getting ready. Stephan, as the best man, had to make sure everything and everyone was where they were supposed to be . . . including the two security guys Stephan hired to cover the entrance.

Lily was already there when we arrived. "Good. You're here," she said as soon as she saw me. "You can help distract me."

"What's wrong?" I asked as she dragged me into a side room. I looked over my shoulder at Stephan as she pulled me away.

"Go easy on her, Lily," he called before Lily shut the door, separating us.

She led me over to a huge mirror that was surrounded by lights. "Nothing's wrong," she said, encouraging me to sit in the chair. "Not yet anyway."

I glanced up at her, confused.

"I just want everything to be perfect, that's all."

"And you're afraid something will go wrong?" I asked.

She blew out a breath. "I don't know. But I can't be out there coordinating things like I usually do at big events, and it's driving me crazy."

That made sense. Lily wasn't used to giving up control . . . unless it was to Logan. She was always making sure everything was just right. And she was great at it.

"Stephan and Logan will take care of anything that comes up." Although Stephan wasn't as good at organizing events as Lily, he was good at fixing things. If something came up, he'd figure it out.

She sighed. "I know. And I'm trying not to freak out, but I've waited so long for this day and I don't want anything to go wrong."

I smiled at her in the mirror and placed a hand over hers. "It won't."

She grinned back at me. "You ready for me to start on your hair and make-up?"

For the next hour, she pinned my hair back, put several creams on my face, then buffed and polished it. At noon, Tess joined us and a woman that worked there brought us some lunch. The three of us sat around talking. I was a lot more relaxed with Bridget gone.

During the rehearsal the night before, they'd had to do some rearranging since there were now only two people in the bride's party and three in the groom's. It was decided that Caleb and Michael would both walk me down the aisle after the ceremony was over.

I couldn't help but chuckle as I remembered Stephan telling Caleb that if he laid one inappropriate hand on me that he'd told me to kick him in the balls. Caleb had gone pale. He looked at me as if assessing whether Stephan was telling the truth.

He was. We'd had a long conversation Thursday night, going over everything having to do with the wedding. He'd ended the conversation by saying if Caleb, or anyone else, touched me inappropriately or cornered me that I was to use my self-defense training.

Caleb had been on his best behavior after that. Not that he was doing anything before that, really, but he was a lot more cautious afterward.

Once lunch was over, Lily finished my makeup and went to work on Tess. "You know, we're supposed to be doing this to you. Not the other way around," Tess said.

Lily pinned Tess's hair back away from her face and reached for her supplies. "Some traditions are meant to be broken."

Everyone, including Lily, was ready to go, except for our dresses by two-thirty. We all took turns in the adjoining bathroom before getting into our dresses. While going to the bathroom wouldn't be all that difficult in our bridesmaid dresses, Lily's was another story.

At three fifteen, there was a knock on the door. "Who is it?" Tess asked.

"Stephan."

My heart skipped a beat at the sound of his voice.

Tess opened the door and let him in the room.

His gaze fell on me and I went to him. I couldn't help it.

He skimmed his thumb down the side of my face, careful not to undo the work Lily had done on my face or hair. "You look beautiful, sweetheart."

"Is there a problem?" Lily asked, coming to stand beside me.

"No. Everything's ready to go and the last guests are being seated as we speak."

Lily took a deep breath. I'd never seen her so nervous, although I guess it made sense. This was her big day, after all.

"You ladies all set?" he asked.

"Yes," Tess said from my other side. "Let's get this show on the road and put Lily out of her misery."

Stephan chuckled. "All right. I'll let the minster know we're good to go." Then he looked at me. "I'll see you in a few minutes."

"Wow." Tess gathered up our bouquets and handed them to each of us. "I'm not sure how you two got so lucky, but I need some of it. All the guys I date are duds."

Lily looked over at me but didn't say anything.

We did a last check of our make-up, and then it was time to go.

The walk from the room we'd been getting ready in and the main room where the ceremony would take place wasn't far. As soon as we stepped out of the dressing room, I could hear the music playing. It got louder the closer we came.

As the volume increased, so did my nerves. I held tight to the bouquet in my hands even as sweat coated my palms.

I can do this, I told myself over and over again. Stephan was standing beside Logan at the far end of the room. I was safe and I was with our friends. Everything was fine.

A hand touched my arm before I became visible to the guests. I jumped a little and turned to see Lily looking at me with concern. "Are you doing okay?" she asked.

I decided to be honest. "Yes. Just nervous. Once I see Stephan, I'll be okay."

She nodded.

Taking a deep breath, I took the final steps that would lead me into the main room. Everyone turned to stare at me, but I tuned them out and found Stephan standing at the back next to Logan.

He never took his eyes off me as I walked down the makeshift aisle. And when I finally reached the front to take my place on Lily's side of the stage, he held my gaze for a long moment and I could see the pride in his eyes.

Tess came to stand next to me, and then the music changed, and everyone turned to watch Lily walk down the aisle. Like me, she didn't take her eyes off her man as she walked. And when she put her hand in his and he led her to stand in front of the minister, a warmth spread through my chest all the way down to my toes.

My nerves fell away as I listened to the words of the ceremony. Logan turned to Stephan and Stephan handed him the rings. Lily beamed as Logan slid the ring on her finger.

When it was finally time for the groom to kiss the bride, Logan didn't hold back. He pulled Lily into his arms, cupping the back of her head, and gave her a kiss that not only sealed their union, but staked his claim as well.

Several people in the audience were chuckling by the time they separated, including the minister. "And now, it is my joy to present to you for the first time, Mr. and Mrs. Logan Mattson."

Logan led Lily down the aisle. Then, Stephan offered his arm to Tess. Once they were on their way, Michael and Caleb got on either side of me and each held out an arm for me to take.

We reached the back of the room and I released Michael and Caleb's arms. It was over. I'd made it through without having a panic attack.

Stephan

By the time I'd gotten to the back with Tess, Logan already had Lily gathered up in another kiss. "You know you'll have plenty of time for that later, right?" I teased him.

He laughed and set her feet back down on the floor. "Yes, but why wait?"

I smiled and shook my head, turning to watch Brianna make her way toward me. She was smiling, but I could tell by the way her eyes were darting around that she was nervous. It was unavoidable given how anxious she was around crowds. She'd done great today and for the remainder of the evening she'd be by my side. The hard part was over.

Caleb kept his hands where they were supposed to be, and when the three reached us, Brianna released them and came straight to me. I pulled her into my arms. "You did great, sweetheart."

She smiled—this one not tainted by fear or uncertainty.

With the ceremony over, people began to move around in the background. Logan and Lily made their way back to the main room to greet their guests and allow the attendees to congratulate them.

"What do we do now?" Brianna asked.

"I'm gonna go check on the food," Tess said, then looked at Stephan. "Can you make sure the band is good to go?"

She didn't wait for a response before walking away.

"Need us to do anything?" Michael asked.

I looked around. "Why don't you see if the minster needs anything. Other than that, I think you're good until the photographer's ready for pictures." I scanned the area and found him hovering near Logan and Lily, snapping random pictures of them talking to guests.

They took off toward the front again, leaving Brianna and I alone. "Number?"

"Four."

I kissed the top of her head. "Let's go check on the band.

As I went to turn, my gaze landed on a lone figure standing in the far corner near the dressing room Lily and the girls used earlier that day.

"What's wrong?" Brianna asked, noticing the change in my mood.

The figure turned to walk away, and I realized who it was. Bridget. How had she gotten in? "I'll be right back."

Leaving Brianna wasn't something I wanted to do, but I didn't plan on being gone long. Bridget was here, and I needed to find out why. I didn't want her ruining Logan and Lily's day.

I followed her into the girls dressing room, but when I got inside, she wasn't there.

Then, the door closed behind me. I turned around and came face-to-face with the woman in question. She was dressed in a black cocktail dress that was a little too short to be considered appropriate at a wedding.

"What are you doing here and how did you get in?" I asked, getting straight to the point.

We'd gotten the test results back from Brianna's water glass earlier in the week. The added ingredient had been alcohol. More specifically, Tequila. That's what had given the water it's yellow tint. And while I knew it could have been worse, that she could have spiked Brianna's drink with any number of drugs, I was livid Bridget had tampered with the drink at all. If I could have her prosecuted for it, I would do so in a heartbeat, but as of yet, we hadn't found the evidence we'd need to pursue a legal case.

None of the bartenders remembered serving her a drink with Tequila in it and none of the video surveillance had shown anything either. I was betting she'd gotten someone to buy it for her, but again, proving it was the issue. Unless we could find the person who'd made the purchase and have them confirm that they'd given the drink to Bridget, we didn't have anything to go to the authorities with. Oscar was still working on it and he also had someone digging into her past. I was hoping they'd find something we could use. I didn't like people targeting Brianna and that's exactly what she'd done.

"I had some unfinished business to take care of." She pushed herself away from the door and toward me.

I stood my ground as she made her way to where I was in the center of the room. She went to touch my chest and I grabbed hold of her wrist. Unfortunately, that didn't stop her. She lifted her other arm, ready to attempt the same maneuver again. I intercepted that one as well.

Bridget tugged on her arms, trying to break free. When I didn't let go, she got a gleam in her eye I didn't like. "You like it, rough? I can do that. I like it rough once and awhile, too."

"You have no idea what I like or want for that matter." I took a step back to put a little distance between us and released her. "Now, answer the question, why are you here? It's my understanding that Lily told you that you weren't welcome."

"There was something here I wanted."

"And what might that be?" I asked, not really caring, but needing to get her out of here before she disrupted the reception.

"Why, you, of course." It came out in what was meant to be a sultry purr, but it did nothing for me. In fact, her actions reminded me way too much of my ex, Tami.

"In case you haven't noticed, I'm with Brianna."

"But you don't have to be. I'm so much better for you than she is." She took a step toward me again. "I doubt she can truly satisfy you. You need a real woman to do that."

I laughed. I couldn't stop myself. The notion that Brianna couldn't satisfy me was insane beyond comprehension. "I think you should go."

"But—"

The door opened, drawing our attention. Brianna looked at Bridget for a long moment, and then came to stand by my side. "You need to leave," Brianna said. "Lily doesn't want you here." She paused, and then added, "I don't want you here, either."

"I'm here for Stephan," she said, overconfident. "He deserves to have a real woman on his arm, not a mouse who doesn't know what she wants."

Brianna glanced up at me, and then back to her. "I know what I want. Stephan's mine and I'm his."

To hear her stake her claim and not be timid about it made my heart soar. Especially with what I had burning a hole in my pocket.

"We're done here," I said. "You need to leave, or I'll contact the authorities and have you arrested for trespassing."

She looked at both of us, huffed, and then turned on her heels to go.

"Oh, and Bridget?"

She stopped and looked back, hopeful.

I was about to burst her bubble. "If you ever come near me or Brianna again, I'll have you investigated for stalking."

Bridget held up her middle finger before sauntering out of the room. I grabbed Brianna's hand and followed her out to make sure she was leaving.

We stood in the foyer, flanked by the two men I'd hired, and watched as Bridget got into her car. "Make sure she doesn't come back," I said to the men before Brianna and I headed back into the reception.

Logan and Lily were still making their rounds, oblivious to what had occurred, and I breathed a sigh of relief. While they finished greeting their guests, I finished the task I'd originally set out to do and checked in with the band. With them ready to go and Logan and Lily finishing up, the wedding party gathered in the front for pictures while the caterers served appetizers to the guests.

Brianna did well with the pictures and didn't seem fazed by what had happened with Bridget. She wasn't nervous standing next to Lily or Tess, and anytime there was a group picture, and she wasn't with the girls, I made sure she was next to me.

By the time the pictures were finished, I was starving, and I knew Brianna had to be, as well. The lunch that was provided earlier had long since left my system.

The wedding party sat together at a long table that had been set up in the front, right in the middle of where the aisle used to be. While it was tradition that the bridesmaids sat beside the bride and the groomsmen sat beside the groom, I nixed that idea and sat Brianna beside me.

"I'll sit beside Tess," Caleb said.

I nodded. "Thanks." Caleb wasn't a bad guy, but he still acted like he was in his early twenties rather than thirty-two.

The servers brought over a plate of appetizers for the table. Everyone put a few on the small plate they'd given us and devoured them within seconds. Luckily, we didn't have to wait long before our salads arrived.

As the meal wound down, Logan helped Lily from her chair and walked her over to where the large cake was set up in the corner. Lily had wanted something spectacular and it was something to behold. The cake was five tiers high and had flowers draping over the sides. Last night she'd explained to all of us all the details and layers of the cake, but it went over my head. It may have made sense to Brianna, but I had no idea what the difference was between buttercream icing and regular icing or why it was a good thing.

We all laughed as Logan and Lily smashed cake in each other's faces, and then Logan kissed her like no one was watching. I heard a few throats clearing, but as there were no children in the room, whoever it was would have to deal with it.

Once everyone was seated again and eating cake, it was time for Tess and me to make our speeches. She went first.

"Lily and I met because she stole my crayon." The crowd laughed. "We were six years old and I'd just moved to the neighborhood. I'd run inside to get a snack and when I came back, my crayon was gone." She glanced over at Lily who was smiling at the memory. "When she heard me crying, she brought it back and we ended up coloring for hours on the front step of my house." She paused. "It was the first of many days like that. And after coloring books and crayons we spent hours together learning how to do makeup and talking about boys."

Tess took a drink of her water, then continued. "So, when she called me to tell me she'd met Logan, I knew I had to meet him. I knew right away he was as crazy about her as she was him. They did that whole starry-eyed thing."

Everyone laughed again.

Smiling, Tess looked down at the couple beside her. "They haven't stopped looking at each other that way and I hope they never do." She raised her champagne glass. "To many happy years together as husband and wife."

Everyone toasted the couple, and then it was my turn.

I stood and cleared my throat. "Thank you all for coming tonight to celebrate Logan and Lily's marriage. Logan saved my life back when we were teenagers, and so when he saw Lily across the room at an event we were attending and asked me to introduce them, I couldn't say no." That got a chuckle from the guests.

"What he didn't know was that moments earlier, she'd asked me for the exact same thing." Laughter filled the space, and I even heard a whistle from the back of the room.

I waited for the noise level to die down, and then continued. "After that night, I knew there was no turning back. They were both smitten and only had eyes for each other. The love and commitment . . . the devotion Logan and Lily have for each other is something we should all aspire to in our relationships." I lifted my champagne glass, which had been filled with sparkling grape juice instead of champagne, and the crowd all raised their own glasses. "To Logan and Lily. May you never lose the qualities that make you each unique, nor your love for each other. Here's to many happy years to come."

"Here, here," everyone toasted and drank from their glasses.

I sat down and Logan turned to me. "I was worried there for a minute. I thought you were going to talk about how we used to sneak out."

Taking another sip from my glass, I peered at him over the rim. "I thought about it.

He smirked, and then got pulled away when Lily's aunt wanted to talk to them both.

Once all the cake plates were taken from the tables, the band announced that it was time for the first song. He asked for the bride and groom to make their way to the dance floor as the lights in the room were dimmed.

In the time it had taken everyone to finish their meals, the stage area where Logan and Lily had said their vows had been transformed into a dance floor. Both times we'd seen the space before tonight it had been set up with the stage and I hadn't realized there was a set of large windows along the back wall that looked out at the lake.

The sun had already set, and the moonlight reflected off the water. It was a breathtaking view and I understood right then why Lily had picked this venue.

Logan guided Lily in front of the window as the band began to play. I heard Brianna sigh beside me, and I knew she was thinking the same thing I was. Patting my breast pocket, I made sure the ring I'd placed there earlier was still safe. I'd been carrying it around all week, trying to find a good time to ask her, but nothing ever seemed right.

"Lily's so beautiful," Brianna said. "She looks like Ginger Rogers in her dress."

"She does, doesn't she." Given both Logan and Lily attended fundraisers on a regular basis, both knew how to dance. They twirled around the dance floor never taking their eyes off each other.

CHAPTER 31

Brianna

It was like a fairytale.

There were strands of white lights hung around the dance floor and the light coming off the lake made it feel magical.

After Logan and Lily finished their dance, the band invited the rest of the bridal party to join in. Stephan stood and held his hand out to me. "May I have this dance?"

"Yes, Sir." I placed my hand in his and he led me to the dance floor.

It felt good to be in his arms again. The day had been crazy and after the ceremony, there hadn't been time for much besides holding hands, even though all I wanted to do was crawl into his lap after what happened with Bridget. I relaxed into him, resting my head on his shoulder. It was almost as good as being in his lap. Not quite. But almost.

"You doing okay?" he asked.

I nodded.

He kissed the top of my head and moved us around the floor. The song ended, but he kept going as other couples got up from their seats and began dancing. I closed my eyes and ignored them.

I have no idea how many songs we danced to, but eventually

Stephan stopped moving, tipped my head up, and placed a soft kiss on my lips. "Let's take a break. It's going to be a long night and I don't want to wear you out."

He led us back to our table and held out my chair for me. "I'll be right back. I'm going to get us some waters."

Almost as soon as he was gone, Tess sat down beside me. She kicked off her shoes. "My feet are going to hate me tomorrow."

"Mine are hurting a little, too," I said.

She motioned toward my feet. "So, take off your shoes. No one's gonna care."

Doing as she suggested, I slipped them off and placed them under my chair. The cool air hit my feet and it felt good.

I must have made a noise or something because Tess laughed. "See. I told you so. There's no better feeling than taking heels off after a long day. Or night, as it were."

"I don't know how Lily wears them all the time," I said.

"Me, neither. You couldn't pay me enough to wear high heels every day."

Stephan returned and set a glass of water in front of me. I picked it up and downed half of it, not realizing how thirsty I was until the cool liquid hit my tongue.

"Did you want something, Tess?" Stephan asked.

"Water would be heavenly. Do you mind?"

"Not at all." He handed her the other glass in his hand. "Here. Have mine. I'll go get another."

"Normally, I'd ask if you're sure, but I'm so thirsty, I don't care. Thank you."

Stephan smiled and went to get another water for himself.

Tess took a long drink. "Lily said you were thinking of going back to school."

I nodded. "I'm registered to start at the local community college in January. It's just my GED, but it's a start."

"She mentioned you hadn't been able to finish high school."

I thought maybe she'd ask me for details as to why, but she didn't.

"We should all try to get together after Logan and Lily get back from their honeymoon."

"I don't know," I said, glancing down.

"No pressure, but I was thinking a girls' weekend would be nice after all this."

I'd done a few girls' weekends with Jade and Lily before that were really fun. And I liked Tess. "Would you mind if Jade came?"

"Nope. The more the merrier." Then she tilted her head down and looked at me over her glass. "As long as they aren't anything like Bridget."

"No. Nothing like Bridget."

Tess glanced around the room. "To tell you the truth, I'm kind of surprised she didn't show up tonight. I wonder what Lily said to her."

"I asked her, but she wouldn't tell me."

Tess took another drink and nodded. "So, did I and I got the same response. Guess we'll never know."

Stephan pulled out the chair on the other side of me and sat down.

"Thanks again for letting me hijack your water," Tess said.

"You're welcome." Then he glanced down at my shoes that I'd tucked under my chair. "How are your feet doing?"

"Better. They will probably be sore tomorrow, though."

He took a sip of his water. "Why don't you leave your shoes off for the rest of the night."

I nodded. Stephan had phrased it as a question, but I knew that was because Tess was there.

The three of us sat there talking until Michael came back to the table and asked Tess if she wanted to dance with him. She slipped her shoes back on and stood. "Guess I'll catch you both later."

Michael led Tess onto the dance floor. It was obvious neither of them were great dancers, but they kept going anyway.

"I think she likes him," I said.

"I don't know him that well, but he seems like a decent guy."

"Better than Caleb?"

I giggled at his scowl. "He's older than I am and acts like he's still in college. He needs to grow up."

The man in question was straddling a chair about fifteen feet away. He was talking to three women I didn't know, but thought they were related to Lily somehow. "He likes being the center of attention."

"Yes, he does." Stephan took my hand in his and played with my fingers. "And he's a big flirt."

I saw him talking to Tess during dinner, leaning into her a little too close. She'd blushed a couple of times, too, which made me wonder what he'd said to her.

"Did you want to dance some more?" Stephan asked, motioning toward the floor. "Or would you rather rest your feet?"

I took a moment to think about it. My feet weren't hurting like they had been. And he didn't want me wearing shoes for the rest of the night. "Can I dance without my shoes?"

"Of course." As if my question was the answer to his question, he got up from his chair and pulled me with him.

We danced through a few more songs, and then it was time for Logan and Lily to say good night. They were spending the evening at a bed and breakfast not far from the event and catching a flight early the next morning to the Bahamas.

Everyone gathered near the entrance and formed an aisle. As Logan and Lily made their way toward the door, everyone blew bubbles. I hadn't blown bubbles since my mom was alive. It was more fun than I'd remembered.

Once Logan and Lily drove off, the rest of the guests began to leave, as well. As the best man, Stephan had to stay till the end.

"Are you sure you don't want me to stay, too?" Tess asked. "I don't mind."

"I'm sure. Brianna and I will stay until everyone's left and make sure things are taken care of."

Tess didn't ask twice. She gathered up her things and headed out.

There were only about a dozen people left, all of them gathered in small groups, talking. Stephan went to let the band know they could wrap up for the night since no one was dancing anymore. Slowly, everyone else besides the band, who was still disassembling their instruments, and the catering staff, headed home.

I figured we'd do the same once Stephan talked to the caterers, but instead he led me back on the dance floor to stand in front of the big windows. It had begun to snow about an hour before, reflecting even more light off the lake. I couldn't take my eyes off it.

"It's so beautiful," I whispered.

"It is."

Stephan's hand came up to cup my face and I noticed it was moist. He hadn't been to the bathroom recently and it wasn't cold, so I didn't think it had come from the condensation on the water glasses.

He swallowed and I realized he was nervous. Stephan never got nervous. At least, not enough that he showed any physical signs of his anxiety. Worry pooled in the pit of my stomach. Had something happened after Bridget's appearance I didn't know about?

I placed my hand on his chest, feeling the firm beat of his heart through his jacket.

With his free hand, he picked up my fingers and brought them to his lips. "I wanted to do this right. You deserve that and so much more."

"I don't understand."

Stephan removed his hand from my face but kept hold of my other one as he knelt in front of me. "You are the most beautiful woman I know. Inside and out. I knew the first time I saw you that you'd change my life forever. I just didn't realize it was because I would fall in love with you."

He reached inside his jacket and pulled out a small box. It was then I realized what was happening . . . what he was doing.

A tear rolled down my cheek as he flipped open the box to reveal the prettiest ring I'd ever seen.

"I can't imagine not spending the rest of my life with you and I want the whole world to know you're mine. Whatever the future has in store for us, we can tackle it together." He kissed the back of my left hand and held my gaze. "Brianna Reeves, will you marry me?"

Tears were streaming down my face as he presented the ring to me. Was this real? Did he really want me to be his wife?

"Sweetheart?"

He was waiting on an answer.

There was no doubt as to what my answer would be.

"Yes."

"Yes?" His smile lit up his face.

I nodded and he released my left hand long enough to slip the ring on it.

There was some clapping in the background as he stood and took my face in his hands, but I barely noticed it. His mouth covered mine in a slow kiss that I felt all the way down to my toes.

When our lips parted, he rested his forehead against mine, the emotion he was feeling there in his eyes.

I couldn't wait to marry him.

Are you ready for another story from Sherri Hayes? Find a complete list of her books at www.sherrihayesauthor.com.

***

Sign up for Sherri's newsletter to make sure you don't miss any of her new releases and sales at https://gem.godaddy.com/ signups/269082/join

After losing her husband unexpectedly, Katrina Mayer decided to open Serpent's Kiss. She wanted it to be a place where she and her fellow kinksters could play and socialize.

Five years after the doors opened, the club is everything she'd hoped it would be. On Friday and Saturday nights, Serpent's Kiss is filled with men and women who share a similar desire to explore the pleasures BDSM has to offer. The club has continued to grow, and over the years, many of its members have become friends.

The one thing Katrina didn't expect when she'd decided to open a club was the human drama that came with it. Learning to balance her life as the club mistress has taken some getting used to, but she wouldn't change a thing.

View the entire Serpent's Kiss series on Sherri's website at www. sherrihayesauthor.com.

SNEAK PEEK OF WELCOME TO SERPENT'S KISS

Katrina Mayer glanced at the clock. She had a few more minutes before she needed to head upstairs. It was enough time for her to glance over the newest membership application she'd received.

The applicant's name was Drew Parker. He was a firefighter and listed himself as submissive. Everything about him seemed fairly straightforward. He was twenty-eight. Single. And looking for a kinky relationship with a female dominant.

As she scanned the rest of his details, two Femdoms came to mind—Madi and Beth. Madi was a regular. The club was open every Friday and Saturday night, and Madi rarely missed the opportunity to have some fun. Every now and then, she'd play with one of the male subs, but it was rare. More often than not, Madi could be found on the dance floor.

Beth was another story. To be honest, Katrina was worried about her. Beth used to come to the club all the time with her longtime sub, Ben. Two months ago, Beth discovered that Ben had a secret life she'd known nothing about. It had left her shattered and heartbroken. She hadn't been to the club since it happened. For the time being, Beth had no desire to get back on the horse. Katrina was hoping that would change with time.

It wasn't her job to be a matchmaker, however. She'd created Serpent's Kiss as a place where kinky people could hang out and play when the mood struck them.

Speaking of moods, Katrina was in the mood to have some fun. She pushed back from her desk and walked out into the hall. After locking the door to her office, she headed down to the main room of the club, where Ali and Brandon were getting things ready for later that night.

Brandon, her main bartender, caught her eye. She tilted her head toward the stairs, and he nodded.

Katrina rarely played while the club was open unless it was to do a demonstration. Things were too hectic, and all too often, she was needed to help with one issue or another. Plus, it was always good to mingle with the club members and make sure they were content.

It was for that reason that she tended to play before the club opened its doors to the evening crowd. Brandon and whichever submissive had signed up for the evening service arrived three hours before the club opened to prep and clean. It was the perfect opportunity for her to sneak upstairs to have a little fun while still being safe. She always kept the door open to whatever room she used, and Brandon was aware that the upstairs was off-limits during those times unless he heard someone yell red.

Ascending the stairs, she entered the first room on her right. All the rooms on the second floor had been turned into playrooms. Each was well equipped with a variety of toys that could be adapted to specific needs for whatever situation arose. She'd tried to make the rooms as versatile as possible.

Ryan was kneeling on the floor waiting. As per her instructions and their arrangement, he was waiting for her naked. His cock hadn't been erect when she'd walked into the room, but as she stood there looking at him, she saw it stiffening.

Katrina had prepared the space earlier that day with all the items she would need for the scene. They were all placed within easy reach at the back of the room. Now, all she had to do was get her submissive in place.

"Stand," she ordered.

Ryan rocked back on his heels and nimbly pushed himself up off the floor and to his feet.

She picked up a spreader bar and nudged his feet apart. With the spreader bar in place, she removed two leather cuffs from the table. One by one, she encircled his wrists and then lifted his arms above his head to attach the cuffs to the chains in the ceiling. Once she was sure they were secure, Katrina stepped back to appreciate her subject.

Ryan was thirty-five and a lawyer. You'd never know he spent most of his time behind a desk. He worked out every morning and ate healthier than she cared to think about. She had a weakness for cake. It didn't look as if he even thought about processed sugar, much less ate it.

Nonetheless, Ryan was one of her favorite submissives to play with. Katrina didn't have a submissive of her own. She had no desire for one, either. At the age of forty-three, she'd found herself widowed. And while she'd loved her husband, he had been vanilla as vanilla could be. Even role-playing in the bedroom held no interest for him.

Her husband's death had been a shock. It had also made her realize how short life was. No one knew how long they had on this earth. That was why, six months after her husband's death, Katrina made the decision to open up a fetish club. Five years later, the club was exactly what she hoped it would be. Every Friday and Saturday night, Serpent's Kiss was packed with members who paid a monthly fee for privacy and convenience.

Katrina's heels clicked on the wooden floor of the dungeon as she slowly circled Ryan. She ran a hand down his chest and could feel the anticipation rolling off him. There was something about seeing a man bound and ready for whatever she wanted to do to him that gave her immense pleasure.

She didn't take her eyes off his face as she moved her hand down over his abs, heading for the straining erection between his legs.

He lowered his head and closed his eyes . . . waiting.

When she brushed her hand against his cock, he tensed. "Have something you wish to say?"

He shook his head.

Taking hold of his balls with her right hand, Katrina squeezed. "Are you sure?"

"Yes, Ma'am. I'm sure." His eyes remained closed, but his breathing had picked up. He knew pain was coming, and what she'd just done to his balls was only the tip of the iceberg.

She released her hold on him. "Very well. Let's get things started, shall we?"

A long table along the wall held a plethora of items she'd selected for their scene. Some she would use. Some she wouldn't. She liked having options.

Running her fingers over the small metal clothespins, she grinned and placed several in her hand before returning to stand in front of Ryan. He hadn't moved—not that he could go very far.

With her free hand, she took hold of one of his nipples and worked it between her thumb and index finger until it was ready to accept the clip she had poised in her left hand. Giving his nipple a hard pinch, she replaced her fingers with the silver clip.

To his credit, he didn't react beyond a small intake of breath. Ryan liked pain. That was good, since she liked to inflict it. Katrina considered herself a sadist. She liked to mix pain with pleasure.

Without pause, she moved to his other nipple and placed another clip on the hardened flesh. He was ready this time and didn't react in any way.

That won't do, Katrina mused. Returning the remaining clothespins to the table, she grasped each clip by the extended ears and pulled sharply.

Ryan hadn't been expecting that, and his reaction was exactly what she'd been hoping for. She saw his jaw flex and then clench.

Releasing him, she gathered up the clothespins again and began placing them where she wanted them. By the time she was finished, he had forty of the miniature clips in various places on his body including his sides, arms, inner thighs, cock and balls. She'd made sure to space them far enough apart for what she had planned.

"How are you doing?" she asked, caressing the side of his face. He trusted her with his submission. She didn't take that lightly.

Ryan opened his eyes and met her gaze. "Good, Ma'am."

"Are you ready to continue?"

"Yes, Ma'am."

While Katrina didn't mind people in the club referring to her as " Mistress," she required submissives scening with her to call her "Ma'am." She wasn't anyone's Mistress. She was the club Mistress, yes, but that was different. The club belonged to her. Ryan and the other male submissives she played with did not.

She nodded and donned a pair of latex gloves. Once they were in place, she lubed her fingers and picked up one of her favorite anal toys. It had three silicone beads that gradually increased in size on one end. The beads were perfect for stimulating the prostate. Where the beads ended, the toy curved around to provide additional stimulation to the perineum. Considering the fun she intended to have with the clothespins, the added pleasure to Ryan's prostate and perineum would have him on the edge in no time.

Without warning, Katrina inserted a single gloved finger into Ryan's ass. She made sure he was relaxed before adding another finger, and then another. Once she was confident he was significantly prepped, she removed her fingers, added some lube to the toy, and pressed it in place. His cheeks flexed around the intrusion, but otherwise he remained still.

That was, until she turned on the vibrations. A ripple went through his body, and he clenched his fists.

She watched his cock grow even harder as the toy continued to work its magic. Smirking, she removed her gloves and then went to the far wall to remove her single-tail whip. When she began researching BDSM, she had known immediately that she was a top. Submission held no appeal for her. Domination, however, was a different story. The first time she laid eyes on the whip she held between her fingers, it had felt as if it belonged in her grasp. She made the decision that day to learn all she could about how to wield a whip properly, and her determination had paid off.

Unfurling the whip, she let the tail dangle against her leg before giving Ryan's backside a quick crack. It wasn't meant to hurt so much as get his attention.

Get his attention it did. Ryan snapped his head up. He'd been so caught up in all the sensations that he hadn't been paying attention to her. Well, that would change.

She stepped closer to him, running the tips of her fingers over the clothespins. "Which one should I remove first, do you think? Hmm?"

His eyes widened as what she was about to do sank in. She'd used the clothespins on him before, as well as the whip, but she'd never combined the two. Over the last few months, she'd been working diligently on her aim. It had been good for the last two years, but she'd wanted it to be excellent. After hours of practicing, she was ready. Ryan just happened to be the lucky one to benefit from all her training.

Without another word, she took several steps back, putting room between her and Ryan. A flick of her wrist later, the whip made contact with one of the clips attached to the inside of his thigh. He jerked when the clothespin detached and landed onto the floor.

She didn't give him time to recover. One by one, Katrina removed each metal clothespin with the tail of her whip, leaving the ones clinging to his cock and balls for last. By that point, he was sweating. Ryan's eyes were closed once again, and his entire body was vibrating with unreleased energy. He looked as if he were about ready to explode.

Tossing her whip to the side, she came to stand in front of him. "Open your eyes. Look at me."

Slowly he opened his lids to stare down at her. His pupils were dark—almost black in the soft light of the dungeon. "You're okay to continue?"

"Yes . . . Ma'am." The words were broken and barely above a whisper. She knew Ryan, though. He would safeword if he needed to.

She lowered her mouth over one of his nipples, grazing it with her teeth. This time, he tilted his head back. He would have been looking at the eyebolts in the ceiling if not for the fact that his eyes were closed. Ryan embraced everything she gave him. It was one of the reasons she enjoyed playing with him.

Keeping her lips on his skin, she reached between them and ripped off the three clips she'd attached to the underside of his cock in quick succession. Before he had time to recover, she wrapped her hand around his length and began scraping her nails along his erection with each pass of her palm. Katrina increased the suction of her mouth, biting down every now and then. He was trembling and completely at her mercy. She loved it.

There were still two clothespins attached to each of his testicles. She switched her mouth to his other nipple, treating it to the same sucking and biting as she had the first. He was close. Very close. It wouldn't take much to send him over the edge.

With her free hand, she began playing with his balls, toying with the clips. His cock was pulsing in her hand. Their play agreement didn't include her having control over his orgasms. He could come whenever he wished. Ryan, however, tended to like to draw it out for as long as he could. He was a masochist that way—another reason he made a good play partner.

She kept up her actions until she knew he was right there, teetering on the edge. Without warning, she bit down hard, sinking her teeth into his chest at the same time that she yanked the two clothespins from his balls.

Ryan arched his back, letting out a strangled cry as he let go. His climax covered her hand, and a few drops landed on the leather corset she was wearing.

With the hand that wasn't covered in spunk, Katrina leaned down and freed him from the spreader bar. Then she stood and walked around to his backside to remove the butt plug from his ass. Once that was extracted and set aside, she reached up and unhooked his cuffs from the chains that held him upright. He sagged a little, but otherwise held himself up. She led him over to the couch along the far wall and draped a blanket over his shoulders.

She sat down beside him, checking to make sure he was coming back down from his high. He seemed fine, so she went to clean herself up.

"I made a mess, didn't I?" he asked.

"Just a little." It wasn't the first time a man had come on her, and she was positive it wouldn't be the last. Sure, she could have stepped out of the way, but where was the fun in that?

When she returned to the couch, she brought a bottle of water and some chocolate with her. He might not be her submissive, but as his play partner it was her job to take care of him after.

He took the offering and downed a good portion of the water in one gulp. "Thanks."

"How are you feeling?" she asked.

Ryan snorted. "Like all my bones have turned to Jell-O."

She gave him a knowing grin. "Relax up here for a bit. I'm going to go downstairs and check on Brandon and Ali's progress. If you need anything before I get back, just holler."

When she moved to stand, he placed a hand on her arm, stopping her. Katrina met his gaze.

"Don't you want me to take care of you?"

While she never allowed her play partners to penetrate her, she did occasionally have them preform oral favors. Ryan was a huge fan of cunnilingus, and he had a very talented tongue. As tempted as she was to take him up on his offer, she had a few things she needed to do before the club opened at seven o'clock. Katrina knew if she gave in and let him pleasure her, one orgasm by Ryan's talented mouth wouldn't be enough.

"Not today. I have some work to do." She placed his hand back in his lap and headed toward the door. "Take your time."

Once she was outside the room, Katrina made a beeline for the stairs. As she descended, Brandon waved her over. "Mr. Monroe called while you were upstairs. I told him you were busy and would have to call him back."

Peter Monroe was the private investigator she used for the club. All members had to pass a background check as well as a medical exam. You could say it was overkill, but most of her members appreciated the care she took with both their privacy and their safety. Even so, the one mistake she'd made in that department plagued her regularly. She'd vowed never to let someone slip through the cracks again. "Thanks. Everything all right down here?"

"We're good. Ali is almost finished cleaning the main floor. Should I send her upstairs or wait a while?" Brandon asked.

"Have her wait fifteen minutes and then come on up. We should be finished by then."

"Will do."

As she started back toward the stairs, Brandon's voice stopped her. "By the way, you missed a spot." He had a smirk on his face, and he was looking in the direction of her leg.

Sure enough, on the inside of her thigh was a small amount of Ryan's cum. She grabbed a paper towel from the bar, dipped it in some water Brandon had sitting close by, and removed the evidence of her afternoon adventures. "Happy?"

Brandon chuckled. "I think the better question would be, are you happy? You've obviously just had more fun than I have."

She gave him a wink. "True. Speaking of which . . . I need to get back upstairs."

He nodded. "Tell Ryan to stop by when he's done. I wanted to ask him something."

"Sure."

Get to know Katrina, Ryan, Daniel, Brandon, and the other members of Serpent's Kiss. Sign up for Sherri's email list at www. sherrihayesauthor.com and get a copy of Welcome to Serpent's Kiss for FREE!

Strictly Professional

A Christmas Proposal

ACKNOWLEDGMENTS

Thank you to Mack and Rae for making sure all the BDSM elements in the story are accurate. The little things can sometimes make all the difference.

Editors are invaluable and they help to make the story the most it can be. Thank you to my editors: Kathie, Teresa, and DeAnne.

ABOUT THE AUTHOR

Sherri picked up her first romance novel when she was twelve and immediately she was hooked. She would stay up reading long after everyone else in her house had gone to bed, needing to see the hero and heroine get their happily ever after. But Sherri never imagined becoming an author.

At the age of thirty, all that changed. After getting frustrated with the direction a television show was taking two of its characters, Sherri decided to try her hand at writing an alternative ending to give the characters the happy ending they deserved.

Since then, writing has become a creative outlet that allows her to explore a wide range of emotions, while having fun taking her characters through all the twists and turns she can create.

facebook.com/SherriHayesAuthor

amazon.com/Sherri-Hayes/e/B004MIO9O4?ref=sr_ntt_s-rch_lnk_1&sr=8-1

bookbub.com/authors/sherri-hayes

patreon.com/SherriHayes